DARKNESS
SAVAGE

ALSO BY RACHEL A. MARKS

Winter Rose (novella)

The Dark Cycle

Darkness Brutal
Darkness Fair
Darkness Savage

DARKNESS SAVAGE

BOOK THREE OF THE DARK CYCLE

RACHEL A. MARKS

SKYSCAPE

SKYSCAPE

Published by Skyscape, New York

www.apub.com

Amazon, the Amazon logo, and Skyscape are trademarks of Amazon.com, Inc., or its affiliates.

ISBN-13: 9781503950306
ISBN-10: 1503950301

Cover design by Cliff Nielsen

Printed in the United States of America

For my daddy, who taught me how to see.

Child of Night, born of angels
with silver blood
and opal skin.

Darkness fair, Darkness savage
now cloaks her soul
with deadly sin.

In the twilight, she will rise
and open eyes
to worlds that lie.

Hungry
to carve castles
from
ash and bone.

Doomed
to crest the ruins
of earth
alone.

Darkness savage, Darkness atoned,
what horror now awaits?
The end
at last
has come.

~ scribbled on the back wall of a child's closet ~

ONE

Aidan

Game on, Demon Dork.

The words appeared several minutes ago as burn marks on the pink paper. A taunt from my sister, Ava. I can't seem to stop seeing the message. Even as I'm led from the clothing store and as the paramedic looks over my wounds—wounds that are already beginning to heal. Even as I scan the other side of the yellow crime-scene tape the police are putting up, wondering where Kara and Raul went.

I can only see the words that appeared along the bottom of the note my sister gave me, the note in my back pocket now smudged with my bloody fingerprints.

Game on, Demon Dork.

Ava, what have you done? That poor woman . . .

My vision clouds with the memory of the death, blood spraying across the innocent woman's face in a red mist as the talon emerged from her chest, the crab-like demon scuttling up her back, perching on her head.

The cops have been questioning people who were in the store when the demon attacked. They've got a cluster of witnesses sitting at the tables outside the coffee shop, across the courtyard of the outdoor mall.

Kara and Raul must've slipped from the scene first thing and hid as the crazy aftermath unfolded. That's good—they need to keep off the radar.

There's a cop standing just to my left, beside the ambulance, his presence chafing my raw nerves. He's waiting for the female paramedic to finish cleaning the deep gouges and cuts on my forearm, and then, he's assured me, he'll have a lot of questions.

Questions I can't answer.

I should've run when I saw the police moving in, but there was so much chaos, and they arrived so suddenly, gathering all the witnesses and looking at me, at my bleeding wounds. Then I heard the store employee talking about the surveillance video, so and I was glad I hadn't run. Runners look suspicious. And I have a feeling that I'm about to be suspect number one as it is.

For now I'm sitting on the back of the ambulance, surrounded by people I'll have to figure out how to lie to.

"You'll need stitches," the paramedic says. She looks over to the cop. "He needs to get checked out in the ER. Whatever that animal was, it bit him or something. The wounds are likely to get infected."

It wasn't a bite, I almost say. Scratches—or gouges, I guess. But it doesn't matter because I can feel my body healing. In about twenty minutes there won't be anything to stitch. If I show up at the ER with only scars, the doctors will just have questions I can't answer.

"I'm fine," I say. "I don't need stitches."

The paramedic shakes her head at me as she finishes bandaging my arm. Her blonde hair is pulled back in a tight bun, making her delicate features seem more severe than they are. She has a glittering gold mark on her soul, on the side of her neck, just under her jaw: it tells me she's been saved by an angel before. I wonder if she knows.

"Can I have a second?" the cop asks her.

She finishes taping the bandage and rises to her feet, pulling off her blue plastic gloves. "You need to get that checked out by a doctor."

"I'll be fine," I say again.

"We'll see what your parents think about that," she says before she walks away.

My insides cringe. Shit, they'll have to call Sid to come and get me. And the guy is so sick. He hasn't been able to stray very far from his shed the last few days—since Ava's return. Whatever his time traveling has done to him, it seems to be getting worse every minute. Eric insists that there's nothing we can do to stop Sid's deterioration, but I can't give up yet.

The cop steps forward. "So, it appears that you got the best view of what happened."

I look him over, his dark-blue uniform, his belt full of weapons; the leather squeaks when he moves. I don't deal with cops. I usually just hide from them.

When I stay silent he adds, "I'm Officer Matson. What's your name?"

"Aidan."

"Do you have ID, Aidan?"

I nod, pull my license out, and hand it to him. My *fake* license that Sid got me. I guess this'll be a good test to see if it works.

I swallow and try to hide my nerves, focusing on the officer.

He's the same height as me, about five eight, and his dark hair is slicked back in a clean, tight cut. His eyes dart from my ID picture to my face, then stop to study intently the marking on my unbandaged left arm.

"So, Mr. O'Fallan, what did you see happen?" he asks.

I saw a demon kill a woman. "There was some kind of weird animal—maybe a dog?" I give him my best confused look and let my nerves out a little to help my voice shake. "It attacked the lady, killed her. I've never seen anything like it." I swallow hard as I recall the woman getting impaled in the chest in front of a pants display. No, I've definitely never seen anything like that. "Then the thing came at me, jumped right on me when everyone was running out the door." I lift my bandaged right arm.

"Then what happened?"

Then I stabbed it with my dagger, and my power turned it to ash. Because that's totally normal.

I hid the dagger in the waist of my pants, so it's not like they caught me with it, but I'm sure they'll see that I fought the demon—animal—in the surveillance feed. And as much as I don't want to mention the blade, the story has to fit. "I, uh, stabbed it. And it ran off." My pulse picks up as I wait for his reaction.

His look hardens. "You *stabbed* the animal?" His gaze rakes over me again. "Do you have the weapon?"

I lift my shirt to show him the hilt.

He steps back a little, out of arm's reach. "Why don't you hand that over, then. For evidence." I pull it out in the least threatening way I can, and he waves another deputy over. "Bag that, will you?" He motions to the blade.

The second cop takes the dagger with a gloved hand and slides it into a plastic bag, then seals it shut as he walks back toward a cop car.

"There was no blood on that blade," Officer Matson says. "Can you tell me why that is—if you stabbed the attacking animal?"

Because it burned off. Of course, even if my power hadn't destroyed the demon's blood, the cop wouldn't have known it *was* blood; he probably would've thought it was tar or something.

"I cleaned it off," I say, "before I put it away."

He studies me, obviously aware I'm not telling him the whole truth. But instead of pushing the point he says, "So, you stabbed the animal, then what happened?"

"Then I . . . I guess the ambulance got here, and you guys. It all happened pretty fast."

"Yes. I'm sure." He holds up my ID between two fingers and says, "I'm going to go check something. You sit tight. I'll be right back." He turns and heads in the same direction the other cop went.

I watch him walk away, and I try to breathe, to slow my heart rate. I consider attempting an escape, but I'm pretty positive that would only end me up in a larger mess. There's a dead soccer mom. They won't let that go with a surface investigation. They'll want answers.

Dammit, what sort of shit storm has Ava tossed me in?

A harsh whisper comes from my right. "Aidan." I turn, and Kara appears from the other side of the ambulance.

"What are you doing?" I glance back toward the cop. "You shouldn't be here. This is bad news, Kara."

"Which is why you need to split before it gets worse."

"Can't. They have surveillance footage."

"Oh, shit."

"Yeah, not good." I take her hand in mine, selfishly needing the contact to calm my nerves. "Where's Raul?"

She steps closer and leans into me. "He's waiting for me at Barney's Beanery. He said he needed chili."

"Chili always helps."

"You gave the cop your ID?"

"Yeah, hopefully it works."

"Sid's guy is the best, hands down. Mine always works fine when I get pulled over."

I give her a sideways look. "That happens a lot?"

She winks at me. "Enough." She seems to recall why we're talking and releases a sigh. "I called Sid. He's ready for whatever."

"You should go, then. You don't need to get dragged into this."

"Just give me the keys to the car, and I'm in the wind, babe." She leans in and kisses me, insistent and urgent, then pulls back an inch and whispers, "Don't let 'em crack you." One more quick peck on the cheek as she takes the keys to the Camaro, and she's slipping away, back into the ordered chaos.

I sit alone for a few minutes, and Matson returns. "The paramedics are going to take you to the ER to get that arm checked out." He hands me my ID, then pulls out a small pad and pen from his front pocket. "I just have one more question. My colleague described some things from the video, namely that it appeared you had two companions with you. A male and female. What were their names?"

"I, um . . ." Shit. "I don't know their names. They were just some kids off the street. I was buying them clothes." I suck at lying.

"How nice of you." And he doesn't believe any of it. He makes a note on his pad. "You're sure about that?"

I nod.

He eyes me for several tense seconds before saying, "Okay, then. Can I get your contact information, in case I have more questions?"

"Uh, sure." So I'm not being held for more questioning, that's good. I tell him my address and cell number, and give him Sid's, too, for good measure. The whole time I have to suppress the urge to lie. Better to tell the truth wherever I can. And I should probably leave it at that, but I can't help prodding a little. "So, do you know what the animal was?"

He looks up from his notepad, and his eyes meet mine. "It wasn't clear in the surveillance footage, more a blur than anything. Whatever it was, it was small." Maybe the view in the footage wasn't any good. No red spark lights his eye, so he isn't lying about the lack of clarity.

"There was something that didn't go unnoticed in the video, though," he adds. "Apparently there was a point where it looked like you could've run with your companions, but you didn't."

I just stare at him like I'm waiting for him to say more. My anxiety shifts back into high gear; I have a feeling my lack of fear in the video during the "animal" attack didn't go unnoticed, either.

"Also, something went wrong with the feed around the time the animal came at you; a glare in the camera. Seemed to make you blink out of the footage for a handful of seconds."

My pulse speeds up as I realize what that *glare* was; it must've been my power lighting up my mark. And it somehow made the camera unable to see me correctly?

All I can manage in response is a shrug, because my brain is going a hundred miles an hour. I never considered how my fiery power might look on camera.

"So, is there anything more you'd like to add to your story?" he asks. I shake my head.

He studies me for another few seconds and then nods. "I'll contact you if I have more questions."

I watch him walk away, and wonder if I should forget going along with the system and just run. But in the end, I sit on the back of the ambulance and wait for the paramedics to take me to the ER, hoping Sid will be able to come get me before they notice I have no real reason to be there.

TWO

Rebecca

I sigh and lean my head on Connor's shoulder as we watch a wave roll up the beach toward us. Just before it reaches our toes, it pauses, then slinks back to tuck itself into the tide again. I take in a deep breath, the scents of salt and sand and sunscreen filling my head, the smell of Connor's skin surrounding me. I revel in the warm sunlight, revel in the calm that settles inside of me whenever I'm with him.

That peace is so scarce now.

"I need to head out soon," he says, his voice breaking the stillness.

The familiar shadow resurfaces inside me at the thought of leaving his side.

"Not yet," I whisper, closing my eyes.

So many things seem to be keeping me unsettled; my fear of what's changed, the hole in my gut since I left the LA Paranormal house, since I passed on my anointing—or whatever it was that linked me to Aidan. I gave that part of me to Kara. I chose to do it—it was my idea to begin with—but now I'm a little scared. What if I gave her everything about me that mattered?

I still haven't tried to draw again. I'm terrified to pick up my pen-cils because it could be gone, that piece of me that was special, that allowed me to escape everything that's happened, my mom leaving, and Charlie . . .

"Aidan and I promised Sid we'd check out a job tonight," he says.

I try not to sound bummed. "You're still worrying about working, even with all the stuff going on with Aidan's sister?"

A seagull hops closer to our bag of snacks, and he flicks sand to shoo it away. "We need to make money. As Sid says, 'The show must go on.' Not everybody has a millionaire dad to pay the mortgage." He nudges my shoulder playfully.

His words sting a little; a reminder that I don't fit in his world.

"Wanna go for one more swim?" he asks.

"Sure." I attempt enthusiasm, but I'm afraid it's not there.

The ache is returning just thinking of going back to my empty life where I have to pretend.

He stands and holds out a hand to help me up. I take it, letting him pull me close. His other hand grazes the bare skin of my back, sending warmth spreading through me. We haven't done anything more than kiss; Connor is a perfectly frustrating gentleman. I wish sometimes that he wasn't so careful with me, but I think he's afraid. He's always saying I'm out of his league, and I'm starting to worry he really believes that.

"I hate to be a typical guy," he says, wrapping me in his arms, "but you look pretty amazing in that bikini."

"Glad to hear it," I say, sliding my fingers over the lines of his arm muscles.

He lowers his lips to mine, kissing me softly as his palms slide down my sides—

A shocked laugh comes from my right. "Oh. My. God!"

I snap to attention, stepping away from Connor, and spot Apple approaching with Samantha behind her. Connor grips my waist, not letting me get away.

"Emery," Apple coos, calling me by my middle name, reminding me who I'm expected to be, "you little slut."

Connor's arm muscles tense against my back.

Samantha gives a small wave. "Hey, guys." Her mousy-brown hair is tied up in a sloppy bun, and she's got a billowy blue cover-up on that could put her in a vacation magazine highlighting a trip to the Bahamas. I know she's wearing it because she's trying to cover a beautiful body that she thinks of as fat.

Apple looks Connor up and down with obvious approval. "I remember you, Jeep Boy. I thought we had a connection when you waved me off the road the other day so you could kidnap our friend, here. Are you trying to make me jealous? Hashtag, so wrong." She tilts her lips and hips suggestively. She's wearing a very skimpy yellow lace bikini that doesn't leave much to the imagination, her straight hair is lightened from the sun, and her skin is perfectly tan. She's Hollywood-gorgeous and she knows it.

Samantha rolls her eyes behind Apple's back.

Apple glides closer and runs a finger over Connor's shoulder, purring, "I'm hurt."

Connor just glares down at her, flexing his jaw. I kind of have the urge to punch her perfect nose.

"We're heading out to have lunch at Sherwood, maybe go for a swim," Samantha says. "Do you guys wanna join?"

"No," I say, maybe a little too forcefully. "We're leaving." There's a reason I've been avoiding these girls the last few days.

Apple gives Connor a sly grin. "Getting a room? Can I join?"

"Apple!" Samantha snaps. "God."

Apple's lips pinch together. "Whatever." As much as she has no filter, she usually doesn't intend to be horrible. I don't think.

Samantha gives me a concerned look. "I just miss you, bestie." Her tone is so genuine; it makes me want to ignore my anger at Apple. "And school's about to start again—we still haven't had our traditional princess pizza party, and it's senior year. A plan must be made."

Apple gives her a disbelieving look. "Seriously, Sam? We're not twelve anymore."

"And this is why we stopped inviting you," Samantha says.

A wicked smile grows on Apple's face, and she turns her attention back to Connor. "I'll come if the sexy surfer boy is going to be there." She reaches out and slides her hand over Connor's pec and licks her teeth.

A surge of possessive rage surges in me, and before I can stop—

I shove her. Hard.

She stumbles back, sand flying up as she steadies herself.

I should be mortified—old Rebecca would have wanted to crawl under the towel to hide. But something new inside me, something I've never felt, makes me step closer with authority, getting between her and Connor. And I grind through my teeth, "Hands off, bitch."

Everyone's eyes widen, including mine. *What the heck was that?*

Apple almost chokes on her tongue in shock; her mouth opens in a gape, and her brows scrunch together in this super cliché way that's almost funny.

Samantha's shocked face turns from me to Apple and back again, like she's worried about what's going to happen next.

Even as my brain is telling my mouth to shut up, to stop, another part of me grins at the sight of the terrified skinny girl in front of me. I grab hold of the anger that spills out, directing it at Apple. How dare she touch Connor like he's up for sale. She's always so bossy and full of herself. I've had enough. Of all of it! No more Rebecca doormat.

I clench my hands into fists at my side and get right in her face. "Stop giving my boyfriend those *fucking* eyes and acting like he's a piece of meat. You touch him again, and I'm going to ruin that nose your daddy bought you last summer."

Apple keeps moving her mouth like she's trying to speak, but only squeaks emerge.

Samantha steps back, obviously more than worried now. She actually looks scared of me. "Oh my God—Emery, what's going *on* with you?"

I reach down and grab my towel. "I'll call you," I say to Samantha, not meaning it, then I throw my beach bag over my shoulder and walk away.

I don't look to see if Connor's following me. I don't wait to take a deep breath and figure out why in the name of heaven I just did that. I don't even consider babbling out an instant apology. I'm too freaked out. Because in that moment, something inside of me surfaced. Something I've never felt before. Like I was suddenly someone else entirely, someone bold and assertive.

And even as a little guilt trickles in, I have to admit . . . it felt *good*.

———

Connor unlocks the Jeep and opens the door for me, not saying a word. He studies me warily as I get in, and then he goes around and throws his board and my beach bag in the back before he slides behind the wheel. It isn't until we've been driving down PCH for a while and we're almost to the 10 freeway that I'm finally able to speak.

"I'm so sorry," I say. "I have no idea where that came from."

"I'm sure she'll recover."

"I totally freaked out. I can't understand any of it—what's going on with me?"

"You're still processing a lot." He reaches over and takes my hand in his, skimming his thumb over my knuckles.

"Yeah, I guess." But that's not right. I'm *not* processing, not at all—that's the problem. And even though I sort of liked being bold, it's as if I don't actually know who I am anymore.

He looks sideways at me. "You sure dug into that girl, though. What's her name again? Pear?"

I laugh and look over to see him trying to hide a smile. I squeeze his hand. "I shouldn't have said all that. She'll never forgive me."

"And why, exactly, do you need her approval?"

I shrug. Who knows. It's just how I'm made. Weak.

But I sure wasn't weak down on that beach. Imagine how my social life would've gone if I'd whipped out those lines years ago.

A nervous giggle escapes my lips.

"The look on her face was pretty priceless," Connor says.

I laugh harder, thinking of Apple's gape. "She looked a little like her head was going to explode."

"Especially when you said I was your boyfriend."

I choke on my giggle and look over at him. "Oh, gosh, I did say that, didn't I? I'm so sorry." *And mortified even more now.*

He glances away from the road, to me, for a second. "So, I'm *not* your boyfriend? How many other guys are kissing you on the beach, then?"

Warmth fills me at his wry tone. He's obviously not too worried about my craziness. "Well, I mean, if you don't count the guy who tapes those church flyers to the ground on the Venice Boardwalk, there's just half a dozen men in line before you."

"Men? I'm competing with *men* now?"

I laugh and rest my head on the back of the seat, watching the shoreline go by.

"I wouldn't mind, you know," he says, quietly. His hand moves up to brush my jaw with his knuckles, and my eyes close at the gentle touch. "I'd be yours forever, and relish every second of it."

Heat travels over my skin, settling in my chest as the shock of his words charges the air. He glances at me again, his features serious.

"I mean it," he adds. And then his fingers trail down the side of my neck, and he grips me, pulling me closer.

I rest my cheek on his shoulder and close my eyes, not saying a word. Because nothing needs to be said. Nothing can be said. There are no words inside of me to fit in this moment.

So, I just sink into his side and let him take me home.

THREE

Hunger

It watches. The demon Hunger watches the human leave the green vehicle and take the boy's hand in hers before walking up the pathway to her house. The girl is called Rebecca. The boy is Connor; a friend of the time child, who now brings death to spirit—a thing once thought impossible.

The two figures remain silent as they walk. The demon keeps behind the female, close enough to influence her mind if need be. She is so close, but still the demon cannot touch her flesh. She may feel rich disdain if it radiated too heavily. It holds back, but the craving is strong, the craving to sink teeth into the skin of the human female. It burns. Jaw aches with need.

The need to tear into her.

She smells the same as before, the filth of purity billowing from her like rosemary. She turns and seems to look right at the demon, as if sensing the loathing. But she can't possibly see. She cannot comprehend the presence of Darkness. If she could, her blood would smell of scorched earth from the terror.

Humans are never prepared for the truth. They believe in only what is before them, what a simple mind can absorb with five elementary senses. No more, no less. They are pathetic. A waste of time and spirit for El Elyon. But this El of the Heavens insists on bowing low for what is merely mud that's been given animation. Mud that does not even know its own mind. Or acknowledge a power such as El. And, still, Love is gifted to the human.

Disgusting.

For a moment the human girl's fingers seem to play at the air where the shadow Hunger stands as she points to a spot just beyond.

She speaks of her father not being home. The boy speaks of wanting to stay with her. He reaches out to brush knuckles against the coral skin of her cheek. He has done this many times, fascinated by her skin, always touching gently, as if she is made of glass.

The desire between them sparks, yearning strong and potent. But the boy holds the urges in check. It's unsettling how controlled he is. Unnatural.

It has watched. The demon Hunger has watched for three cycles of the sun. This is the same girl the master, Molech, commanded for destruction. The orchestrated death of her brother, Charlie—a lion of a boy, who kept her heart strong—that part of her corruption was achieved easily. But the task of crushing her soul was not fulfilled. It was cut short by the child witch called Ava. She cast out the demon, sent it far from earth's realms into the Lands of Separation and Death.

The time child and the child witch are both meddlers and usurpers. Dogs painted with gold. And now tasks are left undone, doors are cracked open, and nothing is following the pattern any longer.

Things in the Shadow Lands are uncertain. The child witch needs to be stopped, but the way is unclear, the path still unseen. Molech will know. Guidance will be given. Surely the master cannot want its reign toppled. Surely there will be new orders. A new task that will heal this rift.

Because now, watching the fire-haired female, it is clear that more than the boy time child has changed. Something is wrong with the girl, something has shifted.

Her soul is not the same at all.

Before, the green light of energy inside of her was restrained with golden threads; an anointing that protected and contained her core power. But that gilded glint of thread—the gold of Heaven that linked her to the time child boy—is completely gone.

Her energy spills from her now, in twisted green rivers. She is free. Untethered. The sight is unnerving.

An interesting and possibly useful development.

"Tell me to stay and I will," the blond boy says.

"I'm fine, Connor. And you have work to do tonight, remember."

A look of pain creases his brow. He's worried that she's broken. He can't see her spilling insides. He can't see her power. If he could, he'd be afraid of her rather than for her.

The shadow licks its lips. The shadow Hunger licks its lips, contemplating her shoulders, her neck, fangs aching again. She is powerful. So powerful. Could her abilities be used? Errors must be fixed somehow. This mistake could be salvation.

It ponders. The demon Hunger ponders. And a shadow claw brushes at the air around the girl's throat where a bit of her energy lifts from her skin. The green thread of light curls around the talon, letting a small amount of Hunger's silver seep in.

A wince surfaces in the girl's eyes, but still she manages to form a bright smile for the boy.

The demon Hunger smiles, too, as the talon slides along the shape of her throat, just a breath from her skin.

Yes, there will be a way to sink teeth and claw, just there, into that creamy flesh.

It would be the demon's reward for saving the world.

FOUR

Aidan

The ER is a madhouse. They wheel my gurney into the main holding area to wait. I sit up on the thin bed and lean my back against the wall, pull out my cell, and check to see if Kara or Sid have texted me.

Nothing. It appears there's no signal, though, so it's anyone's guess what their ETA is.

Things beep in an area behind a blue curtain on the other side of the circular nurses' station that's in the middle of the large room. Doctors and nurses go in and out of the area where the machines are going off, and there's some shouting I can't understand, just as another bloody patient is hurried past me through the ER doors. More nurses swarm around the new arrival, and I'm left to watch it all, taking up space that seems suddenly very valuable.

The nurse who checked me in says something to another nurse, and I watch the two of them converse for a minute before she points at me, and the second nurse heads over.

"Hello, can you give me your name and full birth date, please?" she asks, taking hold of my wrist and looking at the clock on the wall as the second hand *tick, tick, ticks*.

I rattle off my new name, Aidan O'Fallan, and my birth date.

"How bad would you say your pain is?" She points at a chart on the wall behind her with numbered circle-faces in all different colors and phases of grimace.

"I'm not in pain," I say.

She notes something on her clipboard and then asks me to straighten my arm. "Let's get that bandage off and see what we've got."

"I'm fine," I say. "I told the paramedic there was nothing. Barely a scratch."

She glances at the clipboard again. "It says here you have several lacerations, blood loss, and there's a recommendation for stitches."

"Nope, I'm fine." I peel back the bandage to hurry things along. New scars now run alongside old scars, the newer ones tinged pink. I try not to let my nerves show. "See, no open wounds."

She frowns and looks closer at my arm, at the dried smears of blood that haven't been completely cleaned off. "Whose blood is that?"

"It was pretty crazy, people were running, there was screaming—"

"Yeah, okay." She sighs and walks away, obviously done trying to convince me that I need help. She doesn't look happy, but she doesn't look curious, either, so that's a bonus.

My phone vibrates on the bed beside me. It's Kara. "Hey."

"We've been trying to call. I was getting worried you fell down the social services rabbit hole."

"Sketchy signal."

"You're at Community, right?"

"ER, right inside the ambulance doors."

"I had to go pick up Sid, but we're on our way there. Connor was closer, I called him a minute ago. He'll be there any second. Is everything okay?"

"Yeah, everything's fine. I just need to figure out why this happened." I glance around, checking for listening ears, but everyone's occupied with the surrounding madness. Still, I whisper, "That demon broke every rule I know about when it killed that woman."

"Sid thinks your sister has something she's trying to play out."

"Yeah, if she wanted me dead, I think I would be. The demon was weak, so it didn't feel like much of a contest to see who was going to win. That means it was a statement of some kind."

Game on, Demon Dork.

I hear Sid say in the background, "I'd have to agree."

"You're on speakerphone," Kara says to me. "Sid's just getting in the car." Then she says to Sid with a smile in her voice, "Buckle up so we can get going, old man. You're slower than a snail today, and Aidan's waiting for you to sign him out of that place."

"I'm fine," I say. "There're a million other patients here in way worse shape than me. They just looked at my arm and are now fully aware that I don't need to be here."

"Uh-oh," she says.

"They won't think anything of it," Sid says. "People are so unaware of the spiritual in this time, there's no way they'd even guess the truth about you, Aidan."

"Let's hope so," Kara says.

———

Connor comes in through the emergency-personnel access doors behind me with a group of paramedics pushing a gurney. I spot his blond head towering over the others as he follows, as if he belongs with them.

"Where are Kara and Sid?" he asks when he reaches me. "Still not here?"

"They're on the way so Sid can sign me out."

"I got the call after I dropped Rebecca off. What the hell happened?"

I lean close and speak under my breath. "A demon murdered a woman in the Gap. Right in front of me. Fully formed. Corporeal. I think my sister sent it."

"Ava sent it—why?"

"Who knows? A taunt, I guess. I need to get out of here and figure out what's really going on with her." I pull my sister's letter from my pocket and hand it to Connor. "She left this for me before she met with the Heart-Keeper, and she sent me those burnt words since I found it."

"*'Game on'?* What the hell?" He starts to hand it back like he doesn't want to be touching it. As he does, new words appear in a hiss of thin black lines.

Here's your first hint: You're one step closer to the daylight. Out, damned spot!

I stare at it, my heart crashing in my chest.

"Holy shit," Connor whispers.

I try to breathe, to think, struggling to figure out what she means. But all I can think is: *It's started.* As I tuck the one link I have to my lost sister safely back in my pocket, I say, "'Out, damned spot'? Like in *Macbeth*? What the fuck does that even—?"

My voice freezes in my throat as my eye catches something dark on the other side of the nurses' station. A large shadow moves, a black bulbous body and eight skeletal legs with thick hairs growing from them.

A spider the size of a cat.

The creature scuttles, making loud *clacks* against the tile floor, then begins climbing, crawling up the wall behind the nurse I was just talking to.

My body jolts, my power stirring to life as the demon moves its way around a supply cart. I grit my teeth, trying to hold the force inside as my energy sears my bones. People might see it. I can't let that happen.

Connor follows my line of sight. "What is it?" He searches the room, but I know he's not seeing the demon because the spider moves right through a wall. It's not corporeal, which is something, I guess. It won't see me—I have my amulet on.

But then the demon spider emerges through the wall only a few feet away from me, scuttling closer in a sort of zigzag.

I jerk back, the gurney lurches, knocking over a nurse who's walking past.

The spider leaps onto the bed, hissing my name in a demon tongue, *"Fire Bringer."* How does it know where I am?

I scramble away, falling to my knees beside the nurse. The demon lunges, jumping at us, landing on top of the woman. The scent of its darkness crashes into me, filling my head, the chill of it stinging my skin.

And I can't hold my power back anymore. It hits me like a battering ram to the chest, bursting out in a pulse, stronger than I've ever felt it, the fire tearing from me in a rush of heated air.

Screams erupt around us, the sound of movement, of crashing objects. "He's on fire!" someone shouts. But my eyes are locked on the demon, on the nurse. On my fire reflecting in her fully dilated pupils, golden and molten.

Connor's begging me to get up, to run. I can barely register his fear. My power's in charge now. And all I'm aware of is the demon on the nurse's head, clacking its pinchers. Thousands of tiny eyes covering its face seem to be looking right at me, but it's like it can't quite find me.

My power. It must be sensing my power.

The nurse obviously can't feel the demon on top her. Can't see its crunchy black exoskeleton reflecting the harsh hospital lighting, the thick bristles of hair tickling her ear. She just gapes at me, frozen in fear.

Calls of "Fire!" and "Get security!" are chaos around us now. Someone attacks me with a blanket, trying to smother my flames, but I push them off.

The demon hisses in my direction, using the distraction, and slides its hairy leg into the nurse's eye socket.

"No!" I cry, trying to grab the thing as the bulbous body flexes and bends like a water balloon, shoving its head in after the leg, half the demon sinking into flesh in less than a second.

Words start to flow mindlessly from my mouth. I pull my knife, reaching out for her.

The woman jerks away from my hand, from my blade, at the same time someone else grabs me—Connor this time. I shake him off, my power too big as it fills me with its rage.

As I see the demon disappear.

Inside of the woman.

Filling her flesh with its dark, smoky power.

Everyone in the room seems to go still, as if sensing something happening. Something horrible.

The nurse finally reacts. She gags, her face flushing. She coughs and chokes, like she's trying to swallow dust. The room's attention falls on her now.

"Time to run, man," Connor says, his voice shaking with urgency.

But I can't move, I can't take my eyes off the infested woman. "Gotta get it out," I whisper. "Have to get it out." It's my fault she's been invaded. My presence made the thing *need* to find eyes to spot me with.

I grab her with a fire-filled hand.

She gasps, her eyes widening in terror. Black smoke leaks from between her open lips.

"Don't touch her with that!" Connor says.

But I take the woman by both shoulders. And whisper in Aramaic that I'll kill it, I'll kill this bastard of a demon. I'll rip its legs off and shove my blade through its skull.

The nurse's body twitches in my hands. She bares her teeth, her eyes filling with black fluid, her features contorting.

"I sssee you, Fire Bringer," the demon says with her mouth. "She said to find the Fire Bringer. The witch wanted everyone, human, demon, angel, to sssee what you have become."

Ava. It's talking about Ava. *Out, damned spot!*

"Aidan, please," Connor says, grabbing the nurse's arm now, trying to tear her from my grip.

But it's too late. I hold tight, my power surging through my bones, my muscles, my blood, escaping through my skin in a flash of white light. It jolts the air around us with a loud *crackle* when it touches down, finding its mark.

Connor flies back with a cry of pain as the hot pulse of my flames climbs the woman's arm, sizzles over her chest, and devours her neck.

It slides into her open mouth, a scream of agony rips from her throat.

"Release her," I seethe in Aramaic, all focus and rage. "Now."

"The witch is coming for you," the demon screeches through the woman's lips. "She will have you by her side in the end. Watch as the daylight hits you. The humans will see your power and fear you, Fire Bringer. And Heaven will know you belong to her. *Out, damned spot.*" It laughs horribly.

The vivid image rises before me: Ava's small form, her eyes silver white, her arms outstretched to Darkness. And me smiling down on her in pride as the world looks on in dread.

Fury fills me at the thought, and my power focuses into a pinprick. The fire reaches deeper, pushing through the woman like an extension of my own fingers, the tongues of flame finding the monster that's knitting its dark roots into the terrified spirit of the nurse.

My fire grips tight to the demon. Twists. And yanks.

The beast rips away from the core of the human vessel without a sound. The nurse's spirit flickers, and her body falls into a heap on the floor.

I'm left clutching the shadow of the huge spider. It flails and screeches as my flames coat it completely. I don't need a dagger or a conduit. I only need my will and the storm that crashes through me. It finishes off the writhing demon. Leaving nothing but ash.

The flakes float in the air like silver snow. Nothing is left but dried demon blood coating my fist, my arm.

I breathe. And my pulse begins to slow. My power ebbs, sinking away like a fading tide.

And the world clears, my surroundings slowly coming into focus.

The nurse is a limp form at my feet, Connor is tumbled over beside her, silent. And six uniformed men stand at various points around me, one of them aiming a gun at my head.

Terror seeps from every single body in the room, filling the air with the smell of burnt hair. There's yelling somewhere in the distance; someone is ordering people to clear out, to evacuate. Chaos and panic dance around me, as if everyone's worried that I'm a bomb ready to go off.

Suddenly, I feel a familiar energy in the distance. I turn toward it and spot Kara through the glass doors of the ER, Sid beside her, both looking on in horror. Kara's fighting the grip of a paramedic as she tries to get to me. She's yelling something—my name, I think—but sirens scream in the distance, making it impossible to hear. My ears buzz. My head begins to throb as the new sounds of reality fill my head. And I realize Ava's gotten her wish. Everyone sees. Everyone's afraid.

"Don't move!" yells one of the security guards. The one with the gun. "Drop the knife!" That must be a cop; his uniform is different.

I turn back to look down at the nurse's body. I was trying to save her—wasn't I? Did I kill her? I wanted to destroy the demon, that's *all* I wanted. I didn't think. I was . . . possessed by the need to act, by the fury inside me, this power, this need to kill.

I stare at Connor's limp form, terror rising now to nudge out the confusion. What have I done? God, help me. I squeeze my eyes shut. I clench my hands into fists and push down a scream, wishing it all away, wishing my life back into focus, wishing I was miles from this unbelievable mess.

A searing pain shoots through my core. And then my skin is burning, my body stretching out in unending agony as if I'm being torn in half.

There's a burst of light and a sizzle in the air.

Then I'm tumbling, head over heels, through soft ground. Over sand. It flies around me, and water splashes, shocking me with the sudden chill, the salty taste on my tongue.

I blink. Gasp. Staring at the sky as my hands dig into the gooey ground underneath me—

Holy shit, I just teleported. To the beach.

FIVE

Rebecca

I've stared at the box of art supplies on the top shelf of my closet for twenty minutes. I'm sitting on my bed, looking at it from across my room. It's nestled between a pair of roller skates and a stack of old *Vogue* magazines Samantha gave me for a collage project I was working on for my art media class last year.

A week ago I drew more than I spoke. It was like breathing for me, the deepest connection to my true self. But now, thinking of putting pencil to page makes me feel like I'm suffocating. I need to try, though. Especially after what happened on the beach today with Apple. If I don't try, I'm never going to know the answers to the questions circling like vultures in my head: After saving Kara, who have I become? Am I still *Rebecca*?

I slide off the edge of my bed and grab my desk chair, set it in the closet, and stand on it to pull the box off the shelf. I take the box to my desk and pop off the plastic lid. The contents are tucked neatly inside; Margaritte, our housekeeper, insisted on being careful when she packed the supplies away for me. I was going to throw everything away, but she caught me halfway through the process and scolded me about letting the "sorrows of life" ruin my dream. She also reminded me how much Charlie loved my drawings.

He did. He teased me incessantly, but never about my art—that he was always encouraging about.

I pull out a sketchbook and my container of pencils, then I settle on the floor. My heart is pounding in my chest so hard I'm worried it's trying to climb up my throat.

I flip to a blank page, put lead to vellum, and close my eyes. I imagine a tree—that's simple enough to draw. Like the tree outside of the LA Paranormal house, a large oak with twisted limbs.

Once I see it clearly in my mind, I begin. One line and then another, slowly brushing the lead over the paper in light strokes. My muscles recall the movement as the technical side of my brain kicks in. A lighter line here, a thicker one there, and I soon see the image emerging on the paper, like always, nothing childish or unschooled about it. The style feels forced, but the finished product is technically perfect.

Okay, so, crisis averted. Apparently I can still draw.

Then why am I looking at this sketch and wanting to rip it to shreds?

Something is missing, something vital.

I hear the front door close downstairs, and my father's voice echoes up to me. "Emery, I'm home. Are you ready to go?"

I look away from the drawing as he knocks on my bedroom door. "Come in," I say.

He opens the door, staying in the doorway. "You're not ready."

"Ready for what, exactly?" I ask, feeling dazed and tired. The last thing I want to do is go to one of his business dinners—to which he now insists I always tag along. He's only been home from New York three days, what could be so important?

A disapproving frown wrinkles his forehead. "It's the art show finals for the Arts & Media Museum. You made me put it on my calendar months ago. I thought you submitted that angel painting for the internship."

I totally forgot about the contest in all the madness. That was my life before Aidan. The life where I was just trying to recover from losing my brother. Where there were no demons or curses on people's souls.

"I'm not feeling so good," I say. "Maybe we shouldn't go. I mean, they'll call if I win the internship, right?"

My lack of enthusiasm for an event I would normally be thrilled about seems to strike him speechless for several seconds. Concern fills his eyes. "Are you taking your medication, Emery?"

I look back down at my drawing. "Yeah, of course," I say with forced cheeriness, doodling on the tree. It's more like: *No, of course not.* "I think I'm getting that stomach bug that's going around."

"Do you need me to ask Margaritte to get you something special from the grocery store?"

I shake my head. It's gotten too easy to lie to him. I'm a horrible daughter. "No, thanks. I think I just need rest."

"You're drawing," he says, stepping into the room, sounding surprised. "Margaritte was worried about you; she said you tried to throw your pencils and things away."

Wonderful. I've been snitched on. I try to make it into something silly. "It was a temperamental artist thing."

"Oh." He stands over me, looking hesitant as he shifts his weight from one foot to the other. Then he asks, "Is this about a boy?"

My brow goes up. Where did he get that idea? "No, why?"

"Well, there was the young man in the Jeep who picked you up this morning. And he brought you home from the academy yesterday. I'm concerned, since I haven't met him. I don't even know how you know him."

Girls who go to Catholic school don't meet boys the normal way, so I can see why he'd be concerned.

"His name's Connor. He's just a boy from LA Paranormal, and we're friends."

He nods a few times. "I think I need to meet him face-to-face before you start running around town with him."

I release a small laugh. "We're not 'running around town,' Dad. He took me surfing."

He straightens his shoulders at the last bit of information. "I want to meet him, Emery. You aren't going anywhere else with him until I do."

"Okay," I say, trying to use a calming voice. "That's fine. I'll have him come inside next time he picks me up. If you're home, you can meet him." But I really don't want Connor to meet my dad. Maybe because Connor is older. Or because my dad will be able to tell that he isn't from the right side of town. Being from the wrong circles might be fine for Aidan, who saved my life in my father's mind, but when it comes to dating, it's a whole other story.

"When can we make this happen?" he asks. "I'll be sure I'm here."

"Um, tonight, I guess? He's picking me up at nine. We're going to the movies." We're actually supposed to check out the Hollywood sign, because Connor said LA Paranormal was considering it for another shoot, and I mentioned I wanted to go.

And now it's going to be a date, apparently. Hopefully Connor won't mind the third degree from my dad. I groan inwardly, thinking about the moment my dad asks him what university he goes to.

"All right," he says. And then he steps closer and plants a kiss on the top of my head, whispering, "I love you. I just worry about you, sweetie."

"I know." I smile up at him with as much genuine affection as I can muster. I wish that I could tell him the truth about everything. I wish I could find a way so that we could be closer. We've never had a great relationship, but ever since my almost-suicide, he's been there for me. He's trying so hard.

I wish it was enough to be sure that he would believe me. Because there's this part of me that wants him to understand—understand the real me, not the weak girl who tried to kill herself, or the irresponsible girl who likes to shop.

Of course, I'm not even sure the real me is in the building anymore.

But it's time to stop hoping things will get better, hoping someone will fix this ache. It's time to get help where I know that I can, to figure this all out. On my own. I'm just not sure where to start. I've only met one person who knows everything about this soul stuff, who might get what's happening to me.

I pull out my phone and text Holly.

```
What's Miss Mae's address? Please don't
    tell Aidan or Connor that I asked.
```

After a few minutes an answer comes through with the address on it, and:

```
Mum's the word. But YOLO. And that's,
    You Otta Look Out, girl.
```

SIX

Aidan

I walk up the beach toward the cave and ignore my rumbling stomach as much as I can. After that accidental leap through space, I've never been so hungry in my entire life.

I should probably be freaked by the idea of what I just did, but I'm not. I'm over being shocked by my abilities. And right now all I can think about is finding Ava, to get her to stop this madness. She had her minion kill a woman in a Gap and possess that poor nurse, manipulating me in front of a bunch of people in a damn hospital for some insane game. Not to mention the possibly—no, the certainty—of all those cameras. She's officially sucked me in.

And I fucking fell for it.

I'm still not sure what she meant by her *Macbeth* quote about the *spot*—a stain? But the part of her hint that said I'm *one step closer to the daylight* feels pretty clear. That whole ER just got a huge eyeful of my power.

What have I done? Is that nurse going to recover? And what about Connor? He was out cold when I blinked away. As I come to the cave opening, I pull out my phone to call Sid and start to press the screen button with my thumb.

Seawater dribbles out the bottom of the case and the screen stays black.

Shit.

I walk into the cave and go to the wall where the doorway is, placing a hand on the cold stone. "Ava!" I yell. The sound of my anger echoes back at me. Where the hell is she? "Why are you hiding from me? Why are you doing this?" I turn and look at the altar where she was in a dead sleep only a week ago. Only a week ago she was innocent in my mind. She needed me. She was mine to protect.

And now . . .

What a fool I've been.

Bitterness fills my mouth as I think of how much I wanted to save her, how much I was wrong about. I move closer to the altar and run my fingers along the stone surface of the slab.

The air shimmers, like heat just billowed from in front of me over the rock.

I blink, wondering if the salt in my eyes is making me see things.

It shimmers again. And then something appears on the stone.

A small square of white paper. I lean closer and study it, not sure I should touch it. I look around the room and feel for a presence. "Ava?"

When I sense nothing, see nothing, I look back down at the tiny offering. Then I pick it up delicately and read over the bubbly words. That's Ava's handwriting.

Isn't this fun? BTW: I'm winning. ;) My stomach rises at the childlike tone, familiar and horrible. I keep reading, *Okay, next hint: The green witch begins her rise. The first to fall because of fatherly lies. Find her or she dies. Tonight.*

I scan the hint over and over. Find a witch? Who? How am I supposed to do this? It seems so random. And silly.

But if I don't do it, Ava will kill one more innocent person.

———

A breeze picks up as I knock on my great-grandmother's door, and my teeth start to chatter. I'm soaked. And freezing. And terrified.

My grandmother's house is on a bluff, overlooking the Pacific Ocean like a pink 1950s farmhouse in the middle of a man-made jungle. I was supposed to come tomorrow to trim her hydrangeas, so maybe showing up on her doorstep won't be too weird.

I knock again, more insistent. I can ask to use the landline, call Sid to be sure Connor is okay—things better be okay. I need to know what I did, how bad I fucked everything up, and how much worse it's about to get. Someone needs to answer the damn—

The door swings open, and Fa'auma clutches her bright Hawaiian dress to her chest with one hand. There's a box of bandages in her other. "Thank heaven above! You came just in the nick of time, young man." The smell of mildew and acrid air flows out from behind her—the scents of anxiety and fear.

My own worry sparks even brighter, thinking something else is wrong. Maybe with my grandmother. "What is it? What happened?"

She waves me in, and a splashing sound comes from the other room, the kitchen I think. "I don't know how to turn it off. She slipped and fell and I thought it was just a scratch but . . ." She shakes her head.

I walk past her, through the door. "Where is she?"

"She's in the living room, watching her show. I think she's okay—the fall was minor, she didn't hit her head. It appears that it's mostly the Pergo that's destroyed, which has her quite out of sorts. I've called the concierge doctor just in case, but it's the strangest thing, because you're actually here—she started asking for you about ten minutes ago."

My mind is trying to wrap itself around the tangle of things she just said. I pause in the archway to the living room, the splashing sound getting louder in the back of the house.

My great-grandma spots me in the entryway, and her bird arms lift to wave at the air. "Oh, it's you!" She has a bloody spot on her shoulder, showing through her pink nightdress—probably from her fall. There's also a smudge of blood on her arm, her paper skin torn and peeled back on her wrist. It makes her look so fragile, so vulnerable. "I've been thinking about you! Come here so I can look at you and be sure you're all right." She waves her arms again. Her tiny body seems to shrink when it's framed by the large rose recliner she's always sitting in. But she looks spunky as ever, her blue eyes bright and sparkling with mischief.

I move to her side, looking her over more closely. "What happened? Are you okay?"

"No one listens!" She humphs. "I told that man that copper was the devil's tool. Bad luck! But he just thought I was a crazy old bitty. And now there's a lake in my kitchen, hang it all!"

Fa'auma comes up behind me. "I'll keep trying to get ahold of the plumber, ma'am. But maybe Aidan can take a look. Since he's here and all."

Plumber? Copper pipes?

I turn to Fa'auma. "Did a pipe burst or something?"

"Did it ever!" my grandmother shouts at me like I can't hear her at normal volume. She's definitely fine. "It's Niagara Falls in the kitchen right now, all over the new flooring that my husband's foolish niece insisted I get. All she ever wants to do is spend my money."

I decide that the talking isn't going to clarify anything, so I start for the kitchen. "If a pipe bursts, you shut off the valve under the sink, depending on where it's broken, anyway. I'll go check. I just need to use your phone first—can I use your phone?"

"Of course," Fa'auma says. "I'll go get it." She disappears down the hall.

"Be careful not to slip!" my grandmother yells after me.

I follow the sound of splashing water into the wide hall that leads to the bright open kitchen with a small breakfast nook in the corner. The cupboards under the sink are open, all the cleaning supplies that were stored under there now sitting in a puddle to the side. A fountain is spraying from inside the cupboard like a pipe came loose.

It's a normal problem. Refreshing.

I kneel down in the inch-deep puddle on the floor; I'm already wet, so it doesn't matter that the water sprays over my shirt as I duck under the sink to look closer. I find the valve and have to force it only a little to make it turn, shutting it off. The water becomes a drizzle, then a drip, then a nothing.

I actually fixed something. Something lame, but it's something.

Now I just need to find a green witch—whatever that is—before she dies.

Fa'auma splashes into the kitchen and holds out the phone to me as I move my head out of the cupboard. "Oh, goodness, you are a dream, young man. What a bunch of helpless women we've turned into out here. We're a shame, really."

I stand, dripping, and shake myself off like a wet dog before taking the phone from her. "Thanks."

"You're soaked, you poor thing! Where's my head—let me get you a towel." She walks away again, leaving me to drip.

I punch Sid's number into the phone and listen to it ring as my nerves turn raw, thinking again of what Ava is going to destroy next, thinking of everything that could have already been destroyed in five seconds in that ER. Because of my stupidity. The voice-mail message clicks on: "You've reached the Los Angeles Paranormal Investigative Agency. Are your troubles falling into the 'strange' or 'unexplained' category? Don't be afraid to reach out—"

I hang up and dial Kara's number, hoping I'm remembering it right. It goes to voice mail, too: "Hey, I don't wanna talk to you, so just figure it out, or whatever."

I hang up and rack my brain to remember Connor's or Holly's numbers. But I draw a blank. Damn. I try Kara again, praying she'll pick up, but it's still her snarky voice-mail message.

My mind spins, trying to decide what to do. I've got no car, no money.

Eric! His number, I remember. All the times I had to call from a pay phone ingrained it in my brain.

He picks up after one ring. "Aidan, what's happened?" Of course my guardian angel knew it was me. Calling him on the *phone*. A new era of Heaven, I guess.

I breathe out in relief. "There was a demon in the Gap, then the ER was . . . bad—I did something—" I pause because my throat goes tight, thinking of Connor lying there, the woman's scream just before I ripped the demon from her insides. "And then I guess I teleported, because I'm at the beach now. My grandmother's house. But things with my sister are bad, Eric, really bad. And it looks like they're only going to get worse. There was a note, a riddle or something, about a green witch she's going to kill. And she's totally controlling the demons—"

I hear a splash behind me and turn to see Fa'auma holding a towel. There's a look of shock on her face, like she heard what I just said.

Oh, perfect. Just fucking perfect.

I take the towel from her outstretched hand. "Can you make sure Connor is all right?" I ask Eric, still looking at Fa'auma, wondering what her reaction is about to be. "And call me back at this number as soon as you can. I'm freaking out here."

"Of course," he says. "I'll send a car as well."

"Great, thanks. I've gotta go." I hang up and hand Fa'auma back the phone. "Thank you."

She takes it from me slowly, carefully, looking me over with obvious caution as I pull off my soaked shirt and set it on the counter. I dry my face with the towel and pat down my wet torso before I speak. I need to decide if it's even worth saying anything. She hasn't moved, though. She's got the guard dog look on her face, and she smells like a protective parent.

Fa'auma studies me a little longer than comfort allows. "You're a mysterious one, young man. I heard what you said about a . . . a demon?" Her eyes follow the lines of my mark, and I realize she might actually believe my words.

I say carefully, "Not easy to explain."

She nods and keeps studying me like she's considering. After a few seconds, she says, "Thank you for your help with the sink. You were in just the right place at the right time." And then she gives me a wink.

The phone rings, making me jump a little.

Fa'auma holds it out to me. "Probably your friend."

I take it as she turns and grabs my shirt, along with the wet towel, then leaves me alone in the kitchen to talk. I click the "Answer" button and put the phone to my ear, my focus back on what Eric might say. "Hello."

His voice comes over the line, sounding calm. "Connor's all right, Aidan."

I release a shaky breath.

"He's dazed," Eric continues. "It seems your power linked with his spirit—Sid said that your fire connected to him. It's obvious that you didn't read the next under-passage about the power links, and how it pertains to the Lights, but we'll get to that, I'm sure—"

"What about the woman," I interrupt, not in the mood for more Eric riddles. "How's the nurse?"

"The nurse is another story. And you need to understand, Aidan . . . this wasn't entirely your fault."

A chill works through me. "Just say it, Eric," I whisper.

"She died, I'm afraid." When I don't respond he adds, "But you're not to blame, you must understand that. The demon fought, and it's likely that your power isn't totally under control. It was a simple mistake."

"A woman is dead, Eric," I say, an ache blossoming deep inside me. "That's not a *mistake*, it's a fucking nightmare."

A sigh comes over the line, and I can picture him leaning back in his desk chair and giving the ceiling a pleading gaze as if he's asking

Heaven for help. "You need to realize that you can only do so much to save them, Aidan. This is a time for focus. You can't allow yourself to get caught up in the guilt."

"I'll remember that the next time my power is ripping apart a woman's spirit." My stomach twists. I killed her. Another life gone because of me. Because of what I am.

He ignores my cutting remark and says, "When the car gets there, it's going to bring you here, to the club. You can't go back to the LA Paranormal house yet."

I swallow my torment as his words register. "Why?"

"The police are there, asking questions of your guardian."

Renewed anxiety surges into my chest. The cops are looking for me. Of course they are. I killed a woman right in front of them. And now I know what Ava meant. *Out, damned spot,* a quote from *Macbeth,* when the queen was trying to clean the blood off her murderous hands.

I lean on the kitchen counter, staring at my palm, and try not to puke.

"We'll talk more when you get here," Eric says through the thundering in my head.

"Right."

The line goes dead, and I listen to the buzz, my whole body turning numb.

SEVEN

Aidan

I'm not sure how long I stand there before the sound of the doorbell breaks through my shock.

I hear Fa'auma talking to someone, a man's voice answers back, something about Mrs. O'Linn. After a minute or two Fa'auma splashes back into the kitchen behind me.

"The doctor is here," she says. "He's making sure everything is okay with Mrs. O'Linn."

I only manage a nod.

"The plumber will be here soon, too, so I suppose I better get started on cleaning this up." She surveys the small lake on the floor that reaches from the sink and wraps around the right side of the island I'm leaning on.

"I can help," I say. But I don't move.

She doesn't comment, just brings in a mop and a stack of towels.

After a few minutes of working silently, Fa'auma starts humming something. It's a soothing melody and calms my frayed nerves a little. I focus on the notes and her soft voice and try not to think about the nurse who will never open her eyes again. Or the fact that I could've done the same thing to Connor with this freight train inside of me. I could have killed him, too.

I've killed. Again.

Because of Ava. And her wicked *game*. I wonder if she wants me to feel like her, that I belong in her Darkness . . . If so, she's doing a fucking awesome job.

I need to find her. I have to stop this madness somehow, before she kills that witch. Or causes some other horror.

When the floor is somewhat dry, Fa'auma declares to Mrs. O'Linn that there's only one small spot of Pergo that got ruined, and a rug will fix that. I go into the living room and settle myself on the couch as the two women chat about the price of contractors these days. I'm only sitting there five minutes before a plate filled with a tall turkey sandwich and chips is set on my lap. My stomach growls like a bear waking up. I grab the sandwich with both hands and take a huge bite as Fa'auma disappears into the back of the house again.

"Doesn't anyone feed you?" my grandmother grumbles as she looks away from the local news on TV. Her arm has two bandages on it now, and her shoulder, too.

I study her for a minute and then ask around the turkey and lettuce, "So the doc says you're okay?"

"I'm fine," she barks. "Don't talk with your mouth full."

"Sorry," I mutter. I wipe my face on my bare arm, then give her a forced smile.

She humphs and picks up a book of crossword puzzles.

I go back to my sandwich, only half hearing the news on the screen. I'm so engrossed in the meal that it takes me a minute to realize someone just said the name of the hospital I was at. When I look up, I nearly choke. Flashing across the bottom of the TV, I read *STRANGE DEATH CAUSES MASS CONFUSION*.

The screen is filled with an image.

Of me.

It's a bit blurry because I'm far away from the camera, but I recognize myself instantly, perched on the back of the ambulance. Then the picture changes, and it's video taken inside the ER; looks like footage from a phone camera. I'm holding the nurse by the shoulders and shaking her, my arm shimmering. The light blocks my face as it causes that same glare the cop was talking about. The newscaster's voice-over is droning on about "questions" and "some panic on the part of police." Because "how did the assailant escape into thin air?"

Holy fucking hell.

Next, the image on the screen is of a reporter in front of what appears to be the hospital. "The authorities are staying tight-lipped here, Morgan," she says. "No one is sure exactly what happened an hour ago in this ER you see here behind me." She motions with her hand. "All we know for sure is that a woman has died under very mysterious circumstances from an incident that occurred while a victim related to a previous incident in Oakleaf Outlets—an animal attack—was being treated. That patient's name has not been released yet, but we do know it is a male, and we know from an eyewitness that he was being treated for multiple lacerations. As the amateur footage continues to come in, some are wondering who or *what* we are actually dealing with here. The police are clear on one thing, though. They want to speak to this mysterious patient you see in these videos. And it's no wonder, when you watch them. Very chilling, Morgan. Very chilling to say the least. Back to you."

The image switches to a female newscaster in the studio, her face grave. "Thank you, Lisa. Let's fill the viewers in on what they should be looking for." And then a hotline phone number and a bullet point list of "things to look for" appear next to her perfectly styled head as she begins reading the items off one by one:

- *Age: 16 to 20*
- *Hair: dark brown*

- *Eyes: hazel*
- *Ethnicity: possibly Middle Eastern*
- *Lettered tattoo covering his left arm*

They're giving out my description on KVLA.

I swallow the chunk of sandwich that's turned to sawdust in my mouth and glance at my grandmother to see if she's noticed any of what's just been blasted out to the world. She's still busy with her puzzle.

"What do you suppose the smallest penguin species is called?" she asks absently, focusing on the page in her lap. She taps the eraser end of her pencil on her chin. "Five letters."

I grunt in a noncommittal way as my body tingles with adrenaline. I set my plate aside and reach for the remote, quickly turning the channel to a game show.

"Another word for green?" she asks. "Seven letters."

"Verdant," Fa'auma pipes in as she comes back into the room. She sits down on the chair across from Mrs. O'Linn and picks up her knitting. "The plumber called, he's on his way. What're we watching?"

———

Eric's car service shows up just as the plumber does, which lets me slip out without too much of a fuss from the ladies. When I get to SubZero about half an hour later, the sun is setting over the city. I thank the driver and head into the main part of the club. I barely get through the door before delicate arms tackle me, and the familiar smell of vanilla and Kara's sweet energy fill my head.

"You big asshole," she says into my neck. "You scared me half to death. Where'd you go? The cops were everywhere; they came to the house and were there for, like, an hour. I was so relieved when Eric called and said he'd gotten ahold of you."

My nerves settle a little with her touch, hearing her voice, even if it is filled with concern. I kiss her temple and pull back. "Where's Eric?"

"Here," he says, entering the main room of the club, coming from the direction of the back office. "We're so glad to see you're okay, Aidan." He hands me a new phone. "Same number. Try not to go swimming with this one."

"I brought the journal for you," Kara says, pointing to her bag that's set on a barstool behind her. "Eric said you'd need it."

Raul is sitting on the stool next to it; Jax is behind the bar, fiddling with a box full of tiny umbrellas. Sid is leaning on the bar, looking wan and thin, his eyes sunken in, heavy-lidded. His cane is shaking a bit from the pressure of keeping himself propped up.

His choice to stay in this time has cost him, and it looks like it's nearly ready to claim him.

"I'm so relieved that you're all right, son," he says. He runs a hand across his bald head and over his face like he's wiping away worry. "The authorities that came to the house were very persistent. After everything that happened today, this won't go away anytime soon. They will be determined to find you, but we can't let them."

"No," Eric adds. "You'll need to stay here for now. Until we can fix this."

"And how are we supposed to do that?" I ask. "I'm all over the news."

Kara pales at my words. "You are?"

"Infamous," Jax says with a smirk, looking at my wrinkled and sandy clothes. "Too bad you look like shit. Sid said you *poofed* out or somethin'. Seriously wish I could've seen that one. Where'd you go?"

"I ended up at the beach." I look around for Connor, needing to see that he's at least all right. "Near Mrs. O'Linn's house."

"That's crazy-train," Raul says, taking it all in with wide eyes. "Teleporting? Beam me up, Scotty."

I spot Connor standing on the dance floor, leaning against the two-way mirror wall. His eyes are rimmed in dark circles, his skin is almost green in the artificial light of the club, and it looks like a heavy weight is on his shoulders. But he's standing. He nods at me, and I see he's trying to act like everything's fine.

"I can't believe I hurt you," I say, my voice tight. "Man, I'm just—"

Connor waves off my apology. "I'm fine."

"He said that it felt like being electrocuted," Jax pipes in, tucking a pink umbrella toothpick in his thick hair like a barrette.

Kara glares. "Way to rub it in, lame-ass."

Seeing Connor like this . . . urgency fills me that much more. "I need to find some witch, or Ava's going to kill her," I say, turning to Eric.

"You mentioned that on the phone," he says. "I'm not sure how you'd find this woman, but a green witch means a witch who uses earth energy. They tend to be very powerful. Could this be a rival of your sister's?"

"She seems pretty confident about killing her," I say. "This whole thing with a *game* is nuts."

"That message could be a distraction, son," Sid says. "Don't play into her hands and run off to do her bidding."

So, basically, let the witch die.

Ava's always been one of the most stubborn souls I know. And even if she's not the Ava that I knew—not *my* Ava—she's obviously enough like the old Ava to know how to get what she wants from me: put people in danger until I fall into her trap. Sid's right, I can't let her manipulate me. But I don't feel right, sitting by and letting her kill people, either. Even if they are strangers.

"It's my fault," I say. "I woke Ava up after Daniel's warning. I was so focused on having her back that I didn't consider the repercussions. I need to make this right, and I think I better do it alone or more people will get hurt." I can't let anyone else I care about get trapped in this mess with me.

"No, Aidan," Eric says, very matter-of-fact. "Your power is gaining strength. It's not safe to run off on your own anymore. It's not safe for anyone. You saw the truth of that today at the hospital. You need to allow the Lights you've found to take their place, so your power can be balanced."

My gut twists at the reminder of what I've done. *Out, damned spot!*

No, I can't think about it, or I'll crumble. I focus back on what Eric said. "I assumed the Lights were already a thing. I'm living with them, aren't I?"

Eric ignores my question, asking Sid, "How many do you believe you've found?"

"I think there are six now," Sid says. "If Raul is added to the equation." He motions to Raul beside him.

"Mr. Sid got me the fake papers so I can be legit now," Raul says to me, lifting his chin in pride. "Your old room is mine. Since you're shacking up with Kara anyway."

Jax barks out a laugh. "I like this guy."

Eric frowns. "There need to be at least eight Lights to bond you together. Without enough Lights to spread out your power, it could harm them."

"So we're missing two?" Kara says.

Sid's gaze moves from me to Kara and back again. "How do you feel about Rebecca, Aidan? Since the exchange between her and Kara, things have changed, haven't they? Is she linked to you in any way still?"

"What do you mean?" I ask. "Of course she's linked to me." But the answer comes out quicker than it should've, because as soon as the words escape, I realize it's not that simple. Things have changed, and I'm not sure where Rebecca fits. When I'm with her, it's completely different. As if whatever tied us together was severed.

Kara gives me a doubtful look. "You're positive about that?"

I reform my answer. "No, you're right, it's not the same. But how can I tell if the connection's really gone? I have no clue what these Lights feel like. Everyone just seems like a friend. Normal, really. Except Rebecca. She's the only one I felt a strong connection with that I couldn't explain. And now I just don't know."

"Well, let me ask you this," Eric says. "If I had told you that Connor was killed in the ER incident, what would you have felt?"

I glance over to Connor. Just seeing how I hurt him is giving me a million regrets. His eyes seem almost lost, and the smell of weighty exhaustion around him permeates the air. I did that. And I'm horrified. Devastated. So if I hadn't just hurt him, but had *killed* him? I can't imagine.

Eric moves to Connor's side. "Come stand with him, Aidan. Let me show you."

I move hesitantly to obey, my guilt rising as I get closer.

"Hold your marked hand out to Connor," he says. "As if you were going to give him something."

I hold out my hand, palm up.

"Now you, Connor," Eric instructs. "But place your palm above his."

Connor shifts on shaky legs and reaches out, moving his hand over mine.

Instantly the mark on my chest twinges.

Connor hisses in pain, jerking back. "Shit."

"That is the connection," Eric says. "Only it hasn't been solidified yet. You appear to have a very strong bond with Connor, more than the others—besides Kara, perhaps. Most likely because you've spent more time together and there's a true friendship growing between you. And Connor, that feeling you get, that's Aidan's power seeking out yours."

"Like it did with Rebecca that time in the kitchen," Kara says. "You said your power climbed over her skin."

"And now you've taken Rebecca's place in all this, Kara," Sid says, then he looks to me and asks, "How does your power react to her?" motioning to Kara.

I try not to turn six shades of red. I don't really want to answer that in this room full of people. And how would I even form the words to describe the feeling of her touching me, the way it seems to heal me? How do I explain that the last two times I've been *with* Kara, since the exchange happened, the room glows in golds and blues as our energy twists together?

Yeah, my power definitely likes her.

Jax laughs and hits Raul's arm. "Wow, he's the color of Holly's favorite shirt."

"Shut up, asshole," Kara says over her shoulder. But her focus stays on me, like she's worried about what I'll say.

"So your power is affected by her, then?" Eric says quietly, a smile in his voice.

I clear my throat. "It's like my power wants to protect Kara, more than before. As if it's constantly trying to bring her closer."

"It makes sense that Kara would be the Light now, rather than Rebecca," Eric says. "When Rebecca's attachment to you shifted to Kara, the role she was meant to play shifted as well. This could mean her role as a Light was taken away completely, unless a piece of it still remains deep down."

That idea sinks into my gut like a rock. Even if what Rebecca and I had wasn't romance, it was still *something*. I haven't seen her since she left the house last week, after her stay. She was distant and sad. And I'm the bastard who hasn't called to make sure she's doing all right. Some friend I am.

"But that's still only six Lights," Jax says. "Or seven if Rebecca hasn't totally been fired."

And something dawns on me. "Wait a second. If my power is meant to protect, or link with the Lights, then why did it hurt Connor? I don't get how that's going to be a good thing."

"Your power is becoming more dangerous," Eric says. "Especially to your Lights, if they randomly link with you—like what happened with Connor. They will need to be bonded to you and your power in a specific way. You need to allow the hidden passages in the journal to show you the path to accomplish that bond. Then things will balance out again." He motions to where the book is sitting on the barstool. Raul grabs it and brings it to me.

I take the journal and study the worn leather. It's like a counter to my mother's grimoire. I just wish it had told me everything from the beginning instead of doling out answers one at a time. God forbid this destiny stuff be clear.

I try to recall how I revealed the first hidden passage. It had something to do with being pissed off, I remember that. And my blood. I open the book and flip through a couple pages. It did something when I gripped it—

I release a grunt as I hold the leather, biting back the pain as needles stab at the pads of my thumbs again. And then my blood drains out, threading across the pages, filling the space with new text.

I look over the lines as they clarify themselves more. "It's an angelic language." This time the text fills both pages, lighter here, darker there, creating shadows and other shapes within the text itself. A crescent within a larger circle. A cross as the largest symbol, at the upper center of the crescent, along with several other symbols scattered throughout. Wait, that's not a regular cross, it's some kind of a knot-like design. Reminds me of the Celtic symbol for unity. This is no simple drawing, no simple instruction manual. It pulses with heat and power in my hands.

"It's a spell," Eric says. "A bonding spell. But I haven't seen one like this in a very long time."

I really don't want to do a spell that's so freaking huge. I really don't want to cast at all. Ever. Magic is all too unpredictable.

"Bonding powers isn't easy," Eric says, "so I assume that's why this spell reaches such a level. But we need to do it as soon as possible to help protect everyone and disperse your power, even just a small amount."

"Didn't we just say we don't have enough Lights yet?" Kara asks.

"So we find them," Eric says. "As quickly as we can."

I don't want to bond myself even more to people, not with Ava out there, playing this game of wills. I can't let more people I care about be put in my sister's path. And maybe I need to be dangerous right now; I need as much power as I can get if I'm going to stop her.

"I have to deal with my sister," I say. "Before anything else. I can't let this go on. I can't let her game kill anyone else."

"You won't stop her alone, Aidan," Eric says, his tone turning dark. "And this spell might be the only way to protect the people you care about." He glances at Kara and a sharp twinge spreads through my chest.

I turn away, the weight of it all falling over me. Who am I kidding? The people I love are already in Ava's path. And Eric's right, I can't do this alone.

"We know of at least one other possible Light," Sid says, leaning on his cane as he hobbles up behind me. "You need to speak to her, Aidan, to see her and read her, and decide what your heart says."

"Yes," Eric agrees. "If she's still with us, that will leave only one we need to find."

One. One Light in a city of more than eighteen million souls. Is he kidding? Unless that person is already in our circle, there's no way.

EIGHT

Rebecca

This is a crazy, horrible, bad, bad idea. I should *not* be going to the projects alone at night. My dad—and probably every friend I've ever had—would say that I shouldn't be going to the area at all. But I'm not sure what else to do. This last week and a half have been hell. I need to figure this out, and it won't get fixed with me just sitting here.

Connor texted and said that he's not feeling good, so our "date" to investigate the Hollywood sign isn't happening. Probably for the best with the way I'm feeling. My dad went to the office for the evening, since Connor wasn't coming, and I told him that I'm going to spend the evening at Apple's house. My dad doesn't know her parents very well, so he won't call their house to check. He'll stick to texting me.

I've mapped the route to Miss Mae's place, and I'm good. I'll be there and back in plenty of time. No one will know that I was ever gone. I texted Samantha and let her know about my lie, in case my dad calls her parents for some reason. I still haven't heard back from her, but it doesn't matter.

I'm wearing dark, ratty jeans and Charlie's black hoodie, which I'm swimming in. I have three hours before my dad's back home and notices I'm gone, so it's now or never.

After gathering a few things in a bag, including a flashlight, a couple of drawings, and the soul map Miss Mae made for me last time—large splotches of blood on white velvet that I can't understand at all—I head out to the garage and get behind the wheel of my dad's Mercedes. It's brand new and smells like a leather shop. My gut churns, thinking what he'd say—*yell*—if he caught me right now.

I back the car out of the garage slowly, then down the driveway. It takes me a second to see the dark figure in the rearview mirror. Standing right where I'm headed. Luckily I'm only going two miles an hour.

I slam on the breaks, jerking the car to a stop just before the bumper hits the person, who seems to not be paying any attention. What an idiot. I could've run him—*her?*—over, and then I would've dented my dad's—

A knock on the driver's window makes me jump.

I squint at the brown-haired head and roll my window down. "Samantha? You scared me to death, what are you doing?!"

"I'm staging an intervention." She folds her arms across her chest. "We need to talk."

"You're crazy. You couldn't just call?"

"I needed to see your face when I ask you."

"Ask me *what?*"

"What the hell is your damage?"

I lean back and sigh. "Nothing. This isn't something I want to talk about now. I need to go. I—"

I stop talking as she walks around the front of the car to the other side. She opens the door and gets in, settling into the passenger seat. "Then let's go."

I just stare at her, dumbfounded.

"Well?" She gives me a challenging look. "Let's go do this very vital thing at seven o'clock at night. In your dad's brand-new Mercedes. Must be imperative."

"Get out of the car, Sam. You can't go with me."

"Why? Am I not dressed badly enough? What *are* you wearing?"

I growl under my breath and put the car in reverse again, backing the rest of the way out of the driveway. Maybe if I take her into the projects, she'll back off. "Fine. You won't like it, though."

"Whatever."

It's a good twenty minutes before we start getting into the part of town that's not so shiny, and I can see Samantha slinking down more and more in her seat the deeper we get into graffiti-filled streets.

"Are you buying drugs?" she asks in a high-pitched whimper.

"If I said yes would you let me drop you off at the mall?"

"Very funny." After a few more minutes, she seems to deflate. "Please, Emery, I'm really worried. You've been acting so crazy weird, and I can't lose you to rehab or something. You're my best friend, and you tried to kill yourself a month and a half ago! You *have* to tell me what's going on. Why do you keep hanging out with all these rebel guys who punch your friends and carry emo girls from parties, or stalk you in their ratty Jeeps? Who are they? You haven't been the same since you stayed with them. And now you flip out at Apple? You know how she is. She's already putting together a campaign to get you shunned out of the group. This is no way to start off senior year, Emery."

"It doesn't matter what Apple does, Samantha."

She reaches over and takes my hand. "I get that you're sad, you know . . . about Charlie. I'm sorry if I haven't been there for you enough. I'm so dumb, I never know what to say."

"It's all right, Sam. You've been great."

"Not really." She lowers her head. It looks like she might be crying.

My heart softens at her guilt, her self-criticism; she's not just being selfish, she's obviously worried about it all, and I don't want her carrying my stuff, too.

"A lot's happened since Charlie died," I say, not sure how much I can explain right now, or what I can explain at all. "I've closed myself off lately, I know. It's not easy to talk about everything. But I can start with how I got this, I guess." I hold out my arm, bringing her focus to my scar.

She wipes her cheek with the hem of her green cashmere sweater and looks at the mark, the long line of twisted flesh running from wrist to elbow.

"I didn't do this to myself," I say.

She goes still. Even the air seems to be waiting for me to just come out and say it all. But Samantha isn't ready for that yet. So I say the simplest part. "It was a guy that cut me. He seemed to be . . . possessed."

"Oh my God, he was crazy? A crazy homeless man did this to you?"

I release a surprised laugh and shake my head. I forgot how Samantha's brain always fills in a story. "No, Sam. He was one of the boys from the LA Paranormal house. He tried to kill me."

"Holy shitstickles!" She gasps in shock, and then she turns frantic. "You can't *ever* go back there, we need to call the police, what's his name, oh my God, he tried to kill you, thank God you're okay, you could've—wait how *are* you okay? And why in the name of Jimmy Choo did you go back there last week?!"

"Aidan saved me—the dark-haired guy who brought me home from the club that night, the one you invited to Apple's party. He stopped it. And the possessed boy isn't . . . well, he isn't around anymore."

"Oh. Well, still, you need to never go there again." She shakes her head, stunned.

We turn down a street that looks like the one that Kara took to bring us to Miss Mae. I really hope I'm remembering this right. Samantha pushes the button to lock the doors with a *click*. We pull up along the curb, and she gapes out the window at the buildings.

Her breathing speeds up. "So, now that I know you hang out with killers, I'm really not feeling this." She twists the hem of her short black skirt in her fingers.

"Sorry. You're stuck now. I only have two hours before I need to get the car back, so I can't take you home, come back here, and still get it returned in time."

"It's dark, Em. It's dark and creepy."

"It's fine. I've been here before. This lady I'm coming to see is really nice. You'll love her." I'm not sure about that, but I need to get Samantha out of the car somehow. "Come on."

She grabs her Marc Jacobs bag with a white-knuckled grip and slides out, staying kind of hunched over, like she's trying to hide. Or trying to keep her skirt from looking too short. Who knows?

I come up beside her on the cracked and weedy sidewalk and take her hand as I lead her down the center walkway through the buildings. "We love adventures, Sam. Remember when your parents first got divorced and we'd camp out in your dad's backyard in Simi Valley?" I ask. "He had all those huge eucalyptus trees, and we pretended they were monsters."

"You are *so* not helping right now," she hisses at me through clenched teeth.

"We always won, though, right?" I say. "The monsters never got us."

"They were trees, Em. These monsters have guns and tattoos."

I laugh, thinking of Aidan and how Samantha would act if she saw him again, this time all lit up with that fire of his.

"You won't be laughing when we're locked in someone's trunk."

"You watch too much TV." Didn't Kara say something like that to me last time?

A deep voice comes from the shadows on our left, "Hey, it's Ginger."

Samantha grabs me and jumps back, squealing loud enough to make my head vibrate.

Tray is standing there, hands to his ears, when my vision comes clear again.

"Whoa," he says.

Samantha clenches my arm tighter and gasps.

"Hey, Tray." I bite my lips together to keep from laughing.

He smirks. "Who's the terrified white girl you've got attached to you there?"

"This is Samantha," I say. The tension in Samantha's grip loosens. "Sam, this is Tray."

Tray studies her and holds out a hand. "Nice to meet you." And his face lights up with that magical smile of his. He seems taller than I remember, but he certainly doesn't look dangerous. Well, maybe a little. But only in a fun way.

Samantha seems fascinated by his face for several seconds before she notices his offering. She licks her lips before reaching out to shake, a look of apology surfacing on her face.

But when her fingers slide into his grip, instead of shaking it, he lifts her hand to his lips and brushes a kiss across her knuckles. "You have a lovely friend, Ginger."

Sam brightens instantly, and I see her eyes fill with that look she gets when she's checking off boxes to see if a guy's dateable or not—I can also see that she's totally captivated by Tray's beguiling dark eyes. It doesn't look like she's worrying about guys with tattoos now.

I pull Samantha's hand back to her side. "We're here to see Miss Mae, is she home?"

Tray looks away from Samantha and motions for us to follow. "Where's Kara? Do you have an appointment?"

My gut sinks. "No." What if she doesn't let me talk to her because I just showed up? I'm not Kara, she doesn't know me, really.

"Well, this is her busy time of day, so you might have to wait some."

We stop at the door to the apartment, and Tray touches my arm gently, like he's trying to soothe my nerves. "It'll be fine, Ginger. I'm sure she'll see whatever it is that's worrying you and help you sift through it."

I nod, unable to form words that make sense right now. Being here, so close to possible answers, makes all the worry crawl back to the surface. And I don't even care that Tray is calling me Ginger. That's almost as bad as Red—why do guys always do that?

Tray nudges me and says, "Your lovely rich friend can wait with me if you need privacy." He leans close and whispers at Samantha, "I'll keep you safe from all the bad, girl. No worries."

"And who's gonna keep her safe from the likes a' you, Tray?" Miss Mae says as she opens the door to her apartment. Her bright smile greets us, gold teeth and all.

My worry fades a little at the sight of her. She's obviously not too bothered that I didn't make an appointment. She's in a hot-pink housedress with a bright-blue wrap over her hair. The two dozen necklaces she's got around her neck, along with the clacking bracelets, are all especially shiny today, making her shimmer in the dark.

"Well, well," she says, "here you are, surprising me again. And you're so . . ." She grimaces, looking me up and down. "What *are* you wearing, child?"

Samantha raises her brow at me. "See?"

"I need to talk to you about this." I reach into my bag and pull out the rolled-up soul map.

Her eyes widen a little as I try to hand it to her. "Right to the point, aren't you?"

"Kara and I did the—" I glance sideways at Samantha. "Well, I sort of gave her what she needed. But now I feel . . . not like me anymore."

Miss Mae studies me for several seconds, concern growing on her face. "You're scared, aren't you? Thinking you've got nothing left to hold on to, little one?"

Her gentle words, the vocalization of my fears, seem to snap something inside me, and my throat goes tight, my eyes filling with tears.

Miss Mae takes me in her big arms and leads me forward. "Here, child, come inside and we'll figure it out, I promise."

NINE

Rebecca

Miss Mae makes me sit on the couch this time as she goes to the small alcove kitchen and puts a pot of water on to boil. "You're lucky my seven thirty canceled. Sister Vivian can be quite the talker." She bubbles with laughter for a second, then comes in to sit beside me, taking my hand in both of hers. "So your little friend out there doesn't have any vision, does she?"

I shake my head. "I didn't mean to bring her, it just happened."

"Oh, nothing just happens, sweetie." Her eyes twinkle with hidden secrets. "All things are ordered, all patterns are predicted and played out beforehand in the window of fate. She'll be fine out there with Tray. I tease him but he's a good boy, that one." I nod because I don't know what to say to all that. It kind of hurts my brain to think about fate and things being planned out. Especially when I know my fate isn't playing out the way it was meant to.

She clears her throat, sitting up straighter. "So, what can I do for you exactly?"

I unfold the soul map on my knees and stare down at the shapes of dried blood. "I would like to do another one of these map things so you can tell me what's wrong with me. Like, what did I give Kara? How much did I give? Was it everything? I need to know."

Miss Mae turns the map and studies it. "Yes, looking now I see why you made that sacrifice. It's in you, that love, that vital spirit of goodness, it's a part of you. Don't think it all slipped away so easily."

"I still want to know. Can you read me again?"

She moves to the table where she pulls out her stack of cards as well as a fresh piece of velvet, this one a light green. "I chose this color because I'm sensing lots of earth and life around you; green is all over your aura." She goes over to the teapot as it begins to whistle and turns off the burner.

"Oh. What's that mean?"

"Well, the color was more subdued last time, but it was definitely tinted green. Now, it seems . . ." She squints at me, studying as she pours her tea. "It's like someone cut your ties, and so the color's brighter." She shrugs and walks over, handing me the cards to shuffle.

I have no idea what she could mean by all that, but I cut and shuffle the cards and then set them back down, waiting. Miss Mae has me pick out seven cards and hand them over one by one as she sets them in formation. When the last card is placed in the pattern, this odd buzzing starts behind my eyes, in my sinuses, tickling my nose.

She begins turning the cards over with her plump fingers, telling me what each image represents. She says something about the power being in my hands, how the stars are within reach and I will work spells that protect—but I can't really absorb her words. Everything is too foggy in my brain as the vibration gets louder and stronger.

I pinch the bridge of my nose and squeeze my eyes shut, like I'm trying to stop a sneeze.

Miss Mae goes suddenly quiet, and I glance up to see her giving me the oddest look.

"Sorry," I say. "I think I'm allergic to something. My sinuses are going nuts."

"I've seen enough of the cards." She hasn't turned them all, but she pushes them out of the way. "Let's do the mapping right away."

My phone vibrates in my purse, showing an incoming call, but I ignore it. Whoever it is, they can wait.

I watch as she gets it all ready, the bowl of water, a clutch of dried leaves, and that same silver dagger. I roll the pale-green velvet out on the table in front of me and rest my hands, palms up, inside the embroidered golden circle on the surface.

My buzzing nerves start to turn raw as I recall the burning I'm going to feel, the strange ache in my chest. And as she sprinkles the pine-smelling stuff across my hands and slices into my palms, chanting, my heart speeds up, knowing answers are close.

She motions for me to turn my hands over, and when I press them into the circle, the sting in my wounds flares almost unbearably. I let the pain show on my face this time, from the burning as my skin folds back together, healing itself, from the ache in my heart after everything that's happened.

Miss Mae wipes a tear from my cheek and kisses my forehead as the spell works its magic and my blood spreads out into the circle, creating the map.

When she signals that it's over, I lift my palms and look down at the odd shapes on the velvet.

Miss Mae lays out the old map beside the new one and frowns down at it.

Even I can see the differences; the first has more rounded, oval-shaped spots, while the new one is sharper and more scattered. Like there're holes in the pattern or something.

"This is amazing," she says, shaking her head. She goes to a small dresser in the corner of the room and pulls out something from the top drawer. It's another velvet square, this one pale blue. She unrolls it and sets it on top of my old map, beside the new one we just made. "Would you look at that."

"What?"

She points at three spots on the blue velvet. "There, there, and there," she says. And then she points at the pale-green square in three spots. "And then look, it's the same."

I see it, three points on the bloodstain where it seemed the blood reached out, in the same pattern. "What's that mean? Whose map is that?"

"Why that's Kara's map from over a week ago, before the exchange."

"But . . ." Oh my Lord. "That's Kara's soul map?"

"Isn't that interesting, those three anomalies of shape show themselves on yours now."

"What are they?"

"It's the piece of Kara that could trick spirit."

"*Trick* spirit? What's . . . I don't understand. Did a part of Kara go into me?" The moment at the beach with Apple flashes through my mind. *I acted like Kara.*

"It appears so, child. Though it seems it's manifesting different because of your core energy. You see that?" She points at my new map to an area just under the matching pattern. "That's your core and it hasn't changed. It actually seems larger. That's the green I see, the brighter part of your aura. I think you . . . well, it seems you're a witch, child. Like me."

I laugh. "Excuse me?"

"Many souls have this tendency, it manifests in different ways for everyone. When I saw it in the old map, it was small, and just a part of your lineage. Whatever happened in the exchange with Kara seems to have made it dominant. You have casting blood from your mother."

I shake my head, hoping to brush off her words, the confusion they bring. She's saying I'm a witch. A witch. The only other person I know of who's been called that, besides Miss Mae, was . . . Ava. Aidan's sister was a witch. Is.

"Don't be afraid, sweetie. We choose our own destiny."

"Really?" Anger sparks in my gut. "Because I didn't choose this. Not any of it."

A knock on the door breaks through my frustration.

Tray's voice comes muffled through the wood. "I think the Ginger's gonna want to hear this."

Miss Mae rolls up my new soul map along with the old one and hands them both to me. "Don't fear who you are, Rebecca. Allow your spirit to guide you, and know that you are lovely inside and out. That beauty of grace and kindness in you hasn't changed. Not even a little. You just need to allow it to have the space it needs to grow."

I take the maps from her and put them in my purse, feeling numb and confused. "I appreciate your help." I'm not sure what else to say. She did what I asked and has given me answers. But what does it all mean?

I do know that I was right to come. Because it's now obvious that I'm not crazy; I'm *not* the same person. I gave part of myself to Kara, and somehow pieces of her got passed on to me as well. I think of Kara's bravery, how fearless she is . . . I could use some backbone about now.

Miss Mae hugs me before I walk out of her apartment. She kisses my brow, then whispers strange words as she touches my hair. She says good-bye and then disappears back inside, leaving me standing beside Tray.

Samantha is behind him, her face scrunched in concern. "Are you okay, Em?"

"I think Aidan might be trying to call you," Tray says. "My brother texted to tell me that some shit went down, and it sounds like your man got caught up in a bit of a mess."

His words take a second to sink in, but then I think of Aidan in trouble, of Connor beside him when the trouble comes.

I scrounge around in my bag, looking for my phone. It was vibrating, someone was trying to call me. Connor better be okay, he better not be—*he's fine, he has to be fine.*

Aidan's number shows as the missed call. I tap it and wait as it rings. And rings. When I hear a voice come on the line, I blurt out, "Is Connor okay?"

"Uh . . . yeah, he's—" there's a pause. Aidan's voice fades like he's speaking to someone else. "Hey, man, Rebecca's worried about you. Didn't you tell her anything?" Another pause, then Aidan says into the receiver, "Connor is going to call you, but he's fine now."

"He wasn't fine before?" I ask. "What happened?"

"A very long story, but I'll fill you in later. That is if you're willing to maybe help me with something."

I don't like his avoidance, but if Connor's all right, then I guess the details can wait. "What exactly do you need?" I ask, cautiously.

"I need you to come to the club so we can talk. You know the one where we met? Can you swing by?"

"Yeah, I can come. But why?"

"I need to see something . . . I can't explain over the phone. It'll be easier in person. Can you just meet me as soon as possible? Tonight?"

I blow out a puff of frustrated air, feeling like there are a million things that need to be worked out between us before I do him any more favors. But for now, it seems, he's focused on some new problem. "Okay. I'll be there." I should just go home. But he's right, we should talk in person. There are some things we need to talk about. I have to tell him what Miss Mae just said. I wonder how horrified he'll be when he finds out a part of Kara went into me. And that I'm a . . . witch?

I hang up and collapse into the plastic chair on the tiny porch.

"Is everything all right?" Tray asks. "Jax said the cops are after that guy."

My head snaps up. "Connor?"

"No, the magical kid, Aidan."

"Oh." I don't know why, but that doesn't worry me like it should.

"Hey, do you guys smell that?" Samantha asks, sniffing at the air. I'd actually forgotten she was here for a second.

I drop my phone in my bag and stand. "I don't smell anything, but I'm sensing it's definitely time to go home."

Tray lifts his chin and sniffs the air, too. "Wait, I—"

His words are cut off as his body jerks to the side, tumbling to the ground, like an invisible force just shoved him. Hard.

"Oh, God!" Samantha says. She kneels down and hovers over him. "Are you okay?"

My muscles tense. The hairs on my arms prickle and rise. A strange smell billows around me, like rotten eggs and moldy cheese. There's a hissing from under the chair, and a dark shape emerges, something like a hairless dog. Purple and blue veins weave over its thin skin, patches of bristly fur on its shoulders and chest. Its eyes are fully black, as if the pupils took over. The dark holes look at me with a strange giddiness as the creature slinks out into the low porch light and rises up on its hind legs to face me.

My mind goes blank except for one screaming word: *DEMON!* I hear it like a siren telling me to run. But my body won't listen. It won't move right.

I stumble back.

Samantha turns away from Tray to tell me something, but her breath catches, her eyes growing in terror. Tray sits up in a flash, grabbing her by the shoulders to pull her away as he gapes at the thing.

They see it. They see.

Demon. A demon. This is a—

It lunges at me, gnashing its teeth. But I scream, "Back!" And it's as if something hits it on the side of the head, like a punch to the jaw.

The thing lumbers to the side, falling on all fours, huffing yellow breath from its lungs. Its head snaps around, grotesque features full of surprise as it growls at me, confused and angry. *Did I do that?* My eyes sting and my hands tingle, all the emotions and sensations mixed up with terror. I can't tell, I can't tell what's happening.

The creature releases a garbled noise and then tightens its leg muscles, readying to pounce again.

I scramble back just as there's a sizzle in the air in front of me. I sense something, a presence, like a shield between me and the demon. The creature's features shift in an instant from rage and determination to utter terror.

It seems to be staring at something. Something in the space right next to me.

I look around but whatever it is, whatever is making the air change, whatever the demon is gaping at, I can't see it.

TEN

Hunger

It watches. The demon Hunger watches the girl, Rebecca, emerge from the door where the witch lives. Something slinks in the shadows, a beast breaks through them and comes into focus, into the earthly realms, as the boy named Tray begins talking.

The lowborn is readying to strike. It eyes the humans from its hiding place. It doesn't see Hunger, fool that it is, it doesn't realize the master's servant watches. And when its focus lands on the fire-haired Rebecca, it has blood on the mind, a longing for butchery seeps from its thin skin.

The girl doesn't feel it, the shivering air, the corporeal beast made of the shadows, keying in on her. It shifts back and forth while it waits. It gurgles out impatience, wanting to tear flesh from bone with its teeth.

Normally there would be nothing to do but watch and revel in the carnage. Normally the course of action is clear. But this lowborn thing wants Hunger's claim. It thinks itself free to break the pattern and kill flesh without permission from the master.

It must be seeking to please the Ava witch.

The demon Hunger keeps watch as the Rebecca girl hangs up the phone. As the simple-minded Samantha senses something putrid in their midst. And then the lowborn reveals itself, making contact. It shoves at the Tray boy, sending him tumbling to the ground.

Confusion and terror fill the air with a burnt tang the instant Rebecca spots the beast. Paralyzing revulsion hardens her bones, her muscles, keeping her from flight. Realization flickers in the eyes. Green energy stirs unused on her shoulders. And the lowborn readies to lunge.

But before it catches flesh, the Rebecca girl screams a command, "Back!"

Her green energy bursts from her shoulders down her arms, hitting the lowborn in the jaw with a shot of air.

The beast cowers as it scrambles back to its feet. It growls and shakes its head, dazed. But then it gathers itself, even more enraged than before. And it is clear, the Rebecca girl has no awareness of what she's done.

So Hunger moves. The demon Hunger moves into view of the lowborn beast and stakes the claim. Warning and fury at the lowborn's impertinence seeps from bones as a message.

And the lowborn is cowed. It mews and won't look directly in the eyes, knowing its station.

The demon Hunger looms over the weak, shriveled beast of a thing. Rebecca looks on, scrambling for safety. The friends merely gasp and whimper, clinging to each other as they watch the low-beast cower near Rebecca's feet.

Return to your pattern, Hunger growls at the lowborn. *Or I shall give you to the fields of Ash and Shadow.*

You do not know of the one that sent me? She is Queen. All must bow to her now.

No. Return or face the master.

The lowborn garbles out a complaint before it obeys, and Hunger watches it go, the beast slinking back into the shadow pattern, back into the earth where it won't disrupt the order.

"We need to get out of here," the girl's shaky voice says. "I can't believe it, I just—" her words catch in her throat as she helps her friend rise, and the boy takes them both in hand, leading them to a car.

Hunger follows close and finds his fire-haired human's side easily. Finds the space just at the edge where she might hear. The demon waits. The demon Hunger waits for just the right moment of spirit silence. And then . . . there, a chance to whisper.

You are mine now.

ELEVEN

Aidan

Rebecca's voice is frantic on the other end of the line. "It tried to eat me or something, I don't know—it snapped at me and then it just—"

"Are you okay?" A demon tried to attack her. I wasn't anywhere near her, and she was a target. Ava always liked Rebecca. But she's still sending her minions after her? Is it part of the game? Or something else?

"Yeah, I think so," she says. "I didn't have my amulet on—I shouldn't have stopped wearing it. I'm such an idiot. I—"

"Where is the demon now, Rebecca? How did you get away?"

"I don't know where it went. It seemed to get scared. Of something. Something invisible—I didn't see it, whatever it was."

That idea sends prickles of warning over my skin. Scared of something Rebecca couldn't see. Sounds like an angel. Or another demon. "Go get your amulet and put it back on right away. Then just come here to the club. Right away."

"I'm definitely not taking that thing off again," she says. "But I don't think I can come to the club tonight. I just need to get home now, or my dad's going to freak."

"You shouldn't be alone, Rebecca," I say, feeling the distance between us grow even wider and not liking it. "It isn't safe. There's a lot happening and I—"

"Samantha is with me," she interrupts. "And Tray's taking us home, because I'm too out of it to drive. But I'll be okay."

Tray? I've heard about the guy in passing, Jax's estranged half brother, but I don't know why he'd be with Rebecca. I certainly don't know enough about him to trust him with her safety. And Samantha seems fairly clueless from what I recall.

"Connor will want to come check on you," I say, not sure how to ask about Tray, or how to explain everything that's going on. Maybe I should just tell her to turn on the news.

"He can come over tonight?" She sighs like she's relieved. "Oh, that would be—but no, he doesn't have to do that."

"Well, he will." I pause, then just ask, "Why are you with Tray?"

Several seconds of silence pass before she says, "I'm not going to talk about that with you right now. I don't need you getting mad at me along with everything else."

"That's not making me feel better."

"I'm not worried about how you feel for once, other than how it affects me."

The force behind her words jars me, making me pause before saying, "Okay . . . well, just let me know if you need anything. I'm worried about—"

"Yeah, I know," she says, sounding tired. "I'll put my amulet on and see you tomorrow, Aidan." The line goes dead before I can say anything else.

TWELVE

Rebecca

I've been sitting in the living room, staring at the patterns on the Surya rug and chewing on my nails since Tray called an Uber to take him and Samantha home. My treat, since it was all pretty much my fault. I should've never let Samantha tag along with me to see a witch. I can't let her get caught up in all my crazy magical mess. That girl is *not* prepared for reality. In the car on the way home, we didn't even talk about the demon, as if we were all trying to pretend it hadn't happened. And even though we got away, I can't stop wondering: Why didn't it hurt me?

The sound of the doorbell nearly makes me jump out of my skin when it hums through the living room. I hesitate and then realize it's probably Connor come to check on me. The guy needs to learn how to text me warnings in moments like this, after a demon attacks.

When I let him into the house, he steps over the threshold, looking around the wide-open entryway suspiciously before grabbing me and smothering me to his chest. "You need to be more careful. Where was the demon? My God, Rebecca, you could've been—" his voice catches and he squeezes me tighter.

"Connor, I can't breathe," I say into his shirt.

He releases me a little but doesn't let me go entirely, resting his forehead against mine. I kiss his cheek and then tug him to the couch to sit. "I'm okay," I say as we settle in beside each other. "And I'm going to be wearing my amulet from now on, so there's nothing to worry about."

"I can't lose you to this craziness," he whispers. The vulnerable look in his eyes makes my chest hurt. Then I realize how sunken they are, the dark circles under them, how pale he is. Even the smattering of sun freckles on the bridge of his nose looks dimmed.

"I'm okay," I repeat, touching his temple. "But you aren't. You look so sick. What happened?"

He shakes his head.

I scoot closer to him, leaning my head on his shoulder, my fear turning sour at the thought of how vulnerable he is, how much danger he's in sticking to Aidan's side.

"I can't stand this," I say, feeling it all fall on me like a lead blanket.

He just breathes and takes my hand in his, curling his fingers over mine. "I'm so glad you're okay," he says. He shifts to face me, and I find myself studying his features, that lovely sun-kissed face. I want to be the sun and kiss that skin. Always.

I lean in and gently touch my lips to his jaw, tightening my grip in his.

His body stiffens at the soft connection. He leans back a little and looks me in the eye, a question there between us. And I marvel at the way he seems to understand me, the way he cares about me. Because in all this horror, there's this thing between us. It's more subtle than it was with Aidan. It's a secret in my heart that I barely know myself.

I find my body leaning closer again as the thought comes to me. I graze my lips against his and release a sigh, feeling his warmth, his presence, like it could save me.

His hand pulls from mine to touch me, his fingers trailing a path over my leg, gripping my waist. I sink into the kiss, my urgency growing, and find myself getting lost in how much I want more. How much

I want him. My hands turn to fists tugging on his shirt. My body moves as close as it can, pressing into his chest, my breath stuttering, mingling with his as his hands anchor me to him.

His fingers find the hem of my shirt, and calloused palms slip underneath, glide up my side, squeezing my ribs, flickering fire over my skin, bringing it to life. I gasp at the sensation, at the feel of his mouth on my neck.

The sound seems to undo him. He finds my lips again and leans into the kiss, forcing me down against the couch cushion, pressing with his fingertips at the curve of my hip as he settles between my legs. The cautious Connor is nowhere to be found now, his gentleness evaporated, replaced by desperation and need, his and mine. Because I ache everywhere, my whole body pulses with focus. On him, on the tastes and smells, the feel of it all as it consumes me.

I help him pull his shirt over his head. He tugs mine up more, starting to—

"Emery!" The shocked, angry voice fills the room. My father.

I yank my shirt back down and wiggle out from under Connor, my knees coming up to my chest, like making myself smaller will save me.

"What the hell is happening here?" he asks from several feet away. His suit jacket is on the floor at his feet as if he dropped it in his shock.

Connor doesn't react as quickly as I do. His body moves away from mine slowly, his bare chest suddenly very obvious in the dark room. He mutters under his breath, "Shit," and then releases a sigh as he pulls his shirt back on. Only after he's put himself back together does he look at my dad. "Sir, I'm very sorry."

"You bet your ass you are—you're going to be." My dad is so not a tough guy. I can see his face change from anger to confusion as Connor stands—all six feet and broad shoulders of him. That side of my dad that wants to kill Connor seems to be warring with the commonsense side of him that knows he's an investment guy who barely ever works out.

I try to swallow but I can't because my throat's become a desert. "Dad, please," I manage to say, not sure what I'm asking for. *Don't kill my boyfriend.*

"I'm a jackass," Connor says, putting his hands in his pockets and hunching his shoulders. "I'll just go." And he heads for the door.

I jump up and make it to his side, stopping him as he gets to the entryway. "Just wait." Then I look over at my dad, giving him a pleading look. "Dad, can we take a second here?" I hadn't really wanted these two to meet because the idea felt so alien, like then I'd have to choose between the two worlds I've been trying to juggle lately. I certainly didn't want them to meet like *this*. But now, seeing both of them in the same room, my life suddenly seems much more average than it is. It's actually nice to have a normal teenage problem; my dad caught me making out with a guy on the couch.

It's almost awesome.

"Excuse me, Emery, but this young man needs to go," my dad says in a tight voice. "Now."

"His name's Connor. This is the guy you were asking me about."

"Rebecca," Connor says, touching my arm gently, "he's right, I should go."

"*This* is the boy with the beat-up Jeep?" my dad says, as if Connor isn't still standing right there.

"Connor, Dad. His name is Connor. And he's my . . . well, he's my boyfriend."

I didn't think it was possible for my dad's eyes to widen any more, but they do.

Connor rubs his temple and shakes his head. "Rebecca, I'm leaving."

"Stop calling her that!" my father suddenly roars.

Connor jerks back at the sound.

"No one calls her that," my dad adds more quietly. And the thing he's not saying rings loud in the air, *Only Charlie called her that.* My heart squeezes tight in my chest. "This is insane," he says more to himself, running a hand over his forehead.

"Daddy, it's fine," I say, stepping closer, wanting to get that lost look out of his eyes. Because it is fine. And very normal. "I'm good, I promise. Better than good." I want to say, *When Connor's with me I feel like myself again, innocent of pain, like before Charlie died. And I miss that feeling.*

He looks at me for several seconds before asking in a calmer voice, "How old is he?"

"Please stop talking about him like he isn't right here," I say carefully, motioning to Connor.

Connor holds out a hand, like he's trying to tell me not to defend him. "I understand. This looks bad."

"Yes, it does." My dad seems to deflate even more. "It's also a very new experience for me."

"It shouldn't have happened," Connor says, and I know he means it one hundred percent. He feels like he lost control, went too far with me. And he's obviously unhappy with himself about it.

"Don't be ridiculous!" I say, making them both look over at me in surprise. "You two are being crazy. Of *course* it should've happened. I'm a healthy sixteen-year-old girl, I'm not a nun, even if I've been living like one. I *should* be kissing boys and making out with them, but instead all I'm doing is feeling sad and lost, and I'm sick of it." I pause and look between the two of them, but neither one seems to know what to say, so I add, "I'm going to be a normal girl now. I'm going to get into trouble and skinny-dip and get caught by my dad making out with my favorite guy—a guy who makes me happy and safe and whole. Three things I haven't felt in far too long."

Connor's lips tip up in a slight grin.

My dad's mouth has come open a little in shock.

"So, who wants some ice cream?" I ask, straightening my shirt. "After all that, I need chocolate and guilty-pleasure TV. What do you think, Dad? Should we introduce Connor to *Rehab Addict*? And then we can discuss how grounded I am. Man, I haven't been grounded in forever. It'll be fun."

I walk past them as they blink at each other. Silent questions bounce between them as I head into the kitchen.

When they pause only for a few awkward seconds before following me, Dad first and then Connor walking hesitantly like he's not sure what else to do, I find myself considering a future, looking forward to it instead of fearing it, and the warmth that fills me nearly lifts me off the ground.

THIRTEEN

Aidan

When I hear the back door of the house open, I pull out of a sleeping Kara's arms, throw my shirt on, and scramble downstairs to find Connor in the kitchen.

"Is she okay?" I ask. "Why didn't you text me back? I was worried."

"She's fine," he says, looking miserable, and then he puts a palm to his stomach. "But I think I shouldn't have eaten that last tube of cookie dough. My gut is starting to rebel."

"Cookie dough, huh? Did you have a pillow fight in your bras, too?"

He releases a tired sound, unamused. "We were kind of making out and things got—shit, I can't believe I almost let that happen." He shakes his head, looking like someone hit him in the jaw and he's still trying to figure out which way is up. "I'm an ass. I wasn't thinking. Her dad came home when we were in the middle of . . . stuff." He shakes his head again. "Anyway, she was trying to smooth things over with him. Apparently she makes the guy pliable with junk food. A *lot* of junk food and HGTV."

"Shit, man."

"Yeah. Not good." But then he seems to realize something, and backs up with a worried look surfacing on his face. "Hey, wait. What're you doing here?"

"I just snuck in for the night. I'll be gone before sunrise." I couldn't sleep at Eric's place. I tried, but after I talked to Rebecca, it wasn't happening. I kept seeing the nurse's shocked face, hearing her scream, every time I closed my eyes. My brain knows that was the demon screaming, knows her dying wasn't entirely my fault, but my spirit can't seem to rest.

Out, damned spot . . .

Connor raises his brow. "So, you needed a little action, huh?" He pats me on the shoulder with a wink.

My body jolts and a feverish tingle washes over me.

Connor stumbles back, cradling his arm to his chest. He hisses in pain and grumbles, "Shit."

I back up and hold my hands out like a warning. "Fuck, I'm sorry." What am I doing to him?

He shakes it off, like he's trying to rid himself of the feeling of my power. "No, I'm fine." But he's not convincing and red sparks in his eye. "I probably shouldn't touch you until we . . . do that spell or whatever."

"Yeah." I study him as he makes his way out of the kitchen. His breathing isn't steady anymore, and the relaxed energy that surrounded him when he came in is long gone. "Really sorry," I repeat. Apologizing doesn't help, but I don't know what else to say.

Because what *can* I say?

He's almost to the staircase when I realize I meant to ask him something. I walk into the entryway, keeping my distance. "So, what do you know about Tray?"

"He's Jax's brother."

"I know, but that's all I know." Jax was asleep already when I snuck in, so I couldn't ask him for any details. "Is he cool?"

Connor shrugs. "He and Kara were close for a while, a year or so ago. She was going over there all the time, visiting Miss Mae, and he'd always be around. He's a bit of a slick dick if you ask me."

The idea of Kara hanging out with anyone related to Jax, in the way that Connor's hinting at, makes me cringe inside. "You mean, he's another Jax?"

"Older, less of an ass, maybe. But I never trusted him with Kara."

"You never trusted me, either."

"Yeah, and look how that turned out." There's no humor in his voice and I wonder if he's still worried.

"Is Tray like Jax in other ways? Like, does he have gifts?"

He thinks for a second before he says, "Not sure. But Sid asked him to be a part of the house, too. He said no, that he needed to take care of his mom. Or maybe he's just not a joiner."

"I wonder why Sid never mentioned him. He might be a Light."

"Wouldn't that be ironic?"

I raise a brow. "Why?"

"Well because, you know"—he motions to the landing where Kara's bedroom door is—"he was all tight with the Chosen One's girl."

"Don't call me that." I release a sigh and try not to think about any of it. Jealousy is a luxury I can't afford right now. And if I don't trust Kara at this point, I never will. Besides, it's more important to focus on fixing this thing, getting my power under control. "Can you get me in contact with him?" I ask.

"He's not the Mafia, dude. We can just go over there. He's always around the courts in the afternoon."

"How do you know that?"

"He stands around the dealer's corner when his mom gets off of the night shift so he can stop her from buying drugs."

———

Mrs. Marshall gently kisses the top of Ava's eight-year-old blonde head, and I avert my eyes, pretending it doesn't bother me. I have to force myself to not let jealousy take over at the motherly way the kindhearted woman gazes down on my sister, like she's claiming her.

"We don't need to talk about the broken window anymore, Aidan," *she says, stopping the questions I had just started asking.* "Let's have fun at the beach and not upset our little Ava bird on her birthday." *She gives me a tight, shut-up-kid smile.*

I have to bite my tongue so I won't growl out my frustration.

Adults don't like it when you have an opinion. And even though Mrs. Marshall is super nice, she's kind of clueless. She still doesn't understand after all these years that Ava and I aren't like other kids—well, she must be suspicious, but I can see her shake it off whenever I'm around. Which is more often now—now that she isn't worried I'm a bad influence or something.

She leans over and reaches into the bag at the edge of the beach blanket, pulling out a Ziploc full of red grapes. "Let's just have a snack and play, since the sun will be going down and we'll have to be getting you back home soon, Aidan. We don't want to waste our birthday time at the beach fussing over things that can't be changed."

But she's wrong—something's wrong this time. Mrs. Marshall can pretend it's just broken glass, but I can see in the way Ava won't look at me that it's more than that. I can tell by the way her eyes got red with held-back tears when she whispered to me about her bedroom window cracking after she got mad. She looked scared, she smelled scared. And this is familiar, just like her sixth birthday. She's focused on her bucket and shovel now, though, and won't say anything else. Like she's ashamed and just wants to hide what happened from Mrs. Marshall.

I stand and brush sand off my too-big swim trunks that my foster mom got from the Rescue Mission thrift store. "Hey, let's go find some hermit crabs."

Ava's head tips but she stays focused on the shovel for a few more seconds before she nods at the ground. Then she stands, picks up her bucket, and follows me to the edge of the surf. We start to walk, balancing our way over the rocks in the tide pools. *We stop every now and then to search the current for life, a silent exploration, as if we've belonged to the sea all our lives. And maybe we have. Mom always loved the ocean, like she wanted to disappear into it. Instead she disappeared into her mind, leaving us long before her body was crushed.*

Once I think Ava and I are far enough away from Mrs. Marshall, I crouch down and pretend to look more closely at one of the larger pools. Really I just want to get Ava relaxed enough to open up to me.

She sits on a rock beside me and plays with her bucket, acting like everything's fine and this is just another day at the beach. Not her birthday. Not the six-year anniversary of our mom's death. That violent, horrifying death.

I hold in the shivers that fill me, and shove my nausea down as the memory of blood rises, vivid and crimson.

Don't be sad, *Ava says with her mind.* Mommy isn't in pain anymore.

I move a blonde curl that's fallen in her eye, tucking it in her butterfly barrette. I know. I just want to keep you safe. It's my job.

"It's not really your job," she says, a sigh in her voice. "Not anymore." She sounds resigned. And a hundred years old.

"I'm afraid it is, Peep."

She shrugs and plucks a hermit crab from the pool. "Did you know that these glow blue? All the ocean friends do."

"Glow?" I look around the tide pool, but the only light I see is from the sun reflecting off the water like diamonds scattering the surface.

"It's called an a-ur-ra. Or something."

"You mean, aura?"

"Yeah, I think so. It's in Mom's book. It talks about energy and, um, stuff."

That familiar chill related to all things Fiona and her casting works over me. "I thought I told you, you need to bury that thing."

Ava shrugs again, then says absently, "Yeah."

I take her small arm in my hand, trying to let her feel my fear. Promise me. It's dangerous.

She blinks up at me with her wide silver eyes. I know. Mom told me.

———

The sky is still dark when I open my eyes, feeling disoriented. A part of my mind is still there on that beach, the day before the Marshalls died. I wonder why I dreamed about that, the first time Ava mentioned speaking to our mother's ghost. The first time she mentioned reading the grimoire. I thought she buried it soon after the Marshalls' death. I made her promise.

Now she's living in the Darkness, captured by the madness that took our mom. And I'm as helpless to save her as I was to save Fiona. I have no idea how to find her and stop her. No clue how to even start.

I look out the window at the night sky, and my chest aches. Ava's likely killed the green witch by now. Another person lost their life because I failed. It was an impossible task, though—I had nowhere to start. I have no clue why she thought I could do it; I'm obviously missing something.

I reach over and pull my pants off the chair, taking both notes out of the pocket. There's no new message burned into either of them, but Ava seems close right now. Almost as if a part of her just sent me that dream, trying to remind me again of how it's supposed to be: her and me together.

I know one thing for sure. Ava was right in the dream when she said I wasn't meant to protect her. I've certainly done a shitty job.

My chest aches as the weight of the past mingles with the weight of the present. Everything I've done up to this point has only made things worse and put people in danger. Looking for another Light probably won't end any differently, but I have to *do* something while I wait for

Ava to make her next move. Is it stupid to let myself hope that it might be Tray? That the search will be that easy?

The bed shifts and Kara sits up, propping her head in her palm, grumbling, "Wow, your stress is loud."

"Sorry," I whisper, and lean in to kiss her brow. "I have to go back to the club anyway, so you can sleep."

She curls into my side and rests her head on my chest, running her fingers over my mark. She skims along one circle after another with her delicate touch. My power simmers to life a little, yellow sparks flickering at my shoulder and down my arm. "You're not helping with the leaving," I whisper as my body responds.

She props herself on her elbow again and gives me a wicked grin. "Oh, darn."

Then she's leaning in, and we're kissing, finding ourselves tangled together in seconds. Kara's sky-colored essence is cool against my skin, following the trail of her hands, spilling off of her shoulders, down her arms.

My own power entwines with hers, seeking comfort as it finds its way across her back and up her neck, caressing her with invisible fingers. The colors bounce off the walls in blues and yellows like a reflection of water, flickering with each caress. And I wish that she could see it, see with her own eyes how much my heart needs her. Because there are no words to describe it all as things escalate quickly, the unspoken communication between us taking over, our bodies having only one goal, one need, touch and unity. And even though I should leave, I fall into it and let the world slip away.

Which makes it take a second or two before I feel the odd tingle.

A warning buzz echoes in the background of my mind. Followed by a scraping sound coming from somewhere outside.

I break away from Kara and sit up a little, listening intently as a sinking dread mingles with the lust in the room. In an instant, all my senses tick into high gear. I feel the block on the house and move it aside, then I hear something that sounds like someone gasping, and smell a sharp zing of fear.

"What is it?" Kara asks, breathless.

I focus on the location. "I sense something . . . I think it's out back."

She sits up beside me. "Sid," she says, her voice sharp with panic.

We fumble into our clothes and run downstairs. It's clear no one else heard or felt anything. The house is sound asleep as Kara and I rush out the back door. And as we're approaching the shed, I realize something's very wrong with the casting magic in its walls. The vibration I usually feel when I'm close has changed, become even more twisted—if that's possible. It calls out to me, the gravity a million pounds against my skin.

I stumble as it hits me, but keep my feet.

Kara finds him first. "Oh, God," she moans. "Sid, oh my God, no."

I come around, and my hand goes to my mouth. Sid is on the ground, back hunched, just outside the shed's doorway. He grips the frame with white knuckles and huffs air in and out laboriously through his rattling lungs.

The tall green grass around him is speckled with fat drops of crimson rain.

He heaves again, leaning over, vomiting blood at his feet.

"Help me get him back in the shed!" Kara cries.

The way it's pulsing at me, no way anything living should be in there. It wants dark things. It wants death and blood. The door is wide open, and I realize the casting seal has burned through from the other side, still sending up threads of smoke from the charred wood. And there's a new symbol just underneath it, a curse, written in what appears to be a mix of chalk and blood. The paint underneath the chalk seems to be blistering.

"No," I say. "He can't go in there."

Kara starts to argue, but Sid sits up a little and takes her arm. "Aidan's right," he whispers through trembling lips. "Take me to the house."

Kara blinks at him with tear-filled eyes and then gives a jerky nod.

I go to his other side, taking him under the arm to help him up. "We've got you," I say.

We manage to get into the house as the sun breaks violet over the horizon. He has to throw up again and stumbles to the sink as we enter the kitchen. The blood splashes up as it hits the fiberglass. Sid's thin body shakes as Kara and I hold him steady. His arm, his shoulder, is glass in my grip. He teeters on the edge, and death seems to move closer.

I knew it was coming, but it's happening too soon, far too soon. What's gone wrong? Someone drew that curse on his shed. Someone . . .

But I know who it was.

Kara grabs a rag and wipes his face, her tears falling.

Sid reaches up and touches a bloody finger to her cheek, trying to brush the evidence of her pain away. "This is right, Kara. It's how it was meant to be, don't forget." His breath rattles through his words, and she just stares at him, her face draining of color.

"We need to get you on the couch," I say.

I grab a large mixing bowl from one of the cupboards as we pass it and one of the towels hanging from the oven handle.

Once he's sitting, his rasping breath seems to steady. Kara runs to get a blanket, then comes back and fluffs up the pillows, helping him get situated. "You're going to be okay," she keeps repeating. I see flashes of red in her eye each time the words emerge, each time she lies to herself. "And if you leave us, Aidan can just bring you back with his powers."

"No, Kara," he says, "I told you I will have no real body to come back to. Time is tearing me apart."

She shakes her head, not listening.

I had decided the same thing; I planned on trying to resurrect him. But my power only unites body and soul. If his body is decayed or ruined, I'm not sure a resurrection would even work.

"So proud, I'm so proud of you both," Sid says, "and so thankful to have seen what you've become."

"Be quiet with that," Kara mutters. "You're not going anywhere."

He grabs Kara's arm, stopping her words, stopping her from fussing with his blanket. He takes my wrist, too. His peace is a steadying force in the room, calming me.

He looks back and forth between us, the shadow of a smile on his bloodstained lips. Then he brings our hands together, gripping them with more strength than he should have right now. "This is why we breathe. This." He shakes our entwined hands. "This is why you will be fine once I am gone. And you will see why I have done what I have done. And perhaps you will forgive me. Perhaps you will." His eyes seem to grow heavy, and his body sinks farther into the cushions. "I will rest now," he whispers in Chaldean, and his hands release ours, going limp in his lap.

Kara crumples at his side with a sharp sigh. She rests her forehead on the cushion beside him and seems unable to move. I stand over them, watching Sid's chest rise and fall slowly, counting each long pause between breaths.

"He's just sleeping," I say to reassure Kara. Reassure myself.

After a few drawn-out seconds of silence, she lifts her head and says, "He's not safe out of that shed for much longer, I don't think."

"He won't be safe *in* the shed anymore," I say. She gives me a questioning look, so I add, "There was a curse on the door. A new drawing. And something about the energy is different, stronger, more . . . ravenous. The seal on the door was burned through, too. Whatever the casting was meant to do, that curse twisted it into something else. Blood magic can do that—the beginning purpose isn't always the ending force. It felt to me like the curse may have made the initial spell turn on him."

"A curse? But how——?" She stops asking her questions, realizing the answer quickly. She seethes for a few seconds and then says, "Ava's not going to let up at all now, is she?"

I can only shake my head and swallow the ache in my throat.

She takes Sid's hand again. "I would be dead if it weren't for him. I never would've met you." She looks up at me, her tears only dry salt on her cheeks now, but the misery is still clear in her eyes. "We need to help him."

"This isn't something we can change, Kara. He made the choice to stay. Even if Ava hadn't cursed the shed, he'd be leaving us soon, anyway."

"Do you think . . ." She doesn't finish, like she's nervous to say the words.

"What?"

"Your father," she says, making my breath lodge in my throat at the reminder of the ancient prophet. "Could he help us with this? Wasn't Sid his student?"

"I think Sid would have said something if it was that simple." Sid was shocked when I told him about Daniel. Shocked and sad, as if he was disappointed Daniel hadn't contacted him yet.

"Do you have a way to reach him?" she asks, standing up. "Didn't he go to the Middle East or something?"

That's what Eric told me. And like everything else with Daniel, Eric was very stiff when he brought it up, as if the workings of the ancient prophet were secret or dangerous.

"It's not happening, Kara. I wouldn't even know how. And if he wanted to talk to me, he would."

She nods but I can tell she's not letting the idea go. She sits at Sid's side and tucks herself around his arm, resting her head on his bony shoulder, like a daughter might. Then she closes her eyes and a fresh tear escapes, slipping down her cheek.

And I know she's not just going to sit by and let this happen. That's not my Kara.

I lean over and kiss each of them on the forehead, then whisper, "Just rest. I need to get back to the club."

But as I turn to leave, to head back to the warehouse apartment, the reality, the emotions, tug at me, as if the gravity pulling Sid away from us is pulling me back to his side again. A warning. Time's almost up.

FOURTEEN

Aidan

A new message comes just as I'm settling on the apartment couch an hour later. The sun casts its glow over the living room; another day I'm not ready for is already in full swing. I feel the magic in the air this time as the piece of paper on the coffee table sizzles. I watch the words appear, and my pulse speeds up as I read over them.

You are so clueless. But you're also super lucky. Your witch had a card up her sleeve. I'll get her another way. I guess you win that one, but I've got another, buck-o. Hint: Someone sweet will soon be in my soldier's teeth. Save her within the hour.

I stare at the paper and seethe. This is madness.

At least the green witch is still alive, whoever she is. I pace the living room, racking my brain for who I know that Ava might want to hurt next. She already tried to get Rebecca, but maybe she'll try again. Rebecca is definitely sweet.

I pull out my phone and text Rebecca that she needs to call me right away, even though she's coming over later this morning. Her house isn't warded at all. Anything could get in there.

I grab my jacket and head outside for some fresh air, hoping maybe I'll see her arriving. The sky is coated in thin grey clouds as I check the parking lot, and there's a slight chill in the air. Hanna's car is here already. She's probably inside. Maybe I should talk to her about all this, get some advice from a sensible person. I head across the lot to the main part of the club.

As I'm starting to go around the side of the building, I see her. I wave but she doesn't notice me. She's bent down, talking to someone who's sitting on the front sidewalk near the opening of the alley. It looks like a homeless man. She hands him a white pastry bag—she's giving him her breakfast.

She smiles her kind smile at him and tips her head as she says something I can't hear.

And then a hand shoots out from the bundle of rags and grabs her throat.

My body jerks to a halt, my mind unsure what I'm seeing.

Hanna's eyes go wide in shock, her mouth opening, looking for air.

It all clicks into place in a heartbeat, and I spring forward, closing the distance between us. But before I can get there, the man is rolling on top of her, beating her head into the concrete.

She gasps, cries out. And the smell of blood lifts into the air.

I skid into them, grab the man's filthy jacket and yank. My dagger is in my other fist already, coming at him in warning. He tumbles off Hanna's body, the jacket fabric tears, and suddenly it's all I'm holding.

He squirms away and darts down the alley, back toward the warehouse. I'm on him in three paces, tackling him, trying to take him off balance. My foot slips on cracked gravel and we both tumble to the ground, the dagger flying from my hand.

He scrambles up onto my back, pins me, smashing my face into the filth beside the trash bin. The smell of rot smothers me. A sudden fist to the kidney, then another. My skin burns, head throbs. And rage fills me.

I roll, shoving him off with every ounce of strength I have in me.

He goes flying. With a *crack* his body hits the wall ten feet away. Then lands on the ground.

I rise to my knees quickly, ready for the next attack, the next escape. But the man isn't moving.

My power smolders on my arm and shoulder as I try to catch my breath. I can't think. The urge to lunge, to hurt, still courses through me. Everything happened so fast.

I feel someone come up on my left and spin to block a hit. But it's only Hanna.

She limps over to me. "My God, are you all right?" She glances sideways at the man crumpled on the other side of the alley, panic on her face.

Shouldn't I be asking her that? She's the one that was attacked by . . . a man?

I get to my feet and nod that I'm okay. I study her troubled eyes, reaching out to touch her shoulder gently. "Your head . . ." A bruise is already surfacing on her arm, and there's a scratch on her cheek, her hair's spilling from its tight twist, and there's blood smeared on her neck. "Hanna, I'm so sorry."

"Why?" she asks, sounding confused. "Aidan, you saved me."

We both look over to the pile of rags again, and I move closer. I can't see his face.

"Is he possessed?" Hanna asks from behind me.

I crouch down and she protests.

"We have to see if he's all right," I say. Whatever thing that pushed him to do this, inside his skin or out, this is still a human soul. I tense my muscles and reach out to feel for a pulse at his neck. There's a slight beat against my fingers. Relief fills me. I didn't kill him.

I start to roll him over to get a better look—

Three demons the size of rats skitter from under him, like cockroaches fleeing the sunlight. I stop one with a foot, then a second with a hand, but the third slips past Hanna's feet unseen, then disappears under the trash bin.

My power surges, and the two I've got pinned gasp out a squeal as they crumble into ash. Parasites, these things could drive anyone mad. They must've been controlling the man.

A figure appears three feet away with a shudder of air, making my ears pop. Eric.

"Hanna!" He looks around the alley, frantic. He spots her and releases a long breath, then rushes to her. He takes her in his arms, kissing and holding her gently. "I can't . . . I had a horrible feeling—then I felt Aidan's power. My heart, you're all right, aren't you?" She nods and rubs his arm, almost as if she's consoling him now.

He turns and looks at me, then down at the man in rags crumpled beside me.

His features turn hard. A faint shimmer of gold rises onto his skin, human Eric flickering into angel Azri'el for a moment. His scent is fury and malice. It's so strong I wouldn't be shocked to see the asphalt melt at his feet.

I stand up, ignoring my aching muscles, my burning side. Whatever was damaged, I'm healing now. "He's human. It looks like a few pest demons were latched on to him."

Eric stalks over, appearing to grow larger with each step.

I put a hand on his chest, knowing he wants blood. "We need to let this go now," I say. "It wasn't him, Eric. It was the demons. I can just take him and drop him off at the homeless shelter. You can smell the alcohol on him, the guy's likely not going to remember any of this."

His gaze moves to meet mine. His eyes darken. And I wonder if he'll just crack me in half to get me out of the way.

Hanna puts a hand on his arm. "Come on, Eric. Let's go inside, and you can help me clean up these cuts and check my head."

That snaps him back, and his face fills with pain again. He turns to her and they walk together into the club. I wait, let them have their moment, and try to figure out how to deal with this guy.

Eventually Eric comes back out. He's calmer, but he still looks seriously pissed. He helps me move the limp body into a sitting position.

"Is Hanna all right?" I ask.

He clenches his teeth and nods, but doesn't elaborate.

The man groans and his head lulls.

"If you help me get him into Hanna's car, I can drive him to the shelter," I say.

Eric shakes his head. "You shouldn't be out there right now. I'll take him." He pauses before picking the man up. "Ava did this, didn't she?"

I nod. "Her game." The misery fills me again at the thought. "How do I find her, Eric?"

"You won't. She's cloaked herself. Even my own brothers haven't been able to locate her."

"But she and I have a connection. Doesn't that mean something?"

"Do you mean your mother's blood?"

"No, we can speak mind to mind."

He's silent for several seconds, then he says, "I'm unsure how a mind link could help you find her if she doesn't want to be found. She has the control right now, she has the upper hand. That is why you need to work on finding a way for this bonding spell to be done. You'll need as many souls on your side as you can get."

"I hope to go see someone today who might be a Light. And Rebecca's on her way over soon."

"Good." He pulls the homeless man into his arms and stands as if the guy weighs next to nothing. "I'll be right back. Wait here." And then he's blinking away, only to return with a pop of air a minute later. I'm guessing the man is safe wherever Eric took him.

As we're walking into the club again, I remember there's more to be said. "Something happened with Sid early this morning." My throat tightens as the memory fills me. "He's taken a bad turn. I don't think it will be much longer before . . . I'm pretty sure Ava cursed his shed so his spell wouldn't work right anymore."

Eric glances back at me over his shoulder, heading up the stairs to the office. "Perhaps we should place stronger wards over the property. Similar to the ones we placed at your great-grandmother's."

More wards. All we ever have are wards. They're all over this place, and they didn't protect Hanna a few minutes ago. It feels like we're only swatting back a fly when we really should be preparing to fight off a lioness. "I know we need to block her out as much as we can, but I feel like I need to let her in at the same time. How else am I going to catch her?"

He's silent as he opens the office door and walks over to the couch where Hanna is sitting. He kisses one of the scrapes on her forehead and then sits beside her. She holds a cold compress to her head and leans on his shoulder, closing her eyes.

He looks over to me. "And what do you think you will do once you have *caught* her?"

"I . . ." I have no idea. "There has to be a way to change things. Maybe we can put her in a deep sleep again? Just for the time it takes for us to figure out how to heal her, or fix this mess."

"You don't truly believe any of that will work."

I don't. But what else can I do? "If I could manage to get my hands on her blood, then I can throw her into the doorway."

"Don't you think she's thought of that? Maybe this is why she hides from you. In any case, she would just find a way to return, and then the struggle will begin all over again."

I clench my jaw. "I don't know, Eric. You tell me, then. What do we do?"

"I've been looking for alternatives to the only answer I can come up with, trust me. Because I know that answer isn't easy. And it's not something you can do."

"What answer?" I ask, feeling breathless. Because I think I know.

He gives me a steady look. "Kill her." Hanna's features pinch in pain as she opens her eyes, looking up at him. Then he adds, "Destroy her. Annihilate her from existence."

He's right, I couldn't do that.

God, I'm a coward.

"It's all right, Aidan," Hanna says.

"No," I say. "No it's not." I should be able to do what needs to be done to keep people safe. Whatever that means.

But when I think about hurting her, my little sister, cutting into her with a blade, burning through her spirit with my fire . . . my stomach churns. I just . . . I can't.

"How?" I ask. When he gives me a questioning look, I clarify, "She's a Nephilim. How would we even . . . do it?"

"A human would have to sever her head from her body."

I step back involuntarily.

Sadness fills his eyes. "Your power would likely allow you to kill her with a blade through the heart, or the brain."

I choke on a burst of emotion at the vision of it and find myself sinking into a chair. It's gruesome. Horrifying. I breathe through my nose and try to steady myself, hold down my gut as it rises.

"Let me keep looking for another way," he says, quietly. "You find those Lights so we can be sure the others can protect themselves and you can have some backup. All right?"

I give a jerky nod and swallow the sharp pain in my throat.

FIFTEEN

Aidan

Rebecca seems to be in better spirits when she answers my frantic text from earlier. She writes that she's fine, and she'll be swinging by the club soon. There's a heart emoji at the end, so that's a positive sign. And since Hanna was obviously the "sweet" person in Ava's threat, I don't feel the need to say anything else.

I call and check on Sid, and Kara says he's the same, sound asleep; she's filled everyone in on what happened. I hate that I'm here and not at the house with the them. I hate that I'm a walking BOLO. While I wait for Rebecca, I'm back to sitting in the warehouse apartment with books stacked on the teal brocade couch. If there are any answers in the thousands of pages around me, I won't find them. I can't focus on any of it. The ink blurs into grey and black smudges as my mind wanders, and the rest of the morning comes and goes.

Rebecca obviously isn't feeling the same urgency to see me that I'm feeling to see her. I thought she meant she'd be leaving her house in mere minutes when she said "soon." Why would she be worried, though? She has no clue what's happened in the last twenty-four hours.

I should have taken one of Eric's cars to go and get her.

But just as I'm tossing aside a book and going to get my phone on the kitchen counter, it pings with a text.

```
I'm here, where do I go?
```

Relieved she's okay, I type back.

```
In the warehouse. I'll meet you in the
    main garage by the cars.
```

I head out of the apartment and down the stairs to the garage. My rushing footsteps echo in the huge space. I'm so relieved when I see her emerge from the light shining through the side door that I grab her up in a hug as soon as I reach her. "I shouldn't have let you come alone, I'm sorry. After everything, I'm just . . ."

She doesn't return the embrace. She pulls away and frowns at me. "What's going on, Aidan. You're seriously freaking me out."

I step back, and suddenly have no clue what to do with my hands. It bothers me that she pushed me away just now. "Let's talk in the apartment," I say. As soon as we're inside and she's settled in one of the chairs in the small living room, I stand in front of her and say it: "I needed to see you because of my sister. She's finally coming at me. At us."

"Us?" She doesn't seem to like the word.

I tell her a little about what happened yesterday at the Gap and the ER, as simply as I can, and watch as she goes from guarded to *very* guarded. As I elaborate on the media and the police, she starts to smell like fear and bites at her nails.

"So, it was Ava who sent the demon to attack me last night?" she asks.

I nod. "Pretty sure."

Her gaze moves to my pile of books. "I thought Connor was acting strange and wanted to tell me something, but we never really got to talk because my dad showed up."

"I heard."

Her eyes skip back to mine, and her cheeks flush pink.

"But there's another reason I needed to talk to you," I say, ignoring her embarrassment. I start to pace, trying to figure out how to explain. "I'm supposed to find at least eight Lights to do a spell to bond our powers, and I need to see if you're still one of them, or if that connection is really gone now."

"Still a Light," she says, carefully, like she's feeling out the idea. "How do you tell if I am?"

"I'm not sure." I stop pacing and face her. "Do you feel any connection to me? More than just friendship?"

She studies my face. "No, Aidan. Everything I felt for you is gone now."

A red spark lights her eye.

I step closer and crouch to her level. "You just lied."

She leans back. "No, I didn't."

"You may not think so, but you did."

She blinks at me for several seconds, then says quietly, with assurance, "I care about Connor. A lot."

"And I love Kara."

We stare at each other, and her confusion seeps into my skin. The way her chin comes up in defense and the innocent way her cheeks glow as I study her should make me feel more than endearment. I should want to soak in the sight of her curves, the delicate line of her coral lips.

But she's not inside my skin, not like Kara. My feelings for Rebecca are protective, brotherly. And I'm fairly sure she feels the same friendship. So what is it? Why did she lie?

"I'm positive we're not connected anymore, Aidan," she says, her voice stern even as her gaze shifts away from me, to the floor. Her fingers play at the hem of her sundress.

"Why are you so sure?"

She shakes her head. "I just am."

I take her hand in mine, but she pulls it back and cradles it in her lap, leaning back again.

"What's wrong, Rebecca?"

She just stares at me. Her green eyes glisten as her jaw works. Her body is tense. As I watch her walls go up between us, my own worry grows.

"I went to see Miss Mae," she says, quietly. "Last night."

I move to sit a little farther away on the coffee table. Rebecca was at the witch's house last night when she was attacked? "What did she say?"

Rebecca takes in a shaky breath. "I'm not a Light. I'm not supposed to be with you. I'm the exact opposite."

"Miss Mae told you that?" Green witch or not, it's obvious Miss Mae isn't much of a reader of people. Rebecca is *not* the opposite of a Light. I know that much.

"She didn't say that, exactly," Rebecca hedges. And then she stands abruptly and begins to pace "Things have been . . . weird since the exchange with Kara."

"What do you mean?"

"I haven't felt like myself. I haven't *been* myself. I wasn't sure what was going on with me, so—"

"So, you went to Miss Mae for answers. And she gave you some. Just say it, Rebecca."

She spins to face me. "Give me a second!" The green of her eyes flashes. "God, you're so annoying."

My head pulls back in surprise. "I am?"

"Yes!" She throws her hands up. Then she comes at me, her finger pointing in my face. "You're always so perfect and protective and bossy and you care about freaking *everyone*. It's exhausting. And you know everything!" She motions around her to the books, then goes back to pointing accusingly at me.

Oh, boy, is she wrong.

"But I don't know anything," she continues. "I really don't." Her finger pokes at my shoulder. "So let me take a second to think."

I look up at her, her red hair hanging in her face, her eyes fiery, her energy sweet and full of sass, and a strange feeling overwhelms me, like déjà vu. "What's gotten into you? You're acting like—" But my voice freezes in my throat as a very blurry puzzle plays out in front of me.

Her hand falls back to her side, and she looks into me like her brain is following mine down the rabbit hole.

She just keeps looking at me, then whispers. "It's crazy right? I guess some of her went into me in the exchange."

How could I have not thought of this? The road went both ways. "Miss Mae said a part of Kara went into you?"

"She said I got some kind of gift. One that could . . . trick souls."

The air leaves my lungs. "Kara didn't have any gifts. She was cursed." I should have looked at Rebecca's soul after the exchange, checked and made sure everything was all right. But I was so caught up. I was . . . I was being selfish. Rebecca gave so much, she'd only been there for others. And all I could do was let her give and not care about the consequences to her because I was so relieved that Kara was safe. God, what a prick I am.

"Miss Mae didn't act like it was a bad thing," she says. "She just said it wouldn't—*manifest*, I think is the word she used—she said it wouldn't look the same because of how I'm a—"

Her words break off, and her eyes grow a little like she almost let something slip.

"You're a *what*?" I ask, looking her over. What the hell did that witch tell her that's got her so messed up in the head?

She backs up several steps, and her chin goes up in defense again. "She said I'm a witch."

SIXTEEN

Rebecca

Aidan laughs sharply, like a shock just ran through him.

I can't look him in the eye; he seems completely stunned. So I just repeat myself. "She said I'm a witch. Because of blood on my mom's side."

"You're serious." His expression becomes severe. Then he turns and goes to the couch, sinking down on the cushions, shaking his head. "I can't believe it," he finally mumbles under his breath. "I don't even know what to say."

"Yeah, well, me neither."

He sits there for what feels like more than a minute, staring at his hands. A hundred emotions surface on his face, like he's having some sort of silent conversation with himself. Just when I think he's decided he won't be speaking to me again, ever, he says, "If this is true, we need to find out what it means. It can't be a coincidence."

"What do you mean?"

He looks up at me, and confusion and doubt cloud his features now. "My sister knew what you were. She told me to find you."

I stare at him, stunned. That's really not what I expected him to say. "Ava knew what I was?"

He picks up a tiny piece of paper off the coffee table and looks at it, mumbling, "The demon attack. Of course."

"What?"

"I can't believe it. You're like her."

I really don't like the sad tone in his voice. *Her*. Ava. I am so not Ava. Am I?

"This has to mean something," he says. Then he looks up from the piece of paper to me. "Doesn't it?"

And suddenly he's coming at me, grabbing my hand, pulling me from the apartment.

"What're you doing?!" I ask, terrified he's lost it and is about to kick me to the curb.

"Taking you to the man who might know what the hell's going on with all this."

"Who?"

"My guardian angel."

He moves fast, but he stops pulling on me as I follow him down the stairs, back into the large garage. The ceilings are at least three stories above us. A black car is parked off to the right in front of a large roll-up door that he rushes us past, then he's walking down a hall where there's an eight-foot round metal door that looks like the opening to a bank vault. "Your guardian angel is locked up in there?"

"It's Eric, he's my guardian. He owns this place. This is usually where he works at this time of day."

"Oh." I've heard Eric's name mentioned but I didn't know he was an . . . angel. How does an angel *own* anything? Don't they just watch from church steeples or something? Or is that gargoyles?

He punches numbers and letters into a keypad beside the vault door, and there's a thud as it unlocks.

"You can let go of me now," I say as he opens the heavy door. He releases my hand and motions for me to go in front of him. I step inside and have to hold in a gasp. It's a museum. Statues, paintings, huge pieces of pottery stacked along the wall. Rows and rows of metal shelves jam-packed with what look like ancient artifacts, books, and scrolls. The artist in me is in awe; my fingers itch to touch, to draw the timeworn relics all around me. I totally get the vault door now.

I walk into the large space, feeling like I'm entering a temple full of holy things. It smells like dust and paper and oils. The sight, the feeling, leave me breathless for a second before I realize he's talking to me.

"Eric has to know why this came up now," Aidan is saying. "I mean, it's not like the legacy just showed up in your blood. It's been there since you were born. And Ava knew, so it must somehow be connected to what she's doing. It has to be." He pauses, then something seems to dawn on him, and he gets this odd look on his face. "How could you be a Light, then? And you were supposed to be my soul mate?" He sounds disturbed by that idea.

I have to tear my eyes away from studying an unframed painting in the corner that looks like da Vinci could've painted it. "What *is* a Light, really?" I ask.

"One of my soldiers, I guess?"

There's an echo of footsteps from behind one of the shelves to our left, and then a voice says, "They aren't *your* soldiers, Aidan. They belong to HaShem."

A tall blond man emerges from a row of artifacts. All my focus lands on him, his presence in the room like a beacon. He has etched and striking features, but his hazel-green eyes are soft, even kind, as he studies me. If this man is an angel, then angels have great taste in clothes. Samantha would be floored by those shoes. Definitely Italian.

"Hello, Rebecca," he says, his voice quiet.

"Hello," I say, feeling a little vulnerable as his gaze becomes penetrating.

His lips tip in a small smile. "It's lovely to meet you, finally." He walks toward us, and I see there's a woman behind him. I hadn't noticed her at all. He holds out his hand for me to shake it.

I take it, and as his skin touches mine, it seems to glisten with golden flecks. Did I really just see that? He lets go before I can be sure.

"This is a surprise," the woman says. She comes out from behind the shelves. She's beautiful. And tall, almost as tall as Eric. She has a small bandage on her temple and her feet are bare, but somehow she still looks perfectly put together.

"I'm Hanna." Her dark eyes search my face then skip over to Aidan. "Perhaps next time you can let us know if you need something in the vault."

Aidan looks between Eric and Hanna, but only says, "Sorry." Then he focuses all his attention on Eric. "Something else has come up, Eric. I'm not sure what to think."

Eric glances sideways at Aidan as he speaks, still focusing most of his attention on me. He's studying me so intently; it should be intimidating, but it's not.

"Did you bring her here because of something specific?" he asks, nodding to me.

"Miss Mae told her she might be a witch," Aidan says.

"She didn't say *might*," I correct. "She said I had the blood of a witch, from my mother's side."

Eric's brow goes up, and his eyes scan my body, starting at my feet and up, then seeming to eagle-eye my hair. "Interesting."

Hanna comes forward to stand beside Eric and study me as well. "Very curious."

"Yes," Aidan says. "And crazy when you consider that she was supposed to be my soul mate, and that she might still be a Light."

"Why is that crazy?" Eric asks.

Aidan just gapes at him. "Seriously? You know what my mother was—what my sister *is*. Take a wild guess."

His insistence on comparing me to his sister is getting infuriating. "Obviously not all witches are bad, Aidan," I say.

He looks over to me.

"I mean, Miss Mae isn't evil," I add. I don't think she is anyway. She sure didn't seem to be. The woman helped me find answers, and she didn't have to; she didn't ask for anything in return.

"I've never met her," Aidan says.

"And so you think you have the right to judge her?"

"I'm not judging anyone," he says, but I can tell he's forcing his voice to be calm. "I'm just trying to figure out why my sister was, for some reason, directing me to you with her terrifying *game*. She's playing us, and I need to know how, I need to know why. How is she going to use this to cause more death and torment?" He makes a sound of frustration in the back of his throat and goes over to sit in a desk chair, looking defeated. "She tried to kill you, Rebecca. There's something about you that she's threatened by."

His words, the helplessness in his voice, the sheer idea of Ava having some sort of design on me . . .

I shiver.

"Have you looked at Rebecca's soul since the exchange with Kara, Aidan?" Eric asks.

Aidan shakes his head, looking annoyed at himself.

"I think that I would like to see." Eric glances over to me. "Would you mind?"

My tongue is apparently paralyzed. I can only look at the blond man in the expensive shoes and wonder what his reading my soul might entail. I remember Aidan saying that he could see it, that he knew I was a virgin. I'm just not sure when it was that he actually saw my soul—or *how* he sees it.

"Don't be afraid," Eric says.

Aidan seems to realize I'm panicking a little, because he says gently, "You can say no, Rebecca."

"No," I say. "I mean, I'm sure it's fine. I just don't know what I'm supposed to do."

"Nothing," Eric says. "I'll merely look at you and we'll be done." He glances at Aidan and adds, "Though I'm not as talented as our Fire Bringer, I'll have to move into my other state to see the shadow realm, rather than just feel it." He turns to Hanna. "I'll return in moments if you need me. Use the pendant like I showed you if you want to send me a message."

Hanna takes his hand and squeezes it. "How long will you be gone?"

"I'm not sure. There are things I need to take care of on the other side, including protecting the lot and club better, so we don't have a repeat of this morning. Be careful, will you?"

Hanna nods.

Eric turns back to me. "Will you follow me out into the open?"

I glance at Aidan, but he just nods like he's trying to tell me it's all right. I don't feel all right, though. Still, we follow Eric into the hall, then out into the parking lot.

"If I find more answers about your sister when I cross over, I'll send word," Eric says to Aidan once we're outside, then he focuses back on me.

A cell phone rings, and Aidan stops following us. He pulls his phone from his pocket, checks the screen, and puts it to his ear, an urgent look on his face. He waves for us to go ahead and steps back into the warehouse, like he needs privacy. I kind of wish he would tell whoever it is to wait and stay for what's next. I'm not sure I feel good about this intimidating blond angel digging into my spiritual baggage without a little—

My thoughts are cut short as Eric's figure seems to blink in and out of existence for a second, an image projection that isn't quite coming clear.

Then he flickers away. Completely gone. Only a dusting of gold in the air left behind.

SEVENTEEN

Aidan

Holly's voice sounds strained on the other end of the line. "This house is crazy right now, Aidan. The phone's been ringing off the hook all day. Total AF cray-zone. Demons and ghosts and all kinds of creepy-crawlies. Haven't been able write it all down fast enough."

"We can't worry about the business right now," I say. Money and clients can wait. "Can you change the outgoing message to say we've got a waiting list or we've gone on hiatus or something?"

"Yeah, I'll do that. But don't you think this tells us your sister is a busy bee? It's like she's handing out LA Paranormal business cards after her minions wreak havoc. I had three ghosts come to me last night. Three! And they all complained to me about the same thing: demons."

Wonderful. Ava's letting her minions run rampant.

I dare to ask, "How's Sid?" A tiny squeak comes from her, sending my gut spinning, and I ask hurriedly, "He's not—"

She chokes out, "No, he's still here. Kara won't leave his side." Her voice cracks, but then she clears her throat and adds, "He's stopped throwing up now, though."

"What about Connor?"

"He's better, I think." She sighs. "He and Jax took Raul out on a job in Encino, to see if they could help some lady with what sounds like blight in her garden—she thinks it's a land curse or something. The whole thing seemed harmless enough. Everybody's going bonks. I think they needed to be MIA." She sniffs, and her voice wavers again when she adds, "I wish you were here, Aidan. We could really use you."

"I know." I take a breath, trying to still the storm in my gut. "Sorry, Holly." I'd love the distraction of something normal myself, even if it is ghost hunting, but the chance of being recognized and attracting cops isn't worth it for something like that. They're probably safer without me on jobs, anyway.

"Yeah." She sniffs again.

"Will everyone be home tonight? You don't have any classes, do you?"

"We're done for the summer, so no more classes. Besides, there's no way my brain could handle cellular regeneration or neurobiology with things so MFU."

"Okay, then we should have a late house meeting. I'll sneak over after sundown. I need to talk to you guys about a few things."

"I'll let everybody know. Be safe."

———

Rebecca is leaning on her dad's car, picking at her nails, looking bored. Her posture seems so much like Kara's suddenly. It's mind blowing to think that a piece of the girl I love is now sitting inside of Rebecca. I have to wonder what Miss Mae meant about "tricking souls" and pray it doesn't mean anything horrible. She glances up as I walk closer and then rolls her eyes. "Your angel just disappeared. I have no clue what's going on."

I glance around the parking lot and spot Eric at the north edge, looking down the alley. "He's right there." I motion to where he's standing, but then I see he's more golden than human. He's still in his angelic state on the other side.

She glances in the direction I've pointed. "Well, can you talk to him when he's invisible? What did he see?"

Eric turns around and begins walking toward us. As he moves through the Veil, the air of the other world is like a cloak of magic around him. Flames emerge at his feet, flecks of metal spill from his shoulders. He seems a little taller and his eyes are so green it's difficult to look right at him; his skin is so pale it seems to shimmer. He pauses in front of Rebecca and motions slowly to her hair, her shoulders, like it should explain things. I don't get it until I let myself look at her through the Veil, and I see her energy.

No way. No fucking way. She's bursting with power now. A total change from before. It manifests so similar to Kara's energy, the way it spills like water and seems to shape around her in pulsing waves. But where Kara's energy is blue and light, mostly flowing from her when she's focused on me, Rebecca's essence is green—as green as the newest spring growth.

The green witch.

There's a scent to the energy, like the fields right after the rain. A soothing, calming smell. It's so lovely I can barely breathe as I watch it shift and move over her skin. But what does it mean? My mother never had power like that. My sister certainly didn't.

If there was any color at all to my mother's energy when she did spells, it was red mist from the blood, or the faint silver her skin seemed to glitter with sometimes.

There's more than one type of witch power, apparently, because Rebecca's energy doesn't feel bad, whether it's witch or not. As I watch it slide over her, I get the urge to fall to my knees. It's awe inspiring.

I turn to Eric to ask all my questions, but then I remember that we can't communicate with words when he's on one side of the Veil and I'm on the other. He begins to walk forward like he's going to touch my temple, draw me across like he has before, but I step back and lift my hands. I'm in no mood to leave my body right now.

The angel Azri'el tips his head at me, sending more gold flecks spilling off his hair. And then he turns and points at something on the ground I hadn't noticed before. It's no more than three feet from where Rebecca is standing by the car.

A demon's sigil.

I blink at it, shocked. Shocked that I hadn't seen it, that I hadn't smelled or felt whatever it was that left it. And even though I've only seen it once before, I recognize it immediately.

The demon Hunger's mark.

"Oh, shit," I mutter.

"What?" Rebecca turns, following my gaze, seeing nothing but asphalt.

I knew that beast was back. The bird demon that tore me to bits in Hanna's office told me its master had returned, had freed it. But I assumed the thing was after Rebecca because of her destiny with me. That it was after her because she was so important. I assumed that if she wasn't connected with me anymore, that it would be over.

Clearly that was one huge lame-ass assumption.

With that river of power on her skin, how is there any doubt that she's more vital than ever? "You must still be a Light," I say, knowing she won't understand fully what I mean. I barely understand it myself.

Ava wants her dead for some reason; her power must be why. But if Hunger is following her this close, and she's still alive, could that mean Ava and the demon aren't on the same side? Rebecca mentioned that the creature who attacked her seemed to see something it was afraid of, something she couldn't see. Could that have been Hunger?

Tingles work over me when I realize what that means; Hunger saved her life last night.

But why?

Eric motions to the warehouse, and I know he's asking me to watch out for Hanna. I nod and he flickers into nothing, leaving only his gold sparks behind him.

"It's back," I say quietly to Rebecca, wishing the words weren't true. "The demon Hunger is tracking you again."

"Wait, the . . . the demon is still after me?" Her voice chokes, and she looks around frantically, searching the parking lot. It's likely been following her for days.

I move closer. "It's all right." But I'm not sure it is. She's wearing her amulet—how did Hunger know she was here if it's not able to see her?

But then I get another whiff of her power. It's strong in my head, tingling in my chest. Could the demon be tracking her by scent now?

"It killed Charlie, Aidan," she whispers. "I thought that I was safe from it."

"I know," I say, unable to formulate words to make it all better. Words won't fix this. And right now, I'm not sure what will.

———

I follow Rebecca home in Eric's car and walk her to her door, trying to figure out how to protect her better. It's not like she can just come stay at the LA Paranormal house again, not with her dad watching her so closely. And I'm not sure she'd be safe there, either. I'm not sure of anyplace that's safe anymore.

All the way up the walkway she holds my hand. She doesn't let go when we get to the door.

"Tell Connor we'll do family movie night another time," she says absently, eyes searching the yard. "I think maybe he should stay away for now. I'm not safe to be around." Her voice breaks on the last words, and she squeezes my hand so hard it hurts.

"I can ward the house before I leave, Rebecca," I whisper, not wanting to shake the air too much with the sound of my voice. She looks fragile enough to shatter. "I have everything I need in Eric's car." That guy has quite the supply stock in his trunk.

She looks up at me and nods, a small bit of relief surfacing in her eyes.

"But you'll have to let go of my hand for a second," I say with a grin.

She glances down like she didn't realize she was holding it. "Oh." But instead of releasing it, she moves closer and rises onto her toes, then wraps her arms around my neck, whispering into my chest. "I'm sorry that I've been crazy and impatient."

I don't understand her sudden affection until the freshly sprouted scent of her energy blossoms again, weaving over us both. There's love in it, I realize, real love. Not like romance or sex, but friendship and steadiness. Pure and real. Safe. I hug her back and let myself rest in the simple moment.

"You don't need to apologize for anything, Rebecca. You're in this storm just like me. I'm the one who should apologize for being the ass that ignored you and didn't make sure you were okay after you gave so much to save Kara."

She sniffs like she might be crying, but her voice is steady when she says, "I love Kara. And I love you. I'd do whatever I need to do in order to keep you both safe, to save you."

The words are an oath when they fill the air. They settle into my skin and seem to mark us both. And with everything crashing into us, I'm not sure how to feel about the idea.

EIGHTEEN

Rebecca

I release Aidan but not before giving him one last squeeze. This is the first moment I've had with him in forever that I haven't felt horrible. I feel like I can finally see him, and our relationship, clearly. I'm released and free to really care about him now. As a friend.

The front door opens, and my dad is standing there, looking at us both with curiosity.

"Hello, sir," Aidan says, opening up a foot of space between us. "I just wanted to be sure Rebecca got home safe."

"Aidan's going to check a few things around the house, okay?" I say.

My dad looks over the front yard. "Is something wrong?"

"No," Aidan says quickly. "I'm just . . . I was going to . . ." But he seems to have drawn a blank. He looks at me in desperation.

"I was going to let Aidan do a blessing on the house. LA Paranormal was hoping to get a few new clients, and I thought maybe we could tell our neighbors what we think of their services. Is that okay?"

He seems a little confused, but he smiles through it at Aidan. "I, uh, I suppose that's fine. Is there anything I should do to help?"

Aidan smiles. "Not at all. Just go about the rest of your day, and you won't even know I'm here."

"Wonderful," my dad says.

After he goes back into the house, I linger a little, following Aidan down the walk back to the car. "Sorry about that, before," I say as he collects a few things from the trunk of Eric's car.

He shrugs. "Looks like it worked out. I can put up the wards, and I'll feel better about leaving you here."

"That's not what I mean, silly."

He straightens from digging in the trunk. "What?"

"I'm sorry about the hug. I don't want it to be . . . I don't know, I don't want you to think—"

He shocks me into silence by leaning over and planting a quick kiss on my brow. "Stop apologizing. Besides, I already knew that you think I'm amazing. It's fine." He winks, and relief fills me to my toes again.

I laugh and take one of the small sacks from him. "Yeah, that's what I meant. Now teach me about demon recon."

———

I come back in the house once we're done, and my dad calls out to me from his office, "Emery."

But I ignore him until I start up the stairs and he calls again. I pause midstride and take a deep breath before backtracking.

I linger in the office doorway. "Yeah? What's up?"

He releases a heavy breath and pulls off his glasses, rubbing his eyes before finally coming out with it. "Emery . . . I hate to ask this—I can't believe I'm asking this—but are you stringing two boys along at one time?"

I stare at him, wondering where that idea came from. "No, Dad. Aidan is just a friend. A very good friend. I'm still head over heels for the poverty-stricken surfer, sorry."

He closes his computer, and I bite back a groan. He wants to chat. "You think I don't approve of Connor because of his bank account?"

"I have no idea why you don't approve."

"I want you to be happy, Emery. If Connor will make you happy, then I'll find a way to adjust. I just don't understand why—why a young man with no college education, no real *personality*, interests you? The boy barely said two words last night."

"Dad, you were giving him the evil eye the whole time he was here. I know you're upset about what happened, but you didn't even try to get to know him." I raise my brow in challenge.

He sighs in surrender and opens his computer back up. "What time is movie night starting?"

Are we still doing that? I just told Aidan to tell Connor never mind. My dad would probably prefer it if it was just the two of us anyway. "Whenever, I guess."

"All right, well let me know when Connor gets here."

"It's just you and me, Dad."

He blinks up at me through the thick lenses of his glasses and looks so surprised and adorable I want to give him a hug. I suddenly realize how vulnerable he is, sitting there at his desk, talking to me about boys, and he has no idea what's really going on. He has no idea that the demon that drowned his son is now stalking his daughter again. Maybe stalking him.

A shiver runs over me at the thought. I can't let that happen. I can't let that Hunger thing get its claws into my father. I won't.

Something stirs in me as the anger rises, thinking of my dad in danger, and a twinge sparks behind my eyes, making me grip the bridge of my nose from the odd sensation.

"Are you all right?" my dad asks. "Are you getting a headache?"

"Yeah," I say absently. But I'm remembering that I got the same feeling at Miss Mae's when she was reading my cards. I know it's more than my sinuses now. And then, as I pull my hand from my face, I see gold flecks flicker across my palm, and . . . green. A brush of green light hovers at my fingertips.

I jerk my hand down, hiding it behind my back. "I'm going to go get something, to take something. I'm—" But before I can finish the nonthought, I rush out, heading up the stairs, holding my hands in front of me, gaping at the green light coming off my skin.

NINETEEN

Hunger

It watches. The demon Hunger watches the house. The girl is in there. Hunger's girl. The one marked as witch. The one that should be whispered to. Whispers to call a shadow up, to bring a shadow closer. Closer to flesh, delicious flesh.

Hunger paces and growls, teeth aching with longing. Fury forms a dark, sticky cloud, surrounding all things within reach. Rage. Red rage and urges for destruction. Urges to tear through the Veil and be free. Forbidden urges. Lovely urges.

But the Balance must be kept.

After darkness falls, lights flick off in the windows. Waiting will do no good this night; she isn't leaving. Fists clench and shadows move, move toward the master's lair. The city blinks past, the ground a blur beneath. Until it stands. Until the demon Hunger stands outside of the opening to his master's chamber.

Must speak with the All Mighty, Hunger asks the shadows in the opening. They move in a swirling mass before reaching out with long talons shaped from their pitch.

Sharp points slink and scrape across Hunger's skin, they dig in deep and draw their payment in blood. The pain is a relief, it is salvation.

And the shadows sink into the edges of the lair, a cave deep down, in the underbelly of the city, where no light can reach. Water glistens on the walls, making the tar-like surface slick. The scent of rot and decay slithers in the air, the smell of fresh blood up ahead.

A voice emerges from the smells. *You will have a share in the spoils if you tell me that you've at last completed your simple task.*

The demon kneels. The demon Hunger kneels before the rising form of the master. *Your kingdom is vast, oh powerful Molech.*

You disappoint me, Shadow.

A growl fills the space, trembling against Hunger's skin. *Forgive me, Master. I am close to using the fire-haired girl to regaining the Balance.*

The growl becomes a roar. *Do not scrape at my feet while speaking Heaven's words. The shadows will rule this world. It is written. That is Balance.*

But the Ava witch, Master—

I know of her. The Heart-Keeper created her so beautifully, did he not? She is the key, a most worthy child sacrifice. And as he controls her, her power will become ours in the end. He has given much, and so we will honor him and watch this play out. The large shadow of the master seems to grow. *For she is powerful. Delicious.*

Hunger nods at his master, unsure what words to allow into skin as truth.

Only your foolishness sees something to be fixed in such dark perfection as the Ava bird, the master continues. *Thanks to her brother's foolish mistake, she is to be our caged bride, our slave. We shall rule her flesh in her eternal death, as we ruled her spirit in life, and her power will belong to my ranks. She believes she is queen, let the lie sink in, let her sweep across my city, and the next, until blood soaks the feet of Man. Our final battle may at last come through her. And if not her life, then through her blood.*

Confusion fills Hunger, a conflict, a disagreement. It's wrong and unwelcome, but still it comes. The demon dares to ask his master, *And the boy—what of the time child? Is he not more of a threat now that his sister has completed her fall, as he completed his rise?* Perhaps Hunger could be given the task of ripping the boy limb from limb to fix the failure. The head of such a powerful soul would be a prize, would it not—

Fury rumbles in the air, lifting ash from the floor. *The boy . . . my child witch will care for his bones. I am sure of her success. Yours, however, I am not so sure of.* A shadow stretches over Hunger as the master looms closer. *Now, will you gut the fire-haired female before the time child discovers your presence, or shall I send another?*

The demon Hunger falls to its knees, trembling. With rage. With fury. With fear. *I will gut her, Master. I will not fight the Ava bird or the boy.* Sharp fangs grind as the unwanted words emerge into the air.

Hunger bows. The demon Hunger bows a head for the master, Molech. But inside there is only one belief. One need.

Balance. Whether it is a word of Heaven or not, it is needed.

TWENTY

Aidan

I expect a new message from Ava as the day passes, something about the green witch and Rebecca, or something about what happened with Hanna, but none come. As evening falls I feel an urgency to check on Sid, to get a second with him. And maybe talk. Not to ask questions; I feel like I need to tell him something.

Thank you.

Or a million other things, but they all boil down to what I never thought I'd utter to the strange man: *thank you.* I won't be burdening him with any of the stuff about Rebecca's energy. Or the demon Hunger being back. The guy deserves a little peace for once.

I pull up into the long driveway, parking Eric's car behind the Camaro, and decide to try something before I go inside. I pull the note from Ava out of my back pocket and find a pen in the glove compartment.

On the line just under her last message I write: *I found the green witch.* And then I add, *We need to talk. Face-to-face. Please, Ava.*

It's worth a shot.

For now I'll talk to everybody about the spell and figure out what to do about Tray, how to approach him.

I slide out of the car and head for the house. When I pass the shed, I consider grabbing the can of turpentine stacked on top of the paint and pouring it over the rickety shack, then lighting a match. The thing is seriously rank in the casting. There's even a red mist of energy seeping out from under the door right now. The spell circle on the wood has definitely burned through, and the curse underneath it seems to have puffed up like bloody marshmallows, which makes me think there's a secondary problem about to happen from it somehow.

The thing needs to be taken care of, sooner rather than later, before bad gets worse.

Raul is in the kitchen with Jax, the two of them stirring something in a pot like two old women making a witch's brew. "Are you guys on KP for dinner?" I think I'll be fasting tonight.

"Holly isn't feeling it," Jax says, "so we're all feasting on the amazing Campbell's." He looks beat, his shoulders low, and the usual spark of mischief in his eyes a little dimmed.

"And it takes two of you to stir it?" I ask.

Raul smiles, looking relaxed as ever. He's wearing skinny jeans, a colorful paisley, tight spandex shirt, and a long black sweater that nearly hits his feet.

Jax shrugs and pats Raul on the shoulder like a chum. "Newbie here thought I needed more oomph in my swing or something."

"You just didn't seem committed to the task," Raul says in all seriousness.

Holly shuffles into the kitchen, holding her glasses in one hand and rubbing her eyes with the other. She's a bit disheveled, her brown and pink hair falling out of the two braids coiled on her head, her feet in Jax's Wookie slippers. She's wearing a white T-shirt and green stretch pants, barely a colorful thread in sight. "I need someone to give me a neck rub. Answering messages all day in that *cabra grosero* of an office chair is sucktastic on the lumbar region."

Raul taps his stirring spoon on the side of the pot and waves her into the room. "Oh, sweetie, that's my specialty. I'll get you straightened right out."

She plops down in a kitchen chair and groans in relief as he starts kneading her shoulders.

"Do you think everyone's up for a meeting?" I ask them.

Jax gives me an exhausted look. "What, now?"

"We all need to get on the same page about stuff," I say, "like the whole Light spell thing, the plan for Ava, and now Sid. It's going to fall apart fast if we don't work together. Can you go tell Finger to come out of his cave?"

Jax nods, turns the burner off, and sets his spoon down, then heads for the basement door under the staircase, where Finger hides when he's not killing trolls or zombies.

Once he's out of earshot, I turn to Holly. "Are Kara and Sid still—" I realize that I was about to blurt out *saying good-bye,* so I bite my tongue. I can't let my mind head in that direction. Not yet.

Holly leans back in the chair. "Thanks, Raul, that's fine." He stops kneading her shoulders and moves to sit in the chair beside her. She looks up at me. "Kara's barely left his side all day, except to get more towels when he was sick."

"How many times did he throw up?"

"Only one other time. It seems to have stopped now."

An ache fills my chest, thinking of them here all day, scared and unable to call a doctor. "What about Connor? Is he feeling all right? He's not answering my texts."

"He just went straight into the living room when they got back from the job earlier." Her voice wavers. "Been in there ever since, right next to Kara." She releases a long sigh, bowing her head and rubbing her eyes again, this time wiping away tears.

Raul reaches over and touches her knee.

I move closer and put a hand on her shoulder, trying to comfort her even though I have no clue what to do next. "We're going to figure this out." I have to believe that. Or else I'll crack.

She nods, then looks over to Raul, patting his hand. "Thank—" But her words cut off. Her eyes widen, staring at something just past Raul's head. She whispers under her breath, "WTF. It's . . . how is that possible?"

"What?" I follow her line of sight but don't see anything. I let go of her shoulder and lean on the back of her chair, squinting at the area she's gaping at.

"There, it's—wait . . . he's gone. Where'd he go?"

"Who?" Raul and I say in unison.

"A ghost," she says. "One of the ones that came to me last night, but I never see them when I'm awake, that's . . . that's nuts-o."

There's no ghost here; I would've seen it. "A ghost can't get through all the wards on the house." Could Ava have done something to those, too?

No, I'd sense it if they were broken. And everything feels nice and solid.

"They come to me in my dreams, Aidan. That means I see them in my mind's eye. Not here, in the house."

"Oh."

Raul adds, "Like a waking dream."

"Exactly." She stands quickly, turning to me, the chair legs squeaking as they scrape over the linoleum. "Touch me."

I step back. "Excuse me?"

"You put your hand on my shoulder, and the image appeared. Didn't you feel anything?"

I shake my head and look her over, realizing my power must've done something again. Like it does to Connor. But it wasn't the same at all. It didn't hurt her, for one. And I didn't feel a thing.

"I felt a tingle in my nose," she says. "I sometimes get the same zing in my dreams, just before a spirit shows up to interrupt my make-out sesh with Zac Efron. Or on the off nights it's Tyler Posey with that adorbs crooked jaw of his." She grins and gets a twinkle in her eye, thinking about who she dream-dates. Then she shrugs and says, "So, let's try again."

"I don't want to hurt you," I say. "I'm hurting Connor."

"Because it stings?" she asks. "That's nothing."

"I knocked him out," I say, wondering how she doesn't get that's *something*.

"But he was fine on that job thing we went on," Raul adds, not helping at all. "He ate two cheeseburgers and fries from In-N-Out on the way back."

Jax walks in, glancing around the room. "What's with the faces?"

"Aidan's gonna touch me," Holly says, stepping closer to me and holding out a hand.

Jax's brow goes up and he moves to stand by Raul. "This should be interesting. I hope Kara walks in."

Holly whines, "Come on, Aidan, I wanna try to make it happen again."

"Fine," I say, taking her wrist and holding it out awkwardly. "See anything?"

She looks around herself and grips my hand. Then she grunts in frustration. "Nada. Maybe I'm wrong." She moves back to the table and picks up her glasses, sliding them back on her face. "Or," she says dramatically, "we could experiment? We can use what just happened as a baseline for a possible control group, and then—"

"Holly, let's just have the meeting," I say, mostly relieved nothing weird happened. I might be curious, but I'm not in the headspace for any of Holly's experimental zeal, and I don't need anything else to go wrong. "We can figure this out later."

"Spoiler." And she walks out with Jax's Wookie slippers scraping across the floor with each step.

———

When everyone's gathered in the living room around Sid, the air turns solemn. I sense Finger attempting to settle everyone's spirits, but he's got his work cut out for him, and it's not doing much to lift the pall.

I can't let myself look too long at Sid. His sunken eyes, his hollow cheeks, and the sallow color of his skin . . . The blood that's dried in the corners of his mouth. If I don't focus on how he's failing, on the presence of death, maybe it'll leave us alone. Maybe we'll have more time. It's a childish notion—I'm like a kid hiding from a monster—but I can't seem to help it.

Kara said he's even too weak to talk. He's asleep again, laid out on the couch like a skeletal sleeping beauty, looking peaceful.

Looking dead.

Kara and Connor are on the floor, leaning against the couch below him. Jax and Holly are on the loveseat, and Raul is on the floor beside Holly. Finger is hiding in the shadow of the corner.

I'm not completely in the room, leaning on the wall beside the archway, trying to center myself and clear my head. I have to stay focused. Or I won't be able to do this leadership thing. Because how do I get us all working together to fix this? I fake it.

"Okay," I say, "I know things suck right now. Three months ago I showed up, and your whole world turned to shit . . ."

Kara leans forward. "Aidan, stop that. We're all a part of what's happening."

"Yeah, man," Connor says. He's got half a sandwich left on a plate on his lap. Obviously the two cheeseburgers and fries weren't enough. And he still looks exhausted. "We'd never have been brought together if it wasn't for Sid finding us. And he'd never have made this family if it wasn't for you."

This family. The words soak into me, making me pause, and I realize—that's why. It's why I'm so frantic, why everything feels too huge. It's true. When I wasn't looking, they became my family. And I can't stand the thought of losing any of them.

Finger smiles slightly as if he senses my realization.

"I'd be in juvie," Jax says.

"Same," Connor adds. "Prison, actually."

"I'd be dead," Kara whispers, taking Sid's hand in hers. "I'd have made sure of it."

Raul blinks up at me. "I can't even think about where I'd be if it wasn't for you giving a shit about me, *compa*. I had no clue how to be free of that hell. You pulled me out."

Holly's nodding along as people talk, and after it's quiet for a few seconds, she adds, "I'd still be in that mental hospital." We all turn to her as she shares a look with Kara.

"You didn't belong there," Kara says.

Holly stares down at the carpet. "I wouldn't know where I belonged if I wasn't here. With you guys." Raul leans over from his place on the floor at her feet and rests his head on her knee. Jax scoots across the cushion, closer to her, tentatively taking her hand in his.

"We'll fix this," I say again to her; a sad Holly is too painful to watch.

"How?" she asks, obviously defeated.

"We stop Ava," I say. "We find out what she wants and save her if we can. But before we can do that—or before *I* can do that—I think we should discuss this bonding spell. Sid talked about how you're all supposed to be a part of this, and that's why he gathered us together in this house, like Connor said. Eric seems to think that the reason I'm hurting Connor is because that link is becoming stronger, and we haven't done the spell to complete it. So it's like a live wire."

"And in the kitchen you made me see the ghost when you touched me all affectionately," Holly adds, pointing at me.

Everyone looks over at her, Kara and Connor with matching frowns.

I explain, "Holly thinks she saw a ghost when I touched her shoulder."

"Uh, excuse me," she says. "I saw it."

"I wonder what would happen if you touched me," Jax says, his eyebrows high, *"affectionately."* And then he and Raul both seem to think that's funny and start laughing. Holly rolls her eyes, but she doesn't let go of Jax's hand.

"Can we just focus?" I ask.

"Eric said this spell was big," Kara says, sounding tired. "What will it take to do it?"

"I need to read over it more thoroughly as soon as I get back to the club. But we still need to find out who the eighth Light is."

"Wait," Connor says, "who's the seventh?"

"Rebecca," I say. "I'm pretty positive she's still a Light. I read her soul today, and her energy is huge. Now that she's not linked to me."

From the shock on his face, I realize that probably wasn't something I should have surprised him with. I'll have to fix that later.

"And you think Tray might be the eighth?" Kara asks.

"How do you feel about that?" I ask her, trying not to let any jealousy sneak into my tone. "Connor said you know him pretty well. Do you think he could be one?"

She studies my face for a few seconds and then says, "I suppose. I always thought he should join us, but he never wanted to. He has gifts, but he hid them from Sid." She seems nervous talking about it.

"One of you needs to talk to him again," I say. "As soon as possible."

Connor motions to me. "It should be you, Aidan. You're the one he's supposed to be ready to follow."

"The guy doesn't know me, or have any reason to trust me." Not to mention my newfound fame being a problem.

Connor looks over and nods to Kara. "Take her with you."

She gives him a sharp look. After a second of glaring she says, "Fine." She leans back against the couch again. "I'll text him right now." She pulls out her phone and starts tapping at the screen.

"And if he's a green light, then we do the spell," Holly says. "Easy peasy."

Let's hope so.

"Okay," I say. "Then we'll do this as soon as we find out what part Tray plays—what part he's willing to play."

"Sounds good," Jax says. "My brother's a stubborn ass, but he's not likely to pass up saving the world from a psycho Carrie."

My chest twinges at the mention of Ava. Kara looks sideways at me, feeling my pain, my hopeless frustration. But I ignore my emotions. They're not in a sane place right now.

Holly says, "We should talk about the news and this BOLO. Because the infamous Aidan O'Fallan could make this all moot when he lands himself in Hotel Jail-o. The media is having a field day. I did some research, and that woman that died in the Gap was some kind of PTA mom who ran a charity thing. They're already planning the Lifetime movie according to the TMZ website."

"Two days later?" Jax asks, sounding incredulous.

Raul snaps his fingers dramatically. "Hollywood is a hound for blood."

"And then there's the nurse," Holly adds, more quietly.

The room goes still.

"I know how to stay invisible," I say, pretending I didn't hear the mention of my newest sin. I kick the edge of the rug and push against the horror crawling up from a dark place inside. It's ready to consume me.

I bear the mark.

Murderer.

Connor clears his throat and then says, "I'll contact Sid's guy for a new ID. But there's got to be something else we can do."

"Changing your name won't erase those videos popping up all over Twitter," Holly says. "Luckily most of them don't show your face, and the ones that do are pretty blurry."

"You can bet those men in blue got your prints," Raul says.

My nerves spark. My prints would be a huge arrow to the truth.

Connor seems to be following the same horrible logic. "Which will lead them—and then the media—to your actual files."

The words and weight of it all sink into the air, and even Finger isn't able to lift the finality of what it could all mean. If they find the real me, the authorities will realize I've got fake papers, then the system could find all these kids, one by one, and the whole glass tower of lies Sid's built up to shield them shatters.

"You could hightail it to Mexico," Jax mumbles.

———

I hold Ava's hand, watching the policemen, the firemen, going in and out of our house. I pretend it's jelly making our fingers sticky. Not blood. Not Mom's blood.

The woman who brought us water and blankets stands to the side, talking in a hushed whisper to a policeman. The adults seem to want to keep it a secret that my mom is dead, like they don't know that I watched it, that I watched when—when the—

My chest caves in thinking of it, seeing it happen over and over, again and again, in my mind. The fire circle. The wolf. The blood.

She's gone.

There is no pretending about that.

A yellow fire truck blocks the street, and the spinning lights splatter pulsing red all over everything, with the beat of my heart. My heart . . .

My mom is still in the house.

No. Her body. Her shell. Not her.

Where did her spirit go? Will she turn into a white whisper like the ghosts I see? Will she rise like light to Heaven? I want her to be okay. I want a hug.

I grip Ava's hand tighter and try to comfort her with our connection. I try to push into her all the safety I can find inside me. She's so little, and she doesn't understand. Her mind is a tangle of confusion and fear.

The woman with the blankets comes back and kneels in front of us. "So, we're going to go now, okay?" Her voice is soft—she's trying to hide her sadness for us, but I smell it. Like cooked peas.

I want to ask her where she's taking us, but my throat hurts too much. I can only blink at her and shiver.

She rubs my arm as she begins drawing us away from the house. "Let's get you cleaned up and warm. And I bet we can find some hot chocolate." She stops by a dark-colored car and opens the door to the backseat, then starts fiddling with a car seat. When she turns around to pick up Ava, she pauses. Her eyes narrow, locking on the small cut on Ava's tiny shoulder.

Where the demon's claw dug into her skin.

I want to tug Ava back toward me, hide her in my arms. But I stand still, waiting to see what the lady will do. Does she see it like I do? Does she see the silver threads already growing from the angry welt?

"Oh my, little one," the woman says. "You got a bruise. Did you fall down?" And I smell it on her, the anger, I see it in her adult eyes, what she's thinking. She believes our mom hurt us.

I pull Ava away, wrapping my arms around her, and somehow manage to keep my gaze steady, looking the woman right in the eye, trying to warn her, trying to say what my mouth can't: leave us alone. If I could run away, I would. I'd take Ava and live in a deep dark cave, like an adventurer or that Patrick guy our neighbor Mrs. Jenner told us about on green clover day—a cave like the one on the beach that Mom's always drawing.

Was drawing.

I wish I'd put something in my pocket before the police came, a drawing, one of her rings. I wish I'd done more than sit beside her with Ava—I wish I'd put roses in her hair. She liked roses. I'm never coming back. I'll never see her again. Never.

Never.

"It's all right, Aidan," the woman says, taking Ava's hand and trying to pull her away from me, a worried look on her face. The lady says my name like she knows me. Like it's more than letters on one of the files tucked under her arm. Like she's not going to take my sister from me.

I keep my eyes on hers and shake my head slowly. No, it's not all right. It's never going to be all right again.

And I feel that truth, that forever change in my chest, as Ava's tiny form slips from my arms into the hands of the stranger.

TWENTY-ONE

Rebecca

My phone pings with a text notification, waking me up from a foggy half sleep. I groan and swallow the ache in my throat, in my body. Worst. Night. Ever.

I pull my hands out from under my pillow and hold them up to catch the sunlight, studying the skin for sparkles or green glowy bits as I turn them this way and that. Nothing seems out of the ordinary. Could I have imagined it? As soon as I reached my room last night, the color had dissipated, and by the time I'd paced back and forth a few times, it was completely gone. I washed them just in case—in case of what, I have no clue. But it seemed like something to do.

After that I couldn't sleep. There was no movie night with Dad, no fake family fun time. I just told him I was tired when he knocked on my door to ask if I was ready. Then I turned off my light and stared at the ceiling until I couldn't keep my eyes open anymore. Even with my eyes closed, I don't think that I ever actually slept.

I roll over and check my phone. Seven thirty in the morning.

And it's Samantha who texted me. No surprise; she gets done with her first hour of dance around this time.

```
Ok, so I know we haven't talked about it
but WTF is up with this dog monster?
Did we srsly see that thing?
```

How could it have taken her more than twenty-four hours to say something? Maybe her brain wouldn't let it digest at first.

I text back, *I know, it's scary.* My thumb hovers over the "Send" button, wondering if I should say more. I'm unsure how to keep from dragging her into the mess. But then, it might be too late for that now. So I add, *Let me know if you need to talk more about it. You can come over and stay the night tonight if you want.*

I text Connor, *Good morning,* with a heart, and ask him how he's feeling. And then I'm at a loss as to what to do next. I stare more at my ceiling but get annoyed at how useless I am, so I get up and go for my box of art supplies. I toss a tablet, a sharpener, and charcoal pencils on my desk, then I sit in my chair, flipping open the sketchbook and picking up a pencil.

And just sit there.

I close my eyes and breathe through my nose, trying to find something in my brain to draw. But the only thing I'm feeling or seeing is my confusion, my lack of knowledge.

Come on, powers, work.

I'm not sure what I want them to do. Maybe they could show me some answers for once? What did Miss Mae say? That the stars were within reach and the power was in my hands, or something.

Hands that I draw with. Hands that were sparkling only hours ago.

I lower my pencil to the paper, deciding not to think at all, to put everything aside. If the key to all this is in my hands, then I'll shut off my brain and let my fingers take over. I'll wipe my mind clean. Of words, images, even of this blank paper in front of me. I'll think about nothing but black.

With every ounce of will I have, I look. At nothing but slate. Obsidian. Pitch.

That strange twinge surfaces behind my eyes. My fingers twitch, making my breath hitch. I struggle to keep my body from reacting. And I feel it, something creeping over my skin, movement like a small breeze lifting the hairs on my arm. And my hand moves again. And again.

Until it's dancing all over the paper in a frantic pattern. The odd sensation in my head grows with each stroke, but I keep my eyes squeezed shut and don't let myself look until my hand stops moving.

My heart is pounding against my ribs so hard it's making me light-headed. I likely just drew a big scribble. That's what it felt like.

I squint my eyes open and take a peek.

And my body goes numb.

A pentagram? It's an intricate drawing of a pentagram, with depth and shading and everything. Like something on the cover of a heavy-metal album. Or something in a witchy movie. Within the design of the circle that rims the star, there are weird symbols that could be a strange language, and there are four other stars around the circle—Stars of David—each one with its own word underneath. A few weird symbols are drawn at specific points and seem to coincide with the points of the larger star.

A chill works over me as I study the complex drawing—a drawing that I did with my eyes closed. It's completely freaky.

I lift my hands to look at them again, feeling like they've betrayed me. Then I reach down and crumple the paper in my fist. But just as I'm going to toss it in the trash, I decide to take a picture of it. Who knows what it is, but there's a reason I drew it, and knowing the reason might be important.

I flatten it with my hand, take the shot, then realize that throwing it away won't be enough. Not for this. It's a magic thing, witchy magic of some kind, I'm sure. And nothing good from the feel of it.

Don't they usually burn evil things in movies?

I dig in my desk drawer and find a lighter from when Samantha and I snuck her dad's cigarettes. It's pink with a Playboy bunny on it, and it reminds me of two summers ago when we thought that getting asked to a dance was more important than anything else. If only.

I flick the lighter to life and hold the edge of the paper over the flame.

The fire begins to climb, eating away at it as grey ash falls on my desk. Then the flames reach the first point of the pentagram.

The fire hisses and sparks.

I drop the paper on the carpet as it's devoured, curling in on itself. And burning the carpet! I step on the fire, sending ash and sparks up, and when I'm done, the white Berber is spotted black, and my sock is singed grey. Plus, my foot stings; I probably burned it like an idiot.

I try not to panic, try to decide what sort of furniture could be put on top of the ruined carpet to hide it.

A loud beep, beep, beep fills the air. The fire alarm above my bedroom door going off.

The door bursts open, and my dad flies into the room, looking for an emergency. He gasps in air to catch his breath, then spots the burnt blotches on the carpet, my sock. "Thank God. You're okay."

I look down at the mess. I don't think so.

TWENTY-TWO

Aidan

I can't shake the feeling that Ava's eyes are on me constantly. Last night was the second time I dreamed about her, dreamed a memory. Exactly like I used to do with my mom. And that stopped once my mom's ghost was gone.

Now it's happening again, this time with Ava. It makes me think she's sending them.

I get out of bed and go to my jeans on the back of Kara's chair. I dig in the pocket for the note, pull it out, unfold it. And there's nothing, no new writing answering my ink message. I knew it seemed too easy.

I rub my thumb over the pink bloodstained paper and focus my energy on trying to feel her, my sister, the girl in the dream who had no choice when her home was ripped away. She was so little. And I never knew how to help her.

"I'm sorry, Ava," I whisper.

Kara releases a sigh in her sleep and rolls over, settling into a patch of rising sunlight. I was weak and stayed the night after our meeting—I started leaving the house a thousand times but then kept telling myself, just one more hour, then one more, until I was telling Kara if she'd go to bed and get rest, I'd lie there while she fell asleep. She was so tired.

What's happening with Sid seems to have completely overwhelmed her, body and mind, and I have no clue how to help her. No idea what to say to comfort her. All I could do was wrap her in my arms as she lay shivering in our bed, praying that my energy would heal her heart like it's supposed to. Like hers always heals mine.

I should be at the club, staying off the radar. What if the cops come by with more questions for Sid? And here I am serving myself up on a silver platter. But at the same time I can't just run off and hide forever. How will I protect Kara, protect them all if my sister comes to hurt them when I'm away in my hideout? As much as I want this thing to be between me and my sister alone, I know she won't let it. She's made that perfectly clear.

I settle into the chair beside the bed and watch Kara sleep, dread filling my gut, realizing Eric was right. There's only one way for all this to end. Only one way to settle things. And it will destroy people I love one way or another.

I grip Ava's note in my hand and then start to fold it back up. *Where are you, Ava? Why're you doing this—*

Something rattles, knocking my focus back to the room. I glance at Kara, but she's still, sleeping soundly in the morning light. She hasn't moved at all. Maybe it was someone in the other room.

I finish folding up the letter and slide it back into my jeans pocket.

The rattle comes again, like stones clacking together. I'm pretty sure it's near the bed.

I lean forward in the chair, looking underneath. The shadows are shaped by a stack of board games, my duffel bag, and a shoebox filled with Kara's pin collection. I don't see anything that would make that sound.

After there's silence for a solid minute, I sit back up, pull my jeans on, grab my shirt off the end of bed—*clack, clack, clack* comes again. Definitely under the bed. I set the shirt back down and drop to my knees, looking more closely. I pull my duffel out.

When I open it and look inside, it's suddenly very clear. The alabaster box. It's set on top of a folded pair of board shorts, stark white against the black fabric of the bag. If it had eyes, I'd say it was looking at me.

I reach in and take it out, then set it on the wood floor in front of me. It's heavier than I remember, solid. The winged sun carved into the lid reminds me where it came from, how old it is. And who it belonged to.

Eric said that it wouldn't open unless there was something it could give me. And if it rattled, I'm guessing it's trying to get my attention.

My raw nerves spark as I wonder what it might want to give me. What it needs to prepare me for. The last time I opened it and held that feather inside, it gave me a dagger to kill a demon. Which I did. Maybe that means whatever I pull out of there, it'll work?

I take the lid between my fingers. It lifts right up, revealing the white feather inside. I read over the Hebrew lettering of Psalm 91 on the shaft—*He shall cover you in His feathers; and under His wings you will find refuge*—and the night of the cave comes back to me in a wash of emotions and images, the helplessness mixed with determination. No realization of what I was walking into.

I study the feather and wonder what it was that my father used it for. What things in his life brought him to open this box? I pick the feather up by the quill and hold it out in front of me. Dark-brown spots still speckle the afterfeather and shaft; dried blood from when I fought the demon. There's a smell to the object, a dusty rose scent that tingles in my nose and behind my eyes.

And the twinge grows, heating my forehead until I'm squinting. What the hell—?

My fingers spark to life, a flicker of light that pulses up my arm in a quick burst. And I'm no longer holding a feather.

It's a . . . well, it's a pen.

I stare at it in confusion until I realize what I was doing when the box got my attention. I was holding the note from Ava. I move, reach into my back pocket, pulling it out, studying the pen as I unfold the paper. It's a normal office pen from what I can tell. Like the one I got out of the glove compartment and used to write the message.

I smooth out the note on my leg and grip the pen to write—

Shit. Something jabs the pad of my finger before I can get any words down on paper. I hiss in pain and look at my thumb, my finger. And of course there's blood. When I study the pen, I see the grip has tiny needles sticking out.

Not a Bic, apparently.

Blood. It uses blood in the ink.

I sigh and get ready for the pain, then grip the pen again and write, *I found the witch. I need to see you, I need to understand. Please, Ava. No more games. No more death.* It stings my fingers, but it's not unbearable, and the words flow onto the page in black ink and blood.

The page sizzles, and threads of smoke begin curling up from the words I wrote. I stare in amazement as my writing flares, then becomes burn marks. Exactly like the ones from Ava.

The only way to distinguish my message from hers is a light-blue glow along the charred lettering.

I'm pretty positive she's gotten the message now.

————

The house is still asleep when I go downstairs to check on Sid before I head back to the club. My chest feels a hundred pounds fall on it when I look at him. I go into the living room and sit next to Connor while he pretends to read *Huckleberry Finn*.

"Hey," I say. "How did the night go?"

"Uneventful." He looks up from the book and gives me a weak smile. "How's our girl?"

"Exhausted. I'm letting her sleep."

"You're going to go see Tray today?" he asks. "Are you okay with Kara joining you? Because, if you're worried about him listening to you, you could take Jax instead. They don't get along great, but at least there's a history."

"I'll let Kara sleep for as long as I can, but she won't be happy if I ditch her. And I think she'll be okay."

"That's not what I meant," he says. "I meant, are you okay with her, you know, *convincing* him to come over to this mess of ours."

I have to smile at that. "What are you thinking she's going to do to convince him, Connor?"

He grunts in irritation, like I'm not understanding. "You'll see them together and you'll get what I mean."

That doesn't sound helpful. "This isn't about petty shit. And if Tray isn't interested in the bonding spell, then I suppose he goes on with his life, and we go ahead with our plans."

"Eric said the spell needed at least eight for it to work."

"I know, we'll figure it out." I study him, sensing his tension. "Sorry I sprung that Rebecca stuff on you, by the way. How're you feeling about it?"

He stares down at his book and picks at a corner. "I really wanted her to be out of this mess for good."

"Me, too." I glance over to Sid and have to turn away after only a few seconds. "I sent a message to Ava, telling her I want to meet."

"Good. Let me know when we're headed out with knives and pitchforks."

I start to get up, but then reconsider. "Why don't you go to bed, Connor. I'll ask Jax to take a shift before I go. You need sleep in case something else crazy happens."

He grunts and moves his stiff limbs to rise. "Fine. But text me when you and Kara head over to Tray's."

"I will." I lean back against the couch, realizing I still have things to tell him about Rebecca, but I'm not sure how. And I'm not even sure it's my place, so instead I just say, "You should text Rebecca and be sure she's all right before you crash. I think she could use someone to talk to."

"She texted me earlier."

"Is everything okay?"

"Yeah. I guess." But he's still tense.

"What?"

"Is there a reason you didn't tell me right away after you found out she was a Light?"

"No." I give him a questioning look, and the bitter scent of envy filters strong between us. "Are you jealous?"

"What do you think?" His eyes dig into mine. "You're close to her, obviously. And you see parts of her that I can never understand or know. You were her first choice, and she was meant for you. No matter what happened with Kara, Rebecca's got that way about her. And you two would fit. I've seen it."

I lean forward, hoping he *hears* me. "Connor, nothing's there. It never really was. I liked her, she's beautiful, but she's not . . . well, she's not Kara."

He nods slowly.

I pause before rising back to my feet. I can't leave while he has that look on his face. He's obviously disturbed. I decide I need to just tell him everything and ask forgiveness from Rebecca later. "You should know that I didn't read her after the exchange with Kara, and I only did it this time because of something she told me."

"What?"

"She went to see Miss Mae, and apparently the woman told Rebecca that she's actually a witch, and that her energy is untethered now with her anointing, and her connection to me gone." I let the information settle in. "And that's why I read her. That's the only reason. And when I did . . ." I pause, feeling the amazement again at how striking her energy was. "What I saw when I read her—I saw *her*, Connor . . . It was *stunning*. She's not the same. She's nothing like she was—"

"Stop," he says, the smell of his jealousy sharpening into fear. "Just fucking stop."

"Connor . . ." I don't know what to say, though. I don't want to make it worse.

He stands and runs agitated fingers through his hair. "You did this to her, you know. Your choices did this to her. And now, she might—" He seems to stumble on his words, but then says, "I'm sorry, but I won't sit back and watch her get twisted or hurt anymore. I'll protect her, Aidan. From your horrifying sister. Even from you."

And then he's walking away, leaving me to carry the cold realization that even my best friend believes I'm the enemy.

TWENTY-THREE

Aidan

Kara picks me up at the club a couple hours later. "Betsy's ready for our adventure," she says, patting the dashboard of the Camaro as I get into the passenger seat. "Are you?"

"I hope so."

To my relief, she seems much clearer and lighter than she did yesterday. I can't help a smile filling my face as the warm glow of her joy hits me. It smells sweet and rich, like chocolate. Her cerulean energy is slinking down her shoulder and over the seat, reaching for me. She seems so much better, and I have to wonder if curling up with me to sleep really could have had such a huge effect at healing some of her crushed spirit last night.

She pops an 8-track tape in—*The Monkees*, which she explains is Connor's favorite. I try not to think about the conversation earlier with him and just enjoy the feeling of Kara beside me. I let myself rest in the simple moment of it just being the two of us on the road. Even if it is a road that might lead to more disappointment.

After twenty minutes or so she exits the freeway. When we stop at a light, she turns, glances at me, and I realize she's becoming tense the closer we get. I take her hand in mine and attempt to settle her nerves with my energy.

She pulls over, parking along the curb in front of an apartment building. After turning off the engine, she bows her head, smelling like misery. "I was feeling so much better when I woke up," she says. "But now, being out, away from Sid. I'm turning raw again."

I unlatch her seatbelt and tug her toward me as much as the bucket seat will allow. I cradle her face in my hands and kiss her forehead delicately. "I know."

"I'm scared this all could end."

I'm not sure what she means by *this*—the world? The house? Us? I don't think I want to talk about it, but I sense that she needs to, so, for her, I ask, "What?"

"She wants to kill you, Aidan. You know that, don't you?"

A chill works through me. "She wants me to be like her, I think."

Kara pulls my hand from her face and weaves her fingers through mine, squeezing them tight. "You'll never be like her," she says with a sharp edge to her voice.

"I could, Kara. She and I aren't that different." We come from the same blood, the same place, and . . . I'm crushing as much life around me as she is.

"Are you kidding?" Her light eyes glint with frustration as she moves her body to face me. She places a hand over my heart where my seal is. "Listen to me. I know about evil, and you are not even close. You're goodness and light. Your love is inside me, waking my spirit and healing my scars. You're mine, Aidan. *Mine*—do you hear me?"

I stare at her, my pulse racing at her words. I can only nod.

"So, stop saying things that make me want to punch you," she says. "Let's do this. We've got a Light to find." And then she nudges me to get out of the car.

Once we're on the sidewalk and I'm looking around, I realize the location feels familiar. There are dozens of places in LA that look just like it, though. Cookie-cutter projects, all in a row. I follow Kara down the street, along a chain-link fence, toward some basketball courts a block down. We pass a small golem-like demon perched on the fence, facing the courts. A raven is roosting next to it, like they're keeping each other company. I try and hold tight to my power, not wanting it to spark so close to the demon, not wanting the thing to sense me.

The raven stretches out a wing to scratch an itch underneath it, and the demon lifts a hind claw to scratch behind its floppy pointed ear at the same time. The creature's probably watching someone; it must be a scout of some kind.

Kara slows her pace beside me. "What's wrong?"

"There's a demon hanging out with that bird."

She looks at the raven behind us on the fence. "What's it doing?"

"Just . . . waiting." But then the demon blinks its overlarge eyes, zeroing in on a spot on the other side of the fence to its right, to where two young African-American men are playing basketball. A round guy is chasing a more nimble one toward the far basket. The ball is swiftly bounced through legs and then tossed as the rounder guy flails his arms and tries to guard the basket. Giving a valiant effort, but failing.

The bird flies away, and the demon scuttles down the chain-link, making its way to the two guys, obviously here for one of them.

"Tray," Kara says to herself, grabbing the fence. Then she yells, "Tray!"

The swifter boy turns as the ball is coming at him, and it hits him in the head. The rounder boy laughs and points, but the other guy just rubs his head and squints over at us. He's like a tall Jax, with that same stubborn chin, but more muscular, harder around the edges. Recognition fills his eyes when he spots Kara. He waves at us as the demon moves past.

It's heading toward a young man in the shadows who's watching Tray with sharp eyes. The demon comes close to the guy and seems to whisper something, making the young man's body tense. And that's when I see the glint of silver in his fist. A knife.

Oh, shit.

Urgency sparks in my gut with a sudden jolt. That familiar rage my power brings fills my insides as the armed guy stands and begins walking straight for Tray.

Without thinking, I grab the fence and climb, hoisting myself up and over the top, jumping down to the asphalt on the other side, all in seconds. And then I'm sprinting toward them, watching the demon claw its way up the attacking boy's leg and torso, then latch on to his neck with sharp talons, and continue to whisper in his ear. But I'm still more than a dozen yards away.

I hear Kara running behind me, but I stay keyed on the demon, even as Tray turns toward his attacker, his face filling with confusion.

I'm five yards away, then two, and just as the knife comes at Tray's side where he can't see it, I'm on the guy wielding it, tackling him to the ground. My knees and elbows grind against the broken asphalt as we skid. My fist meets the guy's gut just as the blade comes up. But even as the sharp edge slides down again, swiping a hot slice across my arm, the demon that was on the guy's shoulder tumbles right onto mine.

Instinctively it digs its claws into my cheek and neck to stop its fall. Hitting bone and slicing tendon.

I cry out in agony and stumble back.

My power bursts from me with the pain, and I fall to my knees, gripping the thing by the neck and plucking it off me like it's a tick. It shrivels and turns to ash before I can even focus my energy on it.

The agony from the tears in my neck and face ebbs a little. I try to catch my breath, find my center. My head spins. My mark burns. And I know the guy cut me deep, because my arm doesn't want to move right. I hear feet scrambling on the pavement, see a blurry figure running away, and then Kara's at my side, saying my name, putting something that smells like cigarette smoke to my face, my neck, as she tries to stop the bleeding.

Panic hits me at her touch. No, no, she can't be close to me!

I shove her away as the power still courses through me in bursts, making the rage linger, making the fury, the murder, pulse in my veins.

I hear her grunt and she's gone.

"Hey, careful," someone says.

I blink up and see the guy I was trying to save. But he's bare chested now, and he's helping Kara off the ground, putting her behind him, like he's shielding her. From me.

TWENTY-FOUR

Aidan

Tray takes a wadded up T-shirt from Kara's hand and throws it on the ground in front of me. A weird combination of annoyance and fear paints his face. Why is he looking at *me* like that?

"Kara, you need to get out of here," he says in a low voice, while he continues to watch me intently. "Go to Aunt Mae's."

Kara shoves his protective arm aside. "Lay off. He's hurt, Tray." She kneels in front of me and picks up the bloody T-shirt. She holds it to my neck again.

"Sorry I pushed you," I whisper, my voice scratchy and weak. The power is only a buzz in my spine and arm now, but there's an ache left in my chest, in my bones. My skin feels stretched out from the sudden burst of it all. I'm robbed of energy. I'm not sure why or how, but the force of my power has to be getting stronger, even stronger than it was in the ER. It physically hurts right now inside me, as if the explosion of power hit me just as hard as it hit the demon.

But my power wanted to help Tray—man, did it ever. It was like I couldn't control myself, like I didn't have a choice. I didn't just have to save Tray, I needed to get my hands on anything that would want to hurt him. I'm guessing that's a bit of clue; the guy must be a Light.

If I did feel any form of protection over him it's gone now, though, with the way he's looking at me. And he certainly doesn't seem to have any mutual connection with me at all.

"I'm fine," Kara says to me. "You know I'm tough." Then she turns to Tray as she keeps the shirt held to my wounds. "We need to help him up. It's going to be hard for him to walk for a minute."

But Tray doesn't move. "Kara, what the fuck is going on?" He's looking around, cautiously, his eyes sharp. He's containing his fear but I can smell it.

The court's empty now; the knife guy is gone, and the guy Tray was playing basketball with seems to have run off, too. I sense eyes watching from far away, though.

"Apparently Aidan was saving your life," Kara says, a bite in her voice.

Tray's frown gets deeper. "This is Aidan?" He's looking me over, gaze hovering on my mark.

"You're welcome," she mutters.

Tray doesn't respond at first; he just studies me, one predator wary of another.

Kara brings up my hand to hold the shirt to my face, then huddles under my limp arm and tries to hoist me to my feet. But I'm not ready yet.

"I'm okay, Kara," I say. "Just give me a second."

She stands and hovers over me protectively before turning to Tray. "Why would that guy want to attack you?"

"Who, Jeremiah? That guy's just a punk, he's always freaking out about something. He's harmless."

"How blind are you?" she growls.

"Are you seriously going to chew my ear off while the guy who was just lit up like the fucking Fourth of July bleeds to death?" He motions to me casually, like he doesn't actually care that I might lose too much blood.

"That light was his power. And he's healing now." She turns back to me, her voice becoming nervous. "You're healing, right?"

I look down at my limp arm and see the skin almost scabbing over. I'm guessing my neck and cheek are about the same. "Yeah, I'm good."

Tray's frown comes back. "What do you mean, 'healing now'? Like, *right* now?"

"He heals quick," she says.

"Well, great for him. In the meantime, the whole fucking neighborhood saw his crazy ass tackle Jeremiah like a psycho."

"Excuse me?" I force my limbs to move, not wanting to look weak anymore. "That piece of shit had a knife and a fucking demon on his neck. He was ready to stick you a few dozen times, I'm guessing. We'd have been cleaning up your blood instead of mine."

"A *demon*?" Tray scoffs, but he looks over at Kara and asks, "Is your boyfriend sane?"

"Did you hear the part about the knife, Tray?" Kara says, sounding tired.

I finish getting to my feet and brush off my jeans, trying not to show how little balance I have. "Let it go, Kara. I think I've seen enough." We'll have to reevaluate the spell. Maybe there's another way. Maybe having fewer Lights won't matter. I have to hope so. My instinct is telling me that this guy wouldn't follow me anywhere. Definitely not into Armageddon.

Kara groans and grabs the bloody shirt from me, shoving it into Tray's chest. "See what you've done. Why are you always such a clueless jerk?"

He holds up his hands in surrender. "Listen, I appreciate the help with Jeremiah, but you need to give me a beat to switch gears. All I saw was *this* guy running at me full throttle before he basically burst into flames, bled from his face—where no one even touched him—and then shoved you into the dirt. Not to mention the fact that the guy's arm is fucking—*shit*, are you seeing this?" He points at my cut as it becomes a scar.

"Yeah, I see," she says, absently. She folds her arms across her chest and starts to pace, her body tense. "And so does everyone else. Can we take this somewhere else, please?"

I'm feeling exposed, too. I've spent too long in the open. I just can't seem to make myself care, though, with the pain pulsing in my body right now.

Tray doesn't answer, he just watches me intently, still trying to play it cool. "Jax mentioned you were full of juice, but shit, this is nuts."

"We need to have this talk somewhere else," Kara says through her teeth. "Let's go." She starts walking away, toward the opening in the fence that leads to the street.

"Hold on." Tray grabs her by the arm. "What *talk*?"

"Hey!" I bark. "Get your hand off her." I step into his space. He's a little taller than me, but even though I have nothing left in me to fight with, I can still *attempt* to kick his ass.

He stares through me, the hard edge in his eyes impossible to read.

Kara looks back and forth between the two of us, then pauses on Tray. She touches his hand, which is still gripping her arm. "Tray, *please*."

He stops glaring at me and releases her slowly, like he's surrendering territory. "We can talk at my place."

Then he walks away, apparently unconcerned with whether we follow him or not. Kara and I share a look before we wordlessly surrender to the moment and start walking, keeping a few yards behind. I'm unsure what Kara's thinking, but it's clear what she's feeling; she's practically coming out of her skin. I brush a strand of hair from her shoulder as we walk, and when she glances at me, I try and give her a reassuring look. "Never a dull moment," I say dryly.

She smirks as we catch up and follow Tray into one of the apartment buildings. We head up the stairs to the second floor and down a hall. The smells assault me in here: sorrow, desperation, and piss. There's a ghost hanging out in a shadow beside the broken fire-extinguisher box at the end of the hallway, a bullet hole in his head, bloodstains on his shirt and hands. He eyes me, and I wonder if he sees something on me. A threat? The kindred spirit of a killer? I've never had a ghost stare me down before.

Tray stops at a door to the left, unlocks it. He opens it a crack, but before going in he holds up a hand for us to wait. Then he slips inside, and it's a full minute before he comes back out and motions for us to follow.

By then I'm so relieved to get away from the glaring ghost that I forget to lock my walls up tighter. I really didn't want to feel anything personal from this guy's life, but before I can close my insides off, I get a sudden hit of several things clamoring at the air: anger and despair, a recent argument. And, of course, demon energy. I immediately spot a tiny one, about five inches tall, pacing on a shelf above the TV that's by the door. I feel more of them around the space, but I ignore it, like I ignore the mess of drug paraphernalia and spilled Cheetos and Diet Coke on the coffee table. Dirty dishes are piled in the sink, and there's a box of crayons tipped over next to an open Disney Princess coloring book.

"You have a little sister?" I ask.

His eyes skip to mine with suspicion. "Why is that your business?"

"Her name's Selena," Kara says, ignoring his attitude. "She's, what? Five now, right, Tray?" She looks down at the crack pipe on the coffee table. Her brow pinches, and her voice turns soft when she says, "You should've told me it was getting bad again."

Tray walks away, grabs a plastic trash can and comes back, swiping everything on the table into it, including a TV remote. "She's just having a bad month."

It's silent then, no one sure what to say. Kara settles onto the couch and I sit next to her.

Tray moves a few more things around like he's trying to do a quick clean, then he plops in the chair with a loud groan. "So what's with all the dramatic shit? You just wanting to check out how the other half lives?"

I decide to be brutally honest. "No. I wanted to see if you were one of us." I motion between Kara and me.

His look turns even more stony. "One of . . . ?"

"Your name has come up," I say. "And you helped Rebecca the other night?"

Kara tenses beside me.

He tips his head. "The redhead? Yeah, I helped her and her friend get home. So what?"

"You saw a demon."

"Wait." Kara shifts to face me. "What—what demon?"

Tray turns smug. "So, the relationship between you two is going well, I see. You've obviously got great communication skills."

I explain to Kara. "A demon attacked Rebecca the other night when she came here to see Miss Mae."

She blinks at me. "Rebecca came to see Miss Mae again on her own? Seriously? Wow, I'm so proud of her."

I won't mention that it was because Rebecca was desperate. And I won't say what Miss Mae said to her, or how I saw Rebecca's energy, what she might be. Kara does need to know all that. Just not right now; it's none of Tray's business.

He leans back in his chair and puts his feet up on the coffee table, next to a dried soda puddle. "There was some freaky dog. You're telling me that was a demon?" He doesn't look convinced.

"Come on, Tray," Kara says. "You know what Jax is at the house for."

"Oh, you mean the playhouse where you guys con unsuspecting morons into thinking they have ghosts in their attic?"

And there's the family asshat gene.

I have no idea why I'm even here. The more time that passes in his space, the less I want this guy to join us. And how in the hell did Kara put up with him, let alone *like* the guy? Maybe kiss him—

A vision of them wrapped in each other's arms fills my head in vivid detail. Kara's breath catching as he grips her hips, as he kisses her neck, her shoulder.

That's *my* shoulder.

I seriously want to kill him right now.

Okay, so apparently I'm jealous. Very. Jealous. But it's not like the guy actually did something I should be so pissed about.

I glance around for spirits that might be tossing shit my way, and grip my knees. Kara places her hand over mine, brushing my knuckles with her palm in a soothing way, like she can feel me losing it. Because she probably can. People in Orange County can probably feel me losing it.

Tray's eyes move to our fingers weaving together, and his jaw clenches.

"So, I came to see if you have any weird talents," I say, needing to reach the point and get the hell out of here. "Word is, Sid asked you to join the house, so I'm guessing he thought you had certain abilities."

Tray's fear simmers in the air, but his expression doesn't change. "You should go sell crazy someplace else. We're all stocked up here."

A small laugh comes from Kara, breaking the tension a little, then she glances at me and explains, "It's from a movie. Jack Nicholson."

"Our *favorite* movie," Tray corrects.

She turns back to him and smiles, revealing her dimple. "Good times. Noodle salad."

He winks at her. *Winks.*

"Well, this is all fascinating," I say, leaning forward on my knees. They have a favorite movie. They have inside jokes. Wonderful. "I'd still like to know the answer to my question."

Tray's smile sinks back into a smirk. "You don't give up, do you?"

"Not usually."

He releases a sigh, and I can feel his fear again. What the hell is it he can do?

"I can tell you're afraid," I say.

Kara scoots down the couch, closer to him. "It's all right, Tray. If anyone gets it, Aidan does."

"It's not like you have a right to know," he says. He clears his throat. "But yeah, I have similar shit abilities to Jax. They're not exactly useful. All I can tell you is, I hear things. In the ground, or the trees, rocks and stuff."

That's . . . weird. "Things—what kind of things?"

"It's voices, sort of. I mostly ignore it. It's not like they tell me anything I understand. It's way beyond a different language, more like animal sounds. That's why I never joined your weirdo con club. I'm better off ignoring this shit." But a red spark lights his eye at the last part. Either he's lying to me or himself.

"Voices." I repeat, trying to wrap my head around the idea. "In the ground."

It's such a strange gift. He's right, how is that even helpful? Something about his ability seems to be freaking him out, though. He's found a pen in his chair and is fidgeting with it, and his scent is only bigger now that the secret's out. I imagine hearing voices probably doesn't go over well on a daily basis. Some of my irritation and dislike of the guy turns to sympathy.

I know what it's like to feel crazy, to be seen as a freak. I get why he hides it. And maybe a small part of me—a *very* small part of me—gets why he's a bit of an ass.

"Well, we need you, Tray," Kara says. "Things are changing, Sid is . . . he's sick, and—" her voice cracks, stopping her words.

Tray's annoyed frown becomes concerned. He doesn't reach out and touch her, but I can see his need to comfort her exuding from every muscle in his body.

"Sid is sick," I continue for her. "It's a long story, but we need you to help us with something. We need everyone together."

"No," he says. His voice is full of assurance, but his energy is conflicted. "I need to watch out for my little sister."

Hearing him say that, those words I've heard come out of my own mouth a hundred thousand times, my head spins. Pain rolls over me. And I get this crazy urge to tell him never mind. To tell him he's better off ignoring it all, better off in ignorance. Everyone he loves will be better off if he stays away from me and my fate.

"What about Jax?" Kara asks with a pleading edge. "He needs you, too, Tray."

"I get it," I say quietly, not able to look at him now. I'd tell him he could bring his sister, but . . . no. No more innocent lives need to be put in harm's way.

Kara grips my leg in silent panic. "We need everyone together, Aidan. It's important."

"Maybe we could do the bonding spell with less." I try to settle into the idea.

Kara gives me an annoyed look. "But Eric was clear, we need at least eight—"

Tray interrupts her. "What spell?"

"A spell to bond all our powers to Aidan," Kara says.

Tray's expression fills with disbelief. "Don't you have enough power, man? Your body healed in, like, five fucking minutes. And you run like you're not even human. You need more juice than that?"

"No, I have too much," I say. "Too much power. This would be me sharing with you, with the others, not the other way around."

His mouth opens a little in stunned silence.

"Things are a mess, Tray," Kara says. "We really need you to help us."

He ignores her, still staring a hole through me. "You would seriously share that force factory in your skin?"

"I have to, or people will get hurt."

He seems to chew on that for a second, like he's reconsidering, but then his shoulders set in determination. "I can't leave. They need me." He stands and walks over to the door, opening it. "But thanks for the effort to recruit me." The demon on the shelf scuttles to the edge and peers down at him, only a foot above his head.

Kara stands. "But there has to be something—"

Tray shakes his head. The demon's body bobs up and down, and I realize it's shifting the air around Tray, making him feel some emotion that's not his own.

"Maybe we can help," I say, standing and walking around the coffee table. The guy's carrying a ton of stuff, and I know that weight. "Like, with your mom." Finger has his ways with people, maybe he can help get the need for drugs out of her. Raul was much better after only a few days in the house. Of course, I think the demon I killed was probably a big part of his addiction.

"I don't want your help." His eyes move from me to Kara; the loss in them is heavy.

"Well, you know where to find us," I say.

Then I feel clearly what emotions the demon on the shelf is oozing out into the air: jealousy and bitterness.

There's the answer to why I wanted to punch Tray a few minutes ago. I reach up, grab the pointy thing off the shelf, and crush its tiny bones in my fist. My power sparks in a flash of light, consuming the little bastard in three seconds, then sinks away as quickly as it came.

I wipe the ash off on my pants. "I can help," I say. "More than you might think."

Tray glances to the shelf and back at me. "What was that?"

"A demon. Small, but it seemed to be fucking with you."

"I felt it," he says under his breath. "Or I guess I should say, I felt when it was gone." Then he motions to his neck. "Was it the same thing that made your new scars out on the courts earlier?"

"No, that was a different one, but it's dead, too." I think it was watching Tray, probably because he's a Light. I suddenly wish that I could help him more, but it doesn't seem like he'll let me.

I lift my hand and run my fingers over the new scars on my neck and cheek. "There was one watching you out there from the fence when we came in. I'm not positive if it was keyed on you or the other guy, but it's what got Jeremiah to pull the knife. It whispered in his ear."

"And you saw all that?"

"Yeah," I look around the apartment again. "It smells like there's more. Do you want me to check?" I motion to the hall that leads to the bedrooms.

"No!" he says a little too forcefully. "Just stay out of it."

Kara comes from behind me. "Is she back there, your mom?"

He deflates a little. "Yeah. But she's baked. Not a good time to poke the bear. I'm hoping she'll sleep it off so she doesn't miss work again tonight. Selena's at the neighbor's until dinner, so she's finally getting rest."

"You need to let us help, Tray," Kara says, sounding miserable. "Tell him, Aidan."

"No," he says, again quietly, resigned. "Just let me go."

He's not giving in. Not now anyway.

"Kara will text you my number," I say, resting a hand on the small of her back to encourage her out the door. "I can come anytime and check things out more, if you change your mind."

Tray looks away from Kara and gives me a jerk of his chin in answer.

He won't take help, he won't leave his mom and sister just to help us, and I don't blame him. He's stuck. When the door closes behind us and he's still in that apartment, that urgency fills me again to save him. It seems twisted, because I can't do a thing about it. The guy's got free will. It's not like I can kidnap him. Not to mention, I totally get it. Damn, do I get it.

So we walk away. From the lingering demons, the ghost in the hallway, and the guy who might make fixing things impossible if he doesn't surrender to his fate soon.

TWENTY-FIVE

Rebecca

Samantha's in the bathroom getting ready for bed when my phone pings with a text from Aidan.

How are things? U ok?

I read it over and wonder why it's Aidan checking in on me, not Connor. I texted Connor this morning and haven't gotten a response. Did Aidan tell him about the witch thing before I could, and scare him off? Connor did keep telling me I shouldn't go see Miss Mae; maybe he's mad that I didn't listen.

I just don't know why he wouldn't at least let me explain myself. Unless he doesn't want to be with a girl who's a witch. Unless . . . he's disgusted by me now.

Panic and shame rise in me, biting at the inside of my skin. I open another text thread to Connor and type, *I really need to talk to you. Please call me.*

I send that and go back to the Aidan thread and answer, *No troubles. Thanks for putting up the protections on the house. Looks like they're working.* I consider telling him about the image I drew, the pentagram thing, maybe text him the picture I took. But the half-burnt paper is crumpled up in my waste basket now, and nothing bad has happened, so I'd sort of be making a huge deal out of a nothing burger. Aidan has enough on his shoulders as it is.

I really wish Connor would call or text me back.

I set my phone down and stare at the small metal trash can by my desk. I should probably take it to the outside trash bin; it's freaking me out having it in the room. But then I feel like I'm totally overreacting. So, instead, I pick up the can, set it on my closet floor, and shut the door.

Since Samantha came over to spend the night, I recruited her to help me investigate my new problem of witchiness. She barely blinked when I told her why I went to Miss Mae and what the woman said; she just warned me that I better not turn goth on her, because "Black totally washes out your complexion, Em." We've spent the last couple hours searching witch stuff on the Internet—maybe that's what's making me feel so antsy. We looked up everything from Wicca to *The Wizard of Oz*. I now know more about the Salem trials than I ever wanted to. And according to a movie, *The Craft*, most witches wear a *lot* of eyeliner— Samantha went into a style lecture about ten minutes into watching, and then proceeded to explain which color season each of the girls in the coven was. Not helpful but entertaining.

She comes out of the bathroom, garbed in her pink jammies, and plops down on my bed, looking chipper. "Okay, so what's next on the Project Witchy list? Ouija board? Chanting? My neighbor is an old hippie, I think he has chickens if we need to kill one for a spell."

"Wow." I laugh. "How about we just watch another movie—one with more kissing and less creepy."

She seems happy with the idea, so we settle into bed with my laptop and watch a funny romance flick. Eventually we're being normal us again, talking about class schedules, what senior year might be like, gossiping about teachers, and planning our very last bye-bye summer, princess pizza party.

As our easy conversation fades, my mind goes back to the reality of my new twist of fate and how little I know about what it all means. I can't stop thinking about the strange and terrifying pictures and videos from Samantha's research help; the image of a hunched old crone, with a warty nose and claws for hands, who cooked children in ovens; beautiful raven-haired goddesses who cursed men with longing, driving them insane . . .

None of what we found was encouraging.

One image was especially haunting, though. And as I sink into sleep, I feel like it's rising in front of me, coming alive. As if the scent of wood smoke truly fills my head, the crackling of flames filling my ears like wind. And the screams . . . the screams of the woman. Her young form is tied to the pyre, her hair flying up like wings.

The hot flames lick over her body, swallowing her whole.

———

The smell of smoke wakes me. Samantha is lying in bed, facing the window and sleeping soundly. I sniff the air, wondering if there's a brushfire; maybe it's Santa Ana winds come early? But as I roll over, the smell gets stronger, closer, and settles in my lungs, forcing a cough.

I sit up and look around my room, but it's dark, too dark to see anything. I reach over to the bedside lamp and turn it on—

Smoke. The room is full of it, muddying my eyesight to the surroundings.

I cough more and wave my hand in front of my face, my muscles starting to panic. Where's it coming from? I can't see anything.

"Sam." I shake her shoulder but she doesn't move.

Why didn't the alarm go off this time? I've never seen so much smoke.

I roll out of bed, the coughing uncontrollable now. "Sam, wake up." But my voice is a scratch at the air, barely there. I lower myself to the floor, where the smoke is thinner, and feel around for my door. A wave of dizziness hits me as I crawl along the wall. My cough turns sharp. I feel my desk, but I'm all turned around now. I try to yell for Samantha again but nothing comes from my throat.

My hand hits metal and relief fills me—the doorknob! I pull it down, opening the door, praying for clean air. But something's wrong, the smoke follows me, envelops me, like it's alive. It wraps me in its arms, and in the back of my mind I feel like I'm moving, being dragged across the floor until my shoulder hits a wall.

The room spins, my head aches, my chest . . . everything—wait, I'm not in the hall outside my room. I'm in my closet. The shelves are against my back. I grope for the exit and hit metal—the trash can.

And suddenly, I know. I feel cool metal against my palm and I know. This is the drawing, the spell. It's alive again, aware. *And it's all my fault—*

I jerk forward, sitting up in bed with a gasp, pulling a gulp of fresh air into my lungs. I pant, heaving, breathing in and out between rattling coughs and feeling the sting in my lungs as I blink at my surroundings.

I'm back in my bed.

There's no smoke. None. The room is tinged blue from the moonlight coming in through the window, and the air is clean.

I turn and see Samantha sleeping beside me, in the exact same spot as she was a second ago. Was it a dream? All the pictures of burning witches must've gotten to me.

I cough again and pull back the covers, slide out of bed, and head for the closet. Before I open the door, I wait a few seconds, trying to see if I smell anything, any smoke. In my dream something in here was on fire only seconds ago—it felt so real.

I swing the door open and flip on the light, looking down at the trash can. Which is full of charred paper. Black, burnt charcoal paper. Everything inside it has been devoured. And there's a grey ring of ash around the rim of the can.

A chill works through me, and I can only think of one thing to do. I grab the trash can and walk out of the room with it held in front of me, head down the stairs, and out the French doors in the dining room that lead to the backyard. My bare feet hardly feel the cold from the dew-covered grass as I make my way to the edge of the yard where the hill begins to drop off. I step onto a rock, lift the can over the fence, and toss it as far as I can. It hits the ground with a small sound and bounces, the moonlight reflecting off the metallic surface. I watch the glint of it until it disappears into a gully.

And then I keep staring, like it might crawl back out and find me.

TWENTY-SIX

Hunger

It watches. The demon Hunger watches the Rebecca girl's house. Something must be decided about her, a way in, a way to rip and tear out Hope from the root.

No shadows will lend aid against the will of this new queen, Ava bird. Hunger will have to remedy past failures alone.

Something rumbles underfoot. Power breaking free, seeking to be heard.

Hunger looks around. The demon Hunger looks around the lands nearby and senses nothing to answer the interruption in the pattern. But then a ripple of green mist emanates from the second floor of the house being watched.

There, the power is coming from there, the Rebecca girl's window.

What could she have possibly challenged? She seems unaware of her own abilities.

The demon sniffs at the air. The demon Hunger sniffs at the air, finding many things in the houses along the road: lust, despair, joy, and selfish ambition. But nothing smells of casting.

Hello, a cheerful young voice says.

The demon turns. The demon Hunger turns and looks down at the white-haired female child. She sits on the grass with her legs crossed, looking up at the same window where the green mist still slides against the air.

The demon glares at the child, smells the energy. The scent of silver fills the head. Mingled with the smell of a Nephilim.

A growl emerges from deep in the chest, *Ava witch.*

Yes, it's me. And you're Mr. Hunger. I hear you're not a fan.

The demon lunges to grab the witch by the root of her hair and rip her spine from her body. But claws grab only air. The witch now stands on the other side.

You're very predictable, aren't you? she asks.

Hunger glowers. *You broke the pattern, you must be destroyed to reform the Balance.*

Well, your master doesn't agree. She tips her head in a thoughtful manner. *I kinda see where you're coming from, though. I've made a bit of a mess in the ranks. I get it. And Balance is really important, I know. What would you say if I told you that that's what I'm trying to do, too?*

Hunger stares at the child witch in disdain, not accepting the lie.

I am! she says. *I just have a small problem. It seems like you have the same one.* She points at the house where the Rebecca girl is. *Maybe we can team up?*

Hunger releases a growl.

I know, I cast you out before, but obviously you had the power to come back. And I knew that. I just had to put on a good show, right?

Hunger was sent to destroy the fire-haired witch by the master. Though, the desire to do so comes from the deep urge to taste her flesh.

What if I told you that I could help with that, once you've helped me?

Hunger looks up at the window again. The green mist is now dissipated. *How would the usurper child possibly be of any help to Hunger?* Malice laces the thought, but there is a twinge of relenting.

Well, for one, you felt that spark just now, right? She has no idea what she's jumped into. Which leaves her weak.

And I will influence the father to stretch his own neck, Hunger says, *leaving her completely alone. This will cause her to wish her own life over, and—*

You're missing the point, meathead. The small witch releases a sigh of impatience. *She's weak, so I can easily get what I want from her if I can find the right demon to trap her.* She motions to Hunger. *I can get you over there, on her side of the Veil. I can give you flesh to wear and you'll be able to do whatever it is you want to her, as long as you let me have her for a little while.*

Hunger's chest sparks with confusion and sudden elation. So close, the witch would allow him through to get close, where flesh is strongest? Where the demon could touch her. Feel her skin chill under the touch of claws, and smell her hair—

Okay, perv, the Ava bird says. *Slow down that weirdo movie in your head. Yes, I can make you corporeal, but there's something you have to do for me in return.*

TWENTY-SEVEN

Aidan

Another message appears from Ava as the sun sets over the city. I'm back in the warehouse apartment, trying to distract myself with some research on teleporting, trying not to think about how much I want to bang my head into the wall. I turned on the TV for background noise, but that only lasted about ten minutes because *I* was a topic of conversation on the evening talk show.

I feel a crazy relief as the letters burn themselves into the note on the coffee table. I can't understand why I'm relieved, though. Especially after I read my new task.

You are so very clever, finding witches by accident, saving damsels, and sending me messages. You're ruining the fun when you win. :P It doesn't matter, there's no way you'll guess what's next. Hint: The past is coming back to haunt someone you love.

I go to my bag and pull out the blood pen I got from my box and immediately write back, *No more riddles, Ava. What do you want? Just get to the point.* I watch the words burn in and wait.

Nope, comes back as the answer.

I get the urge to shove the paper down the garbage disposal, but instead I just put a book on top of it so I don't have to look at it anymore.

I have to hope the answer to this hint comes to me like the others did. Another life in the balance. And I'm still no closer to understanding why.

It's time to just do this bonding spell and get some control over something. Rebecca was obviously one of Ava's targets, and might still be. She needs more power to defend herself. And so do the rest of them.

I find the journal in my pile of books and flip it open to the bonding spell. It hits me again how big this magic is, all the intricate details and layers. I see several familiar Enochian runes, but most of it—writing and symbols—is completely alien. There are a few notes here and there, some instructions on which oils to use, that sage should be burned in the area, and it very clearly states that no mistakes can be made in the transfer of the drawing. It has to be perfect or it won't work.

I run my fingers over the blood ink, and it vibrates, warming under my skin.

Eric said I need at least eight Lights to distribute my power to, because it'll harm them if it's not spread out enough. So far Tray isn't budging. But maybe there's a way around having eight. If there is, the answer isn't in the journal. And Eric is on the other side of the Veil.

I grab my phone and call Hanna, knowing she's aware of how to contact him. I explain a little of what's going on, and ask her to please pass a message to Eric: Is there any way to do the bonding ceremony with only seven? Hopefully she'll get back to me with Eric's answers quick.

I feel like we're running out of time. This thing with Ava will come to a head soon. But what happens then? Something tells me the game will be a cakewalk compared to the finale.

My phone pings with a text. When I rush to look, it's not Hanna but Holly.

```
It's official. You hv a fan page on FB &
    your very own hashtag: #BurnLikeBlink.
    Get it? Because you "blinked" out?
    ROTFLOL.
```

I sneak over to the house after midnight. When I pull into the driveway, I'm thrilled to see the shed's been torn down. The boards are stacked against the fence just like I asked Jax to do before I left this morning. I want to hug him. The energy in the yard feels much lighter than before.

I heard back from Hanna, and she sent out the message to Eric, so hopefully I'll have answers about the spell soon.

When I walk through the back door of the house and head across the kitchen, I'm stunned to see Sid sitting up on the couch with a plate on his lap and one beside him, both topped with a mountain of food. His skin is still pale, and his cheeks are sunken, but he smiles when he spots me.

"You're not very good at hiding," Holly scolds me.

I make a beeline for Sid, but then pause before touching him. He looks so fragile. I don't want to break him.

"Sit, son," he says in a raspy voice.

Elation fills me at the sound of his voice, him calling me son, and I have to smile. As much as it used to piss me off, I hadn't thought I'd hear him call me anything again after what I saw the other night. I move the second plate of food to the coffee table and sit beside him.

"How're you feeling?" I ask, looking him over closely.

"Tired," he says. "Very tired. But I'm so glad to see your face. And the others. I was lost for a moment there."

"Lost?"

He just gives me a slow smile and pats my hand. "Tell me what has happened. I heard from Jax that you think Tray may be a Light. And Holly said Rebecca was having trouble. Are things better there?"

I don't want to talk about any of that with him. "Let's just sit."

He nods, looking a little relieved.

Kara comes in; her face is lit up. She motions to Sid. "He's better!"

Holly gives me a sideways look. "He's not eating."

"And he's not in a coma, either," Kara snaps back.

Holly rolls her eyes and walks away.

Jax comes in, grabs the remote, then flips on the TV as he plops on the loveseat beside a silent Finger.

"Let's see what the world is saying," he says.

I cringe and start to ask him to turn it off, but Kara grabs my hand. "We need to know, Aidan. We need to know how to get around this."

So I just sit back and close my eyes as Jax flips through the channels, finally settling on one of the midnight gossip shows. They're talking about some actress who took her top off at a nightclub, the cohosts joking back and forth about what her next role might be. Raul walks in and starts adding to the snark like he's a part of the show. He seems to know an awful lot about the people they're talking about. And when Holly comes in, it gets even more ridiculous as they start to argue about who the actress is dating. Jax tells them both to shut up, twice, but neither seems to notice.

I start to doze off with Kara's head on my shoulder and her fingers laced through mine. I let the noise and the familiar sounds of bickering calm me. It's soothing, like home. I smile and breathe, thankful in the moment.

Then someone is hitting my leg.

I open my eyes to Jax's hysterical laughter. "Your superhero name is lame-*ass*, man. Blink Boy, seriously?"

"I liked when the girl they interviewed on the street called him a Titan," Holly says.

Jax snorts. "He's not big enough to be a Titan."

"I like the alien theory," Kara says, kissing my cheek. "You missed when the close-up magician was on, showing examples of ways to disappear a rabbit."

How long was I asleep?

"The television people are having fun with it, aren't they?" Sid says, sounding amused as well. "It's quite interesting to see how they are processing things they can't explain."

"Maybe you should just come fully out of the closet," Holly says. "Go on the show and make a Twitter account, Blink Boy." She grins wide. "I'd sew you an outfit; mask, cape, and all."

"Very funny," I say.

I look over at the TV and see several people sitting on a couch, talking animatedly like they're arguing. They're different people than before so this must be a different show. The bar at the bottom of the screen reads, "Science Fiction Come to Life or Elaborate Hoax?"

"Well, I've had enough," I say, standing. All the weird attention is making me feel even more vulnerable than I already am. They want to pick me apart, understand me, name me. It's creepy as fuck.

Kara stands quickly. "You can't go yet. You've only been here a few hours."

"I can't stay long," I say.

She takes my hand and leads me out onto the back porch and makes me sit beside her on the swing. She curls against me and puts her arms around me. "I need to feel you close. Even if it's just for a little while more."

I run my fingers through her dark hair, let the vanilla smell of her shampoo fill my head, and try to enjoy the night air, as we sit in silence.

"We haven't talked about today," she whispers eventually. "About Tray and everything. Are you okay?"

"Yeah." But I don't know how I feel. As much as we need him for the spell, I'm almost more worried about him joining us at this point. "I sent a message to Eric to see if he thought we could do the spell with seven instead."

"I wonder what it'll feel like."

"What?"

She props herself up on my chest so she can look me in the eyes. "You know, your power becoming a part of me."

"You're a part of me, so it's only fair," I say. I skim my fingers over her jaw and slide my thumb over the dimple in her cheek. "You're so beautiful. Sometimes I look at you, and I can barely breathe. *Love doesn't feel like a big enough word for how my spirit needs you.* I never thought a heart could feel this way, not for real."

Pink rises to her cheeks, and I revel in how my words affect her.

"We're going to get through this," she says, like I'm saying good-bye.

But I'm not. I'm just soaking in the moment. "It doesn't matter," I say.

She frowns. "Of course it does."

"No," I whisper, pulling her in to take her lips with mine. "The only thing that matters is this. Now."

"You're making me nervous," she says, leaning away a little, fear in her voice. "You make it sound like you're going off to war."

"I am. We all are."

She studies my eyes, and I see she's trying to think of some way to say it's not true. But she can't.

So, I kiss her furrowed brow, I kiss her cheek, her lips. I hold her to me and try to help her to understand what I mean without words.

———

I sit on my foster brother's beanbag chair and watch Lindsey Sawyer as she perches on the bed across from me, resting her chem lab book on her lap. She lives a few doors down, so she said we could study together sometimes. And by study, she meant make out.

She seems nervous now that we're alone in my room, and I start to doubt that she'll let me kiss her again. I'm definitely doubting the text she sent me after school today.

```
I wanna try going all the way this time.
   Bring a condom.
```

I almost pissed my pants when I read it. Girls always seem to steer clear of me, making me feel a bit like a leper. I even checked for demons around her when I watched her walk to the bus. Is she serious? She'll just have sex with me after a few "study sessions"? The girl barely knows me—beyond which breath mint I prefer.

And she isn't exactly an easy A. Neither am I, though.

But now something about being alone in this tiny room with her again, thinking of the last few times she kissed me and let me feel her up, what she's going to let me have, it's making her seem much more attractive than when I first met her a few weeks ago. The way her brown hair is twisted up and pinned to her head makes her neck look very . . . kissable. And I remember she tastes like strawberry lip gloss. Which I know is a total cliché, but damn is it tasty on her.

She sets the book aside, pops her gum, and twists her feet inward, knocking her knees together, blocking my view up her skirt. Not that I was looking. I wasn't.

Okay, I may have considered it. But I didn't do it.

"So," I say, feeling the awkwardness emerge between us as we both contemplate what we've decided to embark on. This is it. This is when I finally get a taste of what makes the world turn. I just wish it wasn't in this hellhole of a house, with that rat demon right outside the door that's always following my foster father around.

The air in this room is a little better than in some of the other parts of the house since I cleanse it with sage regularly, but it's still full of the buzzing remnants of my foster father's rampage last night. My cheek and arm have a few marks to remember the tirade by, too. But I can pretend they're there because I fell off my skateboard.

"I only have a half hour," Lindsey says, scooting off the edge of the bed, down to the floor in front of me. "We could just skip some of the first parts since we've done those already." She tilts her head, and I have to wonder if she has a checklist in her brain of all the things she's wanted to try. All the items except one are crossed off, apparently.

"Okay, well . . ." And I'm drawing a blank because she's reaching for the zipper of my jeans.

As she pops the button, I bark out a nervous laugh and scoot back, beanbag and all.

"What? Don't you have a condom?"

"I do. I mean, I will." After I figure out which foster brother to ask. Or which drawer to look in. "But maybe we should kiss some," I add, feeling lame.

"Oh, yeah, sure." She winks and pulls the gum from her mouth, pressing it to the bed frame behind her with her thumb. I have trouble looking away from the green glistening glob for several seconds, but then she's climbing on my lap, looming over me, and sticking her tongue down my throat.

After I settle into the kissing, it's actually kind of nice. I get her nestled into my side so I can be in control more, and soon we're sinking into a rhythm, my hand beginning to roam a little farther than last time, and my mind starting to imagine what it'll feel like when I've finally crossed the line. Because I'm going to cross it. I'm going to fucking laser blast it.

She's moaning and making me feel very masculine again, and I'm just about to—

Something bangs on the door, and my foster father's nicotine-plowed voice comes through the wood. "Fuck-up turd, the phone's for you."

Lindsey unlatches her face from mine, her breath coming in tiny gasps. "What time is it?" She scoots her skirt back down and grabs her shirt off the floor where it landed a few minutes ago. She flips over her phone. "Oh, shit, I'm gonna be late for the movies."

I blink at her as she pulls the gum off the bed where she'd left it and sticks it back in her mouth.

My gut rises.

Last time I kiss her. Ever.

"I told you I only had a half hour." She actually sounds irritated at me.

I grab my shirt and pull it over my head, feeling annoyed right back. "Yeah, well, what can I say, I'm not a fast sale."

When she picks up her chem lab book, I spot a text on her phone from a guy in my gym class, who I'm guessing she's meeting for the movie. Or should I say, date?

"Whatever." She pops her gum. "Your loss."

I want to laugh but it's just too depressing.

"Say hi to Trenton for me," I say as I open the bedroom door, ushering her out.

And I'm greeted by the stubbled, round face of my foster father. The rat demon that's always following him licks Lindsey's leg as she walks by.

He holds out the phone for me. "That was quick, turd. You might wanna practice more."

I grab the phone from him and put it to my ear, my chest aching from the need to hit something. "Yeah," I say through my teeth.

The sound of trembling breath comes from the other end of the line. And a small voice whispers, "There's blood, Aidan. So much blood."

TWENTY-EIGHT

Rebecca

I'm not sure what to think about last night. Samantha leaves early, heading straight to the dance studio, and I'm left alone and confused. I asked her if she smelled anything, fire or burnt paper, or if anything had woken her up, but she insisted that it was the best night's sleep she'd had in forever.

I can't just pretend it's all fine. I've got a demon after me, I've got some hidden witchy power ready to burst out of me. I need to make sure that a repeat of last night doesn't happen. First step, I text the image of the drawing to Aidan and ask if that symbol means anything. Second, I resolve never to ever draw like that again. Whatever was controlling me, my subconscious, my inner spirit, or something *else*, it doesn't seem like it's heading in a positive direction.

Hopefully Aidan will get back to me quickly.

I still haven't heard back from Connor. Instead of hurt, I'm starting to get offended. Why's he being such a jerk? I'm so tired of waiting for a guy to get his crap together. I decide to let out a little of my frustration and go back to my texts, typing in, *So much for dependable Connor.*

After sending it I feel ill, but I try to shove it down. I can't keep letting people walk all over me. It's my new life motto.

Dad's left for work, so it's just me and the empty house, full of questions. Margaritte has the week off, so I end up nervous-cleaning for an hour, scrubbing the ring of ashes off the carpet in my closet and rearranging my art supplies into the Rubbermaid box, sliding them back onto a very high shelf. Then I vacuum my room and dust things that were just dusted.

I'm so relieved when the doorbell rings, interrupting my cleaning binge, that I run downstairs and fling the door open without checking the peephole.

It's a woman in what looks like a Denny's uniform. Her hair's askew, a smudge of ketchup on her cheek. She stares through me, still as death.

"How can I help you?" I ask, hesitantly. The hair on my arm prickles. I shut the door a little, hiding behind it.

"I have something for you," she says, her voice almost robotic. "Can I give it to you now?"

"No, thank you." I start to close the door more. "I'm good." But before it latches, it's stopped by a firm hand.

"I said no, thank you," is all I can think to say as I push with everything I have at the door. It doesn't budge, it just opens back toward me so I can see her again.

"I heard you," the woman says. Dread climbs up my spine, and I'm suddenly aware that this is no woman, no ordinary person. Her eyes are glazed over, almost filmy.

Then I hear something, a *drip, drip, drip* onto the stone. I follow the sound with my gaze and—

A terror-filled moan comes from deep in my chest as I stare at the mutilated possum in her fist, its insides spilling from it, blood, red and shiny, pooling at her feet.

My stomach rises. My breath comes in gasps, the panic fills every muscle. I shove and shove at the door, but I can't shut it, I can't shut the door. The horror burns in my lungs, courses through every inch of me. *What is she?*

Through the fog of dread I hear, "It's just a curse from the queen. Don't be afraid. We can't have all these pesky wards getting in the way." And then the dead animal is plopped on the doorstep with a wet *splat*. A curse. "She wants you to know that you did well against the creature at Miss Mae's. She's been watching you. But it's nearly time to choose a side." The woman backs up a step, and the door shuts with a loud *bang* as she lets go.

I latch and lock the deadbolt, hands trembling, mind panicking.

Even as I stumble away, I can sense the sick rot of the curse through the door.

TWENTY-NINE

Aidan

I slept in Kara's arms again. And now I really need to go. I need to see if Eric has a solution. I check my phone, but he hasn't texted or called, neither has Hanna. I do have a text from Rebecca, though. An image.

The text reads, *I drew this, what does it mean?* I tap on the photo and then enlarge it, taking a closer look.

My breath catches. It's the same symbol burned into the leather cover of my mom's grimoire. A seal of protection from earthly elements, a lock. But parts of the spell were made up by my mom, a cocktail of casting magic and something else. Why would Rebecca draw this? How would she even know about it? She's never seen the grimoire.

I text her back, *When did you draw this?*

Then I get out of bed, get dressed, and give Kara a kiss before heading out.

The morning air is cold when I walk out the back door into the yard, the sky a crisp summer blue over my head. I'm unlocking the car when my phone vibrates in my pocket. I'm hoping it's Eric, but when I pull it out I see it's Rebecca.

I tap the green button. "Good morn—" But I don't get it all out.

"It's dead!" she chokes out. "There's all this blood—oh my God, it's horrifying, I can't—"

"Rebecca, stop," I cut in, panic grabbing me by the throat. "What's dead?"

"I think it's a possum," she whimpers.

My rushing pulse begins to slow back to normal. "Start over, tell me what happened."

So she does. She tells me about how a woman came to her door and tossed a bloody dead possum on the welcome mat. The creepy woman said that the gift was from the queen, and soon Rebecca would have to choose a side. Everything in me sharpens as she speaks, her voice shaking. My nerves burn, my head aches. And helplessness fills me again.

I know what the woman—who was possessed, by the sound of it—I know what she was doing. Breaking the wards that I just put around the house.

A crunching sound makes me turn.

Someone is standing three feet from me, holding up a cell phone. Recording video of me.

I step back, lifting my arm to block my face as I mumble to Rebecca that I have to go. But the man moves closer. He's short, with spindly arms and legs, head topped with a backward baseball cap, his cargo shorts' pockets bulging. "How did you do it?" he asks in a rush. "The readers at Blind Man's Blog want to know: Are you going to come out and let us know the truth, Blink Boy? Why did you kill that woman with your alien powers? What are you hiding from?"

The sound of my lame-ass media name coming from his lips makes me stop retreating.

I come at him, grabbing for the phone. "I have no idea what you're talking about." I yank it from his hands.

He smacks at me like a debutant, yelling, "Hands off the gear!" Then directs his voice to the street. "Help! Police!" As if the cops are waiting just a few yards away.

I chuck the phone as hard as I can, over the fences and the backyards of about three houses.

"Hey!" he yells as he watches it fly away.

I turn on him and get in his face. "Back off."

The smell of his thick fear bursts out between us.

Okay, I could've handled that better than I just did.

"You need to leave," I say in a more measured tone. "You really don't want to be here."

His eyes dart back and forth between the direction I tossed his phone and my face. "This is my job, man."

"To stalk people?"

He shrugs. "Yeah."

I look around again, making sure he's alone. This is bad. "How did you find me?" If this dimwit caught me, then it won't be long before someone else does.

"I've just been watching the house the last couple days—heard the address come over dispatch, so I've been keeping an eye out." He points to a yellow MINI Cooper parked across the street. "I saw when you got here last night. I just waited it out to get the money shot."

"You've been out here all night?"

He shrugs again, calmer now. He's also apparently not in a hurry to leave, only a little nervous as he eyes me. I don't know what to do with him. Technically he's trespassing, but it's not as if I'm going to call the cops. I could shoo him off, but he'd just come back, likely with more curious eyes in tow.

"I can tell your story," he says, his hope sparking when I just stare at him. "I could be the Lois Lane to your Superman."

I sneer, annoyed. "Are you kidding?" I take him by the arm and tug him farther down the driveway so the house will block the view from the street entirely. "This isn't some comic book, dude. You're going to get yourself killed."

"I feel ya, man, you're a rebel to the system. I didn't let the cops know you were here, I swear. We don't need the pigs getting wind of shit. You need to be able to do your thing and let your voice be heard. I can—"

"Shut. Up." My head feels like it's going to explode. It must be nice living in his world, where this could all be some movie plot he can twist to his narrative, like my life is made up of sound bites and Vines he can tweet to make me look good.

"Look . . ." I start, trying to figure out how to say this, "thanks for not calling the cops. But you need to understand, it's not safe to follow me. There are . . . *things*—forces—after me, trying to hurt me. You don't want to be in the middle of this shit."

His mouth opens in amazement. When I'm done, he says in a hushed voice, "Like the government?" He looks around as if there might be people watching now.

I sigh and let the thought stand. "Yeah, sure."

"Oh, that sucks, man."

"Yeah, so don't come back around, or they'll come after you, too."

He looks less relaxed about that, stepping away from me. "Gotcha." But then he pulls another phone from his jacket pocket and taps at it. "Could I maybe still get a quote on the record to go with the video?"

"I chucked your phone, there's no video."

"Haven't you ever heard of a cloud?" He looks up from his screen and gives me a quick sardonic grin. Then holds the phone up like it's a microphone. "Quote?"

I just glare at him. Then I walk past him to the car and slide behind the wheel without a word. As I drive away, I glance in the rearview mirror, checking to be sure he's not going to the front door, but see he's already heading away from the house to his own car.

———

As I head for Rebecca's house I consider whether I should take off the front and back plates of the car now. Since that blogger guy found me, he's got the license number obviously. I'll have to get Eric to scrub himself from the paperwork or something, switch out the numbers to keep his name out of it. But if the guy found the house, then he likely has Sid's name, too . . .

Shit. It's too many connections, too many threads tying us all together.

I call Hanna to give her a heads up, and she says she'll take care of the car's paperwork right away and get some new plates from a contact by the end of the day. But when I ask her if she's heard from Eric, she gets quiet and I can tell she's nervous about something.

"What's wrong?" I ask.

"I don't . . ." her voice staggers. "He always answers me right away. And after the other day, I know he'd want to be sure I was all right. I just . . . if you still haven't heard anything, either . . ."

My anxiety rises, the road ahead of me blurring a little as my head starts to ache, but I say, "I'm sure he's fine. There's probably a lot going on. Ava's not just messing with me, there are demons out there all over the place, so the other side has got to be a mess." She doesn't answer, so I add. "I'll be there in a little while, and we'll send another message." And then I realize something else. If the LA Paranormal house isn't secure at all now, then I can't go back to do the spell there. We'll have to find another spot to do it. "Is there a way that we could do the bonding spell in the warehouse?"

"Of course," she says quickly, then releases a sigh. "I'm sorry that I'm not very helpful, Aidan. I wish that I could do more, that I understood your world better."

"No, you don't," I say. "And don't be sorry. I have no clue what I'd do without you and Eric."

I hang up after reassuring her a little more, but the conversation leaves me feeling unsteady. Why hasn't Eric contacted her? She's right. If he thought something was wrong, he'd have been there the instant she sent the message. And if he's not, then something isn't right.

I've barely set my phone down before it's ringing again. Kara this time.

"Tray's in," she says, relief clear in her voice. "He's a go for the bonding spell."

That was quick. "What happened?"

"Apparently something attacked his little sister when she was playing in the park."

My body goes tense. "Oh, shit."

"She's okay, just some scratches. But she's terrified, obviously. Tray is convinced it was a demon, so he says he's fine with helping us as long as it means he'll be able to protect her better."

"We can't guarantee that, we have no clue what this bonding will do."

"We need him, Aidan. We'll sort all that out later."

She's right, but I don't want Tray to go into this with the wrong idea—thinking I know anything about the side effects. Because I don't. And I know my power isn't all safety and roses. The others get that, I think. They see it. But Tray didn't even know about demons being real until a few days ago.

"So, we should do the spell today," she says, like it's not really up for discussion. "Can you call Rebecca, though? Connor acted weird when I asked him to."

That doesn't sound good. "Yeah, I'll take care of it. Let's meet at the club in an hour."

"The club?"

"I was caught in the driveway this morning by some blogger who's apparently been following me. Don't think I'll be coming around the house again for a while."

She barks out a laugh. "A blogger? Are you joking?"

"I wish. And now I'm probably going to be the headline of Blind Man's Blog tomorrow."

THIRTY

Rebecca

Aidan's going to pick me up on his way to the club. I really couldn't care less about this spell he's so anxious to do, I just don't want to be alone in the house anymore, wondering what the heck's going to get dropped off on my doorstep next.

The truth is, after last night I'm terrified that whatever's going on with me could mess everything up. I'm not like the rest of them, I can feel it. I'm not like Aidan, with his abilities to read people or his powers to kill demons. I don't know what I am, but it's not like them.

If that lady who left the possum was telling the truth, then Ava wants me on her side. And she wouldn't want someone good.

When Aidan arrives, he cleans up the dead possum, and I hose off the porch. I want to tell him everything that happened last night with the fire—or the nonfire, I guess—but I just don't know how. I don't know how to explain it. And I still sort of feel like I may have imagined it all.

Instead, when we're getting in the car, I ask him if he got my text of the drawing.

"Yeah," is all he says. His hands grip the steering wheel tighter.

"You know what it is," I say.

He glances sideways at me. "It's a spell." He pauses but then adds quickly, "How did you know how to draw it?"

I knew it was bad. I can tell from the tension in his shoulders, the pinched skin at the corner of his eyes, that I was right. "I, uh . . . well, it just sort of came to me. I drew it with my eyes closed."

He sucks in a quick breath. "You channeled."

"I did? Is that bad?"

He shakes his head, and I assume he's going to say no, but instead he says, "I don't know. It depends what you were channeling. But it could mean you're able to call up spirits." Then something seems to dawn on him. "Maybe that's what Miss Mae meant by tricking spirits." He sounds relieved at the idea, like there were worse alternatives. But it all sounds pretty bad.

"Maybe, I guess." I don't have a clue what Miss Mae meant. "So, you think this was because of the piece of Kara that went into me?"

"I don't know. Kara's ability was very . . . different."

"What could she do?"

"She, uh . . . well, I guess you could say that she hypnotized people. She was basically able to make them do whatever she wanted."

I sit straighter, the idea unnerving me. "She could mind control people?" No wonder Aidan was worried that I somehow adopted that part of Kara. "Did she ever do it to you?"

He shrugs. "Once, just to show me how it worked."

"Oh." And then I ask, hurriedly, "Did she ever do it to me?"

"No," he says firmly. "She didn't like using it, it made her sick."

"But now it's gone?"

"When my energy healed her curse, that went with it."

"Except the piece that went into me."

He stays focused on the road but reaches over and touches my knee, like he's trying to comfort me. "We'll figure it out, don't worry."

I nod, but my mind is racing, wondering what it all means. I know the part of Kara that I got will be different than it was for her, but how? I'll be able to manipulate spirits. Somehow. By channeling them? I just hope it will be something I can control. I can't seem to control anything lately.

"Why has Connor been ignoring me?" I ask.

Aidan blinks at the shift in subject. "I . . . I don't think he's—"

"Yes. Yes, he is." I fold my arms across my chest, feeling guarded now, embarrassed that I even asked. "Is he ashamed of me or something?"

"Rebecca, Connor really cares about you."

"Then why isn't he picking me up and driving me to this thing instead of you? And why won't he answer my texts?" My stomach churns. I cringe at how much I sound like a petulant girl who's not getting her way. "I'm sorry," I add. "This isn't your problem. I'll ask him myself."

I don't want to, though. I don't really want to talk to him at all right now. I'm hurt that he would ignore me so blatantly, especially with everything that's been going on. And after what almost happened between us . . . if my dad hadn't walked in . . .

I'd kind of like to punch Connor in his perfect abs when I see him.

———

As soon as we get to the club, Aidan has me burn a clutch of sage and walk around the large warehouse to spread the smoke while he checks on Hanna. I take a path around the empty space, not sure what I'm doing exactly, not sure I'm doing it right, but the motion of it is soothing.

After a few minutes I hear the side door click open and then shut. I turn, thinking it's Aidan. It's not. It's Connor.

The sight of him, his hair damp, a fresh tan warming his skin, making his eyes shine—I find myself swallowing hard, my resolve to be angry drifting away like the smoke coming off the sage in my hand.

"Hey," he says. But he doesn't quite look at me.

I turn away, pretending to be focused on my task. "Hey."

"I'm supposed to be getting something from the apartment."

I don't respond. My throat tightens at how awkward it all feels. It hurts. And it's ridiculous. Because I don't even know why it's there between us.

"Rebecca," he says, his voice heavy.

I turn, shoring up my resolve.

"There's something . . ." he starts, but he seems unable to say it. There's pain in his eyes. And I have no clue why. He opens his mouth to say more, but the side door clicks open again, and Jax, Tray, Holly, and Raul all come in, laughing about something Raul is saying.

I don't look away from Connor, though. He's tortured by whatever it is, whatever's keeping him distant. He glances sideways at the new arrivals, but just as he seems to be turning to start up the stairs to the apartment, he shifts directions and walks quickly over to me, leaning in to whisper, "Come with me." His hand wraps around mine, and I feel disoriented as he leads me up the stairs to the apartment, shutting the door behind us, blocking out the others' chatter.

He doesn't let go of my hand. He moves closer, and I tense, thinking he's about to try and kiss me, but instead he just tips his head and gives me a hurt look.

"What's going on, Connor?" I ask. "Why have you been ignoring me?"

His features pinch up. I can't imagine what it could be that he's about to say. I just know it's not going to be good.

"I let myself think I could have you," he says. "I'm sorry."

I shake my head. "What are you talking about, I don't understand."

He releases me then and walks away, heading for the living room. I follow and sit in the same chair I was in the other day when Aidan asked if I thought I might still be connected to him. I said no, because I didn't think I could be. I thought my feelings for Connor had over-shadowed all that. But as I watch him struggle with whatever it is he needs to say, I realize my link to him is barely a sliver of what I thought it was.

Aidan, I can talk to. It's easy with him. But this—Connor . . . he's not making this easy.

"The other night," Connor says finally, "before your dad came home, we almost . . ." He seems to struggle, then turns and looks right at me. "Would you have had sex with me if he hadn't interrupted us?"

Why is he asking me this now? "I . . ." I decide to just be honest. "Yes."

His breath catches. Confusion fills his features. "Even though we barely know each other?"

That cuts me. Is he about to lecture me on purity or something? "What's this about, Connor?"

He sits on the couch and cradles his head in his hands. "I just don't think I'm good for you. I'm not good."

"Excuse me?"

He looks up to meet my gaze. "I'm not a good person, Rebecca. I never have been. I've told you that."

I have no clue how to respond. I could argue, but right now I'm just trying to figure out where this is coming from. And he's right, I've only known him a little while. But I was really starting to care about him. It felt real. And safe.

"I didn't want to get so close, to feel this way for anyone again. I've hurt too many people, I—" His voice cracks, breaking something in me, too. "I've done things. Very bad things, Rebecca. And I wasn't even going to tell you, that's how big of a bastard I am. But this spell today, what we're about to do, I don't know what it might mean, for you, for me, all of us. And I feel like it's wrong of me to keep it all from you now."

I can't speak to even ask what this horrible secret is. It all feels too huge, the emotions, the pain in his eyes as he looks into mine.

His hands are shaking when he finally whispers his confession, "I hurt a girl once. We were both high, and I don't remember half of it, but she woke up with bruises on her arms and her neck. From my hands." He looks at his palms and his voice twists. "She died the next day. The cops said it was an overdose, but I know she killed herself. Maybe because of whatever happened. She'd threatened to do it before. And I just pushed her, like I wanted her to do it. I was always—" He chokes up, and his head falls into his hands. "I don't remember what I did to her that night, why she had the bruises. I don't remember anything. But, I know what I come from; my dad beat me, my mom actually *cut* me when I pissed her off. I'm rotten because of everything they did to me." He looks back up at me, pleading. "I mean, how could I hurt a girl, ever? If that's inside of me . . . I have to protect you, Rebecca. You're lovely and good and . . ." He shakes his head, not able to say any more.

"Connor . . ." I go to him, I can't help myself. I kneel at his feet and take his hands. I swallow the ache in my throat and try to speak. "You're so wrong. You're not rotten. You can't blame yourself for—"

He pulls away. "Didn't you hear me?"

"Yes!" I stand, my frustration rising with me. I get why he didn't tell me, I get why he's pulling away, but it doesn't make it any easier. "You want me to be pissed at you? You want me to hate you?"

He averts his gaze. "Yes."

But I know he doesn't mean it. I move to sit beside him on the couch, not sure what to feel about it all. He says he hurt a girl, I should believe him. But when I look at him, the guy who's more patient with me than anyone, the guy who made me feel like I could be whole again, it's impossible to believe. He's talking about a completely different Connor.

"So you pulled away because you thought you'd hurt me?" I ask, finally.

"I let us go too far," he says, his voice colder now, under control. "I'd made a promise to myself not to get too close, to hold back with you. But I lost control. If your father hadn't come in, I wouldn't have stopped what was about to happen, damn the consequences. You deserve more than me, Rebecca."

I shake my head at his blindness. "Gee, you'd think I'd be able to decide for myself who I want, but I guess not." I stand, the urge to punch him rising again. "There were two people in that moment in my living room, Connor, but apparently I don't count. How weak do you think I am? Do you really see me as some damsel in distress that just needs to be saved, protected? From myself? From you?"

I release a growl and step closer, kicking his shin, surprising even myself.

He grunts out a curse and stares up at me. "What the hell?"

I feel crazy but I want to do it again. "Stop being a martyr and be honest. You're afraid."

"Of course I am!" he snaps.

"But not because you could hurt me, you're afraid because you can't control this." I wave my hand between us. "You can't stay in your stoic shell anymore. And now you're pulling away because you're a coward. You're afraid of getting hurt *yourself*."

He just looks at me, his mouth open.

"Well, I was scared, too!" I say, my voice getting shrill. "But I was ready to take the leap with you. And then you hurt me. Yes, you've *already* hurt me, Connor. So whatever it is you were trying to spare me from, you failed. You've taken my heart. And then stepped on it."

I turn and head for the door, fire coursing through my veins. I need to get away from this, all of it.

He comes after me, taking my arm and stopping me. "Please, Rebecca." He moves to stand in front of me, blocking my path. "I don't . . . I can't . . ." but he can't seem to form words to explain.

Instead he reaches out and touches my cheek. "Please, I need to fix this."

"You need to decide what you want, Connor," I say through the tears filling my throat. And then I push past him and leave the apartment, leave my confusion and my need for him behind.

As the door closes, I tell myself that it's for the best. I think of the green light in my hands and wonder if maybe he's right, we were just going to hurt each other. I could lose myself to this thing growing inside of me. I could already be lost.

I ignore the cracking in my heart and walk away.

THIRTY-ONE

Aidan

I'm hit with Rebecca's heartache as soon as she comes out of the apartment onto the landing that overlooks the inside of the warehouse. She tries to hide the emotions roiling inside her as she comes down the stairs, but they're pulsing from her as she walks toward where we're preparing for the spell.

I rise from my attempt to draw the intricate symbols on the cement floor and go to her, pulling her aside. "Are you all right? What happened?"

She shakes her head, eyes turning red.

I want to comfort her, to hug her, but I know that might give the others the wrong idea. So I just squeeze her shoulder and whisper that I'm here to talk if she needs me.

She nods and looks to the chalk drawing I've started on the floor. "So, is this the spell?" she asks, obviously trying to distract herself.

"Yeah." I turn to the white markings, feeling how unbalanced it is still. "I'm not doing it right, though, I don't think."

"Where are you seeing this? In your mind?"

I laugh and pick up the journal, showing her the blood ink on the pages. "No, these are the instructions."

She starts to comment but then pauses when Connor comes out of the apartment and heads down the stairs. She watches him as he crosses the room, her eyes never leaving him as he walks over to Holly and Raul who are setting up the altar near the row of office windows. Finger is standing close but keeping to the shadows, watching everyone intently and looking very uncomfortable about being out of the house. Tray and Jax are off to the side, talking softly.

Sid's in a chair by the door, Kara standing at his shoulder like a centurion. At seeing me and Rebecca together, he struggles to rise. Kara moves to help him, and lets him lean on her as they come closer.

"Is something amiss?" he asks.

"Everything's fine," I say.

Rebecca points to a part of the image on the page of the journal. "If this is the section you're drawing, then I see what you mean. That crescent shape is at the wrong angle. It needs to tip more toward the oval symbol here." She moves her finger from one shape to another, her features focused, and I realize I shouldn't be the one drawing this. This is her gift, not mine.

I hold out my piece of chalk to her.

She looks from the offering to my face with a question in her eyes.

"You're the artist," I say with a smile.

She gives a little smile back. She plucks the chalk from my fingers, and settles onto the floor with the journal opened beside her. She looks intently over the pages for several minutes, then begins to slide the chalk over the cement.

"Very good," Sid says as he watches her, nodding. "Yes, this is good."

And it is. The confidence she has in her task raises mine. After watching for a while I leave her to work on drawing the complex spell and go over to Tray, make sure he's all right.

"How's your sister?" I ask him and Jax, who's standing beside him. Jax smells even more anxious than Tray does.

"Our mom has her at the house," Jax says, "so the wards will protect them, at least until we can finish this."

Tray shifts on his feet. "I really appreciate your help, man. Seriously."

I nod, unsure sure how to answer. It's not like I'm doing anything. "So, you're sure you're okay with this?" I ask, motioning to Rebecca's growing drawing of the spell. "I have to be honest with you, we're not sure what it'll do exactly."

"It's fine, worth it to try. And I know Kara trusts you. And my brother. So I will, too."

I glance at Jax and wonder what he's said to Tray about me. I'm surprised he's said anything positive. "Okay," I say. And then I leave them and go over to help Holly and Raul figure out the oils and other herbs, which ones to put where. After a good twenty minutes Rebecca's voice breaks through our organizing.

"I think I'm almost done," she says, sitting back on her heels.

I look over to her drawing, and my insides kick like a jolt in my chest.

Everyone steps closer, gazing down at the labyrinthine details of the artwork. It's stunning. Beautiful. Its subtle power hums at the air the longer I look at it. And I know Rebecca's right, it's almost done.

"You rocked this, chica," Raul says.

Holly shakes her head in amazement. "It's crazy detailed."

"Wow," Tray and Jax say at the same time.

Connor stands beside Finger, looking stoic, a shadow over his features, and I wonder again what's going on with him.

"How annoying, Miss Perfect," Kara says with a smirk. When Rebecca glances at her, she winks.

"I may have overdone it," Rebecca says, her cheeks pink from all the attention. Most of them have never seen her artwork.

The floor is covered in different shades of white chalk, making the design look like it's emerging from the ground. As if it's moving and alive. The curves seem ready to rise and cut into the air, the circles have become spheres that could roll away. And the lettering, the runes, could be carved out of the earth. I can almost I hear them each whisper their sounds and incantations.

A part of me wonders how much of the power is from the drawing, and how much was placed into it by Rebecca's hands. It felt as if it was buzzing on the page, but now it feels wide-awake.

She takes the time to work a little more around the edges, then proclaims the piece finished. Holly begins placing oil on everyone's foreheads, and Raul walks around the circle three times with a smudge, like the instructions say. Jax and Tray move closer, and Kara settles Sid back into the chair against the wall so he can watch. They all seem to be embracing the moment; it's a relief to watch. Only Finger and Connor stay on the rim and wait.

Rebecca and Holly are talking about where we should all be standing during the spell when I move next to Connor. I lean on the wall beside my friend and feel Finger's hold on him, like the silent boy's trying to calm Connor's obvious turmoil.

"I ruined it," he says, his eyes locked on Rebecca. "I've lost her."

"She's not that easy to lose," I say, still unclear what could be going on between them.

He looks at me sideways.

"Just trust her," I say.

"Have you ever looked at my soul?" he asks, surprising me. "Like you have the others."

I turn to him and meet his gaze. "Yeah." He seems to be waiting for me to elaborate so I say, "I saw handprints and the mark of a thief on the back of your shoulder—I assumed it was from when you were a drug addict."

He chews on the answer for a second and then asks, "Are there any marks from me trying to hurt anyone? Violence or murder?"

I see he's desperate for the answer, and terrified of it at the same time. "No, Connor," I say quietly. "You don't have violence in you."

He's not sure what to do with my answer, but he nods and looks back at Rebecca, not asking anything else.

Everyone is gathered around the spell now, attempting to find their places in the pattern on the floor. I step forward to see if I can figure it out, but Finger surprises me, placing a hand on my shoulder to stop me. He gives me a look and nods, like he's saying he's got this.

He walks over to the others and, one by one, puts each of them into the crescent pattern in the shape of an arrow, bodies facing at an inward angle. Jax and Tray at either end, just within a hand's reach of each other. Then Raul in front of Jax, and Holly in front of Tray. Connor in front of Raul and Kara in front of Holly. And then he motions for them all to hold hands as everybody faces the large symbol for unity between Connor and Kara.

I realize . . . that's where I'll stand, in that intricate weaving of lines. But Finger still hasn't placed himself or Rebecca.

He takes my hand, takes Rebecca's, and then leads us over to the spot where the unity symbol is. He places Rebecca in front of Connor and me in front of Kara. He situates us until we're facing each other, like a couple getting married, and then he steps back to look at everyone, as if he's making sure it's correct.

I want to ask why I'm standing with Rebecca, facing her, why I'm not alone in the central spot, but I don't. It's not as if Finger could or would answer me anyway. And as I stand where I was placed, I begin to sense the vibrations of the markings at my feet, the hum of the magic now moving up my legs.

Finger settles in front of Rebecca and me, like the tip of the arrow, and I realize he's the one meant to be at the head of the group. He's the link, just like he was when he helped Rebecca give her anointing to Kara.

He nods at me, and somehow I know he's saying for me to take Rebecca's hands.

"What're you doing?" she whispers as I reach for her, giving Kara a nervous glance.

"I think we're still soul mates," I say, shocking myself with the words as they leave my lips.

Her eyes go wide, and the smell of her fear fills the space between us. "But I gave that to Kara."

"Maybe a soul mate isn't like you're thinking," I say. "We're friends." I squeeze her hands and sense her relax a little.

She gives a slight nod. "Friends," she whispers back.

Heat moves through my fingers where we touch. My palms tingle, and I realize the spell's already starting. I realize I can't move. I'm locked in and my power is beginning to flicker to life in my chest. Kara puts her palm on my shoulder, and Connor mimics her, placing his on Rebecca's.

Rebecca's jaw tightens and she blinks like her eyes itch. Her hands grip mine even harder.

"Oh, shit," I hear someone say behind me—Tray, I think.

I wonder if he feels it, too, the air charging, coming to life with electric vibrations. It absorbs into me as the atmosphere in the warehouse hugs my body, pressing in.

Finger places his hand on Rebecca's shoulder. He takes a deep breath, focusing.

And then he puts his hand on my marked arm.

My body jolts, muscles clenching, head snapping back.

A burst of electricity cracks the air. Glass shatters, objects fly across the room and crash into walls, the garage door rattles. A storm of energy rises above us, misty clouds of blues and greens crackling overhead as wind begins blasting the pipes in the high ceiling and shaking the lights. Thunder rumbles, angry and troubled. It shakes the ground and shivers in the supercharged air sliding over my skin.

My power courses through me, over me.

There's a gasp, and then another. Grunts of pain and shock.

I try to move, to look. And the first thing I see is Finger. His whole body is covered in colored light, gold and green, mingling together as it slides in swirls across his body. The gold comes from me where he grips my arm, and the green is spilling from Rebecca's shoulder, joining mine at Finger's chest, where they entwine, only to trickle down like a strange waterfall over his stomach and down his legs, to the ground.

It fills the drawing at our feet in a gleam of marbled light. White rays slice the air here and there around the pattern where the runes are. Each time a burst comes, one of the bodies in the circle reacts, bowing as if they can't stand, shivering and chattering their teeth, or crying out in pain.

The electric storm builds and builds inside the circle, inside of me. The power humming higher, coiling tighter, and flaring brighter. Until it's all too loud, too much. I've gone deaf, the world's gone white, and all that exists is the beat of my heart.

Seconds pass. Minutes. Eons.

Then a pulse of power blasts from the ground beneath us, just before it all falls into stillness.

The hum dies. The air returns to normal.

And all around us pieces of glass and broken plastic *tink* and *ping* back to earth, like odd-shaped rain.

THIRTY-TWO

Aidan

Everyone opens their eyes slowly, their expressions full of hesitancy and trepidation.

Jax breaks the silence first. "Holy fucking hell-tornado, Batman," he says breathless. "What a rush."

We all stare at each other, like we're not sure if we should move, we're not sure of what just happened. Or what it could mean. My body aches, my muscles are stiff, skin stretched out, a more extreme version of how it felt after my powerburst yesterday, when the boy attacked Tray with the knife and that demon's claws dug into me.

Everything around us is in a shambles. It's a good thing that the valuables are in the locked vault, because what was in here—chairs, boxes of stuff, papers—is strewn all over the place. The windows of the downstairs offices are all broken, and the roll-up garage door is bent outward.

Sid is still in his chair, eyes wide as he grips the seat, like the wind tried to lift him out of it.

But we're all okay; everything seems fine.

People start to move from their spots now, feet a little unsteady.

"My skin is vibrating, dude," Jax says, studying his arms.

Tray holds out a hand to show him. "Mine, too."

Holly is running her fingers over her face and eyes. "I need a mirror. I think my eyes are—" Her voice cuts off and a grin grows across her face. "I can see them," she says, sounding giddy suddenly. "It's Frank from my dream last night." She waves at nothing, saying hello.

Finger watches everyone, looking happy, his eyes sparkling. My gaze follows his around the room, and I find myself smiling like an idiot, too. We're all okay.

But then I notice Connor off to the side, like he's trying to back himself into the shadows. His face is scrunched in what appears to be pain, and his hands are shaking, sweat glistens on his brow, dampening his hairline.

"You okay?" Kara asks as she steps toward him.

He shakes his head and moves away, like he's scared of her getting too close. His eyes squeeze shut as he shivers. The smell of misery is like singed air around him.

A flash of silver-white light comes from his fingertips, then sinks back in.

He hisses in pain and folds in on himself. Like he did when my power touched him.

"Connor?" I move closer, urgency filling me. "What is it?"

"I don't know," he grunts. Another flash of white light, and he falls to his knees.

Everyone converges. Rebecca falls to his side and tries to help, but he rolls into a fetal position, yelling at her, "Get back!"

The light pulses in his hands once, twice . . .

In a burst, it surges, an explosion of heat coating his whole body in the white glow.

He screams in agony, and my insides panic, my own power flaring in response. But I don't know what to do, I don't know what's wrong.

Just as suddenly as the light had come, it sinks back into his body.

He gasps, trying to catch his breath. After several tense seconds he tries to sit up, shaking.

Everyone's staring at him in shock.

"That was his ability to heal awakening," Kara says, sounding stunned but sure. "I felt something in me, like . . . like I just realized it. And I knew it was true. Connor will be able to heal us eventually."

"And apparently your thing is that you'll know shit?" Jax asks with nervous laughter.

"Like Aidan," Holly says.

"What about me?" Raul asks, fear in his voice. "What's my crazy thing gonna turn into, *compa*?"

I shake my head, feeling lost.

Hanna rushes in through the side door. "Is everyone okay? I heard a scream." And then she looks around her tattered warehouse, eyes widening. "Oh, my."

"Sorry," I say. "Things got . . . out of hand."

"No, it's . . ." but her voice fades as her gaze falls on Connor, who's still sitting on the ground. "Connor, are you all right?" She walks toward him.

Whatever just happened seems to be over for now. He runs a hand over his face and tries to get up. He won't let anyone help him, though. He gets himself into one of the chairs with a sigh of exhaustion.

Hanna turns to Sid. "Are they all okay?"

Sid just shakes his head, still in shock. I wonder what it all looked like from his vantage point.

"I think everyone's fine," I say, glancing again at Connor. He's the only one who appears to have had an adverse reaction. But if what Kara said is right and that was just a part of his Awakening, then it means his body is accepting his power. If anyone knows the pain of that, it's me. I vividly remember the fire in my skin during my Awakening. It felt like I was being burned alive.

I want to go to his side, but it looks like he'd rather be left alone right now. Except for Rebecca. He's letting her touch his shoulder in comfort.

"Well, let me help," Hanna says. "I can get some coffee, maybe some muffins for everyone or something. You all look very pale and worn down."

"You're TBE, Hanna," Holly says. "That would be awesome. I'm, like, scary starving."

Kara comes over to my side and takes my hand in hers. "Don't worry," she says. "It'll be difficult at first, but this is all going to be good for them."

I squeeze her hand and touch my shoulder to hers. The feel of her skin sends a wave of calm over me. "And you know this, how?"

She shrugs. "Mystery, mystery. This guy I know gave me some of his power, and I'm going to be figuring it out for a while." Then she rises on her toes and plants a kiss on my cheek. "I'll let you know when I do."

THIRTY-THREE

Rebecca

The sun is setting over the horizon as Connor pulls his Jeep along the curb in front of my house. He insisted on taking me home, even when Aidan and I argued against it. Connor still doesn't look too good. Even after a meal and several hours of rest in the apartment, his eyes look tired and his hands are shaking a little. But he was determined not to let me go with anyone else.

I should've been annoyed, or nervous to be alone with him, but I'm feeling surprisingly released from it all. As if the crazy explosion of power we all shared shed something from me.

He didn't say a word during the ride here and neither did I. I could sense that he wanted to, though. I can sense that he's struggling with how to fix it all. I can sense a whole lot more than I could before.

And I can actually smell something odd on his skin, like maybe his nerves are making him smell like burnt coffee. It's weird.

I get out of the Jeep, and he follows, coming around quickly to catch up with me. He walks beside me on the path to my front door, his body only inches from mine.

"Are you going to be okay, Connor?" I ask as we come to the doorstep.

He folds his arms across his chest, looking like he's warding off a chill. "I've handled things with you . . . badly."

"Yes." I sigh, not sure I can have this conversation again. "But what I meant was, are you going to be okay after the spell? Something's hurting you because of it."

"I just can't seem to get it right," he says, like he didn't hear me, like he's not able to let go of what happened between us. "I said I didn't want to hurt you, but I did. I keep hurting you."

"I'm tired, Connor. I'm not sure this can be fixed right now." I try the doorknob but it's locked, so I bend over to get the spare key under the potted plant. "Can we just call a truce?"

"Rebecca," he says, his voice beginning to waver a little. "During the bonding. Your magic. I felt it go through me."

I stand straighter and look up at him. "You did?" The only things I felt during the spell were the storm and the pain; this horrible sting in my skin that was like something sucking my insides out through my pores. It was all so overwhelming.

"I felt *you*. Like I've known you my whole life." He reaches out and his fingers slide over mine. "Your energy smelled like summer. Like a forest after the rain. And even though I know you're not sure about . . . about us. Because of what I said. I wanted you to know . . ." He takes my hand in his and pulls me closer, leaning over me. He presses his forehead against mine gently, letting our breath mingle. "I wanted you to know I'm yours. And I'm completely wrecked that I hurt you."

My heartbeat stutters and I'm filled with confusion. I don't know how to respond. I want to kiss him, I want to run away and cry.

I pull back a little. "Goodnight, Connor," I whisper, the pain clear in my voice. And then I unlock the door and slip the spare key into its hiding place again. I wait for him to move out of my way so I can go inside.

"Connor, please—"

His fingers reach out and graze my cheek, stopping all sensible thought as they slide into my hair, gripping me. Before I can absorb his touch, his lips cover mine, stealing my breath. The meaning flows through me, though. It takes hold of me, as strong as iron, and pulls me close. To him.

And I let him kiss me. I let myself forget the way he hurt me, as his hands move over my shoulders, my sides, my lower back. As his arms hold me to him.

We slowly twist together until we're nearly drowning in the moment. And I know this is desperation I taste on his lips, it's sadness I feel in his skin. And all I can think is how much I want to heal him.

"Come inside," I whisper into the kiss. "Please."

He's breathing hard as he presses his forehead to mine again. "We can't."

He's right. Of course he is. I don't even know what's going on between us right now. But a part of me aches, thinking he's saying no because he's pushing me away one more time.

He kisses me gently, like he knows what I'm thinking. "We need to work this out first."

I nod.

"I need to prove to you that I'm worthy."

"No, you don't."

"I want to," he says. And then he pulls me into him again, his arms strong as they wrap around me, his chest warm against my cheek as he keeps me close.

I take in his scent of salt and sun, and try to banish my doubt. Even when he releases me and walks away, I ignore the dread that fills me. I push back the sense of looming pain. I touch my fingers to my lips and pray that won't be the last time I feel him holding me.

Then I turn back and walk into the house, shutting the door behind me. I lean against it and cradle my head in my hands, trying to breathe and not let myself cry. After a few deep breaths the confusion and desperation still a little.

I try to imagine peace and calm. I even imagine I can hear music in my head. Sad, aching music. A violin drawing low notes across the air.

My eyes fly open.

A violin.

"You're so tragic and adorable," a small voice says over the slow notes. "You and Connor—I hate to admit it—I didn't see that coming." Ava appears around the corner from the living room, her violin pressed to her chin, the bow drawing mournfully over the strings. She wrinkles her face, looking displeased. "You don't think he's a bit . . . weak? I mean, compared to my brother . . ." She smiles wickedly. And begins swaying with the rhythm of her music.

Her wild eyes are almost white, they're so pale. A white sundress with faded yellow flowers flows around her bony knees with an unseen breeze, and thin silver lines web her bare shoulder and run down her right arm, as if her veins were filled with metal. Her bare feet are caked with dirt and muck to the ankles. I wonder suddenly if some of it is dried blood.

I grip the door handle and start to press the top of it with my thumb.

It clicks. Locks sliding into place.

Ava clucks her tongue, lowering her bow and violin. "No, no, green witch. You can't leave yet. There's still stuff we need to chat about."

I slide along the door to the wall of the living room, panic rising. I'm trapped.

She's going to rip me to pieces.

"Yes, I *was* going to kill you," she says, her tone almost playful. "But then you had a bit of luck the other night, and I realized I was being so dumb. Why would I kill you when I could have you as my very own friend?" She shrugs and rolls her eyes, like she's been so silly.

"So," she says, swaying back and forth, heel to toe. "I have a present for you. It's in your backyard, a surprise." She waves behind her to the French doors.

A present. In my backyard? I do *not* want a present from Ava. Terror climbs in my throat as my mind ticks through the possible things it could be.

"Don't guess yet!" she says with a giggle. "Not until I go."

She's reading my mind?

"It's just super big all of a sudden," she says. "You're as loud as my brother now." She shrugs like it doesn't mean anything. "You're probably just lots more powerful than you were. Which is good. It means we'll have more fun." Then a troubled look surfaces in her pale features, and she says as if to herself, "As long as she doesn't learn to block me out like he did."

She blows at her bangs and rolls her eyes again. "Well, your gift isn't going to come get you, so you better scoot." She motions to the back doors again. "I'll see you soon." And then she wiggles her fingers in a good-bye wave, just before the air cracks and she's gone.

The hair on my neck rises and my skin tingles with electricity.

I look around the room worried it's some sort of trick. She just came and went? She didn't hurt me. She didn't leave any dead things.

She left a present in the backyard . . .

Whether in spite of the gnawing fear or because of it, my feet move through the entry, past the dining room, to the doors at the back of the house.

I push aside the white curtain with trembling fingers and look through the glass.

The air freezes in my lungs. My throat fills with a cry of pain, of horror, that I can't find the will to stop.

Because, there, under the willow tree, only ten feet from the bench where I used to sit and read every morning in the summer—the bench that he built just for me—

Is Charlie.

THIRTY-FOUR

Aidan

After Connor leaves with Rebecca, Finger and Sid leave, too, heading back to the house. Finger seems different than before the spell, less afraid, as if he's finally found his place, and my heart feels lighter when I look at him. Before he left with Sid, I asked him if he was okay, and he just gave me a secret smile and put his hand on my shoulder. I didn't think anything of it until I realized—Finger's *never* touched me before—except during the spell.

Connor hasn't come back, and I wonder if he stayed with Rebecca, if he was able to fix whatever was troubling him, but then he texts that he's headed to the house.

He definitely needs rest. Whatever happened—or is happening—to him, it's taken even more out of him than me touching him with my power did the first time. Kara assured me several times that he was okay, but that didn't hold back my anxiety. And he was upset even before the spell. Something is tormenting him.

Everyone else stays at the club, gobbling down everything Hanna feeds us until we're stuffed and flopped all over the living room of the apartment.

I'm sitting on the floor beside Kara, both of us facing the couch where Jax, Holly, and Raul are splayed out. Kara stays quiet as everyone says what they hope to gain from the spell, how fun it'll be on their next job when they get to try out their new abilities—Raul wonders if he even got anything out of it, saying he doesn't feel much different, that there was no aftereffect on his body like there seems to be with the others.

"It's 'cause you're already perfecto, friend," Holly says. She's lying across the couch, her head in Jax's lap, her feet on Raul's.

Tray sits at the small bar that divides the kitchen and the living room. He's called the house to check on his mom and sister three times, and they're apparently fine. Selena has been happily playing Xbox with Finger.

"I definitely feel different," Jax says. "Like . . . aware, or something."

"Yeah," Tray agrees. "Me, too."

"Rebecca's energy was crazy," Raul says. "Did you feel how deep that girl is?"

"Totally," Holly says, nodding emphatically. "And so different from Aidan's power."

"You felt our power?" I ask. "Like you could tell them apart?"

Jax barks out a laugh. "A bit."

Then they all crack up, like the differences between Rebecca's power and mine were so vast there's an inside joke about it. I just smile and feel less alone than I ever have. Like I'm really *known* for the first time.

"Well," Kara says, "we could chat all night, but I think we should leave Aidan to sleep."

The others all look to her like they forgot she was here—she's been pretty much silent since she said goodnight to Sid.

"I don't wanna leave," Raul says. "I'm comfy. And who could sleep after all that?"

"I'd better go check on my mom," Tray says.

Jax starts to rise, but Holly stops him and whines, "No, you guys can't go. We should stay here tonight. All of us." Both Kara and Tray protest, but she cuts them off. "Sid's got Connor and Finger at the house, so he's looked after, Kara. And, Tray, your mom and sister can sleep in my room. We know they're safe at the house, so take a break from all that for once."

"Holly's right," I say. "Just stay here." I reach over and weave my fingers through Kara's. I don't want to be alone yet. I realize I've needed this, this intimacy with all of them. "I'll find some blankets and you guys can fight over the second bedroom and the couch."

It takes a minute but Tray relents. Kara seems content; she leans on my shoulder and listens as the rest of them keep talking, gossiping, and laughing. After another hour or so I get the blankets and pillows from the linen closet for them, then Kara and I break off to my bedroom.

We strip down to our underwear for comfort before we curl into the king-size bed and expensive sheets. We huddle close and kiss for a little while. It's easy, rhythmic and soft, as if we're actually having a quiet conversation. I touch her cheek and whisper with my skin that I love her, she slides her fingers over my shoulder, and I feel her delicate hope in response. After a few minutes we pull apart.

She sighs in contentment and stares at me with her light-blue eyes as my fingers slide through her hair.

"I finally get it," she says.

"What?"

"What it really feels like to be safe."

I can't help the trepidation that stirs in my gut. I don't want to say it out loud, but we're not safe. Not yet.

A soft smile makes her dimple appear. "You don't need to frown, silly. I don't mean physically. I mean in my heart."

I lean close and kiss the tip of her nose gently.

She snuggles into my chest. "There's this peace in me now. It's so strong, like I'm anchored to an unmovable force. And I know, whatever happens, I'm going to be all right."

I hold her to me and feel her heart and mine beat in tandem. I listen to the silence and pray that her hope won't be shattered. I pray for that same peace to fill my skin. And I ask God, ask the power inside of me, to accept her strength, her faith, as my own.

———

Someone's shaking me.

"*Compa!*"

I grunt and open my eyes, squinting up at Raul.

His face is tight with worry, his voice full of urgency. "Something's wrong."

I sit up, instantly awake. I turn to Kara, but she's still asleep beside me, she's all right. "What is it?"

"I think it's that Rebecca girl," he says. "I saw something, I saw her. Like how I see my death visions. Aidan, she was . . ." His voice chokes. "There was pain. You need to find her."

I'm out of bed and pulling on my clothes before he can finish talking. "Can you call Connor?" I ask quickly. "Let him know he needs to meet us at her house. Fast." It's dark outside. Isn't morning yet. I pull my phone out and see it's only 2:00 a.m. There are also three missed calls from Rebecca's dad. Ava's letter, which was in my pocket with my phone, falls to the floor. I pick it up and open it. There's a new message. I missed it with all the stuff going on.

I took my eye off the hovering ax.

Hey, Demon Dork. Tell Connor thanks for getting the green witch nice and upset for me. Barely had to tease her to make her cry. She's about to be perfectly tormented. ;) Hint: What has white eyes, tar skin, and eats souls?

Ice fills my veins. "Oh, God."

Kara slides out of bed without a word. I don't have to say anything, and she doesn't ask questions. She gets dressed, goes straight into the living room, and starts ordering the others to get up and get some supplies together, telling them to be sure to bring knives—which makes me wonder.

Raul stays behind at the apartment, not wanting to go. He's scared. Whatever he saw shook him to the core. Kara drives so I can listen to the voice mails Rebecca's dad left. It takes every ounce of focus I've got left not to let the dread take over. He got home after eleven and Rebecca wasn't there. She missed her curfew, do I know where she is, she isn't answering her phone. Can he get Connor's number, in case the two of them are together? The last two messages are panicked, his voice shakes. In the third he says he called the police, he's going to the station to fill out some papers.

"Why're we going to her house if she's not there?" Jax asks from the backseat.

Kara glances at him in the rearview mirror. "To see if there's a hint where she might've gone."

"And who knows what Ava has planned for her dad," I add. "We need to keep him safe, put up new wards or something." Not that it'll matter if Ava wants him.

"What about cops?" Tray asks, echoing my own unspoken concern.

"It'll be twenty-four hours before the cops get actively involved," Holly says. "Rebecca's only been missing for a few hours, technically. She's a teenage girl who could've run off to her boyfriend's house. They'll let time fix it first, if they can."

My heart clenches at the mention of a boyfriend. Connor's going to be frantic.

When we pull up in front of the driveway, his Jeep is already there. I spot him in the yard, coming around the side of the house, toward us. He looks even worse than the last time I saw him, a few hours ago. His eyes are wild and rimmed in dark circles, his skin pale.

"What happened?" he asks. His anger comes at me in a rush. "Where the fuck is she?"

I flinch at the smell of his rage. So does everyone else, like they can smell the sharp scent, too.

"Her dad said she never came home," I say. "When you dropped her off, did you see her go inside?"

"Yes," he grinds out. "I walked her to the door, I . . ." He shakes his head, miserable, terrified.

"We need to get in the house," Kara says.

"There's a spare key." I point to the pots by the front door.

Holly steps forward. "Wait. What if the dad's back home from the station? I'd prefer not to be arrested."

"I second that," Tray says, sounding distracted. He's looking around the yard nervously.

"Her dad's car isn't in the garage, I checked," Connor says. "I was just about to use the key when you guys pulled up."

Jax moves to Holly's side. "And what are we gonna do when—"

"Shut up!" Tray hisses, his frayed nerves on the surface now. There's a trembling in his skin. He leans in and whispers, "I hear something."

And I realize, he's talking about his ability. He said before that he hears the earth speak.

We all go still and look around. Except Tray, who's now staring at the ground and focusing all his energy on breathing.

"What is it?" Holly asks.

Kara looks at me, like she's trying to send a silent message. She mouths, "He can hear them."

Them. Demons.

Jax stumbles back suddenly, gaping at something above us. "Holyshitholyshit."

We all turn.

And see a very large demon crouched on the roof of the house, leering at us.

THIRTY-FIVE

Aidan

Holly screams, then covers her mouth to hold in the sound. Tray stares up in stunned silence at the hunched creature. Connor and Jax lurch back. Kara grabs my arm, gripping it like iron.

The creature is horrifying, with four spindly legs, pinchers for arms, the torso of a man and the head of a bird of prey, beak hooked and deadly. It sneers down at us, huge black eyes keyed on me. "Ssseeeer," it hisses.

My power explodes out before I can stop it, chest burning white hot as light spills from my skin, brightening the night around me.

The demon springs back.

The others huddle closer, as if drawn to me like magnets.

"It's huge," Holly whimpers.

"Are we all seriously seeing this?" Jax asks.

Tray pulls Jax behind him protectively. "I heard it, like the ground was telling me it was here."

The demon watches us all for several heartbeats, considering. Then it skitters to the side and jumps, landing on the grass several yards away.

Holly screams again and Kara hits her in the arm. "Seriously."

"Everybody get behind me," I say, moving to stand between them and the creature.

It's as big as the bird demon that killed me in the club, maybe a little larger. Its skin is covered in reflective scales. As I move closer, they flicker orange and gold along its thin legs.

"Why are you here?" I ask it in demon tongue.

It tips its head at me and grows the distance between us. "I watch. I wait."

"For what, who?"

Its beak clacks, like it's annoyed. "The father. We wait for the father."

We?

I look around the yard, but I don't see any other demons, don't smell any. "What else is here?"

A low chuckle rumbles across the yard.

"Tell me, *dever*," I order.

"It has no name. But it knows you are here now, and it will perhaps eat you, Seer. Pick its teeth with your bones." The demon sounds giddy at the notion. And even though it steps away from me a little more, it doesn't seem as afraid as it should be. It glances behind me to the others. "You brought us treats?"

This thing is way too confident. It might be large, but once my power touches it, it's toast. "Where is it?"

"Which?" the demon asks. But for a second I don't understand, until—

A familiar cry rips through the air behind me and I spin, seeing everyone scrambling away.

It's Kara.

She's being held by the neck, tight from behind, in the claws of a second demon. It has insect legs like the other, but this one is more man than beast. Except for the long stinger-like spear coming from its arm; a ten-inch, barbed dagger.

A ten-inch dagger that's beginning to slice into Kara's side.

"Stop!" I choke out.

The spear pauses, but it's already in her muscle. I look from one demon to the other, suffocating in the panic. I'm such a fool. How could I come here with them all? What was I thinking?

Kara gasps frantically, trying to see behind her to her attacker, trying not to move. Her skin dampens with sweat. Her pain fills the air like the smell of rotting fruit—it fills my nostrils, begging me to kill something. Everything. And my power surges with it, only compounding the rage.

"The queen said that one companion can die," the first demon says from behind me as I stare helplessly at the black stinger ready to plunge deeper into Kara. I can't take my eyes off it. "And you have brought us so many to choose from. But she is the prize, she will be the one. Because she owns your heart. And she will just be in the way for what comes next." Its sinister laughter rumbles again, and it looks at its companion with a slight nod.

"No!" I rush toward Kara.

But I'm too late.

The stinger shoves up, into her flank.

All the air leaves my lungs.

I falter. Gape in horror. As I watch the thorny spear disappear into her body. She stares at me, a million questions on her face. The whole world seems to wonder: What just happened?

Then the spear slides back out. It glistens red. Shiny crimson. The bitter taste of copper in my mouth. Copper that came from inside her. Copper that drips down the demon's scaly forearm.

I cry out and run to her.

The demon lets go. She crumples to the grass.

She's so still. She's . . .

Holly's crying. Everyone's moving. Tray lunges at the demon at the same time I'm hurtling toward Kara. He's closer, though, and his large body hits the even larger beast, tackling it to the ground in a mess of alien limbs and hair-raising screeches.

When I reach them, Tray's pulled a knife from his pants. He stabs the creature right in the eye with a *crunch*. Its legs twitch. As if it's actually hurt by the blow. Just before it bursts into ash and cinder.

Tray killed it. He *killed* a demon.

Before I can process any of it, I see Connor run past me at full throttle, straight for the first beast. Jax barrels after, pulling his own knife—it looks like one from the apartment kitchen—as a war cry erupts from his chest like he's gone insane.

Tray falls to Kara's side, his expression frantic with confusion. "I killed it, Kara," he says, thickly, "just like you said I would." Holly is crawling to her, weeping openly. I'm almost there, I need to have Kara in my arms. But then I hear Connor grunting, and I turn to see the demon holding him in its pinchers as it kicks the approaching Jax with one of its long, spindly legs, sending him reeling. I rush toward them as Connor slices at it with a dagger. The swipe does nothing but make the demon squeeze him harder.

He bellows in pain as I leap, tackling the creature with a savage strength that cracks its sternum and knocks the air from my lungs.

It turns to cinder with a sizzle just before I hit the ground with its burnt-out shell in my arms. Ash flies up around me. Connor falls to the grass. He coughs and holds his chest where the pinchers had him. But there's no blood.

Blood . . .

I scramble to my feet and rush back to Kara. Tray is picking her up but Holly is yelling at him not to move her. I don't know what to do. My mind goes blank as I fall to my knees at her side, watch her hold the wound in her stomach, blood leaking between her fingers.

She gasps in air and looks up at me. "We n-need . . . in . . . side. H-hurry. P-people w-w-will see."

I take her from Tray and yell at Jax to get the spare key and unlock the door. Connor does it instead when Jax has trouble finding the right pot, then Connor opens the door for me, looking like a ghost, he's so pale.

I race into the house and set her on the couch. My thoughts roil, my heart unable to accept what's happening.

She's dying.

No!

I'll bring her back, I'll just bring her back.

But I can't watch, God help me, I can't watch her leave me.

"It's okay," I say to her, sounding more sure than I should. "We can fix this. We'll fix this."

She shakes her head slowly. "Don't . . . d-don't use . . . y-your power. N-need to . . . save it."

"We need a belt!" Holly yells, "to slow the bleeding—do any of you have a belt?"

The boys all shake their heads and Holly growls in frustration, then takes off running for the stairs.

I reach out with shivering fingers to peel up Kara's blood-soaked shirt. She whimpers in pain, her stomach moving with her stuttered breath. My heart falters in my chest. The hole is at least two inches wide. And I know it's deep. Blood dribbles from it in a pulsing rhythm, her heartbeat pushing the life from her. Crimson seeps into the couch cushion, quickly growing into a dark stain.

The familiar horror closes in on me. The one that rips everyone I love away from me with greedy blood-soaked claws.

"She said Connor could heal us, remember?" Jax says, sounding desperate. He grabs Connor's hand and places it on Kara's thigh. "Do it! Heal her!"

The agony and fear in Connor's eyes nearly undoes any shred of control I still have over my panic.

He shakes his head. "I—I can't," he whispers. "I don't know how." He looks at me with urgency. "How?"

Kara takes his hand and grips it, smearing her blood across his knuckles. "Y-you can't . . . n-not yet."

"We need to call 911," Tray says. "Just sitting here is killing her."

And I know he's right. She's fading before our eyes.

"I got one!" Holly yells from the second-floor landing. "I found a belt!" She rushes toward us, the belt held over her head. She tosses it at me. "Wrap it around her chest. Tight."

I reach out to lift Kara up so I can get the strap underneath her. But before I can get a grip on her shoulder, I'm yanked with a sudden jerk by an invisible hand.

My body lurches back. Then a heavy shove crashes me down.

My head smacks into the coffee table with a loud *crunch*.

Everything goes black for several painful breaths, the sounds of shock filling my head, until I'm blinking up at the ceiling, trying to get my bearings—

A low growl shivers against the air, bringing the world to a halt. The smell of rot and decay burst to life around me.

"Oh, shit," Connor hisses. He's gaping at something on the other side of the room. They all are.

"Oh, no," Holly whimpers.

"Aidan," Jax pleads, "get your ass up. It's coming closer."

My skull screams as I turn to look.

Bony legs stand several yards away. Legs that appear to be dipped in tar. My gaze travels up, over a slicked skeletal torso, to the elongated head of a specter with wide, opaque white eyes. Its skin makes an odd sucking noise as it shifts to look down on me. Its white gaze follows the path of my fire-filled mark, appearing unconcerned.

Ava's message flashes in my head, her last hint: *What has white eyes, tar skin, and eats souls?*

White eyes and tar skin . . .

This is the nameless thing the demon outside was talking about. I thought it meant the demon that stabbed Kara—God, I'm a fool.

"I didn't feel it," Tray says, sounding confused as he looks at the thing, his eyes going distant. "The ground didn't warn me."

"That's not a demon," Holly says, sounding very sure even as her voice shakes.

"You are children," it says. At least, I think that's what it says. Its thin slit of a mouth hasn't moved, and the sound of its voice isn't traveling. "You are not the father of the witch. I was to devour the father."

The others all slap their hands over their ears, groaning, as if the strange voice hurts them.

"Aidan, get up!" Connor yells. But he sounds far away. Everything seems very far away. I turn back to the creature and look into those snowy eyes, feeling them tug me closer. I can only stare. There is nothing else. *What is this thing?* some lost part of me wonders.

It seems to hear my thoughts, tipping its head at me. "I have been imprisoned long. Time would have forgotten my name." It points at my power, my arm that's now molten with gold. "What are you that you are able to carry the Power?"

I look down and watch for a second as the fire slides over my skin. And then I look back into its white gaze and answer honestly. "I don't really know." I'm not sure why I'm not more afraid. It probably wouldn't do any good to be scared, anyway. It would just pull my kidneys out through my gut and then eat my eyeballs for dessert.

The vivid image jolts a spark of terror through me, and I find myself moving, trying to clamber away.

The others have all gone still, each of them just staring at the creature, like they're hypnotized.

"Don't look at it!" I say, forcing my gaze to the rug.

A rumbling laugh comes from the creature.

Then a choking sound comes from beside me.

I turn to see Connor grabbing at his throat, like he's trying to pull off an invisible hand.

"This one is strong," the thing says. "I will devour him first. And then her." Holly gags and starts flailing, a strangled sound coming from her chest. Then Jax and Tray start choking, mouths gaping.

"Stop!" I yell.

It tips its head again. "Why?"

And for the life of me I have no answer. I can't formulate thought. I can't breathe. I can't—

A vise grips my throat. All the air is sucked from my lungs. I try to gasp, to breathe, but it's as if I've been filled with cement. My muscles tremble, weakening, my vision blurs.

The black shadows around the edges close in. And just as I'm fading, I see the white figure of a girl moving to the side of the sticky creature that's about to eat me. Mud and ash and blood cake her bare feet. Silver threads shimmer on the skin of her shoulders. She looks at me with her pale eyes, like she's almost sad. Then she whispers in a singsong voice that I wish I could forget, *Game's almost over, Demon Dork. I've figured out how we can be free. As soon as the green witch gives herself over, I know you'll see. You'll do what you always do, you'll save me. You'll be mine, and we'll be a family again.*

I feel her come closer. A small hand grips my shoulder, cold as death. *Just don't try and stop him when he comes. Let him have them, Aidan. Please. You won't like it when he's angry.*

The voice echoes in my pounding skull and swallows me. It swallows me whole.

———

I walk up the Marshalls' front lawn, dread and anticipation scratching at my insides. What could Ava have seen? She was frantic and inconsolable on the phone, insisting I come right away, that something was very wrong. I can only hope it wasn't because of her powers, I can only hope she didn't break or hurt anything too vital this time.

I linger on the porch, wondering if I should try and open myself up a little to read the place before knocking. I hesitate, keeping my walls up tight. I don't let them down much since Mom's—since she left us. Because I want to pretend to be normal. I want to pretend like she died of drugs or a drunk-driving accident, not believing that—

No. I won't look at it. I shove the memories down to that dark place where no one sees. Not even me. If all those social services minions taught me nothing else, they at least taught me that. Faking it works better than dealing with shit any day. Otherwise adults want you to "talk it through." And there's usually puppets involved. Show me on the doll where the bad man touched your mommy.

But as I stand within a few feet of the Marshalls' front door, the familiar dread slowly trickles in. I feel something deep in me stir. And I know. If it's something I can't block out, then it can only be one kind of thing.

My heartbeat speeds up, making it tough to breathe. Yes, I see demons. I see them all the time. But I've tried to protect this house, Ava's house. I've placed wards around the property when the Marshalls weren't looking. I buried protection pouches and salted the perimeter. How could there be a demon here? If there even is a demon here. How can I be sure? I don't really want to find out.

It's probably nothing, jackass, just knock on the fucking door.

My nerves still at the inner voice. Reason, I need to be reasonable and not freak out over nothing all the time. I'm just paranoid because I've had a shitty day and Ava's birthday's tomorrow. I'll be here for her then and she'll be okay. Everything will be fine.

I shake off the paranoia and reach out to knock on the Marshalls' door.

THIRTY-SIX

Aidan

My nerves jump as the air enters my lungs in a rush. I gasp it in, surfacing from a dark hole.

I'm sitting up, gripping the cushion under me. My nails have dug into the weathered leather and torn it open. My teeth ache.

I loosen my body one muscle at a time and look around . . . the cab of a car. I'm in Connor's Jeep. We're not moving. And from the view out the window it looks like we're parked on a vista point somewhere around Griffith Park. It's morning, the sun just breaking over the city skyline. Connor's behind the wheel, head tipped to the side, and Kara's quiet in the passenger seat in front of me. Tray is next to me—not just next to me, but snuggled into my side. His head is resting on my shoulder, and he's drooling on my shirt in his sleep.

I frown down at him in confusion, wondering where he came from, because last I remember—

A chill sweeps over me as the images and emotions flash inside my head, bringing it all back. I see the demon stab Kara, everyone choking as the sticky black creature strangled us from across the room. And Ava telling me to save her . . .

I lunge forward and lean over the seat. "Kara!"

Tray slides down behind me and groans.

She's wrapped in a white blanket. Stained with red splotches, one very dark red stain where she was stabbed. I touch her cheek and say her name again, but she doesn't stir in response, she doesn't move. Her skin is drained of color, her lips tinted violet. I jump out of the cab and open her door. "Kara!" I shake her shoulder, and her head lolls to the side.

I check her pulse and feel a small flutter in my fingertips, barely there. It's so weak. But it's beating.

I shut her door and go around to the driver's side, opening it and yanking Connor out by the arm. "Wake up! We need to get Kara to the ER!"

I don't know how we got away from the tar creature, not sure why my sister would just let us go, where Jax and Holly are, or how we ended up in the Jeep. But I do know if we sit here much longer, Kara's not going to wake up again, ever.

Connor falls to the dirt and grunts. It takes him too long to sit up and open his eyes. "Get the fuck in the car, Connor, please." My voice breaks as I plead with him to move.

He must finally sense the urgency, because he fumbles his way into the backseat and shuts the door as I'm starting the engine, and then I'm heading out onto the main road.

———

Connor and Tray are wide-awake once we pull into the drop-off. They jump out of the backseat, and Tray opens the door to grab Kara. He pulls her limp, pale body into his arms, and I ache looking at her, I ache knowing I can't follow them inside.

I grip the steering wheel. "Please call as soon as you know anything. *Anything.*"

"We will," Connor says.

"Can you check on my mom and Selena?" Tray asks me.

I nod, and the two of them disappear through the ER doors. This isn't the same one where they brought me. Maybe I could go in and just wait with them, no one has to know I'm with the girl who got stabbed. The cops will be called, but will they really be paying attention to some dumbass in the waiting room? I glance down at my marked arm and I know, if I give Ava the chance, she'll make sure I'm spotted, that I'm caught. I can't walk right into that possibility and put Kara in jeopardy again. I've already done that enough.

Shit. I can't believe how helpless I feel.

We called Jax on the way here. He and Holly somehow ended up in the Camaro off Mulholland, but they're all right. They went back to pick up Raul and then they were going home.

I drive out of the loading zone and circle the parking lot a little. I end up in the parking garage, my phone in my lap, waiting to hear from Connor. I rack my brain to try and think of why Ava wouldn't just kill us all. She's been trying to rip us apart for almost a week now. Why did she tell her demons they could only kill one of the others? The demon implied Kara was chosen because she would be in the way. In the way of *what*? I comb through what Ava said, over and over. I'm supposed to save her like I always do? But then she said someone's coming . . . I'm supposed to let *him* have them. She has to know I'd never let one of her minions have anyone. Still, she's winning her sick game, because I don't know the rules or get the reasoning behind it.

And Rebecca is still missing. Probably taken somewhere by Ava.

I lean on the steering wheel and bite back a scream. My chest throbs, my head hurts. Where would my sister take her? What twisted thing is she doing with her? Ava knew we would come try to find Rebecca, to save her. She knew one of us would be hurt and that the creature in the house would—

I sit up straight as every muscle tenses—holy shit, I wonder if that thing is still there, waiting for Rebecca's dad to get home. The guy is a sitting duck.

I turn over the engine and gun it out of the parking garage, into traffic.

———

What *can* you do about a mind-controlling creature that has no name? I've never encountered anything like it. Obviously, wards won't cut it with Ava's minions running around undoing them ten minutes after I set them. And my power didn't faze the creature at all, so who knows if I can even kill it.

I'll need something outside of my usual arsenal to push it back. Something I'd usually keep away from. Something I've buried. The closer I get to Rebecca's house, the more I feel like it's the only way. If I can just remember how to do it.

I recall far too much about my mom's casting habit. This is the first moment in my life that I'm grateful for those memories. It helps that I don't have the luxury of caution anymore.

I pass the house and pull over a block up the road, parking the Jeep under the shade of a tree. Everything seems quiet, and I didn't see her dad's car parked in the driveway, but that doesn't mean anything—he keeps it in the garage.

After scrounging in the back of the Jeep and getting what limited supplies I can find—salt and chalk and sage—I rub my hands in some sacred dirt and whisper a prayer before shutting the hatch and locking it. Then I make my way back toward Rebecca's house. Remembering that I need flowers for the spell, I gather some rose petals from a bush along the way and put them in my pocket, hoping this isn't a suicide mission.

Instead of going through the front door, I walk up the driveway and slip through the side gate. As I move past the floor-to-ceiling windows that line the back of the large house, I peek through the glass now and then, trying to see past the sheer white curtains. Nothing seems out of place that I can tell. I don't see Rebecca's dad. No new demons. The house is empty from the look of it.

I take a deep breath and then open the door that leads to the dining room. I step in, cautious as I walk through the back of the house. I don't smell anything, don't see anything. But as I move farther in, the energy shifts, our terror from earlier still making the air vibrate around me. Jax's terror, Connor's. All of us. It's all still here.

Including the spot of Kara's blood on the couch. My gaze lingers on it for a moment before I walk into the kitchen, around the island—

My feet go still.

Rebecca's dad is on the floor, eyes open wide in stunned death. There are broken blood vessels on his brow and at his temples, his lips are puffy and blue. His car keys are still in his hand, gripped tight.

All the air leaves my lungs.

"You've returned to me," says the voice from before.

I don't turn around to look. I can't look it in the eye.

"I was told I cannot have you," the voice says, "but perhaps it is what you would want. You should look upon me and tell me what you wish."

I can only stare at the dead man I'd come to save. Too late . . .

"Where's my sister?" I ask, through the sting in my chest.

"She is here, she is there, the little queen is everywhere."

How quaint. This thing should write a children's book.

I close my eyes and try to breathe, try to think of what my next move should be. I open myself up even more and feel around the room, then around the house—

Wait. There! Near the back room, I sense a ghost. And I'm fairly positive it's Rebecca's dad. Which means I can bring him back. A small spark of hope fills me. I just have to rid the world of this creepy-ass thing behind me first.

Easier said than done.

It hasn't strangled me yet, though. Maybe I need to be facing it for that trick to work on me?

I kneel down, keeping my back to the thing, then begin drawing in chalk on the dark tile floor.

"What does the strange human create?" it asks.

My power sizzles in my chest, and I wonder if the beast is getting closer.

Can't think about that. I just keep drawing, trying to remember my mother's spell. I'm doing this, I'm actually doing this. I'm about to cast. What the fuck am I doing?

But I can't think about that, either. I can only focus my energy and sketch the image in my mind from memory. A double circle. Then writing in ancient Gaelic, the numbers for the five stars of the Dagda. And then the symbol for the moon in the West, where the sun sets, and the symbol for the sun in the East where it rises in rebirth once more . . .

This could either save me or bite me in the ass—it's not always the safest thing to weave a small doorway into the unknown.

I start to sense the tingle of magic in my fingers and am shocked at how easily the spell comes to me. A spell my mother performed only twice as far as I know. It's as if it were in my DNA. Like my power. And as I draw the last of the circle on the floor, the energy of it courses though my veins, a part of me. It's in my blood, just like it's in Ava's blood, in my mother's blood, and her mother's before her. The idea terrifies me and awes me all at once.

Ignoring the dark creature still behind me, I finish the drawing and move to the next step, continuing to weave the spell, sprinkling rose petals around the edges of the circle. I place a petal over each of the dead man's eyes so his ghost will stay and won't think to leave through this doorway with the creature.

I let my power loose a little as I take two magnets off the fridge and place one over the East and one over the West. I test my fire energy to see what it does as it mingles with the casting energy. I'm a little worried it's going to be like mixing the chemicals to create a bomb. But the two seem to not care about each other, my power only interested in the creature.

"The strange boy creates something that says good-bye to the man?" the beast asks, still clueless about what I'm doing. I'm shocked it hasn't caught on. Obviously it wasn't hired for its brains. "Is it a way to mourn? There is no need, I will eat the father human soon, and he will be gone."

"Why haven't you eaten him already?" I'm not sure why I'm asking this thing questions, but truthfully, I am curious.

"The flesh is not ready."

"Well, I hate to break it to you, but you may have missed your chance."

I can feel its confusion tickle the base of my neck, and the sucking sound of its skin moves closer, pressing the chill of its energy against my back.

I hold in a shiver and try to remember the right words. The spell is in Gaelic, so I should probably use that. I close my eyes and chance letting my power fill me more. It doesn't hurt my skin this time as I allow it to flow over my chest, across my shoulder, down my arm, before I begin the final stage of the casting.

I listen to the inner part of me, deep down, the piece that usually tells me what angelic words will stop a demon or what will send a ghost home, the part of me that never wanted to touch this kind of magic in the first place.

And for some crazy reason, it gives me the right words to say.

I breathe deep, in and out, as I begin to whisper under my breath, about wind and rain, earth and sky, releasing the energy in me to mingle with the words . . . and for a flash I feel something different than my fire, something under the surface that smells of new life and . . . Rebecca. It smells like Rebecca's energy. And I realize, I must have gotten a piece of her power in the bonding, too.

I reach for the life energy and weave it into the words as they emerge from deep inside me. And even as I hear a voice of warning behind me, I don't stop. I'm locked in the moment now, unable to pause in the casting. Even as something weighs on my shoulder, yanks my body to the side—the creature, trying to stop me—my mind is gripped tight in the magic. I'm not sure my body is even involved at all.

In the background of my senses I smell death, I smell putrid flesh. But I can't let myself look at it. I can't look it in the eyes.

I can't look.

I can only speak the words and feel the gravity of the room begin to gather around me as it closes in on the drawing. And the circle morphs into a place of passage.

Wind begins to whip past me, then tear at me as it gathers, stronger and stronger, looking for things that don't belong, things not meant for this world. The gusts seek out the alien spirits and flesh as the casting births a doorway. And I dare to look at the creature.

In a huge push of magic, the gale yanks on tar-soaked skin, pulling snowy eyes from the skull as it tugs and tugs the beast into the circle, bit by gooey bit. The air roars with the sounds of it all, the thunder of it in my head, in my bones, as I speak the cast and remain unwavering in the assault rushing around me.

I close my eyes again and lift my heavy hands over my head as the torrent rages stronger and stronger. I feel the heat of my mark like it's encouraging me to finish the task. And then I clap my palms together on the last word spoken.

Stillness falls. I open my eyes.

I'm on the floor several feet from where I started. The house is torn to shreds around me, tiny bits of things—paper, fabric, pillow stuffing, I can't tell—it all floats around me like snow, settling on destroyed surfaces, couches, counters, and the dead body of Rebecca's father, a little at a time.

My skin tingles like I just stuck my finger in a light socket. I've never felt or seen casting magic that strong before. And it came from me . . .

I look at my marked hand, but my power's gone quiet. I have to hope it's not all used up since I'm going to need it to resurrect the dead in a second. I just have to get my bearings.

I take a few deep breaths and then reach a little with my insides, searching the house for anything else, any other creatures. Or a ghost. I'm relieved to find him on the landing of the stairs, he didn't get pulled through the doorway.

His energy washes over the room, his story, and I push it back, feeling like it's not my business. But pieces of it trickle into me, secrets he hasn't spoken of—he wanted to tell her, he didn't have a chance to tell her. It wasn't her fault. Images come to me of a lovely blonde-haired woman, but I don't recognize her . . . his wife?

"Stop," I say, holding up a hand, trying to motion for him to settle himself. "Just hold on." I walk over and kneel at the side of his body. Then I close my eyes and touch my marked hand to his arm. I breathe and pray for my power to work. Because she can't lose everyone. *You can't leave Rebecca alone.*

Please, just work.

As I feel the man's ghost come closer behind me, my chest flickers to life, the fire emerging slowly, as if it's just a small trickle now, after that spell. But it's there. And I only need it for a few seconds.

The flames roll over my wrist, down to my fingers, and then they slink along the same spot where I'm holding the dead man's arm. He wasn't supposed to die. He was meant to live a long life with his daughter. If it wasn't for me and my sister . . .

The power answers, a piece of my mark sliding down to wrap around the man's arm, searing into his soul. And as I watch it move and settle in, I feel my energy and strength go with it, my fire weaving his spirit, his soul, back together with his flesh.

It saps me vacant, and I'm pulled down to the ground with a weighty thud.

I lie on the kitchen floor and stare at the lights set into the ceiling, trying to catch my breath. I fight the black as it attempts to take me again; I've passed out enough today. "Stay awake," I say to myself as I wait for the dead man to wake up.

THIRTY-SEVEN

Aidan

I suddenly understand why my mom always seemed so confused and muddled. Casting takes the brain right out of your head. I feel a little . . . buzzed? I've been high once or twice in the past, and it sort of felt like this. Floating confusion. And hunger. Wow, am I hungry. The same as when I teleported.

I'm contemplating digging through the pantry when Rebecca's dad releases a moan. I sit up and lean forward, touching his shoulder in what I hope is a reassuring way.

"Are you here with me? Can you open your eyes?"

His leg moves and then his head tips. He releases another moan and a cough. Another cough, and then he's gasping, bringing a hand to his throat, like he's waking to the last memory in the queue, the one where he was being strangled to death.

"You're okay," I say. "You're all healed up now." I pat him on the shoulder, satisfied that he's good. I mean, he's alive. He's much, much better, at the very least.

Now, time to find food.

I manage to get into a sort of standing position and crunch my way over the debris on the kitchen floor to the very large double fridge. "Okay, let's see what the rich folk eat. Come on, tri-tip."

I open the doors dramatically and start rummaging around. Everything's in plastic containers. I open a few, smell the contents until I hit the jackpot. "Ravioli! Oh, man, this is awesome." Why am I so giddy about ravioli? Something may be wrong with me right now, but I'm too hungry to care. I pluck a pasta pouch out of the container and pop it in my mouth.

Then I have to close my eyes because I think I'm going to cry. It tastes so fucking *good*.

"What is going on?" a scratchy voice says.

I look down, still chewing. Rebecca's dad is sitting up, massaging his throat, and gaping at me.

"Hey," I say. I hold up the container and motion to the open fridge behind me. "I hope it's okay that I just dug in. You kind of owe me, though." Okay, yes, something is definitely wrong with my head. I clear my throat and make a serious face. "How are you feeling?"

"Aidan? What . . ." His voice fades as he looks around his torn-up house.

I eat another ravioli and watch as he begins to recall everything that happened. I can tell he's remembering it, from how he's not demanding information or an explanation, along with the fear and shock on his face. And my guess is he saw the tar creature pretty clearly—when he looked into its snowy eyes and it strangled him to death from across the room.

Which means he's probably realizing he's been a blind man; monsters are very real.

The scent of terror filters into the air as the memories soak in.

He touches his throat again.

"You were dead," I say, feeling myself sober up a little. "It killed you."

His eyes snap to mine and doubt clouds his features.

"It's true," I say, reluctantly putting the lid on the ravioli and setting them back into the fridge. My reading is muddy from the resurrection, so I go to stand closer to him to feel his emotions more clearly. "Everything you think you saw. It's all real."

"But . . . how . . . ?" He tries to stand but he falls back.

I reach down and help him to his feet, letting him lean on me and then the counter for support. "Trust me, you don't wanna know."

"You . . . what are you doing here?"

"I came to stop the creature from killing you," I say, "but I got here too late. I did manage to get rid of it, though. Unfortunately, I also demolished your house."

He stares at me like he's absorbing my words, but then panic suddenly blossoms on his face. "Rebecca! Where is she? Is she all right?" He tries to head from the kitchen, but stumbles and ends up holding himself up against the wall.

And I have no idea how to tell him this next part. I can only speak honestly. "I'm not sure where she is."

His panicked gaze falls back on me. "No . . . you don't know?"

I shake my head.

"I went to the police station," he says in a far-off voice, like he's reminding himself. "What was that thing?" he asks in a rush. "That black, thin thing—" He shivers. "It was so . . ."

"I know. I'm not sure what it was."

"How did you . . . how did you get rid of it?" He looks over at me, awe on his face.

"I used magic."

"Magic?" Incredulity laces his words. Even after seeing things with his own eyes, he doubts them. I guess I don't blame him, but it's going to get exhausting trying to convince him of everything over and over.

"Yes, magic. But all you need to know is, that thing, and other things like it, are why I was here with Rebecca the other day, blessing the house. This place wasn't safe anymore." Hopefully I've remedied that for now.

He just blinks at me.

"I'm serious."

He drops his gaze to the floor, to the mounds of debris around the room. "I'm not sure what to do."

Anger fills me as I look at him, at his forlorn expression, his weak spirit. Because neither do I. I have no clue what to do about any of it.

THIRTY-EIGHT

Aidan

I find out Rebecca's dad's name is Patrick when he's on the phone with the police again, letting them know Rebecca's been missing for over twelve hours, and I also find out he's extremely intimidating when he wants something to happen. After he hangs up, he goes over and sits on his tattered couch. His hand rests near Kara's bloodstain, but he doesn't seem to notice it.

My chest cracks open all over again.

"I can't be here if the cops come," I say.

He nods, somehow understanding.

"I don't want to leave you unprotected, though. Do you have somewhere you can go?"

"My office in the city. But I don't want to leave, in case she shows back up."

Misery fills me for the hundredth time, thinking of what my sister might be doing to Rebecca. The girl I was supposed to protect. The girl who gave up her protections to save the girl I love. "We'll find her," I say. "And I'll try and mark the doorways again to ward off any new things that come around, but there's no guarantee it'll hold."

He nods again, staring at his torn-up living room. Then something seems to dawn on him and he looks up at me. "Why are we in so much danger from . . . strange things, all of a sudden?"

The answer to that question is a million miles long, so I just say, "Rebecca's going to be able to explain that to you. But for now all you need to know is, it's my fault. I can't lay out everything right now, except to say that. It's on me. But I'm going to fix it." I'm going to stop it. Because it ends here. No one else I care about is going to get hurt.

My chest aches with the awareness of what I'll have to do to make that happen. "Just keep yourself alert," I say. "And if you have any scripture, find it and read some out loud."

———

Connor calls when I'm on my way back to the hospital. "It's crazy, but Kara's somehow okay," he says, sounding awed. "She had severe blood loss but no internal damage. They're stitching her up and doing a transfusion."

The heady relief that fills me makes it impossible to speak.

"The doctors had to check her three times, because they couldn't believe it. She seemed to be incrementally healing while she was lying there in the ER."

"What? Did you—?"

"No," he says sounding sure. "I didn't heal her. I wouldn't even know how. She's been tight-lipped since we got here, but I could tell she knew something was going on. She kept telling me not to bug you, that she'd be fine. But she was so pale and all the nurses and doctors were hooking her up and acting like she was going to die. It wasn't until ten minutes ago that I was sure that wasn't going to happen."

"I should've been there." But I can't feel the remorse with all the relief in me right now. She's okay. Kara's going to be okay. "Can I swing by and pick you guys up?"

"No, it's gonna be a while," he says. "She's still waiting on the transfusion, and now that they know she's not critical, they seem to have molasses in their shoes. It's madness in here." His voice grows quiet. "Looking around at some of the injuries, I have to wonder how many of them are coming from all those demons out there. It's brutal. I heard a nurse on the phone turning away patients. Apparently the other three ERs are overflowing, too."

I breathe out a tired groan. There could be hundreds, maybe thousands of people Ava's allowing to be tormented just to please her hungry minions. It's too much for my mind to even process. How can I save them all? "Listen, Rebecca's dad is okay, he's keeping in touch with the cops."

"When did you talk to him?"

"When I went back to make sure he wasn't dead."

"You—you went *back*?"

"He was a sitting duck over there with that black stick-creature. And I couldn't just leave it."

"No, you never can." It's his turn to groan.

"What's that supposed mean?"

"So he was fine?" Connor asks, ignoring my question.

"No, he was dead."

More silence. Then he breathes out. "Shit."

"It's fine, I took care of it, he's back; and the weird creature is gone. I just wanted you to know that the cops are looking for Rebecca now."

"It won't do any good."

Now he's starting to piss me off. "What the hell is wrong with you?"

Heavy silence sits in the air for several seconds before he answers, "I'm tired, Aidan. I'm fucking tired of it all being shit." Then he seems to come to a conclusion, because he adds, "And I'm pissed, okay? I'm pissed about so many things. That Sid is dying. That Kara got stabbed by some horrifying demon thing. That the girl I care about more than anyone is . . . that she's hurting somewhere and I can't help her." His voice cracks with the misery. "And I'm pissed that you didn't fucking *think* before bringing your sister back. Because now we're all living in hell, just waiting to get our guts torn out. So forgive me if I'm a little tense and don't want to hear how you saved someone else. Because. It. Doesn't. Matter. The spiritual world is melting down, and we're all going to end up in pieces if your psycho sister has her way."

I wait a second and then say, quietly, "I know. I'm sorry." Because, what can I say? He's right. And when he doesn't add anything else, I say, "I'm parking the Jeep near the ER entrance. I'll leave the keys hidden on top of the driver's side tire."

I hang up and call a cab.

THIRTY-NINE

Aidan

"She had a heart attack!" Jax shouts gleefully at me when I come in the back door.

I walk to the table where he's sitting with a laptop, and sink into one of the kitchen chairs. Why is he so happy someone had a heart attack?

"Who?"

"The nurse." He angles the laptop screen to face me. "You didn't kill her, she had a heart attack."

Because I ripped a demon out of her. "Am I supposed to be happy about this?"

"The cops can't arrest you for some woman having a bad ticker, dude. You're off the hook." Then he pauses and qualifies that last part. "Well, I mean, the weirdos who think you're an alien might still be a problem. But hiding from nerds living in their mom's basement shouldn't be too tough." He grins happily.

"They already found me." Which means I shouldn't be here. But I have to be close when Kara gets home. I couldn't care less about some shitty blog.

"What?" Holly says as she comes into the kitchen. "Who found you?"

"Some guy from Blind Man's Blog," I say. "I told him I was hiding from the government."

Jax taps at the keys and looks the blog up, reads for a second, then laughs. "They bought it. Sort of. They still think you're an alien, though."

Holly reads over his shoulder. "There's a three-part post on how the government knows we're not alone," she says. "And you're a large portion of the *proof*."

"Holy shit, there's a video!" Jax points.

Holly clicks "Play" and there I am, talking on my phone like a fucking moron while some guy is videotaping me without my knowledge in my own driveway. "Shit."

"QFT," Holly says as she and Jax watch.

That's an awful clear view of my profile. And the shot when he gets me turning, I'm right there in living color, scowling at him before I raise my hand to block the camera.

"Well," Holly says. "I mean, no way will people buy all this silliness."

"Right," Jax says. Then he scoffs, "Aliens? That's just crazy."

"I kill *demons*, Jax."

They just look at me, then at each other. And they burst into hysterical giggles. They laugh so hard they have to lean on each other to keep from falling over.

I'm so glad my unveiling is hilarious to some people.

I sigh and stand. "Thanks for the touching moment, guys." Then I leave them to their amusement and go find Sid on the couch.

He looks up from the book he's reading and smiles at me when I come into the living room. "Sounds like you kids are having fun."

"They are," I say with a smile as I let myself feel the bright energy in the room. Then I notice a woman and a little girl sitting on the loveseat, watching a cartoon on TV. Tray's mom and sister. "Hey," I say, feeling suddenly awkward. I sit down next to Sid.

The mom studies me with caution. She looks a little like a frazzled scarecrow, her hair wisping up with escaped dark curls, prominent collarbones, thin arms. The little girl on her lap smiles—Selena.

She slips free from her mom and bounces across the room to stand in front of me. I think Tray said she was five or six, but I can't remember. Her cheeks are like a doll's and her eyes are bright amber. She's wearing a tutu and cowboy boots, and the thick dark-brown braids on the sides of her head are tied awkwardly with green ribbons, like she put them in herself.

"Hello," she says.

I lean forward so I'm at eye level with her. "Hello, Selena."

She looks surprised that I know her name. "Are you my brother's friend?"

"Yeah."

"I have two brothers." She purses her lips in thought. "Which one do you like?"

"Both."

She smiles widely. "I never met Jax's friend that's a boy. He only likes girls."

Sid chuckles beside me.

"What's your name?" she asks.

"Aidan."

"And what's your favorite color?"

"Green."

"Mine, too! See, I put green in my hair." She tugs on one of the ribbons.

"Wow," I say, "that's pretty."

"I know. I'm always pretty."

I make a serious face. "Oh, of course."

She nods and then looks over to Sid. She points at him. "Is that your daddy?"

I turn to Sid. "Uh, no."

"Do you have a daddy? I don't have one."

"Selena," her mother says sharply. "Get over here and sit. Leave the poor men alone."

"It's all right," I say, not liking the shadow that fills the little girl's eyes when she has to go back to her mom. I try and give the mother a friendly smile, but she just scowls at me, then looks at the TV like she's actually watching the cartoon sponge flip burgers at the Krusty Krab. I give Selena a smile, and she brightens up again.

I turn back to Sid. "You look so much better." And he does, his cheeks are still sunken, but he's less pale, and his eyes are a little brighter.

"I feel better," he says, patting his chest, like he's proud. "I've been a good boy and eaten everything Holly brings me."

Holly comes into the entry, hands on her hips. "Don't buy it! He's been moaning since I made him lunch, saying I'm giving him too much food."

Sid turns to me. "She's going to make me round as a beach ball."

"I can hear you," she says in a singsong voice.

Hurried footsteps descend the stairs. "Do I hear Aidan?" Raul asks.

"In here," I say.

He pokes his head around the archway and motions that he needs to talk. I check with Sid. "You okay for a sec?"

He glances toward Holly. "I'm not sure." But then he winks.

I stand and follow Raul out, relief settling in a little more. Kara's okay. Sid is looking better. Now we just need to find Rebecca.

When Raul and I are heading up the stairs, I notice Finger by his bedroom door, looking lost. "Hey, Finger," I call down. He turns and I see the worry lines in his forehead. "You okay, dude?"

He glances down at the floor, then back up to me. He shivers a little and I sense his fear. But before I can ask more, he just walks away, heading through the door that leads to the basement.

I turn to Raul and whisper so Sid won't hear, "Is this about Finger?" Raul frowns at me. "No, why?"

"I'm not sure," I say, taking another glance over the railing to where Finger was standing.

"He's been acting skittish for the last hour." Raul says, like he's just realizing it.

That's weird. I make a note to talk to him as soon as I'm done talking to Raul.

When we make it to the landing I ask, "What's going on? Why all the caginess?"

"Because I don't want Sid to think *I* broke it. I just got accepted into this club." He opens Kara's door and walks into the room, motioning to the window. There's no glass in the top half of the frame.

"You broke a window? Sid won't care."

"I said I *didn't* break the window, hon. Keep up. The reason I'm showing you is 'cause the way it broke freaked me the fuck out."

We're all on edge, but this seems a little silly. "And how did it break?" I move to the window and see glass shards on the floor and on the sill.

"Some book flew right through it."

I turn back to look at him. "A book?"

He rolls his eyes with an exasperated sigh. "Okay, so, I was sleeping when this noise starts going nuts. Like rattling. It was pissing me off and keeping me awake, and when I followed the noise, I could tell it was in here." He motions around the room. "You guys were gone, so I figured it wasn't you and Kara, ya know, doin' the horizontal hula." He makes another kind of hand motion, and I give him a warning glare. "When I opened the door, the noise just stopped. And then, like, two seconds later, a book flew from under the bed and rocketed out the window." He makes a crashing sound and motions with his hands like something is exploding between them.

"A book came from under the bed and went through the window?" He gives me a look like I'm being clueless.

There's only one book I know of that might possibly fly away. I kneel down and look under the bed. I pull out my duffel and open it, taking out my sister's bag of secrets, realizing it weighs almost nothing. I open it and try not to let the chill take over.

The grimoire isn't in it.

FORTY

Aidan

Mom's grimoire would only fly out the window for bad reasons. Reasons to do with Ava, I assume. But why would she need it? She must have the whole thing memorized by now.

I stay in Kara's bedroom for a while and think about everything that's happening, trying to make sense of it all, trying to figure out what my sister might have done with Rebecca. But nothing becomes clear.

A couple of hours pass and I hear Holly's voice trail upstairs as she squeals a greeting to Kara and Connor. I rush down and burst into the kitchen to see Connor helping Kara through the back door. Tray follows after them, passes through, and heads straight for the living room and his mom and sister.

I take Kara from Connor and hug her close, trying to be gentle but finding it difficult with my relief being so strong. She seems fine, except for a slight grimace.

"I'm all right," she says, patting me on the chest like I'm being silly.

"I'm so sorry I wasn't there with you."

"It's all right." She touches my cheek and some of her bluster fades. "I understand."

I press my forehead against hers and release a sigh.

"She needs to rest," Connor says, sounding protective.

"I will," she says. "Just let me enjoy the fact that I'm not dead for five seconds."

"Fine," he says. "I'm leaving anyway."

Kara and I both turn to him and I ask, "Where are you going?"

He moves in close so only the two of us can hear him. "Where do you think?" he asks through his teeth. "I'm going to go look for my girlfriend. Because I blew off her calls for two days, crushed her, and now she's gone missing. I might *never* see her again. And it's so goddamn ironic, because I was pulling away, afraid I was about to hurt her. Which I did. I hurt her by hiding myself and now I may have fucking killed her because I wasn't paying attention."

"Connor," Kara says, sadly.

His confession hits me sideways. "This is in no way your fault, man. You can't take this on."

"I get it, you know." He shakes his head. "I get how you feel, Aidan, that weight on your shoulders, and I blame you and you blame yourself, but it's all so goddamn unfair. She never should have been pulled into this. Not her."

"I know," I say, because I don't know what else will console him.

"I need to find her," he says. "I don't think I'll ever be able to forgive myself if I don't."

———

Kara and I decide that since she needs to rest anyway, I should go with Connor to look for Rebecca. I'm worried about him, and I also know I won't be able to stomach sitting around waiting and hoping. The more time that passes without news, the more the dark thoughts have closed in. The more I see Rebecca hurting and tormented. The more I think the unthinkable.

We're taking Tray and his mom and sister back home on the way out. Tray thanks me an embarrassing number of times as he walks out the back door with us.

"If it wasn't for you, they wouldn't be safe," he says as we're getting in the Jeep. "You gave me a way to protect them."

Selena holds her brother's finger and looks back and forth between us with her big eyes.

"Just be careful," I say. "And call me if you need anything, or if anything weird happens with your new stuff."

He nods and Selena tugs on his shirt. When he bends to see what she needs, she whispers something in his ear.

Tray smiles and then glances at me. "She wants to give you something so you're not sad."

Her little hand holds out one of the green ribbons she had in her hair. Then she grabs my wrist and wraps it round and round, tying it haphazardly. "Now you can be pretty, too," she says.

When Connor and I drop them off, I watch the three figures walk down the path to their apartment building and feel a twinge of regret, missing my sister. Missing what we could have been. Missing what we were. I hope Tray and Selena's story has a happier ending than mine and Ava's likely will.

Connor and I drive through town, stopping at each place where he and Rebecca have hung out, searching at the beach, a couple of restaurants. We try her school, even wander around campus a little bit, but there's no sign of her. We didn't think there would be, we just didn't know what else to do.

I recall I have the number for her friend Samantha, and text to ask that she have Rebecca call us if she sees her. That it's important. Then we drive around Rebecca's neighborhood again, around the adjacent neighborhoods, too. As the sun sinks into the horizon, we know we've exhausted what we can do in a car, and start back home again.

I don't say anything and neither does he. But we both feel it, the finality of stopping the search, of pulling down our street. I don't know how to have hope at this point. Not anymore. Definitely not after Ava let that demon hurt Kara so brutally. We both know what my sister is capable of doing. How far she's willing to go.

"We could find another way," Connor says. "Maybe there's some kind of locator spell?"

"I don't know one, but we could ask Sid."

"There's got to be something more we can do to—" His words cut off and he cranes his neck, looking at something in the yard. Then he goes perfectly still and the smell of adrenaline leaks into the cab of the Jeep. "Someone's here."

I glance over to where he's looking, and my muscles tense. A man is in the backyard, near the stack of wood that was the old shed. Tall, dressed in what looks like a robe. He appears to just be standing there, staring at the house. "Do you recognize him?" I ask.

Connor shakes his head. "You?"

"No."

We watch him for several seconds, and he doesn't turn to look at us or seem to know we're here. I try to decide how to approach this. He could be possessed. He could be a corporeal demon in human form. He could also be some freak who's looking for aliens. I can't tell from here. It's too dark to see his features clearly, but he's in a long brown robe, his hair pulled back in a tight ponytail, making his profile look severe. Suddenly he shifts and pulls something from the folds of his robe, a small animal of some kind.

He lifts it up, high. And slices down the belly with a dagger in his other hand.

Blood and insides spill out onto his head and face, an anointing of death.

My gut churns.

"Shit." Connor grabs the door handle and starts to get out of the Jeep. "He's breaking the wards."

I stop him with a hand on his shoulder. "Wait." He looks at me like I've lost it. "Text Kara and warn her, let me deal with this."

"Like hell. You have no clue what he is."

"You need to get everyone out of here. This is only happening because something else is coming. And we can't waste time wondering what that could be."

He nods, leaving the key in the ignition as he slips out of the Jeep and heads around the side yard to the front of the house.

I take a deep breath and go in the opposite direction, making my way along the garage, until I'm only two yards away from the guy, staying behind him in the growing shadows. The smell of carnage is strong. As I pause, the sound of his whispers come clear. He's casting a spell, something about shields. But he's not tearing them down, he's putting them up.

I look around the backyard to be sure there's not some other man or thing hiding nearby, then I reach in my pocket and touch my Star of David, whispering a prayer. I can tell that my power is still weak from doing the resurrection, but I don't have much of a choice.

I step from the shadows, toward him, reciting Psalm 91 in Hebrew as I get closer, not attempting to be quiet anymore.

The figure turns, hunching a little. The ghoulish features shimmer with blood as he faces me. The whites of his eyes are almost glowing as they shine through the painting of death. There are bits of guts on his shoulders and on the front of his robes and black T-shirt underneath.

He drops the animal—a cat carcass—and stares at me like I just caught him spying on a naked girl.

He's human. Not a corporeal demon. Possessed?

"Show yourself, *dever*," I say in demon tongue.

The man's brow creases in confusion.

So I pull my dagger free and add in English, "You know I'm going to rip your insides out next, right?"

The whites of his eyes get even bigger, and he lifts his hands in surrender. "Dude, it's just a job."

Now it's my turn to frown. "What the fuck are you doing?"

"It's a spell," he says. "But it's not real." No red spark lights his eye. He motions to the house behind him. "I was hired to scare the guy that lives here, because he owes some dude money. I'm just a witch trying to earn a living."

I lower my dagger and study him, his soul. There is a slight shine of silver on his skin and the blood mist from the spell is still swirling at his feet. "That spell you just did is real. Who hired you?"

"I don't know, some pretty boy with an itch for overkill. He gave me the instructions and then said to call when it was done."

I hold out a hand. "Give me your phone."

He hesitates and eyes the blade I'm still clutching tight in my other hand, then he pulls a phone from his pocket and passes it to me. "I can just go. Don't worry, I won't call him."

A red spark.

I take the phone and throw it as hard as I can in the same direction I chucked the blogger's. It flies over the fence, over two backyards, before hitting the trunk of a tree at Mach 6 and shattering into tiny pieces.

"Shit, dude! That was a brand-new iPhone."

"Leave now or I'm calling the cops." I point at the eviscerated cat.

He gapes at me like he still wants to be pissed about his phone, but then he growls and storms past me, heading for the back alley.

I watch him to make sure he's really gone before I head toward the house. Connor still hasn't come out with anyone, so I'm guessing he was having trouble convincing the others to leave.

I open the back door and step into the house as someone else comes up onto the porch beside me, holding a phone up like a microphone.

"Just one new quote for the readers would be amazing, Mr. Blink," the blogger says quickly. "You're a huge hit."

I push him backward, trying to get away as he follows me into the kitchen. "Put that damn thing away," I say. "You scared me half to death, you stupid—" but my voice freezes. I watch in confusion as a blade comes around from behind the blogger and slices across his throat, opening his jugular. All in half a second.

His phone falls to the linoleum as his hand goes to the wound, mouth opening and closing, his blood spraying across my shirt.

But before I can react or get a look at the attacker, I'm yanked to the side and shoved hard. I hit the table, crash onto a chair, then hit the floor, wrist twisting. My ribs scream, my knees ache. I'm picked up by two figures and dragged into the entryway, then dropped unceremoniously.

I try to catch my breath, to get my bearings, to figure out what just happened—

"Well, well," says a voice above me. "The Fire Bringer seems to be all out of juice from that resurrection. My girl actually did it. She told me you wouldn't be able to resist bringing the dad back from the dead."

I scramble up and realize there's a man in front of me. A very familiar man. The Heart-Keeper. The thing that my mother's spirit trapped. He's free. He's full of power. And I'm not the only vulnerable one here. My heart crushes in my chest as I see the other occupants in the room. They're all in a semicircle: Connor and Kara at the foot of the stairs, Raul and Finger beside Kara, Holly and Jax next to Connor. Bound, hands and feet. Sid is lying on the floor of the living room. His body still. Eyes closed.

I can't to show fear, I have to focus—but I can't stop my legs from shaking.

Two other creeping figures are fading into the shadows—the ones that dragged me in here. They watch in silence, giving their master the room. I can't tell what they are yet, but I sense their Darkness. I feel the death of the innocent guy they just killed. I smell my friends' terror, my own.

And I know all too well the Heart-Keeper's vicious lust for blood.

FORTY-ONE

Aidan

He looks casually around the entry at his audience.

I watch in horror as he moves along the semicircle of my friends. His clothes are the same modern, expensive style as before. So perfect in appearance, it's disturbing. His model features focus as he pauses next to a kneeling Kara.

Then he takes her chin in his hands and sneers.

"Don't touch her!" I spit out, rising to my feet. I'm grabbed before I can lunge, and the two figures in the shadows shove me back to my knees.

I struggle against them, but they only grip me tighter, so tight the pressure vibrates my bones. I search for my fire, for something, but my power sleeps. I'm useless, a desert. I used up everything on helping Rebecca's dad.

"You are a bit of a surprise," the Heart-Keeper says, ignoring my fit, still holding Kara's face, intent on speaking to her. "You healed yourself . . . ? Unexpected. It won't save you, but it is curious." He studies her face like he's considering something. Then he releases her and turns to Connor. "And you, my violent boy. That fire in your belly is only going to grow. Perhaps we should do the world a favor?" And then he winks in a grotesque sign of affection.

Connor cringes.

Another figure steps out of the shadows behind the stairs, a third guard, watching Connor in case he tries to fight or run. It's a woman. Her eyes are black, and there are dark veins running up her neck and one side of her face. A corporeal demon. I can't get a look at them, but my guess is that the two men holding me are the same.

"So," the Heart-Keeper says, turning to me. "I assume your sister told you I was going to come for a visit. *Do as he says, give him what he wants,* and all that. I am surprised you didn't listen and take precautions. You even let an innocent into the lion's den." He clucks his tongue, motioning to the dead blogger in the kitchen. He shakes his head, and his slick hair falls over his forehead a little. "A bit disappointing, but I'll work with what I can get."

His words send chills over me as I realize what Ava meant. She was telling me to give the others over to *this* creature. The thing that had our mother's heart ripped out. "What do you want with us?"

"Us?" he asks in an amused voice. "You're all cozy and bonded now, I know. Really, that's adorable." He sighs and smiles wistfully. "What do I want . . . ? Now that is a question. Is this the part of our tale where the villain rattles off his plan so that the hero—being you, of course—can save himself and his scrappy band of cohorts?" He motions to the others with a dramatic sweep of his hand. Then he steps closer to me and leans in, saying in a conspiratorial voice, "I always found that bit of human entertainment so predictable. Let's do something new and fresh. You know, where I keep my thoughts to myself and you just"—his voice becomes nails digging into me—*"die."* His features shift, their beauty melting away.

The thing is a scaly, twisted alien. It's man and reptile all in one. Huge yellow eyes, wide mouth full of tiny teeth and two very large fangs. Its long and bony fingers are webbed to the knuckles, each one tipped with a sharp claw.

Holly whimpers behind it, and the others shift, the room filling with the smell of their horror.

Those yellow eyes examine me, and the thing bares its thin teeth in a twisted grin. One of its claws comes up and touches my temple. The talon slides gently over my sweaty skin.

Then sinks in, ripping down my face.

I cry out in agony and try to jerk away, but my captors hold me tight.

The Heart-Keeper laughs, the sound raking over my bones. "You won't be so pretty now, will you?"

My stomach roils from the pain, my cheek and neck turn slick with hot blood. I try to kick out, but something sharp springs from the demon holding me on the left and pricks my chest. I struggle and try to see it. It's pressing at my pec, slicing into my shirt. It looks like a tail. A tail with a long, thin stinger for a tip.

"Don't think I won't slice out that heart, Little Flame," the Heart-Keeper says. "It's a prize I've promised to your sister, but if you push me, I'll consider backing out of the deal." His human guise rises back into place, returning his model-like features. He spins around with a flourish to face the others. "So, children. We've come to the moment of truth. Where the music of what you have become must be faced. Now that my little witch has pushed you all to bond, there is one among you who's marked to be mine. The most vital of you that I must *collect*." His gaze scans the six of them. "I won't make it emotional, it's pretty cut and dry; I just need to know which of you is the tip of the arrow."

My chest clenches. I don't let myself look at Finger, not wanting to give him away.

"Speak up," the Heart-Keeper says in a singsong voice. He stops in front of Connor and grabs him by the hair, yanking his face closer. "You seem a promising candidate with all that power ready to come out of you at any minute. Are you the one?" He studies Connor's eyes intently. "You don't have to be cagey. It just means you're first. And you know, it's always best to get it over with. Rip the bandage off, so to speak. Or in this case, rip the heart out." He chuckles at his joke.

"Fuck you," Connor says. And then he spits in the demon's face.

The Heart-Keeper stiffens. He releases Connor's hair and stands straight.

He stares. And a horrible finality fills the room. A low growl shakes the air as his hand reaches out slowly, fingers morphing into claws again.

They hover in front of Connor, playing at the air, like they're trying to decide.

And then they move.

Ripping Connor's throat out.

The shock of it jars my body. Screams fill the room. I stare helplessly at Connor's confused face. The torn flesh gurgles. And his body falls forward. Hitting the floor with a thud.

I pull at the fists gripping me, crying out in fury. Blood pools around Connor's head. The smell of his life fills the room. Horror and desperation are like an ocean trying to drown me. "No!" I yell. I keep roaring it. As if the word will erase what I'm seeing. What I'm feeling. As I watch Connor's spirit coil and begin to lift from his lifeless body. Because it's not true. It can't be real.

We're all crying out in horror, pain filling every molecule in the room.

The Heart-Keeper watches us with a smile. "Yes, get it all out," he coos. "Release the agony." He takes a long breath into his nose and sighs in satisfaction.

Soon the cries become sobs. Kara is hunched over, wracked by her sorrow; Holly's face glistens with tears, her eyes wide and panicked. Raul weeps quietly, and Jax stares on in silent horror. Finger remains still as death, watching the Heart-Keeper like a cat might watch a bird it's about to eat.

"I'm going to burn your bones," I hiss.

"Yes, so you say," the Heart-Keeper mutters, sounding bored. He turns his attention to Kara again. "He wasn't the one, so could it be you?"

"I said, don't touch her!" I growl.

He ignores me, knowing I'm useless, and keeps focusing on Kara. "I was fairly sure it wasn't you, since the green witch wasn't the one. The two girls who hold his heart are meant for other things. But perhaps I'm wrong?" He cocks his head like he wants her to answer even though she's weeping at his feet, not looking at him. "You did come back from the brink of death, though," he says, reasoning through some mystery.

He takes her by her hair now, pulling her up awkwardly into a standing position.

I look desperately at Finger, wondering why he doesn't admit he's the one, the tip of the arrow. Why he doesn't save her. The silent boy just keeps watching with malice clear in his eyes. No fear. No conflict. Just deadly rage.

The Heart-Keeper lifts his fingers in the same way he did with Connor. They morph into claws and play at the air. Kara just stares at Connor's lifeless form.

I jerk against my captors again, yanking one arm and then the other, not even caring when the stinger slides into my chest an inch. "No! It's not her! Just stop!"

The Heart-Keeper pauses, his claw becoming a hand again. He turns to me. "Oh?" He releases Kara's hair and steps closer to me. "Are we about to snitch to save the girl?"

"It's not her," I gasp, my chest stinging.

"Yes, you mentioned that. It's why I'm standing on this side of the room and not ripping out her throat." He rolls his eyes like I'm annoying him. "So . . . ?"

I hesitate, knowing there's no way I can say it. I can't sentence Finger to death.

"It's me," I say, my throat closing even as the words come.

Holly gasps and Jax cries, "Shut up, dude!"

The Heart-Keeper shakes his head, sneering at me. "No, it's not you, fool. It can't be you, you're a part of the hub, like the green witch. You're the power center. Noble of you to lie in order to save these idiots behind me, but it won't work. You're nothing compared to who I seek."

"Please," I whimper, "just stop."

"Not yet," he says.

The demon turns his attention back to Kara, but Finger steps forward, a guttural noise coming from deep in his chest. Determination spills from him. I want to yell for him to stop, not to do this, but . . . how many will die if he doesn't?

Fear shakes my body. How is this happening? It's all spinning out of control.

The Heart-Keeper slowly looks Finger over. Then his thin lips slide up in a wicked grin. "You . . . yessss."

"No," I whisper, my heart crushing in my chest.

The Heart-Keeper steps closer to Finger. He sniffs at the air around him. "You give yourself willingly?" he asks.

Finger nods. And then he looks over the demon's shoulder straight into me. And when our eyes meet, I know, I see why he's doing this. The knowledge and his assurance fill me like a soothing balm. He tells me it's all right, that this is how it was always meant to be, that I shouldn't be afraid. His journey is only beginning. But I can save the others, I can finish it, with this beast, with my sister. But he believes he has to give himself over first for that to happen. He believes that this is what he's been meant to do all along, to start the dominoes falling, to begin the end.

The Heart-Keeper grips the silent boy's shoulder. And grins.

And there's no way for me to stop it, no way to stop any of it.

As the beast strikes.

A *thud* and *crack* fill the air around us, and Finger's eyes go wide. I feel it in my own chest, I feel it all. As the Heart-Keeper tears my friend's heart out. As his life slips away, to follow Connor's. I feel it in my blood, in my bones, the agony and loss. It burns, tearing a sob from deep in my gut.

My mind shuts down, the world goes dim. Everything smells like blood. Everything is the tang of death on my tongue and the scent of charred hope in my nostrils.

"You are stunning, though," I hear the Heart-Keeper say after a minute. Somewhere in the distance, I see him step over a body and move closer to Kara again. He smears Finger's blood on her cheek as he leans in and smells the skin of her neck. "Just because I found my prize doesn't mean you and I can't have a little fun, does it?" His voice turns gruff when he adds, "There is so much I could teach you and your soul. Just as I did the Fire Bringer's mother."

All Kara does is stare past him, into nothing. Like she's left us already, before he's done a thing to her.

"Your lover was a fool to heal your soul wounds. They were lovely, dark and vicious. I could help you create more." He pauses, then asks, "Would you like that?"

I have nothing left in me to speak or fight. I watch helplessly as she looks into his eyes. Her gaze seems to urge him closer.

"No, Kara," I whisper, hope slipping away.

The Heart-Keeper smiles again. "I knew you would bend for me, evil little—"

His voice stops and a dagger point sticks out the back of his neck.

And suddenly Kara's tackling him, pulling the blade back out of his throat and shoving it into his eye, screaming at him as she stabs him again and again. As she pours her rage and revenge over him. My heart yells for more, my sleeping power sparking a little at the sight. But there's no black blood, no death. His face just looks like sliced-up putty as he laughs maniacally, letting her stab him, his arms wide.

His disguise protects him. He knows he's safe.

Or believes he is.

The woman demon guard lunges at Kara to pull her off her master, just as I yell, "Shed your visage, *dever!*"

The Heart-Keeper's laugh fades, his guise beginning to shift away. Kara raises the dagger one more time. And just as the female demon guard grabs for her neck, Kara plunges the blade down into the scaly lips of the horrifying creature before he can move.

She's yanked off and tossed to the side. But the power-infused blade has already done its job.

The Heart-Keeper's head caves in with a small sigh. And the body crumbles into ash.

FORTY-TWO

Aidan

Kara hits the edge of the kitchen archway and lands next to the dead blogger. She moans in pain, the sound telling me she's still alive.

The guard demons all pause, unsure what to do. They look at each other, they look at the room full of weeping humans, at the husk of their dead master. But the three of them don't seem upset about it all. They just seem confused.

The female demon begins to pace. "This ends nothing," she says. She motions to the pile of dust that was the Heart-Keeper. "Molech still expects the prize. We can rise from this ash."

The demons that are holding me shift, uncertain.

And I know there's only one way for me to do what Finger believed I could. One way to end this. One way to bring him and Connor back.

I steel myself and start fighting my captors again, shoving them off. "I'm going to kill you!" I snap, baring my teeth. "I'm going to burn you all!"

The demon woman just chuckles at me, like I'm a child. "With what power?"

I start to chuckle with her and her smile fades a little. And then I scream in Aramaic at the top of my lungs, Zechariah 3:2, *"Isn't this man a burning branch snatched from the fire?"* I howl it at her, the question rising from my lips over and over, a warning, a promise. *"Isn't this man a burning branch snatched from the fire?"* I laugh and scream and lose my mind, letting all the horror in me loose. I open the floodgates and allow it to spill out, hoping it'll drown these bastards if my fire can't help me.

"Shut him up!" the female guard growls, coming at me.

My right arm bone snaps with a jarring crack from the tightening grip of the demon holding it. The stinger at my chest sinks in even deeper. But adrenaline numbs me. I yank, fighting maniacally.

I kick the female demon as she gets closer, sending her stumbling back. "Shed your visage, *dever!*" I spit at her. "Fight me or kill me, you fucking bitch!"

She snarls as her thin disguise melts away and her bony, scaly form comes clear. Smoke emerges from her slit nostrils as she huffs out her displeasure. Around her feet a ring of the wood floor bursts into flames. "I have my own flames, Fire Bringer."

"We aren't supposed to kill him," grunts one of the demons.

"Oh, we won't," she says. "We'll just melt his face off." The blaze follows her as she steps toward me, then it spreads out in a slow circle of heat.

I see Jax move in the background; he used my distraction to free himself. He's trying to cut Raul and Holly's bonds. He runs over to grab Sid next, but . . . Sid is gone.

"Run!" I scream at him over the crackle of flames. "Just run!"

Holly, Raul, and Jax scramble away, trying to avoid the flames, avoid the dead bodies of their friends. Jax gathers Kara in his arms and then all of them make it out the back door.

Relief fills me as they disappear into the night, just as the flames rise around us and begin to chew at the living room wall. I watch the tongues lick at the mail on the entry hall table and slide against the glass of a picture frame—an image of Sid and Connor on the set of a job.

A fist crashes into my sternum, right beside the spot where the stinger's embedded.

My vision blurs and air whooshes from my lungs. I gag. I choke and gasp. Pain bleeds through me. And the heat of the demon's flames stings my legs.

I'm sure she's stopped my heart, but then there's a grunt, and suddenly I'm falling to the side, collapsing on a pile of ash.

"Get up, dammit!" It's Jax. He just killed one of the demons holding me. He hovers, dragging me toward the front door, away from the two demons leering at us from the flames. He's come back? Why did he come back?

"Get out!" I holler at him. He was safe. He can't be here!

"Fuck that."

I stagger to my feet, push him behind me. "In three seconds you better be out of this house, or I'll come back and kill you myself. Make sure Kara's safe." I shove him toward the front door, then lunge forward, tackling the demon with the deadly tail.

Grabbing meaty shoulders, I scream in its face. And with a heavy thrust, the alien spike instinctively impales my chest, cracking ribs, tearing flesh, puncturing my lung, exiting through my back.

I gasp in horror and relief.

The lizard woman panics. "What did you do, you fool!" She grabs her companion and yanks him out from under me, ripping the stinger out, rending my chest cavity as she tosses him like a rag doll. Then she tears off his head with a roar.

Agony. I can't . . . breathe. I can't . . . I'm drowning, paralyzed. The glow of flames rises around me.

The smoke-obscured creature hovers. The crushing weight grows.

"You fool," the blur over me says. "You will be doomed as much as I. The student queen is a thousand leagues more terrifying than the dreaded master." And then the blur is gone.

Shadows gather in my vision, blocking out the orange light of the flames. Someone takes my arm. I'm being moved but I can't tell where. All I see is black smoke. Then cool air hits me as my vision fills with midnight, stars pricking the darkness. The sky.

There's scrambling and crying far off. It hurts filtering through me. It hurts. Everything. And I can't . . . I can't . . . bre—

FORTY-THREE

Rebecca

My skin aches with cold. Damp, icy cold. The smells of dirt and night fill my head. I start to shiver. My teeth chatter, my stiff limbs protesting movement as if I've been asleep for years. I blink at my surroundings. Outside—I'm outside? It looks like a park or something. Around me the misty night settles in soft greys over the backdrop of black shadow trees and spidery ferns. A winding silver path through the brush is edged in shadows. It weaves off into the distance, but I can't tell where it leads in the darkness.

I'm under a large oak, on a patch of tiny white flowers; a twisted root is jabbing me in the rib cage. Why would I be in a park?

I try to sit up straight. My head pounds once, painfully, blinding me for a second. I rack my foggy brain, trying to remember what happened, how I got here, I—

I ran. I remember running. I ran like my feet could save me. Because I . . . I saw Charlie.

Pain fills my whole body at the memory. Oh my God, I saw Charlie. He was standing right next to our bench. But . . . that wasn't Charlie. Because he's dead. I knew that wasn't really him, it couldn't be. No gift from Ava could be that beautiful.

I think I wanted to believe it at first, though. I opened the back door and I stepped outside, for a second, didn't I? I let myself think it could be real. Believing the miracle was possible. Just for one stunning moment.

Until my feet touched the cool grass and something shifted on his face. When I felt that same odd twinge in my forehead again and Charlie seemed to change, become a beast with horns and claws and eyes made of suffering and agony.

So I ran. I ran from the demon shadow of my brother. I ran from Ava. Until my lungs burned in my chest.

I lost my mind, I didn't think about where I was going, I couldn't. So somehow I ended up . . . here? Wherever here is.

I try to rise but pain surges through the soles of my feet. I hiss in a breath and look down, seeing the raw things that carried me here. My soles are coated in dried blood and soil and leaves. The heavy beat of my heart is pounding in my skin, throbbing in my head.

I lift a hand to my forehead, trying to stop it, and my stomach rises.

Something scratches at my cheek as my arm moves, and when I bring my hand down, I see my palms are covered with leaves and dirt, too. All stuck to them with dried blood. My feet could be raw from running, but my *hands*? The skin is swollen and tender like it's been burned.

I sit up the rest of the way, trying to gently wipe some of the bracken off on my shirt. It stings like crazy, and pieces of skin peel off with the leaves, as if my palms were healing around the debris. I need water to clean them, something to soak them in. I look around me, trying to figure out where I am, where I should go and look for a phone. I'm covered in mud and leaves, for heaven's—

As I turn, my gaze freezes on the tree at my back. The girth of the trunk is huge, at least five feet, the gnarly branches twist at odd angles above me as they reach for the stars. It's like something out of an old faerie story. A creepy faerie story. But that's not the reason I can't stop staring.

The symbol that I drew the other night is burned into the tree, and two palm prints are sunk into the thick bark on either side of it.

I lift a hand, shock gripping me as my palm slides right into the imprint, as if made to rest there. A small vibration hums against my hand from inside the tree, and the smells of earth and sea air fill my head, things blurring—

I jerk back.

I'm shaking again, teeth chattering, this time the cold seems to be deep inside the core of me, as if ice crystals are forming along my bones. What's happening? What did I do? It was evening when I ran. How long's it been? Couldn't be more than a few hours. But I did something to this tree? It doesn't make sense. And my dad—oh my God, my dad must be freaking out.

Dread fills me, thinking of all the warnings Aidan and Connor have given me about the magic and witch stuff, how much anxiety and fear I always felt from Aidan when he used to talk about it.

I should've listened. Ava has made something go terribly wrong.

I hear birdsong above me, growing louder, making me look up. A flock of tiny sparrows bustles above my head. Wow, that's a *lot* of birds, especially to be out at night. And they seem to keep arriving, more and more nestling into the branches, their cacophony rising.

Something under me moves, sliding along my leg. I look down at the ground to see the small white flowers under me shifting, growing. One bud and then another lifting from the ground, then opening in a burst. I can't move as I watch them appearing. I'm immobile with confusion, my brain unable to believe what I'm watching.

Then the flowers begin growing out, creating a small line, like a trail. Until it reaches . . .

Everything in me goes still as I register what I'm seeing. It's a woman, but it's not. She's a glowing figure, ten feet from me, but she's a million miles away. It's as if two realities have suddenly presented themselves to me at the same time, and I can't tell which one is real. And for some crazy reason I'm not afraid. In fact, all the fear and confusion I was feeling a second ago is gone, washing into the ground beneath me.

She's lovely. She's delicate and sad and so, so lovely. A ghost, a spirit, a wisp of memory that stares at me, standing in a cluster of shifting and growing flowers. I see the trees and the path behind her through her sheer body, a white shimmer in the cold night air. A young woman, only a few years older than me. Her light hair is long, half braided and half spilling over her shoulders. A pale-colored dress hangs on her thin body, and her bare toes curl into the green beneath her like she's enjoying the feel of it.

Forgive me, she says. But the words aren't aloud, they sound muffled through cotton, like they're in my head. *I wanted to help you if I could.* I wonder who she is, where she comes from, and she answers instantly. *I am Fiona, a mother, a spirit. I found my way back from a long journey, to try again and mend the broken things, to do what your mother could not.*

There's so much in her words, so many layers of meaning. "What are you saying?"

I will show you, it will be easier. And she slides closer, the flowers following, more growing from the ground she passes over.

I lean back, unsure. When her ghost fingers touch my forehead, a million images and feelings pass over me, through me, marking me with her story.

A girl, a boy, and a broken heart full of regret. Magic, corruption, and the fall of innocence. I see it all play out before me, and tears fill my eyes, an ache fills my chest as I watch her give birth to a son, as I watch her joy twist into agony when her heart is broken, and then I feel her lose herself to the Darkness. She tried to redeem her mistakes, she tried to save her daughter, to save her son, but she failed. Until she returned to try again, taking the horrible monster with her into the void. She was caught there, between worlds, deep in the pit of Sheol. But then she escaped when the river of time shook . . .

Fiona, Aidan's mother. Ava's mother.

Yes.

"Why . . . why are you here with me?" I ask.

You share my gift of understanding, but you use it with more wisdom than I. I felt your power, felt you call to me in the void with your hands. They drew me to you. I wished to help you, to keep you safe from my daughter if I could.

My hands . . . ? My drawing. The pentagram design.

A spell to protect. My spell. I felt it come alive again, my magic, and I knew I had found an opening to mend a piece of the future I'd cast into being. Perhaps in helping you I have done that.

But . . . "I don't understand."

I came to you in the night, but you couldn't hear me. It wasn't until my daughter pushed you, when the demon Hunger tried to take you, that your fear opened a window. I was able to reach in . . . I am sorry. Her delicate features twist in pain. *I couldn't ask your permission.*

A thousand questions pop into my head. The fire, could that have been her trying to speak to me? And the demon? The thing trying to be Charlie, it terrified me and made my pain unbearable. That created a window for her to *reach in*? But she couldn't ask for permission. "Permission for what?" I ask finally as my head spins.

She seems to hesitate, then says, *To possess your body.*

A shiver runs through me, my insides crawling. My stomach rises and the ground tilts.

Forgive me, she says again, this time I feel her regret in the words, though. *I couldn't let the demon harness your gift and allow for my daughter to gain that much power.*

"You possessed me?" My voice shakes. "How long?" What did she force my body to do? What did she make my hands touch? I was a puppet, a shell, totally without will. But she saved me. She kept the demon from getting me. Somehow she ruined Ava's plan.

It makes me wonder—where did the demon that was masquerading as Charlie go?

You need to return to my son. You need to be by his side when this comes to a close. Her emotions are pleading now, desperate. *He needs you, Rebecca. He needs your strength.*

I shake my head. I don't feel strong enough to fight off a fly.

The demon still stalks you, she says, turning to look off in the distance. *I have held the creature off for a moment, but its hunger is powerful, and my daughter has given it physical form for a time, she has made sure the amulet won't hide you any longer. My time is short here. You must destroy the beast. I cannot.*

Destroy the demon—what? How am I supposed to do *that*? Just the small glimpse I saw of Hunger beneath the mask of Charlie was beyond horrifying.

The answer to destroy it is inside you. In your blood. It seeks you out now, the magic. And I see you fear it, but you mustn't. Her ghostly form leans over, gently touching my tear-stained cheek, like a mother would. *Your heart is pure. You won't fall.* A sad smile fills her silver eyes. And then she's floating into pieces, becoming smoke, sliding away, a part of the wind.

The tiny white flowers curl in on themselves like they're sad, then they sink away, disappearing into the grass again.

And I'm left with a similar feeling, the need to tuck myself away like a disappearing flower and hide from everything heading toward me.

FORTY-FOUR

Rebecca

My feet are on fire. Oh my God, they hurt. It would've been nice if Aidan's mom had gotten me some shoes to wear while she possessed me. I find a path into a town after what I'm pretty sure is more than an hour walking. I thought I was in a park, but if I was, that was one very large park. And even as civilization appears, nothing looks familiar. I'm definitely not in LA proper. There are pine trees everywhere, and so far the only businesses I've come across are a Taco Bell and a gas station—which I'm hoping will have a public phone.

I make my way across the street, as delicately as possible, my soles screaming with each tiny stone that presses into them. I'm slow for more reasons than that, though. My body is so exhausted. Everything in me aches.

I go into the store attached to the gas station, the bell on the door dings, making the scruffy man behind the counter look up from whatever he's reading. He's got on a grungy baseball cap with unkempt hair sticking out the bottom, and he obviously hasn't shaved in several days. There're smudges of dirt or grease on his cheek and neck, and his large fingers are tinted darker, like he's soaked them in ink. There's a patch on his shirt that says *Bill*. His eyes widen as I make my way to the counter, they rake over my grimy figure and then his gaze drops to something behind me.

"Your feet," he says with an odd tone in his voice. "They're bleedin'."

I look down and see red-brown footprints following me on the white linoleum. "Yeah, it hurts." Then I look back up at him. "Do you have a phone I could use, maybe? I need to call someone." I guess I'm throwing caution to the wind here, but this guy can obviously see I'm wounded and vulnerable. Hiding the fact that I'm stranded seems pointless.

He looks out the window like he's searching for something. Other people that might see him hurt me? Other people I might be with to pull some prank on him?

"Please," I add, hoping he's a decent guy. "I just need a phone."

He nods and motions me to come around behind the counter. I hesitate for a second but then decide I'm low on choices.

"What town is this?" I ask.

As I step through the opening, he's looking me up and down all over again, and my stomach churns.

He's a lot bigger now that he's standing. "Arrowhead." He points to the phone on the wall beside the window behind him, but his gaze stays locked on my chest.

I shiver and reach for the phone, hurriedly dialing my dad's cell number. I fold my arms across myself and scoot as far away from the man as I can, pressing my back into the glass of the window.

The phone rings and rings and I close my eyes, feeling tears rise. *Please pick up.* But it goes to voice mail and I have to release a shaky breath to keep from bursting into tears. I try to dial again, my fingers trembling as they punch the number in, doing it wrong, having to start over.

"You not gettin' an answer?" The man asks, going back to his reading.

I look out the window as I listen to the line ring in my ear, trying to calm down. I'm way too freaked out right now. Not everyone's out to get me.

But then a smell filters through the space around us. Like rotting flesh and sour milk all mixed together.

I stiffen. Hear movement behind me. I turn and see the man is coming closer, blocking my escape. He licks his lips and starts whispering something under his breath. Something's different about his eyes; there's a far-off look in them now.

I need my dad to pick up the phone. Why does it just keep ringing?!

My teeth start chattering and I can barely breathe as my dad's voice mail picks up again. I press into the glass window at my back.

"You're pretty," the man, Bill, says, his voice scratchy. He's only a foot away now, well within arm's reach.

I shake my head, having no ability to speak as the terror crawls up my throat. There's a demon in the room, or a demon in this man, I just know it. I can feel it, smell it, the Darkness. The voice mail beeps for me to leave my message, but I can't move to hang up or redial. The receiver slides from my ear to my shoulder. *Hit him with it, Rebecca!*

But I can't move.

He reaches out slowly, gently running his stained fingers over my hair. He swallows hard. "Are you a fallen angel?"

His question and demeanor are so strange—threatening, but not. It's almost as if he's so mesmerized he has no choice.

"Please," I whisper, shivering so hard it jars my bones. I can't move, I can't think, I can't—

His eyes are distant as his hand moves to my arm, gripping it hard.

I choke on a sob as he pulls me closer, and I know what's about to happen, I know with sudden clarity that he's about to kill me as his meaty fingers reach out and curl around my neck.

Stop! No, no, no, please, no.

He squeezes. Light sparks in my vision. I try to scream, to fight, but it's as if my body won't listen, just going stiff, my mind retreating. He presses me back against the glass, his raspy breath in my face. I gag, push back with flailing arms, hands seeking purchase against his chest, his shoulders, his face. Panic fills me. The finality of the moment taunting me.

Until the rage comes, the fight billowing up in a rush.

A silent cry rips through me. My nails digging into flesh.

GET BACK!

With a sudden burst of air, I'm free, stumbling forward. Sound explodes around me as I gasp and choke and try to find a way to get oxygen back into my lungs.

And finally my scream comes; I scream so loud I go numb as it bursts from my lungs, pushing me to my knees. The noise blasts around me, crashing, breaking, thundering. It goes on and on, alive and powerful.

I don't know how much time passes as I hug myself, rocking back and forth, my tears spilling out with each wracking breath. Silence falls slowly. I open my eyes and find myself alone in a mess. Glass and food and papers scatter the floor. I look around but can't see the man, so I lift a shaking hand to the countertop and pull myself to my feet. My unsteady legs nearly buckle when I realize what I did—because I know beyond a doubt that I created the wreck in front of me.

The store is torn apart, shelves knocked over, refrigerator doors cracked, soda bottles exploded. And the man, Bill, is in a heap against the bathroom door on the other side of the room.

I shake, trying to figure out what happened. How did I do this?

It takes me several seconds to realize something's ringing. A phone. Sounds like it's coming from the mechanic's garage outside.

I turn to look at the phone on the wall behind me and see a red light flashing. I rush to it and push the button beside the blinking light. I pick up the dangling receiver and press it to my ear. I open my mouth to speak but only a small whimper emerges.

"Hello?!" The word comes urgently through the line. "Did someone call me from this number?" Elation and pain fill me at the sound of my dad's voice. "Hello?"

"Daddy," I manage to scratch from my throat as the tears start again.

There's a pause before it comes back, raw and vulnerable. "Emery . . . oh, God. Thank God, I found you." Tears fill his words and he makes a sound like he's in pain.

I cry harder and can only say again, "Daddy."

"Where are you, sweetie? Let me come get you."

"I don't know," I say, finding it hard to breathe again. "I'm at a . . . a gas station. He said we're in Arrowhead."

"What kind of station, what company? I'll look it up. Tell me what's around you."

"A Taco Bell," I say. "And I think it's a Chevron."

"Don't hang up, okay. Stay on the phone until I can get there."

"Okay." I look around the demolished store. "Daddy . . ."

"Yes, baby."

I slide down to the floor cradling the phone, hoping the man across the room won't wake up. "Please, hurry."

———

A hundred years pass. A hundred years of listening to his voice, unable to speak. Every once in a while he gives me an update on where he is, but apparently Arrowhead is a solid thirty-five-minute drive from the city. I can only marvel at the fact that I walked here somehow.

He's not asking me questions; I think he knows I wouldn't be able to answer. He tells me he filed a missing person's report this morning, explaining that I've been missing for twenty-four hours, instead of just a couple, like I thought. He mentions that Aidan was at the house but doesn't elaborate, and I can't muster the energy to ask questions or hear the lies Aidan had to tell my dad. I don't know how I'm going to explain the wreckage I'm sitting in, wreckage I created somehow. With my terror? It felt similar to when I yelled at the demon that attacked me outside Miss Mae's. I must've actually pushed that thing away somehow. And I did it again? But on steroids. There's something inside me that can . . . destroy an entire store.

"I'm pulling off the highway, sweetie," my dad says. "I think I'm here. I see a Taco Bell."

I drag myself off the ground and look out the window—part of it is missing glass, I realize. Headlights appear and a Mercedes pulls up, parks beside the building. My insides shake, seeing him emerge from the car as he looks around, his phone to his ear.

"Where are you, baby?" he asks.

"Inside."

He looks at the window and sees me. He rushes to the door, but when he tries to push it open, it hits against a fallen rack. He's trying to shove it hard to create enough space to squeeze through when I see something move in the parking lot out of the corner of my eye.

Charlie. It's Charlie, his copper hair reflecting the streetlights. He's walking toward my dad.

No. That's not Charlie. No. It's something *else*.

"Dad!" I yell. "Hurry!" I scramble from behind the counter, over another shelf, crunching over bags of chips and cookies. I have to get him away, away from the pretend Charlie. I try and push the shelf that's blocking the door but it's too heavy, it doesn't even budge.

I stand and put my palms to the glass. "Daddy, run!"

He stops trying to shove the door and turns to look where I'm gaping. He stumbles back, seeing his dead son, seeing the trick, and I know what he's feeling, the confusion, the pain, the doubt. The wishing.

"It's not Charlie, Daddy! Run!"

He steps back, obviously struck with terror.

"Stop!" I scream at the thing, seeing the predator in its eyes—those aren't Charlie's eyes. "Don't hurt him!"

The pretend Charlie stops three feet from my dad and looks at me. "Come to me or I will tear out the spine."

"Okay!" I cry. "Just, please, don't hurt him."

"No, Rebecca, run!" my father demands. "Don't listen—"

The pretend Charlie grabs him by the throat and its other hand comes up, covering my father's chest over his heart. Five dots of blood emerge where each fingertip is. "I shall rip this out in five seconds."

"No!" I scream. My mind becomes frantic, I have to get out! I search the space, looking for an escape and see the door into the mechanic's garage. I lunge for it, feeling nothing but the need to get to them, no pain in my feet or my neck. I'm all focus as I stumble into the closed-up garage, then find the exit in the back, burst out into the morning air, run along the building to the front, and cry out, "I'm here! I'm right here, please stop!"

The fake Charlie shoves my dad to the ground with a hard thrust. He hits with a sharp release of breath, and I hear a *crack* as his arm bends awkwardly. My dad shouts in pain and cradles the arm to his chest.

"Come," the thing that looks like Charlie orders, motioning me closer.

"No, Rebecca," my dad groans.

I kneel at his side and kiss him, hug him, feeling lost, knowing I'm trapped. I swallow my tears and stand, pulling away from his arms when he won't release me. "I'm okay," I lie to him. I've gotten too good at it, I almost sound like I mean it.

The fake Charlie tries to grin, and I want to cower in fear at the sight of it. "You will see her again," it says to my father. "She will be a work of art, carved to perfection."

My knees weaken and the world tilts but I manage to stay on my feet.

And then I let the pretend Charlie take my wrist and lead me away from my father's frantic voice calling my name.

FORTY-FIVE

Rebecca

As soon as the fake Charlie reaches the line of trees, I consider running, but it turns as if it senses my urge and holds out a hand to me again.

I step back and shake my head. I shook its grip loose as soon as I could. The chill of rough, scaly skin against my wrist was more than I could handle on top of everything else. I know I'm going to die, I know a part of what it wants to do to me, but the thought of touching the claws, set to rip me apart, makes my head spin.

"You must touch me if we are to travel."

I blink at it. "Where are we going?"

"My queen wishes for you to give something back, and then we will discover what we may do together, for she has promised me your flesh before your full transition will occur."

My skin crawls and my stomach rises. Oh, God, what does it mean?

"Come," it says, its voice becoming low and dangerous. "Your will is mine now, Fire Child."

The assurance in its tone almost makes me believe I have no choice. But I can't give up just yet. "I haven't taken anything from anyone. What is it you need back?"

It steps forward, grabbing me by the arm, and I see the features of my brother loom over me, scarred with the rage and darkness of the monster underneath. "You will obey."

And then my body is ripping in half.

I scream, but no sound comes from inside me because there is no *me* anymore.

When I find myself again, I'm falling, crashing to my knees, my stomach emptying as my body remembers itself. I gasp and gag and feel like I just died a hundred horrifying deaths.

"Stand," comes the voice of my tormentor. What did it do to me, why doesn't it just kill me? "You will not be weak."

Like hell I won't. I blink at the blurry ground, trying to get my eyes to work. Either I'm crying or I'm going blind, I can't see. It looks like grass underneath me.

A scaly palm slides over my skin and grabs me, then yanks me to my feet, nearly pulling my arm from its socket.

I whimper and look around, more things coming clear. We're not at the line of trees anymore. Somehow we're in the spot where I woke up, in the forest, standing beside the tree that has my handprints embedded in the bark with that odd symbol.

"Why are we here?"

The fake Charlie ignores my question and shoves me at the tree. "Open."

"I . . . I don't know what you mean."

It growls low in its throat. "Open."

What's it talking about? Open a tree—how do I open a tree?

It takes my wrist in its fist and holds my hand out in front of me, showing me my wounded palm. "Open. Now." And then it points to one of the handprints burned into the trunk.

I just have to put my hand back on the tree?

I stare at the markings and then look over at fake Charlie. I'm positive now, this is the thing that killed him, that drowned him, and it's wearing his skin. It's so wrong. I want to rip the mask away and make the creature beneath suffer. I definitely don't want to blindly do what it asks.

It must feel me contemplating rebellion because it says, "Your father is not far from my grasp, Fire Child. I can return with his head if you wish, for encouragement." It leans in, putting my brother's face only an inch from mine. The putrid smell of its breath swells around my head, choking me as it runs something sharp over my cheek. "Then I shall begin to cut away this soft pink flesh, inch by inch, peeling it from muscle and tendon as you scream for me to stop."

My pulse roars in my ears.

"What would you choose, if given the grace?" it asks. It nearly touches its lips to mine. "Obedience or agony?" Then its head moves back to look me in the eyes, watching for an answer.

I shiver and stare right back, forcing myself to look, trying to see past my brother's familiar features to the truth of what this thing is. And as I focus, begging for things to come clear, its eyes seem to become larger, changing shape and turning oily black. Its nose becomes sharp at the tip, and thorns emerge from its widening jaw, teeth lengthening to a point as the head grows, thick horns sprouting out. And I see it, a seven-foot beast, a creature from nightmares, cloven feet, claws as large as my head still gripping my arm.

I curl my raw toes into the grass beneath me to keep from sinking to the ground. There is no choice in this moment of truth, where I finally see the face of what's been haunting me, chasing me. It's ready to do whatever it needs to do to force my will.

But I *can't* do what it says. Even though I don't want to suffer, and I don't want my dad to die. Because once I've done what it asks, what then? It's not as if it will just release me to live my life. It's been promised my flesh. And it's going to take it.

"I won't do anything for you," I say, my voice hollow.

Its beastly features twist, and I'm so relieved that it's not wearing Charlie's face anymore that I barely register fear.

"You shall obey," it says. It grips my arm tight enough to crack the bone beneath, and the pressure inside me rises, the twinge rushing behind my eyes.

The beast releases me suddenly and I stumble back, the pain in my arm growing as the blood starts flowing again. "I can't," I say through stuttering breath. "I won't." And I know with everything in me that's the truth. I won't do it.

The demon's large eyes seem to search me, like it's seeing a part of me that I can't. "You are stubborn. Powerful." It growls low in its chest. "Very well. The queen will have to find another way to retrieve her property." It moves to the side, beginning to slowly pace like a lion. "And so, we must finish this dance." It licks thin lips. "It is what I've waited for. What I have longed to take hold of. So much that the jaw aches, teeth hungry with need. Because you are to be mine, little witch. So lovely, so pure of heart, and I have been gifted the chance to devour pieces of you." With each word, its triumph seems to grow until I imagine that I can feel its elation stinging my skin.

I shake my head, stepping back.

"Yesss," it says with a hiss. And its demonic form widens even more, muscles thickening, jaw opening to bare its fangs. "Mine." Then it huffs out a smoky breath from its nose.

And lunges.

I barely escape its grip as I dodge to the side, then slip on the grass, falling to my hands and knees. I'm crawling, scrambling into a standing position again so I can run, but the ground shakes as it stomps closer, making me falter.

It grabs my ankle. And yanks.

I flop to my stomach again, head bouncing off the ground as it slides me across the grass, the pull lifting my shirt, baring my back. A cloven hoof presses into my shoulder blade, crushing the breath from my lungs. The air around me rumbles with the demon's satisfaction.

And a talon scrapes a trail from the back of my neck down my spine, forcing a scream from my lips as its cold sting sears my skin.

"Delicious," it purrs.

"Fuck you," I say, my skin burning, adrenaline filling my limbs in a panicked rush as I realize how trapped I am. The horror crashes down on me as I wait for the first deep slice, the first jarring agony to fall.

The beast laughs. "Ah, my witch, you will see. Soon I shall be your master and your power will belong to the queen. Then you will beg to feel my claws rake your skin."

I squeeze my eyes shut and block out its words. Whatever it means, I'm not going to let it happen. I'm going to be sure I'm not alive to feel it, to see any of it come to pass. Somehow, I need to make the beast kill me. I won't just sit by and let it torment me. I force myself to struggle, to twist my body, even as the edge of its hoof digs deeper into my back and presses me harder into the ground. I scream into the dirt and tug at the grass. I writhe and kick and force it to crush me.

"I have an eternity to twist your soul, to tame you for her." The pressure on my spine lifts. My ankle is gripped, and the beast yanks my legs again. "Fight as much as you'd like."

I gasp, trying to catch my breath, and as I stare at where I was lying a second ago, a part of me goes still. Pink flowers speckle the ground in the shape of my body. Flowers. Flowers that weren't there before. Did I do that somehow? Like Aidan's mom made the white flowers grow?

I focus inside myself again, searching for the power that tossed the man across the room, hoping those flowers mean something, maybe that I'm not as helpless as I feel. How could I be helpless if I destroyed an entire convenience store?

It was when I closed my eyes and thought of nothingness that I channeled the drawing, and that same feeling of dark nothing captured me just before I caused the tornado in the store.

I go still, not fighting the demon's grip on my ankles, even as I feel something tie them together. "I will take you to her soon," the beast is saying. "She can assist me in tearing away your humanity. I think the little witch would like that." It places a knee on either side of my hips, straddling my back, then grips my wrists, yanking them above me, and begins tying them as well. "Perhaps then you will see her cause is just. Perhaps you will assist her in other things."

I close my eyes and search for it, my empty dark place, where I feel nothing, no pain, no terror, nothing . . .

My surroundings fall away. I let the emptiness rise in front of me and fill my mind. I float in the stillness of it as it spreads, as I breathe it in and let it envelop me.

Save me, I plead. *Or consume me. Just don't allow this thing to have me.* And I wonder who my heart is begging for help from, even as I feel my answer rise.

Like a lullaby it sings over me in a hundred sounds; birdsong, the wind stirring the leaves, the rushing tide. *Receive a new anointing, child of Earth. The years the locusts have stolen will be returned to you; the Seed of Eve will follow your line, as it was meant to. Do not fear your future any longer.*

In a wash of white light, the nothingness becomes everything inside of me, my sight full of its shimmer, my head full of its rosy scent, and my mind engulfed in its peaceful presence.

Just breathe, it says. *And hear the songs of salvation.*

And the white expanse reveals an entire universe within me, as if it cracked open my insides and there was so much power there, it took up an entire sky. And I know its message, what it's trying to convey, without any explanation needed. I understand.

When I open my eyes, I'm no longer on the ground. I'm dangling over the grass. Hanging from the tree by my bound wrists. The ache in my shoulders surfaces first, then the pain in my chest and my back. I gasp in air, but my lungs are too constricted to breathe right.

"I am glad to see you return," says the demon. It stands a few feet from me, a large form surrounded by night, almost blending into the shadows. "I thought that I had broken you already and was disappointed. Perhaps I have been . . . overzealous. It has been a very long journey to this moment." It steps closer, baring its teeth at me.

I try to kick it away but am reminded my ankles are tied together. I still feel the light lingering inside me. And as the demon closes the distance between us that light seems to pulse a little brighter.

The demon's wide brow creases. "What has happened? Your energy . . . it's changed. More . . . focused."

I say through my teeth, "One step closer and I'll show you." Brave words because I have no idea how I'll end this thing, no matter how true the threat feels inside me.

The words must feel true to the creature, too, because it pauses and looks me over more closely. "Something . . . is shifting in your soul. What have you promised, witch? What spirit have you contacted?"

I only stare back at it, the familiar twinge behind my eyes surfaces again.

It growls deep in its chest. "You are mine."

I shake my head. The twinge in my brow becomes a rush of heat, spreading down my neck into my chest and stomach.

"Who, then?!" Its voice becomes a roar. "I will destroy it! I will destroy you for your folly!" And it steps closer, talons raised to strike.

My insides crack open again. But this time I see the strange colors of my power emerge from inside me with my eyes wide open. I feel it in every molecule that hums with the push of its force. A wash of green and gold and pink pours from the center of my chest, reaching out in curls of light like a blossom made of energy and heat. It slithers up my arms in a rush, at the same time spilling down my legs to the ground.

I sense everything above and below me come aware, as if it's waking from a slumber, raising its focus. To me.

The branch holding me creaks. The ground three feet under my toes groans.

And then I watch as a root bursts from the grass, slides into my bonds, cutting them, at the same time a branch grows above me, slicing through the ties holding my wrists.

I fall to the ground with a huff of air, but the energy that's flowing from inside me has me rising to my feet again, facing the demon. Hunger.

Its rage stings my skin as it towers over me, snarling like a cornered dog, shoving its putrid breath at me. But it doesn't attack. I'm stunned, because some part of me wishes it would.

I hear words in the back of my mind, stirring in my throat. I know I'm supposed to speak them. And I'm supposed to create my spell, just like the one I drew without thinking. I let my feet take me, knowing my instinct will guide me.

I begin walking around the beast. One circle, then two, as I let the words escape from my throat, a lyrical chanting in another language, as I go round and round the creature that wants my soul.

It seems stunned, trapped. It doesn't try to escape or move.

Once I've walked the circle three times, I stop and face the thing that killed my innocence. This is the creature that tore my brother from me, tried to steal my sanity. I focus my energy on it, sensing the air around me move. "No more," I whisper. "You've caused enough pain."

The green and gold light still pulses from my chest with each beat of my heart. But now it seems to choose a direction. It spills down my legs and seeps over the grass, like water. It follows the path of the circle I made, then reaches in, closer to the beast.

Hunger moves, frantically trying to escape the light as it closes in, but it can't leave the circle I've created. "You cannot destroy me. I am always here. Always."

The ground shifts, cracking open with a burst of roots, tentacles of life uncoiling, reaching out, wrapping around scale and spike, grabbing horns and talons in a fury of movement, pulling the demon down to its knees, then its back, forcing it to submit. And then it yanks with a crack of bone. It tears leather skin as it tugs down, wrenching limbs from each other. Screams of agony and rage billow from the demon's chest, but the life merely coils around its head, gagging it as roots slither down its throat.

And then the earth shifts again, opening its arms to the beast. With one last jerk it pulls the demon beneath the dark soil before the ground closes over its head. The grass regrows across the healing ground in a swirling pattern of green. Until all that remains is the circle.

With three pink blossoms in the center.

FORTY-SIX

Aidan

Stillness. Peace.

I sigh deep in my chest and keep my eyes closed, letting the smell of tranquil air seep through me. It's so lovely. So right. I don't remember ever feeling like this before. I drift in it for days, for months . . . maybe years . . . before I open my eyes. I slowly allow the light into me, each sliver of gold piercing my vision, blinding me for a second before the vast expanse appears above me.

The night sky. It's not the same, though, not like it was so long ago. Now it's clustered with blue and green stars, a twinkling array of light. It's close, so close that I can almost touch it. I reach out a tentative hand and feel the heat on my palm.

I know I'm dead. It's an awareness inside me. But I don't really . . . care. I also know that I'm not in any kind of afterlife. I'm in that between place before I move on: not here, not there, not alive, not dead. I am nothing. I've been here before. I've hated this place. But this time seems different. It seems right and good and meant to be.

I know I should be fighting, that I should try to get back, like I have before. But for now I just want to rest.

And I want to watch the sky.

"I've broken it all," I say to the stars. "I should just move on and leave things alone."

The stars blink in answer, but I don't know what they're trying to say.

"What happened?" asks a voice beside me.

I sit up slowly and realize I'm inside the house. The roof is missing. I turn to the voice and see the blogger, kneeling beside the kitchen table, looking down at something on the floor. His body.

He turns to me, confusion clouding his features. "Who are you?"

I wish that I could forget the answer to that question. "Don't worry," I say, looking around at the frozen world. "I can send you back to your—" I stop, realizing my body isn't beside me in the entryway where I thought I fell. I look around the room and memories come back to me like fists to the gut. Chaos reigned last time I was in this space. Death was master here. But everyone's gone now. Connor's body. Finger. It's a charred space, half the floor missing to my left, with flames frozen in a trail up the staircase, along the living room ceiling.

I stand, panic sparking. I came here to save them. But where are they?

"Connor!" I yell, but the sound of my voice muffles as it leaves my mouth. I turn to the blogger again. "Did you see anyone else? Was there anyone else here?" The fire hasn't touched much of the kitchen in this frozen moment, but the living room and the entry are blackened and grey, the place where Finger's body was lying, where Connor was beside him, it's completely consumed.

The blogger looks down at his body then up at me again. "I don't know. I think so. I remember someone singing."

I walk past him and open the back door. But I freeze, unable to move outside. There's no yard. The sky greets me, the same stars above me, now in front of me and below, as if the burnt-out house floats in a void.

"I don't like this place," the blogger says.

I shut the door slowly, trying to think. "Me neither." Am I stuck here? Have I stayed too long? I move to the side of the dead man and kneel by his body. His throat is cut open, a thick slice that gapes on the side where his artery is. Blood soaks his band T-shirt, his cargo shorts, and pools around him in thick splotches. I'd be surprised if he had any left inside his body.

"You should've already crossed over by now," I say. "But since your body's still here, I can send your spirit back. Do you want to go?"

"Send me back?"

"But I need something from you."

He moves away a little. "What?"

"I'm going to need you to focus. Focus on me, on my face, on this moment." I reach out and my ghost hand meets the center of his translucent chest. "When you wake up, I need you to remember everything. All of it, the magic, the feeling of being dead, and the feeling of resurrection. Can you do that for me?"

A frown creases his brow. "Resurrection?"

"Just say you'll remember."

"I will," he says, hesitantly. "I'll remember."

I remove my hand from his chest. "Do you understand why people can't know? This isn't something they can understand, and it's worth more than a few hits on a blog."

He nods.

"What's your name?" I ask.

"Daxter." But he says it like a question. And then, more sure, he says, "Daxter Jonas Banks. But my friends call me DJ."

"Okay, DJ, don't be afraid." I reach out to his dead body and touch his temple, then look back up at him. "Can you feel that?"

His eyes have gone wide and he nods, reaching up to touch the same spot with his ghost hand.

I keep my fingers on his temple and focus my energy on my mark, on my power, finding it easily, the flames instantly sliding from my ghost chest and down my arm. In this place it seems I don't have any confusion or trouble controlling my abilities.

"Just try not to stalk me anymore, okay?" I say. Then I push my fire into the skin of the dead man and watch as a line from my mark slithers off my wrist, onto his face, trailing to wrap itself around his neck, over the gaping wound. His ghost disappears, the blood soaking back into him as the slice in his neck seals back together, healing in seconds. And in a flash of light his body's gone.

And I'm alone.

I stand again and look around, wondering what to do next. The sky above still blinks at me, stars pulsing, but no blue light appears like last time to slide across the sky and take me home. No power seems willing to send me back.

I return to the spot where I died and study the charred wood floor. I can still see a part of the large stain from my blood, along with the ash remains of a demon. Then I notice the shadow of crimson smears and drops trailing away. I follow them with my eyes, seeing they go into the kitchen and out the back door. Someone took my body outside. Logic says they took Connor and Finger, too. But there's no way to know for sure. I'm trapped. Am I dead for good this time?

Is this really how it ends?

It can't be. Connor's dead, Finger . . . and Rebecca's lost. What were all the warnings and talk of Lights and spells and—well, all of it—what was all of it meant to be about if this is how it ends?

You always ask this question, a voice says. I look to my right then my left, but I know I won't see anyone. The voice came from above me. It came from inside of me. It's a voice made of falling rain and thunder, vastness and power, but somehow it's a quiet stillness, the soft current of a river, at the same time. *I wonder at how quickly you forget my eyes upon you. Have patience, Little Flame.* It could be a rebuke, but the tone is gentle.

"I need to—how do I get back?"

Have you not asked the power within you to return you into the realm of gravity and time?

I'm not sure what it means. Ask my power?

The power within you is the same that created your world, the same that set the stars above you, a piece of eternity, and it was gifted to you. Not for your withholding, but for the purpose of my Will. Still, you choose to remain weak?

I look down at the mark on my arm, and the awareness of this voice, the truth of what—of *who*—it is, ripples through me. I should fall on my knees, hiding my face. I should beg for mercy. But there's no anger or disapproval in the presence. Merely concern and maybe a sliver of sorrow.

Something brushes gently at my shoulder, as if a hand is resting there. I turn to look but there's no one. I'm alone.

I cannot show you my face. So understand, I am not absent, I merely come to you in other ways.

My eyes are drawn back to the sky, my heart full of questions.

There will come a day when you will understand. Do not despise your very human mistakes, or feel remorse for following after what you thought was right.

"You're going to send me back." I don't say it as a question, because I feel the decision in the air around me.

I am.

"Is that really what you want? I'm not . . . I'm just breaking every-thing." I think of the nurse, of Lester. Of Connor and Finger, of Rebecca and so many others who have been lost because of me. Because I exist.

There's a pause in the presence, and the stars above me seem to shift. *Man cannot break what I have set in motion. In pain there is healing, in death there is life, all things are rebirth, a circle returning to its origin. All things will find balance. And in the end, peace will find you. I will always find you.*

The words soak into my skin, etching something secret and comforting into my bones. And I realize, I'm going to go back. I'm still stuck walking through the minefield my mistakes have created. "I came here to save my friends. Where are they?"

I know who you seek. One is here with me, and one has returned.

No. "Who? Who's with you? I was weak, I couldn't stop their deaths. But they can't die. Please. Not yet."

It will be their choice. I will ask them what they wish.

"But . . ."

That is all I can do. And if you seek answers, they will only come in the land of the dead. Not here. If you wish for me to take you forward to be with your friend, I will. But I see your heart. You would rather return and save the others. Your soul yearns to make it right. Allow it the journey.

I look up at the sky again, feeling torn, lost. The voice stirs something inside of me, it reminds me of the comfort of my mother's arms, the soothing rhythm of her voice as she sang Ava to sleep. It reminds me of home. And I crave it.

You have stayed too long with me, it says. *Your hold on earth is fading. But know that if you lose your grip on flesh again, your ability to return will be weakened even more. You may remain Between. Do you understand?*

"I won't be able to resurrect again if I die?"

No. And when you return in a moment, time will have passed. Powers will have shifted. Whatever comes to pass, allow your heart to settle into living once the tide of Darkness fades back into the shadows. The voice pauses and a thin curve of teal light begins to emerge in the dark sky. It pulses brighter, like it's following the beat of a heart as it moves closer, slinking across the expanse toward me. Something in me struggles, not wanting to leave yet, not wanting to have lost either of my friends.

Trust that it will be well. There are things I have not shown you yet. And soon your father will come to you again. I would ask you to be kind.

He has been struggling in his return to flesh. Remind him of my forgiveness. Remind him of the love I have for him.

I watch the beat of the glow as it widens, feeling it in my chest.

Perhaps this love can come from you.

The fluorescent sky is all around me now, the heat of it, the pulse of it, pressing in as it grows hotter and hotter. A scorching mass moving closer, enveloping me with its sharp sting of fire, pouring over me. Until all that remains is the blaze against my skin, sinking in with its pounding beat, heavy and forever. As it pushes through my lungs.

And I'm submerged in the fire of it, a cry of pain tearing from my chest.

FORTY-SEVEN

Rebecca

I'm numb as I walk back through the trees. I know my feet are torn to shreds, that my skin is tight with the chill settling inside me, but all I can focus on is finding my dad again. I have to keep moving.

I stumble, grabbing onto a tree for support, then I take a few deep breaths and continue walking. I have to keep . . . moving. So I take one more step, then another, ignoring my bleeding knees, ignoring my bruised wrists. Instead I think of how relieved my dad will be to see me, how amazing it will be to take a shower. I don't let my mind go to the man at the gas station. Or the fact that I trapped a demon in the ground with some magical ability to control nature.

Instead I picture Connor, the way he looks at me, and I promise the universe if I see him again, I'll only scold him a little for pushing me away, or maybe not at all. If I could just feel his arms around me, hear his voice . . .

"Rebecca!"

My name. Someone's calling my name. The sound travels through the trees, muffled by the soft ground and the surrounding brush.

"Rebecca!" Closer now.

I open my mouth to call back, to say where I am, but my voice won't work. I stumble again, stubbing my toe on a rock, falling to my hands and knees. More deep breaths, and then I find my way up, holding on to whatever I can reach for support.

"Rebecca!" Connor. I hear Connor.

Here! my mind screams. But it comes out of my mouth as barely a breath. *I'm right here.*

I slide down to the leaves, my leg muscles done holding me up, but I crawl for several feet before my arms won't hold me anymore, my eyes won't stay open, and I can't . . . keep . . . moving.

I collapse and curl into a ball, holding my legs pressed into me to keep warm. Feet crunch on the ground nearby, close, then closer. Then they stop.

"Rebecca!" Instead of a shout, it's a gasp this time. Then the sounds of scrambling and someone's beside me, lifting me off the ground. "Rebecca, can you hear me?" His voice sounds raspy and weak. Fingers press into my neck and a sigh of relief escapes him, then lips press to my forehead. "Thank God, oh, God." Am I dreaming?

You came, I say to him without words, so grateful. My Connor. He cradles me to his chest. He smells like salt and heat and I want to open my eyes but then the dream of him will leave me again. And I don't want to wake up.

———

"We should be taking her to the hospital," I hear my dream Connor say, his tone odd, like he has a cold. He lulled me into stillness until he set me down a moment ago, laying me on something that chilled my skin. It's so lovely to hear his voice, even if it is raspy and frustrated.

"I have a doctor who will come to us," a second voice says. It sounds like my dad. "The ER will take too long. Just drive to the house."

"What about your arm?"

"It'll have to stay broken tonight. I'll wrap it up for now, then I can go get it set once we're sure she's all right."

An engine revs and I feel myself moving even though I'm lying down. Where am I? It smells like coconut and seaweed. It doesn't make any sense. I chance a peek through my eyelashes to the back of a seat.

My head pounds the wider my eyes get, but I look up, see Connor's profile. There's something wrong with his neck, a bandage. But with him close, I couldn't care less how much my head aches. It wasn't a dream. And my dad! I sit up with a lurch, realizing he's in the passenger seat in front of me, but then my gut surges, and I lower my head with a groan.

My dad turns around and touches my arm, like he's making sure I'm real, too. "Rebecca, you're awake." He seems relieved, but then caution laces his tone. "Just relax, sweetie. Try to be still, all right?"

I consider a nod but it hurts too much.

"I grabbed a couple of waters at the gas station," Connor says to my dad. "Shoved them under your seat. She might be dehydrated."

My dad leans over and pulls out a bottle of water, then opens it before handing it to me. "Drink it slow."

I take it from him, sipping a little. As soon as it touches my dry lips, my skin seems to cry out for more, but I only drink a little before putting the lid back on and resting my head on the seat again. I hug the bottle to my chest, sighing in relief. Everything is a mess inside me right now, but the simple rocking of the Jeep, the sound of the road beneath us, and the feel of my two favorite people with me settles it all. I close my eyes again, drifting in the calm, until I'm falling back to sleep.

———

Someone's carrying me. I hear the sound of doors opening and closing just before familiar smells wrap around me, and I'm being set down on a soft surface. I open my eyes and see my purple duvet, then look up to

Connor, amazed again at his presence. He sets my water bottle on my nightstand and just stands there, staring down at me as I look up at him.

I motion to my neck while looking at his and manage to scratch out, "What happened?"

He just shakes his head.

My dad comes in the room, and Connor steps to the side, giving him space. Dad kneels beside the bed and puts his hand gently to my forehead. Then he kisses me, and I feel his tears on my cheek. "I'm so glad you're all right."

I give a little nod as he pulls away, but I can't seem to manage words yet. *Am* I all right? I don't know. I have so many questions, about what happened, about my dad and what he's thinking, what he saw. How is he so calm about it all?

He rises and pulls my blanket off the bottom of the bed, laying it over me, tucking it around my shoulders with his good hand. His other arm is bound against his chest, tied with a makeshift sling made from what looks like a linen kitchen towel. "Just rest for now. We'll clean you up later." Then he kisses my head again before he turns to Connor. "Will you sit with her while I make some phone calls?"

Connor gives a small nod and watches my dad walk from the room, his troubled look deepening as he faces me.

I reach out a hand to him.

He comes closer, taking my fingers in his. A part of me wonders if he's scared of me, if he knows what I can do somehow, but another part of me doesn't care. Because I want to forget all the tension from before and have him close right now. I scoot slowly over and pull him toward me, urging him onto the bed.

He pauses, taking his fingers away. "I can't Rebecca," he says. "Your father."

I part my dried lips. "Please."

His features crumble and he doesn't hesitate anymore. He lowers himself onto the bed beside me, settling a foot away, his back against the headboard. He reaches out and touches my shoulder gently. "I'm so glad you're okay." His voice sounds strained, like mine. Like it's hard for him to talk.

I want to ask him what happened again, why he has a bandage on his throat, but I'm just so relieved to be home, to be safe beside him. I tip my head toward his thigh and close my eyes, feeling his fingers slide across my shoulder, into my hair where they run through tangled strands, delicately pulling leaves and needles from them one at a time, until he's just touching my temple, the rough pad of his thumb brushing over my eyebrow.

My emotions stir with his gentle caress, all the terror and shock and pain of the last twenty-four hours welling up in a rush. Tears fill my throat but I don't want to show them, I don't want him to pull away. I just can't seem to stop it. It shakes my body, forcing me to curl tighter into a ball. I press my forehead into his thigh and try to hold it all in, try not to feel it.

Connor scoots down and pulls me closer, cradling me to his chest. He wraps his arms around me. He kisses my filthy hair as he whispers over me, "I'm here."

———

I'm almost asleep again when I hear my dad come back in the room. Connor has me cradled in the curve of his body, his strong arms holding me tight. Safe.

My dad comes around to the other side of the bed so I can see him, and I realize his features are shadowed. Connor is obviously asleep because he doesn't move at the sight of my dad—his breathing stays steady and soft against the back of my neck. After a second of staring my dad looks at the ground and starts to pace back and forth in front of my window seat.

I manage to find my voice a little easier this time, though it's barely a whisper. "Daddy."

He stops and turns, moving to the side of the bed. "Are you okay?"

I nod and reach out a hand to him, urging him to sit. "Don't worry. Are you okay?"

He takes my hand and sits as he shakes his head. "I thought I'd lost you, little girl." His thumb caresses my knuckles. "I don't know what I would've done."

"I'm so sorry."

"I should've been here. I didn't know . . . I was still letting myself get buried with work, I wasn't paying attention."

I don't know what he means, but I squeeze his hand, trying to comfort him. "It's going to be okay now."

He frowns and looks away. "I'm not sure."

My pulse stutters at his words. And I know he's hiding something from me.

Connor shifts behind me and his breath changes, then he goes still against me before slowly moving away as he sits up. "Sir, I'm sorry. I feel asleep."

My dad doesn't seem to be paying attention, though. His eyes are trained on the window, and he's obviously lost in thought. Just when I'm going to try and ask him what's wrong, he turns back and looks at me. "Let's get you cleaned up, sweetie. And some food. Do you know when you ate last?"

I shake my head, wishing he wouldn't glaze over things and pretend like he's not disturbed by something. Not now, not after everything.

"And you can stay, Connor," he adds.

Connor goes tense in response, like he's unsure how to respond.

"Rebecca would want you to," he says. Then he stands from the bed and releases my hand. "I'll go make sure the doctor's still on his way."

He leaves. I feel unsteady. Why is he acting so strange? I have trouble rising, so Connor helps me to my feet, then he supports me as I walk across the room to the bathroom, but I pause in the doorway, realizing I won't be able to take a shower. I can barely stand. The thought is depressing because I desperately want to get clean now that I'm more awake.

"Do you have a bathtub?" he asks.

"My dad's master does."

"Well, we'll just have to do that, then."

I don't miss the *we* in his statement, but I'm too tired to comment. I let him search my closet to find me something to change into, and then he leads me to my dad's room. We stagger into the large bathroom, and he sets my clothes on the counter, lays out a towel on the floor, then turns on the water to get hot. Once the water is steaming, he plugs the tub and pours soap in, creating pillows of white bubbles. He's keeping himself busy, not saying anything as I sit on the stool by the vanity, watching. I wonder why he hasn't gone to get my dad. Or why my dad has disappeared—not that I'd be more comfortable with him seeing me naked, but I'm sure he wouldn't be a fan of Connor helping me bathe.

Once the tub's full, Connor cuts off the water and turns to me. "Okay . . ." He studies me for a second, then averts his eyes. Now he seems to feel the awkwardness that he was ignoring before. "Maybe I should go get your dad for this part."

"Yeah." But I just want to get in the tub and wash off all this mess. As he starts to leave, I say, "Maybe if you just close your eyes."

He swallows hard, not moving.

I'm done waiting, so I grip the counter and try to get to my feet. I hiss in pain before I can stop myself—they're so raw.

Connor rushes to my side and leads me to the edge of the bathtub. I stand in front of him, both of us facing the water, and lift my arms. "Just close your eyes and pull up," I say.

And then I feel the fabric slide along my sides, but I don't check to see if he's following the other part of the directions. Once I've wrangled myself out of the crusty tank top and then slip off my bra, I lean back in exhaustion and Connor's hands go to my waist to hold me steady. I can't hide the sharp intake of breath at his touch on my bare skin. We both sway and I feel a little dizzy.

I look up at his face and see his eyes are still closed, but he looks very uncomfortable.

My body should be in too much pain to feel turned on right now, but his restraint, the feel of him fighting not to look, almost makes me forget the word *should* ever existed. Because I should be embarrassed to be naked in front of him. I should be mad at him for pushing me away. And I should shy from this intimate moment. But all the *should*s seem to have gone right out the window.

"I think I can just get in with the bottoms on," I manage to say. Because there's no way I can picture him helping with my shorts, and then my underwear, without it becoming excessively awkward, eyes closed or not.

He nods, a small bit of relief on his face now.

I hold on to his upper arm and step into the warm water. Instantly the ache in my foot becomes agony, forcing a gasp from my throat. But I just clench my jaw, grip him tighter, and get all the way in, sliding down so the bubbles cover my breasts.

Connor just stands there for a second, eyes still closed, forehead now cradled in his hand. "This is killing me. I can't be in here with you, Rebecca."

"It's okay," I say through my emerging tears. "It just hurts my feet and hands. But they have to get clean."

"I'm sorry," he says. "I'll just be out there." He points toward the bedroom, and then he opens his eyes, staring at the floor as he turns and walks back into the main room. He slides the bathroom door shut, leaving a small gap, then disappears from view.

FORTY-EIGHT

Rebecca

I grit my teeth, trying to ignore the pain as I pull my shorts and under-wear off in the water and set them on the side of the large tub. I study my hands and see the swelling has gone away almost entirely, even if they still hurt. I pick up the soap and begin scrubbing my arms, my chest, my knees, feeling like everything is caked in mud and blood and sweat. Next I start on my hair, washing out the bird nest it's become. After a few minutes in the water the sting in my feet dims, too, and my body relaxes a bit. Once I'm done with my hair, I rest my head on the back of the tub and close my eyes, letting the warmth soothe my aching muscles for a while.

When I feel like I've had enough, I pull myself up and grab the towel, wrapping it around my middle to cover myself, then I sit on the side of the tub.

"Can you help me out now?" I ask, hoping he's still close by. There's no way I'll make it out of this bathroom on my own. "I have a towel on," I add just in case.

The door slides open and Connor comes in, helping me into the room, settling me onto the ottoman at the foot of my dad's bed. "Is this okay?" he asks.

I nod and ask him to get me my clothes. He walks back into the bathroom and brings them to me, then turns around. "I'd leave but I . . ."

"It's okay, Connor." I pick up the sundress that he pulled out of my closet and manage to get it on over my head without too much trouble, then I somehow pull up my underwear while sitting on the edge of the seat without falling on the floor. Thankfully when I glance at Connor, he's still turned away like a gentleman. "Okay, I'm good," I say when I'm put together.

He turns back around, but instead of coming to sit by me, he stands there and shifts his feet. "I can go," he finally says. "If you want me to."

"Why would I want that?"

"Rebecca . . . I'm . . . I'm so sorry."

"What? Why?"

He starts to pace, running a hand through his hair. "I wasn't watching. I left you here and you were vulnerable, I should have—"

"Oh, please, you can't possibly—Connor, would you please just come sit down, for heaven's sake?"

He stops pacing and moves slowly to my side.

When he's settled next to me, I take his hand in mine. "I'm all right. It was . . ." I swallow. "It was terrifying. But I'm okay." I try to give him a smile, but my bones ache, my feet burn, and I'm exhausted. I sort of want to cry again.

He hesitates but then asks the one question I'm not sure I'm ready to answer. "What happened, Rebecca?"

I release a heavy sigh and just tell him in the simplest way I can. "I was possessed."

Heavy silence fills the room, but he doesn't move away. "A demon?"

I'm surprised by how calm he is at the idea of that horror. "No, not a demon, it was a ghost. The ghost of Aidan's mom. She said that she took over my body to protect me from the demon. And from Ava. But

I think when she went into me she also . . . I don't know, flipped some sort of switch on my power."

"Your *power*?"

"I sort of demolished a convenience store. With my mind."

Concern fills his features.

"I also . . ." God, how do I say this? I trapped a seven-foot demon, with fists the size of my head, in the ground with magical roots. No biggie. Instead I keep it simple. "I fought that demon, Hunger. And won."

He turns to face me, so he can look me in the eyes. "You have powers like Aidan."

"I don't think so."

"Yes, you're his balance. Like in the spell."

I shake my head. "I threw a three-hundred-pound man across a room with nothing but my brain, Connor."

He makes a face like he's impressed. "Nice."

"How are you not freaked out by that?" I ask, amazed at him.

"Because . . ." He shrugs. "It's you. The guy probably deserved it."

I laugh in surprise.

He takes my hand slowly in his and then brings our joined fingers to his lips, brushing a kiss over my knuckles.

My insides melt, and I'm reminded of how tired I am. "What happened to you, Connor? What's with the bandage?" I need to distract myself from wanting to kiss him. I'm not sure I'm ready for that right now. And I can tell he doesn't want to talk about whatever got him that bandage, which means he needs to.

He clears his throat and looks away. He sits there for several seconds, just staring at the floor, and I wonder if he's going to speak at all. He's suddenly tense, like he wants to bolt. Then he seems to steel himself. He releases my hand and reaches up to the bandage on his neck, pulling it off.

I gasp. A twisted scar runs down the front of his neck in a thick mass of flesh. It's pink and irritated. A wound that's healing. But that's not a wound you recover from.

Then I notice the smear of dried blood on his collarbone. My hands shake as I reach out and pull his shirt aside at the neck. More blood on his shoulder.

"I died," he says, sounding far away.

Died . . . he *died*? "Like dead, died?" I ask stupidly. It doesn't make sense. He's here.

"Something happened, and . . ." He shakes his head and then hunches over, rubbing his forehead with his palm. "Finger's dead." A small crack of pain breaks his voice and then the words spill out. "The demon ripped into him and he never came back—it fucking ripped his heart out. My God. It tore into me first, nearly got Kara. If Aidan hadn't—" Another shard of pain hits him and he chokes on his words.

My body goes numb, listening to him, realizing what he's saying.

"The house is ash," he continues. "It's gone. Everything Sid worked for, it's all burned to the fucking ground. And he's so sick—he's gasping for breath now like he's drowning."

My throat clenches. It's suddenly hard to breathe. "Wait. Aidan, is he . . . ?" But I can't ask that, I don't want to—

"He's dead," Connor whispers.

The small words hit me hard, knocking the air from my lungs. No. No, that's not possible. He can't be dead. I'd have felt it. I know I would have.

"His body is at the club," Connor says. "This guy that was stalking Aidan—some blogger—he got himself killed in the chaos, too, and then he came back to life, saying Aidan resurrected him. And I woke up healed somehow, so . . . we think he might still be able to come back. He's . . . he's died before. But it's never taken this long for him to wake up."

I don't know what to say, how to process it. "He'll come back. He's not gone." I say it with so much conviction I think Connor even believes it. I have to believe it, too.

"But Finger . . ." Connor shakes his head in misery.

I think of the silent boy, think of him being gone. And it feels as if a part of me went with him, far away.

Connor and I sit in silence and lean on each other as the weight of what was destroyed falls over us. He puts his arms around me and I curl into him. We both let the tears come then. We cry for the loss of a boy, for the loss of a home, and eventually we find ourselves lying side by side on the bed. As the tears ebb, I cling to him, realizing he almost left me. He was almost gone from me forever, just like Charlie. The idea shakes me to the core. I can't lose him. I can't.

"I need you," I say into the side of his neck.

He kisses the top of my head, his fingers combing through my damp hair. After a pause, he whispers, "I'm falling in love with you, Rebecca. And it's terrifying."

I grip his shirt and hold him even closer, knowing exactly how he feels.

FORTY-NINE

Rebecca

We're woken up by my dad when the doctor arrives. I sit up in the bed and Connor moves to the ottoman. My dad doesn't comment about how he found us. He seems so glad to have me home, I think he could've caught us naked and it wouldn't have bothered him at all, at this point.

The concierge doctor comes around the bed and kneels on the floor, then frowns at my feet for the next five minutes, asking a whole bunch of questions I'm not sure how to answer. Especially when he asks me where I went when I disappeared, because I have no clue. I just tell him I somehow ended up in Arrowhead, which makes him start looking in my eyes and asking questions about if I've ever lost time before, or forgotten how I got somewhere.

I look to my dad for some help in answering, but he's obviously very uncomfortable, his feet shifting nervously when the questions start, until he's eventually rubbing his left temple, which usually means he's beyond stressed. It looks like the doctor gave him a real brace for his wounded arm so that's good. Hopefully he'll go in for an X-ray as soon as I'm settled.

"I'll bandage your feet," the doctor finally says to me. "And I think you need a couple of stitches for that cut in your knee, but I'd like to schedule you for some more testing about the memory loss."

"What kind of tests?" I ask, even though I know they won't help answer his questions. I'm guessing ghosts don't leave evidence behind.

"An MRI, I think. And perhaps some psychological testing to determine—"

My dad stops him. "Thank you, that's enough. Just stitch her up, please, and I'll go get your check." And then he's walking out of the room, not even sparing any of us a glance.

Connor and I share a look.

"Let's bandage you up, then," the doctor says, seemingly fine with not digging deeper into my memory loss. He pulls out some white gauze, some tubes of medicine, and packages of several different sizes. Then he starts slathering clear goo on my soles, laying pads of cotton over them, then wrapping the gauze round and round.

It's when he gets to my knee that the nerves start buzzing under my skin. He doesn't look at me or speak, he just begins using Q-tips to clean out the cut and—ouch! Ah, man, it hurts.

Connor comes over and sits on the other side of the bed, taking my hand and letting me squeeze the life out of his fingers as the doctor sticks a needle into the cut several times, telling me it's going to help with the pain.

I release a tired laugh, but he doesn't seem to get the joke.

I'm just glad he's a quick stitcher, because we're done after only a few more minutes, the last bandage securely in place. I'm relieved that my hands have healed so quickly. Something tells me that's related to the magic that made the burns in the first place.

Once the doctor's done with everything, he gives me a lecture on dehydration and getting plenty of sleep, and hands me a bottle of pills, saying they're for the pain, just in case. Then he leaves, and Connor and

I are left alone again until my dad walks in five seconds later, going back to pacing the carpet without a word. He has an envelope in his hands.

I glance at Connor. "I think I need to talk to my dad. Can I come to the club later? Maybe I can see . . . maybe I can see Aidan?"

"Sure," he says, hesitantly. He stands from the bed but then lingers. "I can come back in a little while and drive you." He glances at my dad, but he's not paying attention. So Connor kisses my forehead softly. "I'll come back in an hour."

I nod and watch him go, knowing he'll probably just wait out front in his Jeep.

My dad still hasn't looked up from the floor.

"Are you all right?" I ask.

He lifts his gaze to mine and I see how tortured he is. My pulse speeds up.

He releases a shaky sigh and sits on the side of the bed. "I need to talk to you about something."

"What's wrong?" I ask.

This strange tingle of memory filters through me. I go cold, recognizing the look on his face. It's the same . . . the same as the day he told me about Charlie.

He sets the envelope that he's holding between us. My name is written on it in delicate curly script, *Rebecca Emery*.

"What's that?" I ask, but it sounds like the question came from someone else.

"I've been lying to you."

My gaze skips from the envelope back to him.

"I've been lying to myself, too. I hoped it would all just go away, that you would never have to know. But after what happened . . ." He swallows hard, shaking his head. "You need to understand."

"Dad, what—?"

"Just let me . . . let me speak. It's difficult. I've been pretending for so long."

"Okay," I say in a small voice. I feel like I'm suddenly six again and Charlie is telling me a story about how Dad found me in the backyard growing on a tree, that I was never born. It scared me to death, thinking my whole life of six years had been a lie. I was actually an orange, not a girl.

"Your mother, she . . ." He takes a shaky breath. "She didn't . . . leave us, she didn't leave you. Not by choice."

I stay perfectly still, letting the words sink in. But I have no idea what to do with them.

"She's been in a mental hospital for most of your life."

A small sound comes from deep inside my chest.

"Your brother never knew, either. I wanted to protect you both, to keep you from knowing what . . ." He chokes on his words. "She struggled with the choice. We both did. It was a very difficult time. I thought . . ."

A tear slips down his cheek and my stomach clenches. I want to squeeze his hand, to comfort him, but I can't move. And I don't understand any of it. How could he lie for so long?

He breathes deep, like he's running a marathon, and tries to continue. "She was sick—I thought she was sick. Even she believed she was." He shakes his head. "I was blind. I know that now."

"Where?" I ask, amazed my voice works with all the pain in my throat. "Where is she?"

He looks over at me, his eyes full of agony. "She died in Mercy Hospital a few months ago."

Dead. She's . . .

Months ago?

He whispers, "It was the week I told you I was going to Paris. I was actually in Connecticut, with her."

I suck in a breath.

"And when I got the call from the hospital here, saying you'd tried to cut your wrist . . . that you'd . . ." But he can't seem to say the rest.

He just looks at me with so much anguish that I feel like my insides are caving in.

We sit in silence for several seconds, maybe minutes. Questions roll through me, but the shock of it all won't let me form any coherent thoughts.

Then the words float from my mouth before I can tell they're even there. "I didn't try and kill myself."

He stares at me.

"A boy was possessed with a demon, and that's what tried to kill me." His mouth opens a little in shock, but he doesn't look doubtful so I keep going. "And the same demon that was after me is the one that killed Charlie."

And then he says the strangest thing I could've imagined. "Did Aidan destroy it?"

I'm not sure I heard his question right, but I answer, "No. I trapped it. How do you know about Aidan?" How does he know about any of this? And how is he not shocked about Charlie?

"Things happened when you were missing. Aidan, well, he saved me. And then seeing that thing that looked like Charlie take you away in the parking lot . . . it all became so clear, what you've been dealing with, what Aidan can do, what your mother . . . what she was seeing. It's all connected."

"Wait," I scoot closer to him, something like hope welling up inside of me. "So you know, about all the demons and how Aidan can fight them? You know about me?"

"I know some things, enough to open my eyes to your strange behavior. I had a gut feeling that something was off a few weeks ago, which is why I went back to the East Coast to visit your mother's family. That's when your grandmother gave me these." He touches the envelope with my name on it.

"You weren't working, you were visiting my grandmother?" I have a grandmother?

Wow, he's a really good liar. I never even suspected him of weaving so many tales. I guess now I know where I get it.

He ignores my question, saying, "The hospital gave these to your grandmother, saying your mother left them for you and Charlie. They're letters; she wrote them over the years, when she could—I never knew about them. And I haven't read them." He stares down at the envelope, touching the edge of it with his finger. "I never told her that Charlie . . . that he was gone. I didn't want to hurt her."

"What was wrong with her?" I dare to ask.

He releases a long breath. "The episodes came on suddenly when she became pregnant with you. She claimed she saw things, that these strange beings would come to her in her sleep, and she would hear voices when we went out. She didn't want to take medication because she was worried that it would hurt you, so she made me promise to restrain her if she became too upset, and she made it through the pregnancy. It was very rough on her physically, though, and when you were born, she nearly died. After the birth she seemed better, more herself again. But then the episodes came back, right around your third birthday. That's when she insisted on going home and seeing her mother's doctors. Not long after that, she was committed."

He rubs the back of his neck, looking agitated. "They wouldn't let me see her. It was wrong, I know it was, what they did to her. She should have been with me."

"I wish you would've told me." Maybe I could have met her. The idea of all those lost years, the lost moments I could have had—I could have at least met her and had one memory . . . it was all stolen from me.

"It was wrong of me to lie," he says. "I've been a fool for so long. Then you disappeared and Aidan helped me and . . . I just understood. It all became clear."

There are so many things to say, so much I need to tell him still, but I'm tired. "I need to think," I say. "And sleep." I want to sleep forever, to put all the mess of the last few days behind me. I want to understand how everything he said could be true. A part of me is relieved; it answers so many questions. But it raises a hundred more. I was blessed by an angel, and my mother was cursed.

"Please believe, I'm very sorry, Emery."

I lie back in the bed and pull the duvet over me, sinking into the mattress. "I know." I don't want to talk about it anymore.

"From now on I won't lie to you."

I close my eyes and wish I could promise the same.

FIFTY

Aidan

I sit up in a rush, gasping, coughing. Fiery air rakes through my lungs, burning in my chest. I try to open my eyes but I'm blinded by dark splotches. I hear movement, a chair scraping against carpet and footsteps running away.

"You've returned," a calm voice says. It's deep and steady, and completely unfamiliar.

I turn my head and squint at whoever spoke. The figure is a blur of light-brown clothes and dark hair. But as my vision begins to clear a wave of dizziness overtakes me, and I have to close my eyes again and sink back down to my elbows. It's like my body can't quite understand what to do.

Quick footsteps come closer and Jax's voice says, "Aw, shit, the bastard's back!" And then he laughs along with someone else. But the laughter ebbs quickly. "Oh, uh, no offense, man."

I open my eyes again to Jax and Raul. Jax is looking timidly at someone standing on the other side of the room. I'm in a bed. The warehouse apartment.

I focus on whoever made Jax get that uncomfortable look on his face. My muscles tense.

Daniel. My father is standing next to my bed. My deathbed. He stares at me with a steady look in his light-hazel eyes.

I stare back, my head spinning again. What is he doing here?

Holly comes through the bedroom door, pushing Jax and Raul out of the way. She falls on me, hugging me tight. "You big dummy! What took you so long?"

I pat her on the back a few times before she pulls away.

"Where's Kara?" I scratch from my throat.

"Right there," Raul says, pointing to my other side. I turn and realize Kara's right up against me, sleeping. She's tucked so well into the blankets I didn't see her.

Holly touches Kara's shoulder. "Hey, sleepyhead."

Kara turns her face up, stretching, dark circles around her eyes. She blinks and scrunches her face, like the small amount of light in the room is too much.

Holly nods toward me and Kara moves her head to look.

She makes a strangled sound in the back of her throat and covers her mouth with her hand, quick tears filling her bloodshot eyes. She gapes at me like she's having trouble believing what she's seeing. "Oh my God," she says, weeping openly now. Then she hits me in the arm just before she leans in, kissing me full on the mouth.

"Oh . . . kay!" Jax says, standing and walking out. "I'm gone."

"PDA overload," Holly says. "Seriously."

Raul releases a happy sigh. "So romantic."

She tastes like her tears, like salt and sadness. It reminds me how close I was to leaving her, and my heart clenches. I made it back, though. I'm here.

I grip her before I pull way, so she'll know how much I need to be close to her. I don't want to stop focusing on her, or let her go, but I'm all too aware of the man standing a few feet away on my right. I sit up and lean my back against the wall and encourage Kara to settle against my chest.

Then I look over to Daniel. Why is he here?

This is a man who hasn't had more than one conversation with me, a conversation where he warned me about my sister before he took off on some secret mission. And I haven't heard from him since. The words from my death keep ringing in my ears, the presence telling me to remind my father that he's loved. Looking at the ancient prophet, I can see he's worn and weary.

I rub Kara's arm and turn my attention back to her. I swallow, trying to soothe my dry throat. "Sorry I was gone so long."

She touches her finger to the large new scar on my sternum, staying silent. But I can smell her fear, her sorrow. I can't imagine what she was thinking, lying beside my dead body. Again.

"How long?" I ask.

"Six hours," Holly says.

Kara's fingers grip my side tighter.

That's a long time to be dead.

"It was horrible," Raul says. "When Jax dragged your body out of the house, your chest had a hole in it. We thought . . . because of Finger that—" but the pain spills from him and stops his words.

Finger.

"Did . . ." I can't seem to ask it. "Did he not . . . ?"

Holly and Raul shake their heads.

He's the one who stayed on the other side. My gut hurts, thinking of it. It's too much to let in.

"What about Connor?" I ask through the emerging pain.

"He came back almost immediately, even before DJ did," Holly says.

Connor's okay. Somehow he came back, just like the voice said. He chose to return. And he did it without me. "So the blogger's all right?"

Raul releases a small laugh. "He's a spaz, and he's fine."

"Cray to the sixth power," Holly adds. "But he's indebted to you. He told us he saw you in a dream and you brought him back from the dead. He has a creepy scar on his neck, so that'll be a good reminder of how much he doesn't wanna screw with your reputation anymore."

"Plus, he thinks you're dead," Raul says. "He saw your body, and I know he was itching to take a picture, but he didn't. I don't think."

I let the news soak in for a minute, relief about Connor and pain from knowing Finger's gone mixing in my blood. But then I remember. "Where's Sid?" His body, it was missing at the end.

They all look over at Daniel, and then Holly mumbles, "We'll let him explain. I still don't get it." She touches my shoulder. "But you need to rest. Raul made some tamales, so I hope you've got an appetite."

Raul smiles. "I'm discovering that I want to cook when I'm stressed."

Holly and Raul leave the room but Kara stays. And Daniel. He just stands there.

I study him, wondering why he's suddenly here in my life again, after trying so hard to stay away. His back is straight, shoulders square. The streetlights come in the window behind him, softening his edges and making him almost glow. He's wearing tan linen pants and a shirt that could be called a tunic, and he has a thin layer of dust on him, lightening his dark hair, as if he just crawled out of a cave, or the desert.

Kara shifts and pulls from my arms. "I'm gonna let you guys talk." She kisses me, then slides off the bed. She looks back several times as she leaves, like she's making sure I'm still awake.

"Why are you here?" I ask once she's slipped out.

Daniel turns away to look out the window. "I was pulled here by Ezra—your teacher, my student. I believe you call him Sid. I ignored his tug when it began, but then I felt the shift in the scales, and I knew you'd been cast down, so I came to your side."

Even though his words are vague, I know what he means. "You felt me die."

His head bows and he studies his hands. "I did."

"But I've died before since you've . . . come back, and you didn't show up."

"You fell very far today, Aidan. I lost all sight of you. I thought you wouldn't return. To be gone so long on the other side . . ."

I sit with his words for a minute, struggling to accept them. One, because even though I know it logically, it terrifies me to realize again how close I came to staying dead. And two, because it sounds like he's been keeping tabs on me. Which shouldn't surprise me, but it does. I assumed he'd decided to let me go.

"I was gone a long time," I say quietly.

"You were."

"And you came here to be sure I was all right?"

"I did." He seems embarrassed by it when the words come. "And I stayed for Ezra as well. I wished to say good-bye to my old friend."

"Why do you call Sid, Ezra?"

"I gave him the name Ezra when he was a boy and I took him under my wing."

"What happened to him? Where is he? He was there in the house and then he was just gone."

"He traveled to the spot where he knew he could pull me to him—a place you call the Devil's Gate Dam. There is a time doorway there. He thought I could help you if he was quick enough. But the single journey cost him much, and he needed to be close to the doorway to reach me . . . it tore away at him."

He teleported. "Is he . . . gone?" I swallow hard.

"Not yet," Daniel says. "But I am surprised he's still here. I think he was holding on in the hopes that you would return."

"I need to see him," I say, sliding off the bed and attempting to get my legs under me. It takes an amazing amount of energy just to stand, but with each deep breath I find myself more and more centered. This isn't like the last time when the bird demon killed me. There's a part of me not quite caught up with being in the land of the living again. A physical taxing I didn't have last time. Not fatigue, but . . . weight. As if gravity is a million times stronger.

Daniel comes around the bed and lets me lean on him as we walk to the door. His smell, the feel of his strong arm holding mine, fills me with sudden emotion. "I am glad you were able to find your way back," he says quietly as he leads me into the open area of the apartment.

I can only nod.

As we're passing through the living room, the front door opens, and Connor and Rebecca come in. They both freeze. And I stare back, a shock running through me when I see Connor's horrible scar.

"You're alive," Rebecca says quietly. She comes at me, grasping me in a hug tight enough to crush me. "I knew you wouldn't stay gone," she whispers into my shoulder.

"And you're here, too," I say, attempting to hug her back with my weak arms.

Connor takes me next and Daniel releases me, letting me lean on my friend.

"What happened, Connor?" I ask. "I couldn't find you when I crossed over. You weren't there."

He steps back a little and gives me a curious look. "I thought I heard your voice." He shakes his head like he's not sure. "I'm not positive what happened. I was in this place where everything was dark. I felt myself needing to find Rebecca. And then I was sitting up and choking on blood." He takes Rebecca's hand and she gives him a surprised look.

"You came back for me?" she asks.

"Of course," he says.

She moves to touch his arm, but then winces in pain, looking down at her feet. "I need to sit down."

He helps her to the chair, and I see her discomfort now, realize there are bandages all over her. "What happened to you, Rebecca?"

Connor gives me a look, like I shouldn't be asking so directly.

But she releases a tired sigh and leans back. "A lot." I can tell she's not willing to elaborate yet.

My thoughts stumble, and I realize I have no idea what's next. I have no clue what my sister is doing now that her master is gone. That single event could change so much. She could have run. She could be trying to find me. She could believe I'm dead for good now. I have no idea if we're out of danger or not.

Who am I kidding? We're not out of danger.

"If you wish to say good-bye, Aidan . . ." Daniel says, reminding me why I'm out of bed. He nods to the second bedroom. The others are in there already, like they feel it, too.

Connor helps Rebecca up and Daniel helps me, and I search for my waning courage as we all make our way to my mentor's side.

FIFTY-ONE

Aidan

I move slowly to the bed, the presence of death a fog of silver in the room. My heart hurts, looking at him. He's become a wraith, his body terrifyingly thin, his skin now grey, stretching over jutting bones. He blinks, and I see the white coating his irises. He's blind.

He looks around, like he heard me approaching. "You're okay, boy," he croaks out in Chaldean.

Kara's sitting beside him on the bed, and Holly is beside her, Raul and Jax are in the corner, like they're trying to hide.

Kara takes Sid's skeletal hand in hers and looks at me with an ocean of sorrow in her eyes.

"I am," I say, moving closer, despite my fear.

"Daniel, you see what a powerful young man he is," Sid says, sounding very proud even in his weakness.

"I do," Daniel responds in Chaldean. "You have done well, Ezra."

Sid grows a satisfied smile. "Yes. I think I have." He pulls in a difficult breath and then motions for me to take his hand. I obey and kneel beside the bed. "I wanted to save you," he says, this time in English, so everyone can understand. "All of you. I am sorry I failed in the end."

"You didn't fail," Kara says hurriedly.

He attempts to squeeze her hand. "Thank you, daughter."

Fresh tears spill down her cheeks, and she leans over him and kisses his forehead, whispering, "I love you."

We sit in silence, the only sound his labored breathing. Everyone seems to feel it, the way death is filling the room now. We stay close, all wanting him to know we're here. Even Daniel moves to the foot of the bed, touching his student in comfort. I make myself watch the end come, as the last breath leaves Sid's lungs. I watch his spirit coil into a ball of light and lift above his body, I make myself stay in the moment with him, and silently thank him. I thank him for saving my life. For giving me Kara. And for being the man who let me become who I am.

When he's gone, heavy sorrow fogs the air. We stay close, not ready to let go. It's a while before Connor moves the blanket to cover Sid's face. The sun is rising in the sky when we all step away, numbly moving into the living room, holding hands, looking silently into the past, into a future without our keeper. We huddle together like wounded animals. Like a family would. And as I see the others begin to look to me for comfort, and ask me what's next, I can almost feel Sid watching, giving me his look of *I told you so*.

———

A few hours later Daniel motions to me that he needs to leave. "Will you walk outside with me?" he asks.

I follow him out the door and down the stairs, then into the late-morning air.

"You seem . . . tired," I say. As I watch him, a piece of me that I hadn't known was there rises up inside me, like I'm a boy wishing his dad would save him, protect him from all the horror around him. It's a need that I know will never be realized, not with Daniel. Because this man is never going to be my father. But I chance the question anyway. "Where have you been?"

He studies my face like he knows what I'm feeling. "I cannot speak of these things with you. My role is not to be played out for many years. For now, I merely prepare. And wait."

"For what?"

"The end and the new beginning."

I swallow as the truth of his words sinks into me. "Because you're the Harbinger."

"One of many. Your sister is one as well."

"What does that even mean?"

"It means that I am here to prepare the way."

Wait, he said *years*. Does that mean my sister isn't going to end the world? "When does the end come? How?" *Is it my fault?* So many people have died because of me.

"You must understand now that all things are fluid," he says, like he's trying in some strange way to comfort me. "This is what I wanted to tell you, Fire Bringer. What was written *can* shift, as your existence attests. Though HaShem is unchanging, Humanity and its fate are not. Otherwise this world would have long since passed into dust. We are like children beginning to walk, only to take a step and fall, then we rise again and learn how to take the second step. This is what you have done. Grace carries you when you cannot carry yourself, and Hope presses at your back, urging you always forward. To save them." He motions to the warehouse. "To save her." And I know he means my sister.

The pain in my heart grows.

He moves closer, like he's trying to impress on me the importance of what he's saying. "Free will is both a curse and a gift. With one hand it creates, with the other hand it destroys. It is the reason you and I stand here in this place and time, today. It was my will to love your mother that created you. Your mother's will kept you alive. Sid's will to stay in this time is the reason he died, and he knew that would be the end result. In the end, his will to preserve your power also allowed for the making of your sister." He pauses. "And your will could save those you love. You are very powerful, Aidan. Not because of the fire within you, but because of the force of your love. You care deeply and sacrifice for those who most people would deem unworthy. With just the spirit of your will you have changed much."

His words swirl around in my head and I don't know where to put them. He's telling me it's not my fault. That free will brought us here. But still, the people I love keep getting hurt, and I can't see anything that I've changed for the better.

"I sense your disbelief," he says. "You cannot know what might have happened if you'd not been born, but I can. And those souls in that warehouse would be living in darkness—if you see nothing else in your existence, see that. Your sacrifices have been pure, Aidan. That will not go unnoticed."

"By who?"

He just looks at me as if he thinks I already know the answer to my question. Which I guess I do.

"When I was dead . . . a voice spoke to me about you," I say quietly, not sure why I'm telling him this. "When I was dead. A presence came to me and said you felt lost."

The thick wall he's got around himself cracks, and something flickers in his eyes that looks like surprise.

I think about the words he spoke to me the last time I saw him, how I should acquit my mom, let go of Ava. And forgive my father. But I'm not sure how.

"I feel that I am cast adrift in a storm without a rudder," he says under his breath. The vulnerability in his voice is jarring.

"Yes," I say, his words voicing my own burden.

Our eyes meet and an understanding passes between us, a connection of pain that makes my chest ache with longing.

"I would regret my actions," he says, still holding my gaze, "but I cannot imagine a world where I would regret you. I mourn the years we have not had together."

My eyes sting and my throat burns with his confession. I can only nod and try to hold it all tight, try not to let it take me over.

He looks into me for several seconds, like he wants to be sure I feel the truth of what he said. "Good-bye, Fire Bringer."

Panic hits me for a second, thinking I need to say more, that I need to ask him what's next. But as I study him, I realize he's given me everything I need already. He's given me understanding. I'll accept that and allow it to be enough.

"Good-bye," I say as he backs away.

He gives me a sad smile and then disappears with a pop of air, leaving me alone.

FIFTY-TWO

Aidan

I stand in the parking lot, staring at the asphalt where my father stood only minutes ago, and absently rub the green ribbon Selena gave me between my fingers. It's still tied to my wrist but now it's stained with blood. I can't decide whether to go back upstairs or not. I need to think, to process everything that's happened. I feel like I need to fix something, that I should be searching, but even if I went looking for my sister, I don't know what I'd do with her when I found her.

There's been so much death.

A click comes from behind me, and I turn to see Hanna coming out the warehouse door. And then I remember, we're still waiting to hear from Eric. By her disheveled look, I'd guess there's still no word.

"Aidan, you're all right." Sad relief fills her eyes as she comes to me, taking me in her arms. "Oh, thank heaven. I was so scared. When they brought you here—" She holds me tighter. "I was praying so hard." She squeezes my shoulder gently, then pulls back.

"Your face . . ." She touches my cheek and my hand reaches up, too. I feel a bump of flesh running from my temple to my chin. Then I remember the Heart-Keeper marking me with his talon.

"I'm okay," I say, trying to smile for her. Just one more scar to join the rest.

"But Finger . . . that poor boy." She shakes her head and looks away. "I'm having my guys take care of everything. We'll find him a place to rest."

"Thank you, Hanna."

"Of course."

"Sid is . . ." I clear the emotion from my throat. I feel like all I'm doing is crying. "We said good-bye a little bit ago."

"Yes, Rebecca told me. I have a bone box for him; it's what he wanted. Is Rebecca all right? The bruises on her wrists and arms, and her poor feet—should I call a doctor to come in?"

"I'm not sure."

The door squeaks behind us and we turn. Rebecca's limping from the warehouse, looking nervous.

"Sorry to interrupt," she says. "Can I talk to Aidan?"

"Certainly." Hanna takes me into a hug one more time, then kisses my cheek before she pulls away and goes back into the warehouse.

"Sorry, I just feel like I shouldn't wait anymore," Rebecca says, faltering a little in her steps. "I need to tell you what happened."

I go to her, seeing her obvious pain. "Let's go inside," I say. "You shouldn't be walking around like this."

"I'm fine," she says, not liking me fussing over her, but she takes my arm and lets me lead her to the bench in the alley where the club workers go for smoke breaks. She sits with a sigh, and looks down the alley to the street. "This sucks. I hate being helpless."

I wait for her thoughts to settle a little before I ask anything. But as I look over her bandaged knees and feet, the bruises on her arms and neck, urgency forces the question from me again. "What happened to you, Rebecca?"

"Your sister," she says, darkly, still watching the cars zip past the mouth of the alley. "She came to me with Hunger."

I start to ask what they did to her, but then I realize I'm not ready for that answer yet, so instead I ask, "Where did they take you?"

She shakes her head. "No, I ran. And . . . your mom helped me."

I stand and face her. "What?" I couldn't have heard that right.

"Your mom. Her ghost helped me escape them."

I blink at her, speechless.

"Remember how you said I can channel? She came into me and protected me from the demon. For a little while, anyway. That's why I was missing."

"Her spirit went into you?" If that's true, then . . . then she's not trapped in Sheol anymore. As the realization settles in, a weight I hadn't even realized I was carrying lifts off my shoulders. She saved Rebecca. Like she saved me.

"She was lovely, Aidan. And kind. She loves you very much."

My throat goes tight and I stare at the ground, nodding.

"And the demon, Hunger, is gone now. I trapped it."

I lift my gaze to her face. "How?"

"I knew what to do and I . . . I just did it." She looks at me like she can barely believe it herself.

I consider what that means. Could it be that Ava's truly alone now? Weakened? I start to pace a zigzag in front of Rebecca and she grabs my hand, stopping me.

"Stop thinking," she says. "Just take a breath, rest."

"I can't."

She pulls me closer to the bench and gives me a dramatic frown, ordering, "Sit."

I look down on her and feel her fresh energy. A part of her is inside of me now, a part of each of these souls I call friends is in me, making me whole again. I grip her hand back and start to move to sit—

Something shifts around us. The air shivers and my skin prickles with the energy.

"Aidan . . ." Rebecca says, voice wavering.

And I hear something. Behind us in the parking lot. Music filters softly in the air, rising in pitch as my heartbeat begins to thunder.

A violin.

Before I can move to grab Rebecca and run, before I can turn to see it, the sizzle of energy in the air pops, shaking the ground around us.

I stumble to the side, grabbing the bench for support. Wings rustle behind me. I'm gripped tight by the back of the neck. And yanked into a storm.

FIFTY-THREE

Aidan

I'm released from the torrent, falling into sand, then I thud into a rock.

All the air whooshes from my lungs.

Before I can catch my breath, I'm wrenched like a rag doll and tossed into a wall. Bones fracture, a rib gives way with a crunch as it hits.

Heaving breath fills my ears, echoing off every surface around me. Growls and tortured snarling. I squint my eyes open just in time to see a fist coming at me. Thorns protruding from the knuckles dig into my jaw as they hit, slicing through skin and tissue. Agony fills my face, my whole body pulsing with it.

"Enough!" a voice barks. "Tie him up before she returns."

I'm dragged sideways, sand scraping at my flank, then I'm pulled up, stone cutting into my back. My arm is tugged, stretched out, one wrist bound, then the other side, and the ankles, until I'm splayed like an X. My shirt is ripped from my chest. Muscles tear in my back and shoulders, forcing a cry from my gut.

And I don't understand. What just happened? I heard a violin, I was taken. But the thing kicking my ass isn't Ava.

A few seconds of torment pass with only the sound of shuffling. My refreshed power slinks over me, miraculously numbing me a little as it begins the healing process. I hiss and gasp air through my teeth, each tendon and torn bit in me resealing itself.

I blink back the fog in my head, the splotches of darkness speckling my vision.

And my surroundings come clear.

I'm in a cave, the beach cave, somehow held off the ground, bound to the wall across from the gateway. The uneven edges of stone dig into my back and wrists as I look around. And see my attacker.

It's Jaasi'el. But it's not Jaasi'el. The creature standing five feet in front of me is no angel of Heaven. Its massive wings fold behind it, a pale grey, just a shade lighter than its shadowed skin. The once-green vines growing over its arms and legs, creating gauntlets and shin guards, are black now, each thorn tipped with a silver glint. Its hair is no longer a thick bright red, instead it's thinned and gone totally white. Larger ears poke out on either side of its head, and its jaw is wider, teeth long and silver through its snarling lips.

It's the eyes that strike terror through me, though. They've become a strange molten ash color, as if they're embers in a dying fire. The remade creature stares at me through those eyes, so much hatred and viciousness coming off its eerie grey skin, I know it's dying to rip me to pieces.

A fallen angel, in all its glory and fury. Ava's father seems to now be her minion. I thought it was dead.

By the way this thing is looking at me, if it has its way, I definitely will be.

When I pull my eyes from the horror glaring at me and look around the cave, I see we're not alone. There's a man as large as a mountain standing guard on my right. A corporeal demon or a possessed human. He's bald and covered in tattoos, playing with a large knife, flicking it in his hand, over and over, like he's itching to use it. My only salvation is that my power is at its full strength right now, so whatever the thing is, it can only cause me pain. Unless I figure out a way to get my hands free to burn it to a crisp. It's keeping a safe distance, though.

I can tell the wounds on my face are almost healed, and my shoulders only ache now. The fallen archangel, Jaasi'el, watches my power pulse over my skin more in curiosity than trepidation. It's obviously not worried about the flames harming it.

I try and make my fire burn through the ropes, I struggle in my bonds, but it's all useless. I'm stuck tight.

"What am I doing here?" I ask.

The looming angel stares back, unmoving.

"Where's my sister?"

Its lip curls up in a snarl. "She comes."

And just as the words vibrate from its lips, the cave walls shiver, dust and tiny rocks rattle loose. The air breaks with the familiar sound of someone or some*thing* traveling. I close up my walls, trying desperately to block my mind in case she tries to link to me.

My sister appears just beside the altar to my left. Her feet settle gracefully, her hair drifts back down to her shoulders. She smiles at me like a hello, just as another form appears beside her, sand kicking up as the person falls forward and lands in a heap, red hair covering her face like a shroud.

My whole body jerks in my bonds. "Rebecca!"

She tries to get to her hands and knees before she heaves, throwing up into the sand, gasping and crying in pain. Fear grips me tight as the smell of her power hits the room. The green spills from her in rivers, sinking into the sandy floor beneath her, like it has no choice.

I turn to my sister, who's watching Rebecca with impatience.

She's Ava, but she's not. She's no longer the little girl who played in tide pools and loved the color purple. Her skin is white, with a web of silver and black veins showing through on her neck and half her face, down her right arm. Her eyes are so pale there's almost no more color at all. Her skin is filthy, coated in dirt and grime, the smell of her pungent. She's thinner, too, bones jutting from her shoulders, jaw sharp.

"Ava, what've you done?" I ask.

She sighs. "What I had to, Aidan. Sheesh."

"Leave Rebecca out of this. She's not a part of you and me."

She clucks her tongue. "Don't be silly. She's your soul mate. And now that I'm free from the Heart-Keeper, thanks to you and your humans, we're going to be a family." She tosses something to the ground. Pieces of wood. A broken violin. "But first I need her to learn some manners." The violin's neck is snapped, the strings the only thing holding it together. "No respect. Especially after all I've done for her. I even let her have that Hunger freak after our mom gave her the grimoire and locked it in a tree." She shakes her head like a disappointed parent.

She directs her words to Rebecca now. "Do you really think I didn't know what you'd be able to do? I knew you'd get that demon bound. I just wanted you to believe it. And now you realize how powerful you are."

"Shut up!" Rebecca screams.

"What a fuss," Ava says, then she turns to me. "She's so ungrateful. After everything I've done to help her. And did you know that our traitor of a mother went against me? That bitch, Fiona, chose the redhead instead of me to give her legacy to. The redhead!" Her features twist in a frightening scowl and her pupils dilate. "I'd rip Mother's head off if she had one." Then she bends over and screeches in Rebecca's face. "We're on the same side! We're the same!"

"The same what?!" Rebecca yells back.

"The same genetics, dummy, the same blood. Same. Not human, derp."

Ava's words jar through me and Rebecca just stares at her, dumbfounded. "What?"

Ava sighs in exasperation. "We're not *human*." She says the last word slowly like we're all dense.

Then Rebecca asks so quietly I can barely hear, "What are we?"

"The children of angels, obviously." When Rebecca just stares at her, shaking her head, Ava adds, "Okay, maybe I shouldn't say *we*. I'm way more powerful than you, obviously, but that's just because my father was so huge." She motions to the stone-like Jaasi'el. "Yours was . . . uh, not so much." She gives an apologetic smile. "He was what they call a Brethren. They kind of live in both worlds, unlike real angels. They're more like, um . . . faeries!" Her eyes brighten like she's happy with her description. "It means you're not human, though. Not really. And it's time you accept that."

A shadow passes over Rebecca's face. "I'm like you?"

My heart beats so hard in my chest I can barely breathe. What is Ava talking about?

"Don't listen to her, Rebecca," I say. "Look at me!"

Ava doesn't take her eyes off Rebecca. "I can teach you and we can rule together. We'd be unstoppable." She grins wickedly.

Rebecca doesn't move, she just stares at Ava and shivers. I smell her confusion, her distrust. But I can also tell from the look in her eyes that she believes every poisonous word coming from Ava's mouth.

"Leave her alone!" I yell.

Ava glances up at me. "Will you shut up? You're ruining the moment." And then she nods to Jaasi'el, who steps closer to me, its huge grey wings rustling in excitement.

I pull back but there's nowhere to go to get away. "Ava, stop. Please."

"No, Aidan. You may have freed me from that horrible creature, but you need to learn how to behave. Just like your soul mate." She nods to her father again, and Jaasi'el slowly reaches out a gauntlet-encased fist and places it on my chest. It presses in, the thorns at the knuckles digging. But only a little. I know it's waiting for something.

My power slides over my left arm, swirling around the seal on my chest with the beat of my heart. As the pulse speeds up, my stomach rises, my body shakes. And the angel watches with magma eyes.

It grins. Its fist heating, crushing more and more into my sternum, blood slicking my stomach now from the thorns. Then the vines begin to shift, to grow. They reach out from the wrist like tentacles.

Five sharp ends pierce my breast.

Hesitate.

And then slither like thorny snakes under my skin.

I cry out. Rebecca screams with me, like she can feel it, too, as the world goes black. My agony fills the air. My body jerks, sharp stones cut into my back. Burning, tearing, flesh giving way, pulling from the muscle. My voice rakes through my throat, turning it raw.

"All right, Father," Ava says, "that's enough." And the thorny snakes pull back, leaving my skin.

I choke, I gag, the pain so huge in me I can't see anything else.

"It's okay, Aidan," Ava's voice says through the fog. She places a gentle hand on my leg. "Just breathe. You'll heal in a minute."

"Please," I whimper.

"I need you to understand that you belong to me."

My skin begins healing as the words sink in. "What?"

"We're a family, Aidan." She comes closer like she's trying to make me see. "You're mine. It'll always be you and me against the world. I told you that."

I meet her eyes. "No," I say with more vigor than I thought I had. "You're evil. And you are *not* my sister."

She looks at me like I hit her. "How could you say that?" She takes a step back. "I didn't want to have to do this, you know." Then she says in a guttural voice, "Bring him in."

I turn my eyes to the cave entrance and see the bald guy with the knife walk out. Fresh panic fills me as I wonder what's next. And after several torturous seconds I hear feet shuffling through the sand, I smell sweat and pain.

And I watch as Eric stumbles into the room, shoved by the bald man.

"No . . ." My gut clenches, my heart breaks. *Eric . . .*

A thick metal ring circles his neck, cutting into his nape like a huge manacle. It has symbols etched into it, and I realize by their meaning that the brace has kept him captive, stopping him from using his powers to escape. His hands are bound behind him, chest bare and covered in dried blood, skin woven with marks that look like they were made by the same vines that tore into me. One of his eyes is swollen shut, and his lip is cut. He's broken, his spirit barely a spark in him now.

"No," I say again through my teeth, jerking against my bonds.

"Afraid so," Ava says. "Do you realize, I've had him three whole days and no one noticed? He was on some errand for you. About me, right?"

She motions to the bald man. He's now carrying a five-foot-long sword in his fist and holding Eric by the back of the neck brace.

"Victor had some fun with your Eric. I'm training the human, you see. I think he's turning out well so far. Look how good he did on your guardian." She says the words with giddy satisfaction as the man smiles down on her, obviously her servant.

A human. Not a demon.

"Yes," Ava says, stepping closer to the man named Victor. "I know you're thinking a human is weak. But they can be just as vicious as any demon. And against you, they're perfect. To stop him you'd have to kill him. And we both know how mopey that makes you." She laughs like it's funny. "Always trying to save everyone, but people sure do drop like flies around you, don't they?"

She motions to Victor, and he shoves Eric to his knees with barely any force. The sword in his hand reflects the low light in the cave, he holds it out like an offering to Ava, and she mutters something under her breath, then touches the blade with her dirt-caked fingertips. The silver metal coats in blue flame. The light flickers over the walls and plays in Eric's eyes as he stares down at it, then he looks up at me and seems to be silently accepting his fate.

"Don't, Ava," I say, my voice barely audible.

Victor positions himself behind the kneeling angel. Readying the blazing sword. His eyes fill with greed. A hunger for more power, for more blood.

"Please." Helplessness washes through me again. I can't watch another friend die. I just can't. "No."

"I don't want to do this," Ava says, "trust me. I'd love it if you would just give yourself to me and promise we could be a family again. But I know you, Aidan. You're too pure and righteous. I'll need to bloody you up quite a bit to be sure you feel the force behind what you are. Because we don't belong to this world. It shouldn't matter if people around us die. We're above them, we're better."

"I'll do whatever you want." I look over at her, trying to plead with our connection, to make that bond mean something again. "Just don't hurt him, please."

She sighs, sounding tired. "Oh, Aidan. I wish that I could believe you. I don't think you want to be with me for reals yet. And Eric here is in the way. He's between us."

"Love doesn't work this way," I say.

She scoffs. "Love, what a silly idea. I want dedication, loyalty."

"Not if you do this. I'll never be with you. Never."

She looks over to Eric and seems to consider. "I'm not sure that's true." She shrugs.

And Victor steps back. Then thrusts the sword through Eric's back. My lungs freeze.

Flames burst from the center of Eric's chest. His mouth gapes, eyes wide in shock. Before the blue tongues spread out, coat his body. And eat him alive.

"No, no, no!" I cry.

Eric is gone. The only thing left of him is flying ash the color of the sea.

FIFTY-FOUR

Rebecca

The sound of Aidan's cries pound at my head, begging me to act.

I stare through my hair at the grains of sand under me, unable to comprehend it all. I can't watch, I can't allow my heart to feel it, can't let it all be true. The death, the lies. I am stone. I am stone. I am . . .

Not human.

But Aidan's agony presses into my skin, not letting me hide. It's begging me to do something. Pleading for an end to the misery.

"There," Ava says to Aidan. "Now you're free of Heaven's thumb. You can do whatever you want."

"What did you do?" Aidan spits. "How could you? Eric . . ." Sobs wrack his body, shaking it against the rock wall at his back.

I look for my magic, searching inside myself, but all I feel is Aidan's pain. Could I have used too much trapping the demon, Hunger? I have to stop this somehow, I can't just sit here.

She killed him, she killed Eric . . .

Ava smiles like she didn't hear Aidan's protests. "Listen, we'll start slow. Once you've been blooded and are safely at my side, you can keep your humans—you know, since the house burned down, and all. I promise not to try and kill them anymore. And we'll only play games every once in a while. You'll like it! You can help me tame some of the demons—you have no idea how annoying they can be."

She's freaking crazy.

"Just stop," Aidan says, all the fight gone from him.

Her voice turns sinister. "There's more I can take from you, you know. You love a *lot* of people."

He goes still and stares at her. He swallows and seems to consider, eyes full of fear. "What do I have to do?"

Ava smiles.

She moves to take Victor by the wrist and pulls him over to stand in front of Aidan, then asks the bald man to kneel. He obeys without question.

"Jaasi'el, cut my brother down from the wall," she says to the huge angel who's been silently watching from the shadows. The beast of a creature steps forward and yanks on Aidan's bonds, tearing him free.

Aidan falls to the ground in a heap, and Jaasi'el helps him into a standing position, holding him under the arm. I watch in dread when Aidan just stands there, defeated, not trying to fight. Could he really be that far gone?

"So, this is the final round of the game," Ava says. She nods to Jaasi'el again, and the angel creature pulls a dagger from its side, holding it out to Aidan.

Aidan just stares at it.

"You know what you have to do," Ava says to him, motioning to the man named Victor, who's kneeling reverently now. "Show me you understand. Make this right, Aidan. Balance the scales like you were born to do."

Aidan's bloodshot eyes move from his sister to the dagger. His jaw works, and I feel his heart struggling.

Ava gives me a sideways glance. "Watch this. It's going to be beautiful."

My pulse speeds up as Aidan takes the dagger with a limp hand. Jaasi'el lets go of his arm, stepping aside. After shifting on his feet for a second, Aidan steps closer to the kneeling killer, and I see the fury growing in his eyes.

His grip on the dagger's hilt tightens as he stares down at the man who destroyed his guardian angel.

And I know he's giving in. He's going to kill. And no matter how much I'd love to see the guy stop breathing, I can't let Aidan be the one to make that happen. It'll ruin him.

My magic sparks at the thought, the familiar prickles starting behind my eyes. And I feel the warmth of the green glow swirling to life inside me. I nearly sigh in relief, but I bite my tongue and make myself focus. I've had enough of the waiting.

I look over at Ava, watching to see if she notices when I let a little of the energy loose. She's too fixated on Aidan to see anything but her victory unfolding before her.

I release more of my magic and see it sparkle over my hands, down to the ground. It seems to have a will of its own as it leaves me, as if it *wants* to go to Ava and wrap her up like the demon Hunger. The magic brightens as it trails over the sandy cave floor to Ava's feet. It's heavy in me, growing even as it pours out. But I need it not to touch her yet, I need to hold it steady.

The green and gold threads become an extension of my senses, as if they're feelers. They sink into the sand and I know they're swiftly sliding up the walls of stone, inside them, looking for something that grows, a plant, a tree, anything to control. And as it finds them, it takes hold of the roots and leaves, infusing them with awareness.

Then it waits, wanting to act. Just like me. The stone around us groans.

Ava looks up at the ceiling, hearing it. But then she focuses back on Aidan. "It's all right," she says, like she's consoling him. "I know how it feels, but you don't have to fight it. You'll feel so much relief when it's done." She directs her attention to Victor, who is waiting calmly for the verdict. "Tell Aidan what you felt when you killed the guardian angel, Victor."

The man moves his gaze to Aidan's. "Ecstasy."

Aidan growls under his breath.

"And what else?" Ava asks.

"Bliss."

Aidan snarls and puts the dagger to the man's chin. My magic presses out, the stone around us creaking again.

"How many children have you killed?" Ava asks, her voice scraping at the air.

Victor answers without hesitation. "Three."

Aidan's breath falters. His eyes move to Ava.

But I can't wait to see what he'll decide, I release the magic and let it do what it wants.

FIFTY-FIVE

Aidan

The whole cave erupts, the walls exploding in a barrage of debris, spraying out from every angle.

I'm knocked aside as something scrapes across my chest, ripping into my skin. I collapse to the sandy floor, Ava pulled away. A creature's captured her, its groan mournful and terrifying.

The man, Victor, is pressed into the floor of the cave, Jaasi'el trapped against the wall, the beast holding them captive.

No, that's not a beast. It's . . . a tree. Tree roots. They wrap around Ava, pull her off the ground, like a boa constrictor preparing its meal. She's lifted above us, over the altar, struggling against her bonds. But they hold strong and only moan at her.

I look over to Rebecca as the shock hits me. I can sense her magic so heavy in the room it's a force of nature. Her face is pained, like she's tormented by what she's doing, but I feel her determination.

And her sorrow. Her confusion. It's coating the magic, directing it to kill.

"Rebecca!" I yell over the din of cracking stone.

She shakes her head like she knows what I'm going to say, but even I don't know.

Three seconds ago I was going to shove a dagger into a killer's skull. I was going to find solace in blood and retribution. But then my sister asked a question about children, how many the man had killed, and I knew. If she used him, knowing what a creature he was, she was the one who deserved to pay for his sin.

Because she orchestrated it all. She played the game that killed the nurse, that killed Finger. It was because of her that Connor, that Rebecca's father, were nearly lost.

She's the one who should meet justice. And now, Rebecca is giving it to her, and as I watch my sister dangle over the ground, strangling in the hold of the tree, I find relief that it's not my hands having to strike the killing blow.

But then I hear Ava, chanting a new spell, working her Darkness in smoky tendrils. With each word she grows stronger, silver and red mist filtering out around her body as the blood magic takes hold.

Her eyes go full white. Even as the root covers her mouth, I know it's too late.

The red and silver mist takes shape, threading through the air, swirling around the roots that hold her. The tendrils harden and stop moving. They groan in protest. *Crack.* Then shatter, shards of wood exploding into the cave.

Ava still hovers, looking so much like when I woke her it sends shivers over me. She casts away the last of the roots and directs her attention to Rebecca. "You," she hisses, her teeth elongating as she snarls her fury. Shadows paint her features in sharp edges, making her lips twist, her white eyes shimmer with silver. Her small fingers turn into claws, long talons that reflect the light. Her dirt-caked feet seep ash. And thorny vines begin to grow from her boney elbows, twisting and growing around her forearms to create black gauntlets.

I step back. She's not human. Not at all—I knew that. I knew she wasn't Ava, not my Ava. But . . .

I can't save her from this.

Rebecca stumbles, hitting the cave wall as the Ava creature fixates on her.

"I'll destroy you, little witch," Ava growls out through her mouthful of sharp teeth, her voice like shattering glass. "I'll destroy you and steal your power in the end."

Rebecca's repulsion and dread fills the cave like the smell of charred earth.

I'm shoved into the wall, the freed Jaasi'el trapping me in the same spot where it was held by the thick root only seconds ago. It locks me against the rock with an iron forearm pressing across my chest. Its fist comes at my head but I duck, and it crashes into the wall beside me, sending stone shards spraying. They slice into my neck and cheek. Dust from the ceiling above falls like sandy snow.

My power flares and bleeds from my skin in thick waves of light, but the angel barely seems to notice. It's not going to burn this twisted creature like I need it to.

Instead I focus on the massive chest in front of me and gather all my strength, pressing my head into the sternum.

And then I shove the power out through the top of my head with a cry of exertion.

The air pops and the fallen angel spasms, body stunned from the jolt of power. It releases me and tumbles back, like Goliath. I ram my body into the angel and do it again. And again. Until my skin stings and my muscles ache.

And the giant beast collapses to the sandy cave floor.

The Ava creature screams in rage from her perch on the altar, staring down at the limp body of her father.

She hisses air in and out through her teeth. And then she turns to me and seethes, spit and black ooze dripping from her mouth. "I'm going to tear your heart out," she says. But it's not a human voice that speaks. It's a nightmare.

Her white gaze trails over to Rebecca. "By ripping her to shreds."

Ava flies toward Rebecca and I lunge, tackling my sister from the side.

The two of us roll in a tangle, hitting the gateway with a thud. The air knocks from my lungs. Claws come at me, searing across my cheek, digging into my neck. Teeth sink into my nape.

I scream in pain and gasp, then pin her to the wall with my body. I scramble for the dagger strapped to my ankle. Find the hilt.

She snarls and squirms and tears my arms to shreds. Blood slicks us both.

I pull out the blade. Not able to think, to feel—all I see is red. As I turn the weapon in my hand instinctively.

And plunge it up, into her chin.

She settles . . .

The air stills.

Her arm twitches against mine.

A wave of anguish hits me. I slide the dagger free, and watch her features return to normal, watch her eyes clear of fog as they search blindly.

Her slack mouth moves as she tries to say my name, blood leaking from between her pale lips.

My walls fall as I look at her and I hear her whisper with her mind, *Why?*

Oh, God, I'm so sorry. My heart's stopped beating.

Her brow pinches as my fire touches her skin at the back of her head. *It hurts, Aidan.*

I know.

Her eyes glaze over, closing. *I want to go home now.*

I ache. I shatter. And I let go of my sister. I let my power take her. I watch it crawl over her shoulders, her chest, I watch it fill her. And I feel it pull the Darkness loose. It tugs all impurities free and captures her spirit, weaving it back into the right shape, even as the light threads gather into a ball of energy, as I say good-bye.

Her body stays whole, and my fire slips away, sinking back inside of me. I hold her, and my mind drifts as I rock, whispering a prayer for the dead as I shake, as I go numb, my tears falling on her upturned face.

My whole world becomes this moment. And I plead for my life to end, just so it won't be true. I'm so lost I don't hear the cracking until the wall in front of me is caving in.

I look up through the haze of my misery and watch the gateway begin to grow fissures, up and up from a spot on the floor.

I shift my foot and realize Ava's blood spilled into the sand and touched the doorway.

As the first shard of stone sucks into the vast expanse behind it, Rebecca yells my name.

The wind comes like a scream, whistling through the breach, swallowing her voice as she tries to tell me to move. She's tugging on my shoulder, trying to force me.

But I'm stone, holding my sister. Watching the world end again.

I smell Rebecca's energy before I see the green light come at me, pushing me sideways away from Ava's body. I grip the edge of the altar and try to decide if I should get up or just stay here on the floor of my mother's secret cave forever. The sorrow in me is a weight in my bones, dragging me down to the bottom of the ocean. And I just want to let it drown me.

"Aidan!" Rebecca's in my face now, shaking me. "Snap out of it, please! This is bad, very bad. I can feel it. You have to get up!"

I reach out to her, running a bloody finger over her cheek. "I'm sorry."

"Come back to me, Aidan. I need you. You can't leave me here alone."

I sense her desperation. Her determination. She's so strong. She's like a rock in the storm. I decide to hold on to her.

She helps me to my feet, and the scream of the wind shifts. A loud groan emerges from the walls, like a protest of what's about to happen.

The fissures widen and indent with a *thud*. And the moaning surrounding us turns to a rolling thunder.

Until the wall releases. And we're standing by the altar, staring eternity in the face.

The wind whips at our hair, our clothes, as the expanse pulls at us.

"Oh my God," Rebecca whispers.

I feel her heartbeat in my skin, echoing mine. Her energy mingles with the ground and shattered walls surrounding us. Some of the broken roots on the floor begin sprouting new life as her green mist pushes out at every surface.

"It's her blood," I say. "We need to use it as the key to close this thing."

"What is it?" She presses her back into my chest.

"It's everything. And nothingness."

"You killed her," comes a growl behind us, over the din. "You killed my queen."

I turn and stumble back, having forgotten about Ava's human who was held to the ground by the tree roots. He . . . he killed Eric. And I want to rip him apart. He stands on the other side of the altar, a mass of muscle and rage.

"Now you die," he says, focused on me like a weapon ready to fire.

I grip my dagger as I move to the side, pulling Rebecca behind me. This isn't a demon, but that doesn't mean it isn't a beast.

Victor makes his way to the other side of the altar, never taking his eyes off us. He pauses when he reaches Ava's body and looks down on her, his features twisting in outrage. "You won't have her," he says. "And you won't have your key to save yourselves from what's about to come." He crouches down then, and shoves Ava through the open doorway, into the expanse.

My body jerks, wanting to rush after her, but Rebecca holds me tight.

I watch my sister's body get sucked into the void, the storm taking hold of her and swallowing her up. *It's not her. It's not her.* It's just a shell.

Victor stands and faces us. "Now I peel the skin from your bones," he says, stepping closer.

I nudge Rebecca around the side of the altar next to the cave entrance. "Run," I say, hoping she'll listen. She could get away if she goes fast enough. The angel killer just wants me.

She pushes back against my hands. "I'm not leaving you with him, Aidan."

"Your soul mate's kinda stubborn," Victor says.

I could teleport us out of here, but I need to find a remnant of Ava's blood and close that doorway before something horrifying climbs through. From where I stand, I can't tell if there's any still there, where her body was.

I step forward, moving to the left. Rebecca stays behind me as I place myself between Victor and the gateway. His large figure is framed by the storm, fists clenched at his side. I need to keep my eye on those fists. Getting hit by one could end this quick.

Rebecca tries to pull me back, toward the exit, but I don't let her. I have to get Victor out of the way. And . . . I want to kill him. I don't care if he's human. He needs to die.

I rush forward, keeping my dagger low.

Victor swings and I swerve, slicing the dagger across his side. He barely flinches. His forearm comes down on my shoulder blade.

My lungs clench and I stumble. I use my fire-filled elbow to jab his kidney as I fall in front of him, onto my knees. He grunts and swings, knuckles slamming into my cheek.

Splotches cloud my vision and I slash wildly with the blade, trying to keep him away. I hear Rebecca yelling something at me, but it doesn't register. I need to get my dagger through this man's gut—no, I have to focus, I need to get to the blood. I move my other hand through the sand, searching for something damp.

A boot meets my ribs, kicking me over.

The thud of pain rings in my head as I land. The storm of the gateway roars at my back now. It whips at my skin as I swipe forward with my blade again, this time hitting flesh.

Victor growls. He grabs my dagger arm and slams my wrist into the stone altar.

The bones shatter. I grapple with my other hand, trying to escape his iron grip. I kick with my power behind it, shoving him back hard, but he doesn't let go of me. I fly with him as he hits the wall beside the doorway.

"Enough!" he grinds through his teeth, getting his face close to mine. "We both go down, Chosen One."

Before I can get free of him, he wrenches me sideways, tossing us both toward the swirling darkness.

I twist, making him fall in first as I'm pulled, my fingers just barely grabbing hold of the archway as we plunge. I hold on to earth as Victor dangles from my broken arm.

The wind hits me hard. It rips at me, stinging, burning, my skin tearing from the force of it. I cry out and hold the wall, willing my body not to give up as I kick him, trying to free my other arm from his insistent grasp. The gravity is too strong. It's yanking Victor, yanking me, screaming, filling my head with its sharp whispers, like talons in the flesh, ripping me away from everything. It wants. It wants me.

My fingers bleed, my arms pull. I'm being torn apart, but I can't let go of the doorway. I can't . . . I can't hold on.

Something wraps around my earthbound hand, and I'm suddenly being pulled in two directions. I look up and see a root gripping my wrist. Rebecca's at the edge, the storm whipping her hair into a frenzy. Her mouth is moving, but I can't hear her words. It's all sinking away, my will, my life, the wind is cutting it from me with each desperate tug. And Victor still holds fast, helping it take me.

Rebecca kneels down, her hand entering the chaos. Her fingers splay over my arm. Her skin warms mine. And her energy reaches out for me, letting me feel *her*. The part of her inside of me that was passed on in the bonding spell.

The green light brightens and trails past my head, followed by another root. It slides over my shoulders, down my other arm, to the man trying to kill me. The green light gathers where Victor grips. It slips down along his arm to his shoulder, the root reaching.

The tendril pauses. Sharpens to a point.

And then impales Victor in the eye, breaking out the back of the skull.

The dead man jerks, then releases my arm as Rebecca's power yanks me free of the storm, tossing me back into the cave.

I reorient myself as quick as I can, trying to sit up. I gasp and hold my chest, the burning from my torn skin almost unbearable now that I'm not in the torrent. Rebecca staggers to me and collapses at my side, still staring at the storm.

"Have to . . . close it," I manage to say. "Demons. Hell."

"What do I do?" she asks, frantic.

"Blood . . . Ava." God, I hope it's still there.

She scrambles up and searches the ground. "The sand all blew away. I don't see any blood!"

No.

I try to get to my knees and crawl over. "We only need a little."

"Aidan, this isn't going to work. We need—oh, shit! Something's coming!" She stumbles back, tripping over me as she tries to get away from the opening.

I'll just kill it, I think as I search the ground for any sign of my sister's blood, trying not to analyze what I'm doing. It won't just be one demon coming through this thing. Any minute we'll have hordes pouring out in a river.

And I see nothing, no blood. I turn to Rebecca. "You need to run!"

"No!" Fear fills her eyes but she's still got that set to her jaw. She won't listen to me. And she'll get herself killed.

"Please, Rebecca! I can fight them, but you can't."

"Did you not see what I did to your sister? And Hunger!"

I shake my head, knowing she's not prepared for what might be coming. I'd love to keep arguing, but we don't have time. I can't think. I don't know what to do. Even as the first claw grabs hold of the archway. Huge. The fingers as thick as a child's arm.

I move back and we both watch as the massive creature pulls its way into the cave, its head like a bull, its hairy shoulders as wide as a truck. It growls and yellow saliva flies at us. I'm going to have to move toward it, but my feet are stuck.

Holy shit, it's huge.

It hoists up a leg, shaking the ground. Then the second leg, and it rises, hunching so its horns don't hit the ceiling. Its black eyes stare at us like it's not sure what we are.

"Aidan," Rebecca whispers. "Kill it now, please."

Another smaller demon that looks like a tiny troll scrambles up the big one's leg, as if it hitched a ride. It spots us and grins wide. Then leaps.

FIFTY-SIX

Rebecca

The demon's body hits Aidan's raised arm, his fire slicing it in half right before it bursts into flames.

The huge bull creature grunts and moves to the side, then starts walking out of the cave, like it's trying to avoid us. But Aidan scrambles up and grips its tree trunk leg.

His power sizzles over the thing's skin, and the beast roars loud enough to shake what's left of the walls, as the flames move, slow at first, like there's too much of a meal, until they're rushing up to the thigh. The demon stumbles, falling over the altar, breaking it in half.

Still Aidan hangs on, skidding across the sandy floor.

Another creature emerges from the wall and my magic instantly sends a root at it when my nerves spark. The branch pierces the demon through the mouth and the back of the head. It just blinks and looks confused, but it doesn't die.

"Aidan!" I yell, feeling useless. "The doorway!"

"I know," he grunts. The bull demon is half-consumed, so he lets go. He spins, scrambles to pick up his dagger from the ground, then shoves it into the demon I pinned, disintegrating it.

He studies the doorway, his face panicked.

The bull demon growls and tries to roll over, still not dead, its head and upper torso untouched.

"What if we break it?" I yell over the mess of sound and storm. "Can we just bring the cave down?" I've already got it started.

"Break it?" he repeats, but I can tell something's dawning on him. The realization in his eyes sparks hope in my gut. Until he says, "You have to leave. You can't be here when I try this."

I shake my head. "Just tell me what you're going to do."

He moves close and takes me by the upper arms. "This isn't something you can help with, Rebecca. Please. Run up the beach to the house. The ladies will let you in if you tell them you know me."

"Aidan . . ." I can't leave him. I just can't.

He growls in frustration, and I'm suddenly being pulled through time again, stretched out and twisted. Then I land in a huff of air, my sore feet screaming in pain as I collapse. My head clears just in time to see Aidan let go of me and pop from existence, leaving me on the bluff, near a pink house.

I gasp and try to not let my stomach empty itself from the instant travel this time.

"Dammit!" I should have known he was going to do that. If I wasn't so terrified for him, I'd kill him.

FIFTY-SEVEN

Aidan

As soon as I return to the cave, I stab the huge demon blocking the entrance and watch it quickly dissolve. Then I drag the still comatose Jaasi'el to the gateway and push it in. Another demon is climbing out as I shove the massive angel over the edge. This new one is tall and thin. I jab my blade in its claw, casting it into ash, then rise and grip the archway, and get ready to tear down some walls.

I know my power packs a punch, I just hope it's enough. Rebecca's roots have done half the work already.

Part of me knows that shutting the gateway won't be as simple as collapsing the cave, but my gut is telling me that if I can just get my power to link with the energy in the opening, I'll be able to destroy the porthole altogether. It's a crazy idea, but it's the only one I've got.

I take a deep breath in and pull at my power, willing it to fill my muscles, my bones. But I don't let it out. Not yet. I hold it, allowing it to grow. And grow. I clench my fingers tighter against the white stone as the sting in my skin builds. I keep the fire captive, setting it like a spring. I grip, grip tight, to the wall, the power, my sanity. To everything. Even as I hear wings rustle, sense creatures below, growling beasts coming closer, ready to come through the gateway. Even when I feel like my skin is about to be flayed from my bones to get the power out. I count my slowing heartbeat.

One . . . two . . . three.

And then I let it go. Pushing the force out with everything left in me. Into the stone around me, and through the gateway.

A clap of thunder crashes, shattering the walls. Rock and dirt spray in, shards fly in a mass of chaos, from the sides, from above and below, as the world explodes around me with a crack of air—

And then freezes. Becoming stillness. The moment of destruction paused midriot. And I know my power's linked in, weaving through whatever it is that created the doorway, freezing time somehow. Sound sucks away in a low buzz. Electricity prickles my skin. Air stops moving in my lungs.

I'm stuck in the time lapse, unable to move, an observer noticing the droplets of blood spraying out of my arm where I'm cut . . . the levitating pieces of the altar . . . the shard of rock heading for my eye.

It all hovers around me for a blink. As my power tugs and tugs, harder and harder, at a piece of the air, as if pulling a thread. Pulling, pulling, ready to unravel it all. The air tightens around me. Pressing in.

Then I hear something, sound returning quickly in a vibrating hum. And I feel time returning in my core. I know my power's done it, it's destroyed the doorway. And I also know if I don't get my body out of this moment—this position—before everything resumes, I'll be dead. For good.

The hum grows, and my lungs begin to move again, my limbs able to break from the pause just a little as the prickles of electricity sting my skin.

And then time hits. The air cracks with thunder once more. My brain tells my body to spring sideways, but my muscles are half a second too slow. A huge rock slams into my stomach, shoving me toward the cave entrance. I hit hard on unsteady ground. The earth fractures and pushes up around me as I cough and try to orient myself again, try to scramble to my feet. I see the opening, daylight. I focus on it, trying to push myself up to move.

I can make it to the entrance, almost free—

The ground disappears underneath me and I fall. I go blind, dirt and stone wreckage pelting my face. I hit earth and slide, scrape over stone for what feels like years. Until I'm punched by a wall of water, the ocean finding me. I'm shoved back, thrashed by it, my body spinning as I curl in a ball to protect myself. And then the tide turns and I'm pulled. I'm sucked through, tugged mercilessly, farther and farther, over jagged edges, salt and brine filling my mouth, my nose.

And then it slows, the deep waters accepting me as I'm embraced by the open sea.

I let the water take me. It's almost a dance as I join the rhythm of back and forth. My body sinking, deeper and deeper. Into stillness and nothing. I breathe in the water, my lungs not even fighting as they fill with lead. I feel my shattered bones, the torn muscles in my broken body. And I revel in it. As long as I feel pain, I'm alive.

I'm alive.

I open my eyes and watch the dusk of the deep. Shadows shape the distant expanse of ocean around me. Shards of sunlight break the surface high above. But I sink deeper and keep to the cold darkness as the truth falls over me.

It's over. It's all over.

THREE MONTHS LATER

Rebecca

"He's not going to give up, is he?" my dad says, watching Connor haggle with the woman selling necklaces a few yards down the beach.

I smile at Connor's sun-soaked figure in silent satisfaction, thinking how lovely he looks framed by the blue Mexican sky. The ocean crashes behind him, foamy crystals that wrap around his ankles and sink him into the white sand with each turn. But he's determined. He's trying to ask a local woman to make a green necklace for me, but his Spanish is horrid. His hands wave at the palm trees in desperation, and the woman just keeps shaking her head.

"Should we tell him it's *verde?*" my dad asks.

"No, this it too much fun." I smile. "I think she's pulling his leg, but he's more stubborn than I thought."

My dad releases soft laughter and sips from his coconut. "His argument with the cab driver when we got here didn't clue you in?"

"Connor was right, the guy was cheating us."

"I'm paying."

"He's trying to be polite, Dad."

My dad squints out at the water. He's quiet for a few seconds, then says, hesitantly, "I heard from the lawyer this morning."

I turn to look at him, my heartbeat speeding up. That can only mean one thing.

"Your grandmother has agreed to meet with you," he adds.

I panic a little inside, feeling torn. "What should I do? Should I go?"

He sighs, heavily. "I can't say that she's the nicest woman. But she might be able to help you with all these . . . abilities you have now."

"I've been practicing with Aidan and that's been helping."

"Except for the wall you exploded in my garage. And don't forget the tree that's growing in our living room."

"I'm trying," I say. "Really." I know this has been hard for him. And even with his own fears and insecurities, he's been so patient, so present for me. I don't think I'd have gotten through the last few months without him. After everything with Ava, with the discovery of my powers, I needed time to just be me.

My dad decided on this vacation after the living-room-tree incident, saying it was time for me to hang out somewhere more salty, and that he needed to get out of the traffic. I'm sure it wasn't totally an excuse, though; he probably did want to get out of the city. With all the roadwork and reconstruction going on after the earthquake that Aidan caused when he destroyed the doorway, the place is a madhouse. Even more than normal. But my dad also invited Connor because he knew how happy it would make me.

"I'm willing to consider something new," I say.

"I know you're more comfortable with Aidan, but he tried and it's not working."

I nod and look back over to Connor. My throat stings now, watching him, my comfort fading as I think about the future. If I do this, go see my grandmother, I'll be leaving him behind. I'll have to do it alone.

"I still haven't opened the envelope," I say, quietly. "With the letters."

He reaches over and takes my hand. If Ava's right and my real father is someone—some*thing*—else, I don't want to know. Because this man is the one I choose.

"You'll know when you're ready," he says.

Connor comes back and kneels beside me, holding out a green necklace. "For you."

I lean over and let him place it over my head. It's lovely, abalone shells woven through with green thread. "You did it," I say.

"I did," he says with a grin. "Mission accomplished. I called Holly, and she talked to the woman."

I laugh. "You cheated."

"I adapted." He kisses my cheek and moves to sit in his own chair, lying back and tucking his hands behind his head. "I'm bummed we have to go home day after tomorrow."

"Me too," I say.

"Yes," my dad says, longing in his voice.

Connor looks over to us and directs his words to my father. "Thank you for letting me tag along, sir."

My dad sets his coconut drink down and starts to get up. "Time for another piña colada." He stands and walks by, pausing when he gets to Connor, resting a hand on his shoulder. "Call me Patrick, son." And then he leaves us in stunned silence.

"Did he just call me *son?*" Connor asks after a few seconds.

"And he gave you the patriarchal anointing—he patted your shoulder."

Connor laughs. "I suppose that means we're going steady now." He takes hold of the base of my chair and pulls it closer to line up with his.

"At least. You may owe my dad a goat, though."

He leans close and says in a low voice, "Then we should probably seal the deal." And he licks the tip of my nose.

I giggle and push him away, but he's stronger than me, and in a few seconds he's got me wrapped in his arms. I smile and sink into him and try not to think about what comes next in my life, try not to think about leaving him. I force myself to keep smiling as the next two days pass. As we shop in the market and make dinner with my dad in the small condo's kitchen, as we play cards and talk late into the night.

It isn't until Connor and I are standing in front of my house, saying good-bye three days later that I let the guise fall.

"We'll talk every day on the phone," I say, tucking my face into his neck and smelling his warm, salty skin before kissing his scar softly.

"And you'll text me pictures of all the East Coast blue bloods." He rubs my back and squeezes me tighter against his chest. He wasn't happy when I told him that I was going to my grandmother's, but he understood. He's seen my frustration as I've tried to get my abilities under control. He's had struggles of his own, too. Even though Kara said he'd be able to heal the others, he still hasn't figured out how. And every once in a while the sudden flashes of pain will come back.

"You send pictures, too," I say.

He pulls away a little and looks down at me with a smirk. "Of what? The traffic or the long lines at Starbucks?"

"Of you guys. Of the jobs and stuff. I'm going to miss you."

He pulls me back into the hug. "I know."

I try not to let the sting in my throat take over as I confess, "I'm scared to face this, Connor."

He kisses my cheek and runs a hand over my hair in comfort. "You're amazing. And brave. And you'll be back with us before you know it."

I nod and take his lips with mine. I fold myself into his arms and let myself feel his warmth, his tenderness, as we remind each other what it means to be in love and let the rest of the world fall away.

Aidan

"That's not where those go!" my great-grandmother shouts at Kara, who's trying to help me repair some of the quake damage to the beach house.

Right now, Kara is rearranging some potted plants in the yard so I can set up a spot to paint the wood that's going to replace the old trellis. Kara might as well be building the Empire State Building with Stalin in charge. She's rolling with it, though.

She moves the fern more to the right. "Better?"

My grandmother huffs, steps over to the pot, and hoists it with her bird arms. The thing has to weigh almost as much as her. But she clambers off the cement porch, over to the flagstone, and plops it down. "There! That's where *Abacopteris penangiana* goes. Alphabetical order, young lady. How many times do I have to tell you?"

Kara bites back a laugh. "At least three more times, Mrs. O'Linn."

"Sassy thing, aren't you?" She scowls, then barks, "Aidan!"

I step out from behind the hydrangea I was hiding behind. "Yes, ma'am."

She waves me over, closer, until she can grip my shirt. She leans in so she can whisper. "Where did you find this wild girl?"

I glance at Kara, who's just standing there looking smug. "Uh, well . . . I guess you could say we work together."

She frowns. "Do you think she's pretty?"

"Yes."

"Are you dating her?" she snaps.

"Uh, yes."

She releases the front of my shirt and pats my chest. "Nice to see you have good taste." And then she pats my cheek. "Now stop peeping at us through the bushes and get my trellis back up so I can have my roses nice and lively again."

"Yes, ma'am."

I get back to work with a smile and leave the women to themselves. Now that I see Kara can hold her own, I feel better. And I hate to think it matters, but knowing my great-grandmother approves of Kara makes me almost giddy. I didn't admit it to Kara—I barely admitted it to myself—but I brought her today to see how they would get along. Even though Mrs. O'Linn is in the dark about our family connection, neither of these ladies will be leaving my life anytime soon.

After another hour or so, Kara finds me just as I'm finishing up cutting the wood. I'm not sure I'll be getting to the painting today, since we've got to pick up Jax and meet Tray for a job later, but I want to get to a good stopping place.

"Hey," she says, looking me over. "How are you doing on time?"

"Almost done."

She leans on the wall and watches me stack the pieces of wood. I feel the heat coming off of her as she gives me a crooked smile, showing me her dimple. "You look pretty sexy all covered in sawdust."

I pause to wipe my face with my shirt. "Oh? How about sweat?"

She laughs.

"Your lady friend is a tough taskmaster," she says.

"But she pays well."

Kara looks surprised. "She pays you?"

"In food." I wink.

"Boys." She pulls her phone out of her pocket and reads the screen for a second. "Tray's ready when we are. Did you get those protection pouches finished last night?"

"Yeah, but we ran out of wolfsbane." I drop the last piece of wood on the stack and pull off my work gloves. "Let me just say good-bye to Mrs. O'Linn and we can go."

"Should I factor in enough time to eat a meal while I wait in the car?"

I rest my arm on her shoulder as we walk around the house to the front door. "Or two."

"Ugh, you weren't kidding about the sweat." She pushes me off her and makes a face.

I chase her with my armpit for a minute until I've got her giggling madly. And then I tickle her until she agrees to come inside and eat.

———

The house is quiet when we get back from the job. We're living at Eric's Malibu place now, with Hanna. Over the last three months she's become the den mother to our raggedy crew. At first we were there more for her than she was for us, so she wouldn't be alone, but as time's passed and the business of life has taken over, she's given us steadiness in the midst of all the change and helped us forget a tiny bit of the sadness each day as she's become the glue that holds us all together.

The house is huge, with a slick modern look to the style and architecture. Like Eric, I guess. I see him in the pieces of ancient pottery framed on the walls, in the Indian rugs. I see him in the view outside the wall of windows that faces west; a peek through the Santa Monica Mountains, the Pacific a blue ribbon in the distance. Right now the sky is painted in pastels as the sun sets into the horizon. It's the first thing

I notice when we walk into the house, and immediately I want to go outside and watch the night rise. So I can see her. But not yet.

Holly and Raul are sitting at the kitchen table. Holly's helping Raul study for a test—since he's started at the high school, Raul's had his nose in one book or another. Happily, just like Holly. The two of them are peas in a pod now, baking and braining like pros.

Kara convinced Tray to come over for dinner tonight after the job. The house feels empty since Connor left on vacation with Rebecca, and now that Tray's mom is out of rehab and doing better holding down a job, he feels less of a need to be guarding Selena so closely. Kara's been working overtime to convince him to move in, but he's not budging.

After the earthquake, his neighborhood was one of the ones that were pretty bad off. There was a lot of looting in the aftermath, and several deaths related to riots over the lack of clean water and electricity. I keep telling myself that no one died the day of the quake, so it's all right. But they did die after. Of course, a lot *more* people would've died if I'd left the doorway wide open. It's all numbers and semantics when I think of it that way. The vicious truth is that, whichever way you slice it, it's too huge a tragedy to measure.

"Hanna's at the club, so we can eat junk food for dinner," Jax announces when we walk into the kitchen. "I vote that we order pizza. And rolls. And large loaves of bread slathered in butter—God, I miss gluten. Hanna's idea of healthy kinda sucks. I feel fit. But sad." He plops down at the table beside Raul. "What're we studying tonight?"

"Tolstoy," Raul says, holding up a fat book. "And how he saw the Napoleonic era."

Jax rolls his eyes. "Speak English, this is America."

"I could go for pizza," Tray says.

Holly pushes her glasses up her nose as she looks around the table. "Who said you two could sit here?"

"Your heart, baby," Jax says, kissing the air. "You're welcome."

"I'm gonna shower, then I'll call in the pizza order," Kara says. "No one kill Jax while I'm gone—I don't wanna miss it."

And then everyone's settled into their tasks, except me. I watch them for a few minutes, smiling at how they all play off each other and laugh, how they live in the moment. But soon I find myself drawn to the outdoors.

I walk out the back and down the deck stairs into the yard. The sunset paints the sky pink and orange, and the hills around the house start to take on shadows, coyotes and mountain lions emerging from their hiding places to rule the darkness. An owl's already started calling from the tall eucalyptus trees that rim the property as I make my way to the edge of the yard where it drops off into a steep hill. You can't smell the ocean from this far away, but I imagine that I can. I pretend I can taste the salt on my tongue as the wind picks up through the canyon.

It's peaceful out here. And I know she'll come soon. So I wait. I watch the night rise, the moon appear, and listen to the subtle sounds the darkness brings. I let the damp air chill my skin and remind me that I'm alive as it bites into my lungs.

Until I feel her presence. The soft press at my back, the tingle at the base of my neck.

I turn slowly and see her standing under the oak tree that clings to the bluff. The shadows of night play over her sheer form, so familiar. So close I could step three paces and touch her small shoulder, where her silver hair lifts now and then in wisps, floating with a ghostly breeze. She holds her violin and bow at her side as she rocks back and forth from toe to heel.

She wants me to know that she likes my haircut.

I tell her about my day and she smiles, a light of joy in her eyes. I don't remember her smiling at me when she was alive like she does now. I don't remember her having peace like what drifts from her when I see her in our moments. She's told me several times that she's forgiven me. She wishes she'd seen more clearly, that she had revealed more of her secrets. And she doesn't understand why she chose the Darkness. It troubles her still.

We've tried to sort through it all, to figure out where I went wrong, where she was lost to me. But it always ends with a single dark realization; there's no changing it.

So tonight I don't let my mind take us down that path again. Instead we listen to the rustling in the brush and try to guess the animal. We watch as the stars appear overhead and the moon takes her place. Then we name each pinprick of light in the sky, until Kara calls me in for dinner. And I say good-bye again.

Ava's pale figure looks on in peaceful silence as I walk back to the house. The smell of her energy follows me, reminding me to return.

And her violin begins to sing, her toes curling in the clusters of tiny white flowers at her feet.

ACKNOWLEDGMENTS

There's a village of people that are summoned to help a writer finish a trilogy; something I've discovered is a massive undertaking. But I was blessed to have had an ocean of support and encouragement. I'm so thankful for everyone who stood by me through this adventure. The patience it takes for the friends and the loved ones of a writer on deadline is a true test of sacrifice. I am blessed.

So many thanks to my agent, Rena Rossner: lady, you are kick-ass (plus, you put up with me). And as always I am so grateful to my pro team at Amazon Publishing's Skyscape, who are wonderful at challenging me to go further and do better than I thought I could. Marianna Baer, you, my dear, are amazing. If these books are any good, it's because of your guidance and story wisdom. Courtney Miller, you took the leap with me—thank you so much for letting me go on this adventure with you. What a ride! Adrienne Lombardo, you're a gem. Bunny-lovers rock!

A million blathering thank-yous to my very patient and supportive writer friends who keep me going, on Codex and LB, you know who you are. You are angels, truly. To the Panera Posse, you have kept me solid and grounded in the storm of chaos and reminded me how much fun writing can be when things went nutty. A special thanks to

Catherine, who read like a speedster, helping me talk through the edit of this monster third book and get everything happening in the right place. You were a godsend, chicky!

To my most amazing bestie, Cayse (you too, Dave), who keeps my feet firmly planted where they should be. God knew I needed you, my friend.

To my mom, who has become a permanent taxi driver over the last year. My kids would get nowhere without you! Plus, you buy me coffee. And listen to all my complaining. *hugs*

My kids . . . you crazy beasts. You were and are and will always be my most precious creation. You are each unique, you are vital. Don't forget, you have a voice. Mommy loves you with her whole self.

To my soul mate, my true heart, my husband; I am so grateful. We celebrated our twentieth year together while I was in this process, and you set aside your goals and your needs for me to reach this dream. May you reap what you've sown, my love. You are the best part of this gift called life.

But, most of all, all glory and love to my creator, Elohei Kedem, my Light in the dark places. Keep my daddy in your arms. And give him a hug from his little girl.

ABOUT THE AUTHOR

Photo © 2014 Rachel A. Marks

Rachel A. Marks is an award-winning writer, a professional artist, and a cancer survivor. She is the author of the Dark Cycle series—including *Darkness Brutal, Darkness Fair*, and *Darkness Savage*—and the novella *Winter Rose*. Her art can be found on the covers of several *New York Times* and *USA Today* bestselling novels. She lives in Southern California with her husband, four kids, six rabbits, two ducks, and a cat. You can find out more about her weird life on her website: www.RachelAnneMarks.com.